BY JAMES S. A. COREY

The Mercy of Gods
Memory's Legion
Leviathan Wakes
Caliban's War
Abaddon's Gate
Cibola Burn
Nemesis Games
Babylon's Ashes
Persepolis Rising
Tiamat's Wrath
Leviathan Falls

STAR WARS™

HONOR AMONG THIEVES

STAR WARS™

HONOR AMONG THIEVES

JAMES S. A. COREY

RANDOM HOUSE WORLDS
NEW YORK

Random House Worlds
An imprint of Random House
A division of Penguin Random House LLC
1745 Broadway, New York, NY 10019
randomhousebooks.com
penguinrandomhouse.com

2025 Random House Worlds Trade Paperback Edition

Originally published in hardcover in the United States by Del Rey,
an imprint of Random House, a division of
Penguin Random House LLC, in 2014.

ISBN 978-0-593-97483-4
Ebook ISBN 978-0-345-54686-9

Printed in the United States of America on acid-free paper

1st Printing

BOOK TEAM:
Production editor: Abby Duval • Managing editor: Susan Seeman •
Production manager: Chanler Harris •
Proofreaders: Rachael Clements, Drew Goter

Book design by Edwin A. Vazquez

The authorized representative in the EU
for product safety and compliance is
Penguin Random House Ireland,
Morrison Chambers, 32 Nassau Street,
Dublin D02 YH68, Ireland.
https://eu-contact.penguin.ie

For Scarlet

THE ESSENTIAL LEGENDS COLLECTION

For more than forty years, novels set in a galaxy far, far away have enriched the *Star Wars* experience for fans seeking to continue the adventure beyond the screen. When he created *Star Wars,* George Lucas built a universe that sparked the imagination and inspired others to create. He opened up that universe to be a creative space for other people to tell their own tales. This became known as the Expanded Universe, or EU, of novels, comics, video games, and more.

To this day, the EU remains an inspiration for *Star Wars* creators and is published under the label Legends. Ideas, characters, story elements, and more from new *Star Wars* entertainment trace their origins back to material from the Expanded Universe. This Essential Legends Collection curates some of the most treasured stories from that expansive legacy.

DRAMATIS PERSONAE

BAASEN RAY: smuggler (Mirialan male)

C-3PO: masculine protocol droid

CHEWBACCA: copilot, *Millennium Falcon* (Wookiee male)

ESSIO GALASSIAN: astrocartographer (human male)

HAN SOLO: captain, *Millennium Falcon* (human male)

HUNTER MAAS: thief (human male)

LEIA ORGANA: rebel, Alderaanian princess (human female)

LUKE SKYWALKER: rebel pilot (human male)

R2-D2: astromech droid

SCARLET HARK: rebel spy (human female)

SUNNIM: pilot (Bothan male)

WEDGE ANTILLES: commander, Rebel Alliance (human male)

A long time ago in a galaxy far, far away. . . .

STAR WARS™

HONOR AMONG THIEVES

CHAPTER ONE

FROM THE IMPERIAL CORE to the outflung stars of the Rim, the galaxy teemed with life. Planets, moons, asteroid bases, and space stations peopled with a thousand different species, all of them busy with the great ambitions of the powerful and also with the mundane problems of getting through their days, the ambitions of the Emperor all the way down to where to eat the next meal. Or whether there would be a next meal. Each city and town and station and ship had its own histories and secrets, hopes and fears and half-articulated dreams.

But for every circle of light—every star, every planet, every beacon and outpost—there was vastly more darkness. The space between stars was and always would be unimaginably huge, and the mysteries that it hid would never be wholly discovered. One bad jump was all it took for a ship to be lost. Unless there was a way to reach out for help, to say *Here I am. Come find me,* an escape pod or a ship or a fleet could vanish into the places between places that even light took a lifetime to reach.

And so a rendezvous point could be the size of a solar system, and the rebel fleet could still hide there like a flake in a snowstorm. Hundreds of ships, from cobbled-together, plasma-scorched cruisers and thirdhand battleships to X- and

Y-wings and everything in between. They flew through space together silently, drifting closer in or farther apart as the need arose. Repair droids crawled over the skins of the ships, welding back together the wounds of their last battles, sure in the knowledge that they were the needle in the Empire's haystack.

Their greatest danger wasn't the enemy, but inaction. And the ways a certain kind of man coped with it.

"I wasn't cheating," Han Solo said as Chewbacca bent to pass through the door in the bulkhead. "I was playing better than they were."

The Wookiee growled.

"That's how I was playing better. It's not against the rules. Besides, what are they going to buy with their money out here?"

A dozen fighter pilots marching past in dirty orange-and-white uniforms saluted them. Han nodded to each one as he passed. They were an ugly bunch: middle-aged men who should have been back home on a planet somewhere spending too much time at the neighborhood bar and weedy boys still looking forward to their first wispy mustaches. Warriors for freedom, and terrible sabacc players.

Chewbacca let out a long, low groan.

"You wouldn't," Han said.

Chewbacca's blue eyes met his, and the Wookiee's silence was more eloquent than anything he might have said aloud.

"Fine," Han retorted. "But it's coming out of your cut. I don't know when you went soft on me."

"Han!"

Luke Skywalker came jogging down a side corridor, his helmet under his arm. Two droids followed him: the squat, cylindrical R2-D2 rolling along, chirping and squealing; and the tall, golden C-3PO trotting along at the back, waving gold-chrome hands as if gesticulating in response to some unheard conversation. The kid's face was flushed and his hair was dark with sweat, but he was grinning as if he'd just won something.

"Hey," Han said. "Just get back from maneuvers?"

"Yep. These guys are great. You should have seen the tight spin and recover they showed us. I could have stayed out there for hours, but Leia called me back in for some kind of emergency meeting."

"Her Worshipfulness called the meeting?" Han asked as they turned down the main access corridor together. The smell of welding torches and coolant hung in the air. Everything about the Rebel Alliance smelled like a repair bay. "I thought she was off to her big conference on Kiamurr."

"She was supposed to be. I guess she postponed leaving."

The little R2 droid squealed, and Han turned to it. "What's that, Artoo?"

C-3PO, catching up and giving a good impression of leaning forward to catch his breath even though he didn't have lungs, translated: "He's saying that she's postponed her departure twice. It's made a terrible shambles of the landing docks."

"Well, that's not good," Han said. "Anything that keeps her from sitting around a big table deciding the future of the galaxy . . . I mean, that's her favorite thing to do."

"You know that's not true," Luke said, making room in the passageway for a bronze-colored droid that looked as if it had barely crawled out of the trash heap. "I don't know why you don't like her more."

"I like her fine."

"You're always cutting her down, though. The Alliance needs good politicians and organizers."

"You can't have a government without a tax collector. Just because we'd both like it better if the Emperor wasn't in charge, it doesn't make me and her the same person."

Luke shook his head. The sweat was starting to dry, and his hair was getting some of its sandy color back.

"I think you two are more alike than you pretend."

Han laughed despite himself. "You're an optimist, kid."

When they reached the entrance to the command center, Luke sent the droids on, R2-D2 whistling and squeaking and C-3PO acting annoyed. The command center had taken a direct hit in the fighting at Yavin, and the reconstruction efforts still showed. New panels, blinding in their whiteness, covered most of one wall where the old ones had been shattered by the blast. Where the replacements ended, the old panels seemed even darker by contrast. The head-high displays marked the positions of the ships in the fleet and the fleet in the emptiness of the rendezvous point, the status of repair crews, the signals from the sensor arrays, and half a dozen other streams of information. None of the stations was staffed. The data spooled out into the air, ignored.

Leia stood at the front of the room, the bright repair work and grimy original walls seeming to come together in her. Her dress was black with embroidery of gold and bronze, her hair a soft spill gathered at the nape of her neck in a style that made her seem both more mature and more powerful than had the side buns she'd worn on the Death Star. From what Han had heard around the fleet, losing Alderaan had made her older and harder. And as much as he hated to admit it, she wore the tragedy well.

The man she was talking to—Colonel Harcen—had his back to them, but his voice carried just fine. "With respect, though, you have to see that not all allies are equal. Some of the factions that are going to be on Kiamurr, the Alliance would be better off without."

"I understand your concerns, Colonel," Leia said in a tone that didn't sound particularly understanding. "I think we can agree, though, that the Alliance isn't in a position to turn away whatever help we can get. The Battle of Yavin was a victory, but—"

Harcen raised a palm, interrupting her. He was an idiot, Han thought. "There are already some people who feel that we have become too lax in the sorts of people we're allowing into our ranks. In order to gain respect, we must be free of undesirable elements."

"I agree," Han said. Colonel Harcen jumped like a poked cat. "You've got to keep the scum out."

"Captain Solo," Harcen said. "I didn't see you there. I hope I gave no offense."

"No. Of course not," Han said, smiling insincerely. "I mean, you weren't talking about *me,* were you?"

"Everyone is very aware of the service you've done for the Alliance."

"Exactly. So there's no reason you'd have been talking about me."

Harcen flushed red and made a small, formal bow. "I was not talking about you, Captain Solo."

Han sat at one of the empty stations, stretching his arms out as if he were in a cantina with a group of old friends. It might have been an illusion, but he thought he saw a flicker of a smile on Leia's lips.

"Then there's no offense taken," he said.

Harcen turned to go, his shoulders back and his head held high. Chewbacca took a fraction of a second longer than strictly needed to step out of the man's way. Luke leaned against one of the displays, his weight warping it enough to send little sprays of false color through the lines and curves.

When Harcen was gone, Leia sighed. "Thank you all for coming on short notice. I'm sorry I had to pull you off the training exercises, Luke."

"It's all right."

"I was in a sabacc game," Han said.

"I'm *not* sorry I pulled you out of that."

"I was winning."

Chewbacca chuffed and crossed his arms. Leia's expression softened a degree. "I was supposed to leave ten standard hours ago," she said, "and I can't stay much longer. We've had some unexpected developments, and I need to get you up to speed."

"What's going on?" Luke asked.

"We aren't going to be able to use the preliminary base in Targarth system," she said. "We've had positive identification of Imperial probes."

The silence only lasted a breath, but it carried a full load of disappointment.

"Not *again,*" Luke said.

"Again." Leia crossed her arms. "We're looking at alternatives, but until we get something, construction and drydock plans are all being put on hold."

"Vader's really going all-out to find you people," Han said. "What are your backup plans?"

"We're looking at Cerroban, Aestilan, and Hoth," Leia told him.

"That's the bottom of the barrel," Han said.

For a second, he thought she was going to fight, but instead she only looked defeated. He knew as well as she did that the secret rebel base was going to be critical. Without a base, some kinds of repair, manufacturing, and training work just couldn't be done, and the Empire knew that, too. But Cerroban was a waterless, airless lump of stone hardly better than the rendezvous point, and one that was pounded by asteroids on a regular basis. Aestilan had air and water, but rock worms had turned the planetary mantle so fragile that there were jokes about digging tunnels just by jumping up and down. And Hoth was an ice ball with an equatorial zone that only barely stayed warm enough to sustain human life, and then only when the sun was up.

Leia stepped to one of the displays, shifting the image

with a flicker of her fingers. A map of the galaxy appeared, the immensity of a thousand million suns disguised by the fitting of it all onto the same screen.

"There is another possibility," she said. "The Seymarti system is near the major space lanes. There's some evidence that there was sentient life on it at some point, but our probes don't show anything now. It may be the place we're looking for."

"That's a terrible idea," Han said. "You don't want to do that."

"Why not?" Luke asked.

"Ships get lost in Seymarti," Han said. "A lot of ships. They make the jump to hyperspace, and they don't come back out."

"What happens to them?"

"No one knows. Something that close to the lanes without an Imperial garrison on it can be mighty appealing to someone who needs a convenient place to not get found, but everyone I know still steers clear of that place. *Nobody* goes there."

Luke patted his helmet with one thoughtful hand. "But if nobody goes there, how can a lot of ships get lost?"

Han scowled. "I'm just saying the place has a bad reputation."

"The science teams think there may be some kind of spatial anomaly that throws off sensor readings," Leia said. "If that's true, and we can find a way to navigate it ourselves, Seymarti may be our best hope for avoiding Imperial notice. As soon as Wedge Antilles is back from patrol, he's going to put together an escort force for the survey ships."

"I'd like to go with him," Luke said.

"We talked about that," Leia said. "Wedge thought it would be a good chance for you to get some practice. He's requested you as his second in command."

Luke's smile was so bright, Han could have read by it. "Absolutely," the kid said.

The communications panel beside Leia chimed. "Ma'am, we've kept the engines hot, but if we don't leave soon, we're going to have to recalibrate the jump. Do you want me to reschedule your meetings again?"

"No. I'll be right there," she said, and turned the connection off with an audible click.

Han leaned forward. "It's all right, I see how I fit in here," he said. "The weapons run from Minoth to Hendrix is off. That's not a big deal. I'll just bring the guns here instead. Unless you want the *Falcon* to go along with the kid here."

"Actually, that's not why I wanted to talk with you," Leia said. "Something else happened. Two years ago, we placed an agent at the edge of Imperial space. The intelligence we've gotten since then has been some of the most valuable we've seen, but the reports stopped seven months ago. We assumed the worst. And then yesterday, we got a retrieval code. From the Saavin system. Cioran."

"That's not the *edge* of Imperial space," Han said. "That's the middle of it."

Chewbacca growled and moaned.

"It's not what I would have picked, either," Leia said. "There was no information with it. No context, no report. We don't know what happened between the last contact and now. We just got the signal that we should send a ship."

"Oh," Han said with a slowly widening grin. "No, it's all right. I get it. I absolutely understand. You've got this important guy trapped in enemy territory, and you need to get him out. Only with the Empire already swarming like a hive of Bacian blood hornets, you can't risk using anyone but the best. That about right?"

"I wouldn't put it that way, but it's in the neighborhood of right, yes," Leia said. "The risks are high. I won't order anyone to take the assignment. We can make it worth your time if you're willing to do it."

"You don't have to order us, does she, Chewie? All you have to do is ask, and we're on the job."

Leia's gaze softened a little. "Will you do this, then? For the Alliance?"

Han went on as if she hadn't spoken. "Just say *please* and we'll get the *Millennium Falcon* warmed up, skin out of here, grab your guy, and be back before you know it. Nothing to it."

Leia's expression went stony. "Please."

Han scratched his eyebrow. "Can I have a little time to think about it?"

The Wookiee made a low but rising howl and lifted his arms impatiently.

"Thank you, Chewie," Leia said. "There's also a real possibility that the whole operation was compromised and the retrieval code is bait in a trap. When you make your approach, you'll need to be very careful."

"Always am," Han said, and Luke coughed. "What?" Han demanded.

"You're always careful?"

"I'm always careful enough."

"Your first objective is to make the connection and complete the retrieval," Leia said. "If you can't do that, find out as much as you can about what happened and whether any of our people are in danger. But if you smell a trap, get out. If we've lost her, we've lost her. We don't want to sacrifice anyone else."

"'Her'?"

Leia touched the display controls again, and the image shifted. A green security warning flooded it, and she keyed in the override. A woman's face filled the screen. High cheekbones, dark eyes and hair, V-shaped chin, and a mouth that seemed on the verge of smiling. If Han had seen her in a city, he'd have looked twice, but not because she was suspicious. The data field beside the picture listed a life history too complex to take in at a glance. The name field read: SCARLET HARK.

"Don't get in over your head," Leia said.

CHAPTER TWO

THE SAAVIN SYSTEM floated in the air above the display panel, tiny colored balls representing the various planets rotating around a bright orange star. A small blue world nestled in a swarm of Imperial ships and independent stations. Cioran, bureaucratic heart of the Empire. Or if not heart, kidney. Maybe small bowel. Another world, a large, bright red planet toward the edge of the system, swelled even larger when Chewbacca waved a paw at it. The Wookiee growled.

"That's the point," Han said. "It's on the edge of the system, and it's a big ball of useless gas. No one lives there. There aren't even any gas miners. It'll take a little longer to fly into Cioran from there, but it's a nice quiet spot to take a look around."

Chewie growled and crossed his arms.

"Look, this is Empire central. I don't want to drop out of hyperspace on top of a Star Destroyer."

Chewie turned away and began prepping the *Falcon*. He carried on a low rumbling conversation with himself, his back to Han.

"You're gonna thank me when we slip into the Saavin system without anyone noticing us."

Chewie grunted, and Han pulled the lever to shut down

the hyperdrive. The streaking white of hyperspace that had filled their cockpit viewport snapped back into a steady starfield, the bloated red of Saavin's gas giant filling half of the view.

"See, now we just—" Han started.

"Unregistered YT-thirteen-hundred, this is the Imperial Star Destroyer *Ravenous,* respond immediately."

The *Falcon* began blaring collision alarms as two TIE fighters took flanking positions next to her. The massive dagger shape of the Star Destroyer drifted into view from her port side.

"Unregistered YT-thirteen-hundred—" Han killed the comm. Chewbacca turned to look at him, not saying anything.

"This is not my fault," Han said, looking for an escape route and finding nothing. "What are they doing out here?"

Chewie growled and reached for the deflector controls.

"No, wait," Han said, grabbing the Wookiee's arm to stop him. "I can handle this." Chewbacca barked out a laugh.

"Hello, *Ravenous,* this is Captain—" Han racked his brain for one of the names on the list of fake registration codes he kept. "—Boro Mandibel, of the light freighter *Vortando*. How can I help you today?"

He put his palm over the mic and said, "Chewie, better turn on the registration broadcast. Make sure it's the *Vortando* codes."

"*Vortando,*" the reply came after a few moments. "You're broadcasting a nonstandard registration—"

"Sorry about that," Han interrupted with a heartily false laugh. "Hired on a Wookiee mechanic, and he's been using nonstandard parts on all the repairs."

Chewie growled dangerously from behind him, and Han covered the mic again. "If he understands Wookiee, that little remark is going to get us in a lot of trouble." Chewbacca rumbled a response that demonstrated a lack of remorse.

"Destination and cargo," the Star Destroyer demanded.

"Uh, going to Cioran with Corellian brandy and Sacorrian wines. How are you guys doing today?"

There was a pause that felt as if it lasted hours. Han began plotting a course to get them out of the system as fast as possible. The two TIE fighters hung next to the *Falcon* like an unspoken threat.

Han turned off the mic and said, "Chewie, this isn't working. Get ready to angle the rear deflectors and make a run for it."

"*Vortando,*" the Star Destroyer said. "Proceed to Cioran on the following course. Do not deviate. We're seeing an incoming load, and we don't need you disrupting the landing queue."

"Received, *Ravenous*. You guys have a nice day," Han said, then laid in the course. Chewbacca bayed his disbelief.

"Yeah, I know. Star Destroyers directing traffic," Han replied, bringing up the drive. "Welcome to the Empire."

THE *RAVENOUS* HADN'T been lying. The *Falcon* waited for two standard hours to get a landing assignment. To pass the time, Han checked the charge on his blaster, and Chewbacca stripped and cleaned his bowcaster. Han pulled on a long coat that covered his weapon. He knew that Cioran's warm climate didn't warrant a coat like that, but he figured it was better than wearing the blaster where everyone could see it.

"You know," he said, pacing and twisting in front of his cabin's mirror to make sure the blaster stayed hidden when he moved, "this is the heart of the Empire. I don't know how many Wookiees with energy crossbows are going to be walking around. You might want to aim for subtle."

Chewbacca growled, and Han put up his hands. "I'm

just saying this isn't our usual run-and-gun. We're here to blend in. Move unnoticed." Han turned suddenly, watching the swirl of the coat to make sure it didn't open up too far. Chewbacca coughed out a laugh.

"Hey!" Han said, hurt in his voice. "I've blended! I can blend. And if I don't—" He swatted at the coat, pushing it away and yanking out his blaster in a lightning-fast draw. "I'll improvise."

THE DOCKING BAYS on Cioran looked exactly like the docking bays on a hundred worlds Han Solo had seen during his travels, only clean. Unsettlingly clean. The same repair gantries and loading cranes. The same fuel tanks and repair droids and inspection clerks, but without the lived-in look. No fuel spills on the decking, no broken droids sparking in the corner, no grease spots on any of the inspectors' uniforms. It felt vaguely funereal. Like a memorial to the idea of a docking bay.

A small, stout droid was waiting at the bottom of the crew ramp, ticking quietly to itself, a vaguely humanoid head on top of a square body sporting too many arms and sitting on rubber treads. When it saw Han, it perked up with a lurch.

"I am R-Four-Two-Seven," it said in an annoying chirpy voice. "The Cioran Port Authority and the Trajenni Dock Management Collective welcome you to Cioran!"

"Thanks," Han said, and tried to walk past it. The rubber treads whirred to life, and it darted in front of him.

"The Trajenni Dock Management Collective hopes we can be of service to you during your stay on Cioran!"

"Great," Han said. "I don't really need—"

"May I assist you with your bags?" R-427 continued, undeterred. "Or perhaps you would like a licensed Trajenni

Dock Management Collective repair droid to look over your ship? Our refueling services are available at extremely competitive rates, and—"

Chewbacca growled and walked toward the droid. It backed up.

"We'll let you know if we need anything," Han said with a smile and a wave of dismissal. Chewbacca continued to advance on the droid until it finally spun around on its treads and sped toward the door.

"The Trajenni Dock Management Collective welcomes you to Cioran and hopes you enjoy your stay!" the droid shouted as it fled, its last words almost inaudible.

Chewbacca chuffed out a quiet laugh as it disappeared around a corner.

"The drop's someplace called Staton Park," Han said, walking to the dock's street exit. Chewbacca followed with a low grumble. "Yeah, I don't know why we aren't meeting in a bar, either. There's a way you do these things. Sometimes it seems like we're the only professionals left."

The exit led out to a wide pedestrian walkway with air traffic flying thick overhead. The speeders, landing ships, and personal speeder bikes moved in crisp lines that exactly matched the ground-level roadways. Imperial craft kept a watchful eye on the procession of vehicles, prominent laser cannons a visible warning against violating the traffic rules.

"It's all very . . . *orderly*, isn't it," Han said, looking up with a sigh.

The Core reminded Han why he'd fled to the backwater planets on the edge of the galaxy in the first place. The massive walls of steel and glass that rose on both sides felt like a cage. He wanted to tell himself that this was what Imperial control looked like: order enforced at the end of a blaster. But any government was going to have traffic laws. Before the Emperor, the Republic had enforced its edicts at the laser-sharp edge of a Jedi's lightsaber. It was the way the universe worked. That didn't mean he had to like it.

"Let's get a drink."

EVEN THE BARS stank of Imperial order. The gleaming chrome tabletops and uncomfortable chairs didn't allow for much lounging or relaxation. A dozen patrons sat quietly at their tables drinking heavily and unenthusiastically. A few of them stared at Chewbacca when they came in, but no one challenged them. A small knot of men and women who looked like off-duty soldiers occupied one corner, their heads hunched close together, talking in whispers.

He found a table at the corner farthest from the Imperials and put his back to the wall. Chewbacca sat next to him, staring at the tabletop and rumbling quietly to himself.

Han caught the attention of a chrome-and-gold protocol droid standing behind the bar, pointed at a bottle of Corellian brandy, held up two fingers, and pointed at his own table. A few seconds later they had their drinks and Han flipped a coin to the droid, who caught it out of the air without a word.

Chewie growled softly at the droid's retreating back.

"I hear you, brother. Not my kind of place, either," Han said, then took a long swallow. "Booze isn't bad. You see anyone following us?"

Chewbacca barked and lifted his chin.

"Me neither," Han said. "So that's a decent start."

He pulled the disposable datapad Leia had given him out of his pocket and laid it on the table. It connected to the local network, updating its information with the most recent publicly available data and cross-checking it with what little the Rebel Alliance knew. Maps of the city flashed by in rapid succession, laying out the route from their current location to the park. Danger spots were marked in red: known trooper posts, Imperial government buildings, cams.

"Not going to be easy," Han said. The dead drop location was a memorial to some Imperial bigwig at the center of the park. Security droids wandered the park day and night, looking for malfeasance. Imperial troops patrolled the streets and skies, and possibly the park, as well. Observation posts dotted the city at intervals as regular as grid markers.

Chewbacca pawed at the pad, scrolling the map back and forth and grumbling.

"Wouldn't be my first choice as a drop location, either," Han agreed. "But maybe that's the point. If it's a trap, I'd put it someplace that didn't look like one. This Scarlet Hark character is supposed to know her business, so I guess we back her plays until we learn otherwise."

Chewbacca grunted agreeably and pushed the pad back to Han, who hit the button that melted the insides with a quiet sizzling sound and a tiny curl of smoke. He tossed it into a disposal unit in the wall.

"Well, we're earning our pay on this one. And maybe we have to get past a couple hundred Imperial troops, dozens of cams and observation points, and not draw attention to ourselves on one of the most heavily controlled planets in the Empire, but there's a silver lining to that."

Chewbacca cocked his head and growled.

"Nobody who works for Jabba's going to be here."

CHAPTER THREE

THE STATON MEMORIAL PARK and Recreation Area was twenty-five hectares of green on the roof of the massive Imperial Water Processing Authority. Half a kilometer of bureaucracy rising from the street level of Cioran, topped by a sward of hydroponic grass, trees, and fountains. A flier station perched at the building's edge, and thin, sleek machines docked or hovered, waiting to ferry citizens of the Empire to their next hygienic, clean, constrained appointment once their recreational period was done. Han felt about as inconspicuous as a Messian flame lizard.

"Will there be anything else, sir?" the flier intoned as he stepped off it.

"No."

"I can provide the menus of the park's food and drink vendors, if you are in need of refreshment."

"Thanks. No."

"Perhaps a guide for the statuary and memorials that adorn this, the most lovely of the recreation centers of Greater Cioran?"

Chewbacca lumbered up out of the flier's too-small seats. It was probably only Han's imagination that the vehicle floated a little higher afterward.

"We just want to explore it all for ourselves," Han said, trying to sound like a tourist.

"The Jaino Personal Transport Collective thanks you for your business. We hope you'll keep us in mind for all your travel needs," the flier said, then pulled out of the slip and joined the line of hovering machines waiting to carry people away again. Han stepped to the park's edge and looked down. The building was like a chalk cliff, pale and huge and windowless.

"Please step back from the edge, sir," an automated voice said. "For your safety and comfort, viewing platforms are at the northwest and southwest corners of the park."

Han gritted his teeth at the little service droid in something like a smile. "Why, thank you," he said. "I'll just go take a look."

"Please enjoy your stay at the Staton Memorial Park and Recreation Area," the droid said, cheerfully. It waited for Han to walk away first.

Chewbacca grunted amiably, stretching his massive arms.

"Yes, getting here did go very well," Han said.

Chewbacca growled again, craning his neck and smiling under his fur.

"Makes me nervous, too. I don't know. Maybe we caught a break."

The park was beautiful. Trees lifted their boughs a uniform six meters above the colonnades, and half a meter more in the open field. Grass so green it hurt to look at grew up four centimeters from the gel mats that took the place of actual dirt. All the paths formed perfect right angles, and discreet service droids lurked politely in the shadows, waiting for a bird to make a mess so that they could swoop in and clean it away. The soft cool breeze smelled of nothing.

Han had dealt with enough spies and criminals to understand that how a person worked said a lot about who they were. The profile on Scarlet Hark didn't have much character to it. Data and history, but nothing about who she was or how she operated. That she'd chosen the park for her dead drop told Han more about the woman than an intelligence profile could. The place was everything bad about the Empire. Every single element was regulated, controlled, built to specification, and then eliminated if it didn't meet standards. She'd picked it, he figured, because she'd fit in here among the pinch-faced Imperials in gray uniforms. He tried to imagine how it would feel, living someplace like Cioran where everything was kept exactly in place, everyone was watched and monitored, and order was enforced with a false politeness that only barely stretched enough to mask the threat of violence. He'd been in prisons he liked better.

Han felt his jaw growing tight as he and Chewbacca made a slow, careful turn around the whole place. There were maybe two dozen people in the park. Four old men sitting at dejarik tables, playing with the grim focus of sappers trying to defuse a bomb. Two younger women sitting on a bench that overlooked the vast canyons of the city, not speaking to each other. Some men playing a complex game on the turf, their expressions angry and joyless.

"Not as much security as I'd expected," Han said, once they'd made the first full turn through the place and come back to the paved court by the flier station. "So that's good."

Chewbacca moaned low.

"Of course they're all looking at you. You're a Wookiee."

The reply was a bellow.

"They probably haven't. I told you Saavin's not the kind of place that attracts a lot of Wookiees. Did you see the memorial? I think it's that black thing in the middle there."

Chewbacca chuffed.

"Why don't you let me take this part? You can go stand over there and . . . do something distracting. Sing, maybe."

Chewbacca looked at him silently.

"As a distraction. If they're all looking at you, they won't be looking at me, and it'll be easier to get the packet. This is basic stuff, Chewie."

The Wookiee sighed and made a show of lumbering away. Han waited a few seconds, then headed back toward the great black structure in the center of the park, pausing a few times on the way to admire perfectly unadmirable flowers and planters.

The fountain stood as high as the trees, symmetrical laminar jets of water arcing from it like rods of bent glass. In the center, the black stone statue of a human man stood heroically, his right hand over his left breast in salute. Han looked around innocently. A thick-faced man was buying a bowl of chaka noodles from a bright yellow stand. An old woman sat on a bench at the statue's left, looking disconsolately out into nothing, a service droid hovering at her side. Han ran his fingers over the memorial plaque, pretending to care what it said. CHIEF MOY STATON OF THE IMPERIAL RESOURCES COUNCIL IMPROVED EFFICIENCY OF SUBJECT SPECIES ASSIMILATION FOURFOLD AND WON SPECIAL MENTION BY THE EMPEROR and so on and so on. Han looked over his shoulder. Chewbacca stood about twenty meters away in a stand of manicured trees. Han nodded at him. Chewbacca didn't move. Han nodded again, the motion a little larger, and Chewbacca's voice lifted in a melodious howl, his wide, furry arms spread like an opera singer's.

Han leaned forward, steadying himself on the plaque, and sank his arm into the cold water. Smooth stone with gummy sealant at the joints. He shifted left and then right. His fingers touched something out of place and hard, and he dug at the place where it was adhered to the stone. It popped away with a satisfying click.

The case was brown and about the size of his palm. Han slipped it into his pocket and strolled away to a bench while Chewbacca finished his performance, then applauded politely as the Wookiee stalked over, sat beside him, and growled.

"If that's the worst thing that happens to you on this run, we'll have gotten away with something. Now let's see what we're working with."

Chewbacca grunted and whined.

"Yes, I'm opening it here. Look, if they noticed us, they'd follow us anyway. And if they didn't, then we might as well."

Now that it was dry, the cover of the case had a deep, almost iridescent sheen like an insect's shell. Han ran his thumbnail around the edge until it caught against an invisibly thin seam. He twisted once, leaning into the motion, and the cover snapped open. A tiny pad glowed a soft but forbidding red. He carefully entered the passcode, and the pad chirped happily, shifted to green, and swung open. The small compartment behind it was empty. Chewbacca groaned accusingly.

"How could it *possibly* be my fault," Han said as Chewbacca plucked the case from his hand. "I wasn't there when she put it in the drop."

Chewbacca tapped the case against the arm of the bench hard enough to make the metal chime, then peered into the space again.

"All right," Han said. "There's nothing here. So this is probably a trap, and we just took the bait. When they stop us, we stick to the story. We found the thing, we don't know what it is, and they're welcome to have it if they want it."

Han looked around the park, trying to seem casual. No stormtroopers were flooding into it yet. He had to fight the urge to draw his pistol and sprint for the fliers. Chewbacca moaned.

"I wouldn't believe us, either."

"Solo."

The voice was unexpected, calm, and friendly. Han twisted in the bench. The Mirialan walking across the grass toward them was broad and thick. His yellow-green skin was darker now than it had been when he was younger, and he had a few more tattoos on his chin and cheeks, but not many. He walked with a rolling gait that made him seem halfway to drunk, though as far as Han knew he never drank to excess.

"Baasen Ray? What are you doing here?"

"Waiting on you, apparently," Baasen said. "Chewbacca. Good to see you again. Been too long."

The Wookiee groaned and bayed. Baasen's expression went pained.

"What'd he say?"

"He said you're looking good," Han said. "He was just being polite, though."

"Sorry," Baasen said, nodding to Chewbacca. "It's my hearing. Got a hard enough time making out all the words even in my own language. So blast it, man, but it's been a long time. Guess you really are working for the rebels, eh?"

"What makes you say that, friend?"

Baasen rolled his eyes. "That when Hark called to get pulled, you showed up at her drop. Doesn't take a genius to add those two sums, does it? Truth is, I was more than half expecting you. Takes a madman or an idiot, flying rebel spies out of the Core, and . . . well, word gets about. Who's working for who. Like that."

"Really? I haven't heard much about what you've been up to. Last I heard, you were running the slow loop out of Hoven."

"Hard times. Hard times. Turns out I'm getting pulled by the same strings as you. Rebel Alliance. 'S why I'm here now. Watch the drop. Make contact. All of that."

"*You're* the message at the drop?"

"Well now, the woman's not an idiot. You didn't really expect her to leave written instructions on how to track her just lying about in public, did you?"

Chewbacca pressed the case into Baasen's broad hand with a chuffing groan.

"Sorry, what?"

"He said that we should get out of here, and I think he's right. You have transport?"

"Transport's what I do best," Baasen said. "Follow on, then."

Baasen trundled off to the north, not looking back to see whether they were coming. The men playing their game on the green ignored them as they passed. At the building's edge, a gray transport floater hovered over the empty air, its docking ramp clinging to the pavement of the park. The same droid that had ordered Han back from the edge, or else one just like it, was squawking at a lifting droid and being magnificently ignored. As Baasen stepped onto the ramp, the park droid shifted its outrage to him with as little effect. Han and Chewbacca stepped around it as they passed, and the lifting droid turned to follow, hauling up the ramp after them.

"I have to tell you," Han said. "After Caarsin Station, I'm a little surprised to see you."

"Everyone's got history," Baasen said amiably. "Man still has to work, whatever's in his past, eh?"

The interior of the transport was almost reassuringly musty and cobbled together. Three men squatted in the back. Two had the look of mercenaries; the last was thinner and more nervous about the eyes. They all wore blasters openly, and while they were cleaner than the average soldier of the Rebellion, they weren't anywhere near as crisp as the usual citizen of Cioran. Baasen knocked twice on the door to the pilot's cabin, and the transport swept out and down. Baasen, humming to himself, flicked a switch on the wall and tapped in a code on a keypad. Han nodded to the three men. They didn't smile. Han's belly went a degree tighter.

"Who're your friends?" he asked Baasen, his eyes on the men.

"Hmm? Oh. Garet and Simm there are part of my crew. Have been since forever. Japet, on the end there? He's a new friend. Just met him recent."

The rumble in Chewbacca's throat was a warning, but Han didn't need it. He dropped his hand casually toward his holster, getting close to the blaster without going for it.

"Good to meet you," he said with a disarming smile.

"Now, none of that," Baasen said. A blaster had appeared in his hand, and Han hadn't even seen him draw it. "We'll need your weapons."

Chewbacca bared his teeth with a bloodcurdling howl, but Baasen's aim didn't waver so much as a millimeter.

"You know how this is going to go," Baasen said. "Shoot it out here and now, and you take a couple down with, but you're still a dead man. Play nice, you maybe find a way out later."

"It happened last time," Han said.

"And maybe that's part of what this is about. History and all that," Baasen said with a grin. "So best you give us your weapons now, and no one dies for a time, eh?"

Chewbacca growled, looking from Han to Baasen and back again. Han weighed the chances. Baasen would die. And at least one of the others. Maybe two.

"Do as he says, Chewie," Han said, raising his hands.

"Good man. Live to fight another day."

"You used to be better than this, Baasen. Working for the Empire is low even for you."

"Oh, that's not me. Hand you over to them, and they'll

likely shoot me for my troubles. No. I got nothing against the Rebellion. It's just the Hutt's money's too good, and times are hard."

"Says something when Jabba is more trustworthy than the Empire."

"Does, doesn't it?" Baasen said as the hired gun he'd called Simm took Han's blaster.

"What happened to Hark?"

"Nothing I know of. Imagine she'll be disappointed that her ride never showed, but word is she's a resourceful one. She'll land on her feet."

Chewbacca stared at Simm and bared his teeth in a silent promise of violence. The man swallowed, but he still took Chewie's bowcaster and bandolier. The transport hit a patch of turbulent air, the car shifting a little and the drives whining to compensate. Simm handed the weapons to Garet and pulled two pairs of cuffs out of a blue plastoid toolbox.

"What about the message at the dead drop?" Han asked as the cold, heavy restraints clicked around his wrists, cycling tighter until the pressure was just on the edge of pain.

"Put it in the recycler, didn't I?" Baasen said. "Likely it's halfway to being paper for some sad Imperial toilet."

"Then there was one? She did leave a message?" Han said. "Written instructions on how to find her just out in public after all?"

"Of course she did," Baasen said. "It was that or trust the locals. Woman's not an idiot."

CHAPTER FOUR

THE WAREHOUSE WAS tucked off the flight hangar. Brushed-durasteel walls and impact-resistant ceramic crates were stacked as high as the ceiling in some places, dropped down and rearranged to serve as seats and tables in others. It was cold as a refrigerator, and the air was sharp with the stink of coolant and volatiles. Han sat on the floor. The wrist cuffs glowed blue, and the magnetic fields of the clamps made his joints ache. Chewbacca squatted a couple of meters to his left, scraping idly at one of the crates and ignoring Han, Baasen, and the two thugs entirely.

"Don't," Garet said, holding up his palm to Baasen. "I told you this before we left. I could stay and prep the ship, or I could go to the drop. You said come to the drop, so I did. Now I'm prepping the ship. Can't do everything at once."

"Hurry is all," Baasen said, brushing the back of his hand across the tattoos on his chin.

"I've put in for clearance to go. Sunnim's heating up the engines. We'll get out when we get out," Garet said. "You can try rushing the Empire if you want. I'll wait here."

Baasen shot a sour glance at Garet but didn't say more. He seemed to have a pretty small crew: the three human toughs from the back of the transport and a brown-furred Bothan pilot with a face like a sad goat—Sunnim, apparently—who'd been driving it. Han twisted the cuffs. They didn't even flex.

Garet walked away, the wide loading dock door hissing up to let him pass. Han caught a glimpse of the hangar. An ancient Sienar NM-600 squatted on the pad, the little freighter looking like a dirt clod against the shining backdrop of the dock. The pilot was standing beside it, speaking to a gray-clad Imperial functionary. Han wondered what would happen if he shouted for help. Nothing good. The loading dock door hissed down again. The other tough, Simm, yawned.

"Hoy, Chewbacca," Baasen said. "Leave that crate be."

Chewbacca looked up, answering with a complex howl.

"What'd he say?" Baasen asked.

"He thanked you for your kind suggestion," Han said, not even pretending it was the truth. If Sunnim the Bothan was halfway competent, it wouldn't take more than an hour to get the ship ready, even if it was dead cold. And once they were on that ship and out of the dock, Han didn't have much hope that they'd ever make it back.

So whatever he was going to do, it had to be done in the next few minutes. He looked over at Chewbacca, who was running his claws over the crate's hinge. If the Wookiee could pull the hinge bolt, he might—*might*—be able to short the magnetic coils in his cuffs. It wouldn't unlock them, but it might reduce the fields to the point that Chewbacca could bend them open by brute strength.

If there was just some way to tell him without the others figuring out what they were doing . . .

Han craned his neck. Chewbacca's blue eyes met his. Han glanced down at the crate, willing the Wookiee to follow his gaze. To *understand.* Chewbacca's sigh was so soft, it was nearly silence. He lifted a brown, hair-draped arm to show Han the hinge bolt hidden at his side.

Ah, Han thought. *Right. He'll need a distraction.*

He stood up. Simm and Baasen both raised their blasters.

"Obliged if you had a seat," Baasen said.

"I'm stretching my legs," Han said. "And you're not going to shoot me. This is the Core. You start firing blasters in here, and there'll be a hundred stormtroopers drawing down on all of us in about three minutes."

Baasen grinned ruefully, lowering his blaster but not returning it to his holster. Han walked to the far wall, turned, and sat on a crate, his body loose and comfortable. He shook his head.

"How did we get to this, Baasen? Used to be we were the guys who prided ourselves on ignoring the authorities. Now we're hunting each other down. And for what?"

"Money," Baasen said.

"Pretty much the money, yeah," Simm said, nodding. "It's good money."

The high screaming roar of an engine rose and fell as a ship left the hangar. Not theirs, but one fewer in the line that blocked their departure. Chewbacca sat forward, his expression disconsolate. His wrists vanished between his knees. Baasen sighed.

"Still, yeah. Know what you mean. The good days were good."

"You remember when Lando tried to buy that load of Caskan wolf-snake venom from you? Only you said he had to try a sample first to make sure it was the real thing?"

Baasen's eyes lit up a little, and his belly shook with silent laughter.

"He was seeing little pink fairies for a month," Baasen said. "But that was before, old friend. And it was before Dusty."

"Would it help if I said I was sorry about her?"

"Wouldn't hurt," Baasen said, then shook his head. "But it wouldn't help any, either. She did what she did because she did it. You weren't anything but the occasion for what was going to happen anyhow."

Simm shot a glance at Baasen, but if the Mirialan noticed, he chose to pretend he hadn't. Then Simm looked at Han, who shrugged. Chewbacca's shoulder twitched forward violently, and he bared his teeth in silent pain. No one but Han saw it.

"What about you, boyo?" Baasen said. "Rebel Alliance? I'd not have picked you for one of that kind."

Han grinned. "What kind's that? Idealist?"

"Government man."

"Hey now," Han said, surprised by how much the words stung. "No reason to get ugly."

"Call it what you want, old friend, but it comes to the same thing. The rebels get their way, and they step back in where the Republic used to be, and then who are you?"

"Look, I only took the work to help out some friends. If it pisses off the Empire, that's just a bonus."

"Friends, eh? Strong word for a man like you."

Han thought of Luke. It *was* strange that he'd taken to the kid as much as he had. All his life, he'd had a lot of people he got along with, a few he liked. There hadn't been many he'd put himself in the line of fire for. He found himself hoping that the kid's milk run as Wedge Antilles's second worked out. And hoping that he and Chewie would be back at the rebel fleet to hear the kid talk about it.

Another drive roared to life, rising and then fading away. They were running out of time. Chewbacca wasn't looking up from the glow of the cuffs in his lap, and Han couldn't tell where he stood with them.

"Anyway, friends are a weakness, aren't they?" Baasen said. "That's where your Hark failed out, too."

"How do you figure that?"

"The rebels, they're going up against the Empire. Wrong side of the law, them. But that don't make them *criminals*, if you see. Honest people with a different view of how things ought to be. Upstanding. Hell, heroic even, some of them. They're looking to change the galaxy. They win—not that they stand a chance, but *if,* y'know—then they turn into the law. You and me, now. Even little Simm here—"

"I'm not little anymore," Simm snapped.

"—we're *criminals,*" Baasen went on as if the other man hadn't spoken. "Not looking to make anything about the galaxy better except our little part. Put us in the Emperor's palace, we'd sell all the furniture before we took off."

"And Hark?" Han said. "Which one's she?"

Baasen's lips twitched into a faint smile. "Can't say quite. Bit of one thing, bit of the other. Only seen her once, but I can say I took a shine to her."

Behind the two men, Chewbacca strained silently but hard. His massive arms trembled with the effort, and Han had to fight not to look at him directly. Simm shifted on his crate, and before he could glance back Han stood again. Simm's eyes turned back to Han. And the muzzle of his blaster did, too.

"How do you figure Hark for making my same mistakes, then?" Han asked, pretending to ignore the weapon. Truth was, it made his neck itch.

"She made her mistake picking friends," Baasen said. "Not seeing the difference between an honest rebel and a criminal who don't mind working politics. Not as she had much choice, true. Cioran ain't got a deep pool of rebel underground to draw from."

"But everyplace has criminals," Han said.

"Needed someone to help her, picked a wrong crew, said a wrong thing, and instead of keeping her secrets for free, gentleman sold 'em."

"To you."

"Paid best."

"No, you didn't. The Empire would have paid a thousand times anything you could manage. He can't go to the Empire any more than you can," Han said, pointing his hands at Baasen in feigned anger. Chewie paused, his chest working and his teeth bared. Simm's blaster shifted another degree. Han's mind raced, grabbing for something to say. Anything, really.

"Japet," he said. "He's the one, isn't he? You said you'd just met him, and he's not here now. He was the rat."

Simm's eyes went a little wider, and he glanced at Baasen. The old smuggler shrugged. "Figured that out, did you? Well, no point fighting about it. Yeah, Japet knew she was working for the rebels, knew she was calling for transport off."

"How'd he know it was gonna be me and Chewie? Hark didn't call for us in particular."

"Didn't know, did he? That was me keeping ears to the ground. Captain Solo gone rebel. Alliance needs someone brave and crazy enough to come to the Core. Don't have many of those."

"You'd be surprised," Han said.

"Wouldn't. Politicians. Soldiers. They're the good people. They don't think like us. Can't make us out. Mistakes get made is all. No blame for it."

Han remembered Leia at her conference on Kiamurr, and the factions that were going to be there. It was a secret meeting of the enemies of the Empire, but Baasen was right. There were going to be plenty of them who would have been just as opposed to the Republic. Trust the wrong one, and they'd all be fed straight to the Empire. Leia. Luke. All of them. It was the nature of the game.

The door hissed open, and Chewbacca hung his head, pretending to be lost in dejection. The Wookiee could be astonishingly good at looking meek when he wanted to. Garet stepped in, keeping carefully out of range of Han's cuffed wrists. Behind him, the freighter's engines were the pale blue of hot standby, and there was no sign of the pilot. That wasn't good. The door hissed closed, and Han bit his lip. This was getting a lot closer to too late than he liked.

"Tower puts us ten minutes from out," Garet said, looking back at Chewbacca.

"What flight path?" Baasen asked.

"Commercial five," Garet said. "It was the best I could do. They could have gotten us commercial two, but it would have meant another hour."

"Commercial two is much better, though," Han said. "I don't mind waiting."

Baasen sighed and hauled himself to his feet. He looked old. Worse than that, he looked mean. There had been a joy in him once, and the universe had pressed it all out of him until this was left. In other circumstances, Han might have felt a little sorry for him.

"Get the cell ready," Baasen said. Garet nodded. The door opened, then closed behind him. "Time to go, old friend."

"There's another way," Han said. "Rebellion has a fair amount of money in it, one way and another. I have some friends in very, very high places. And this isn't a mission they want to see fail. Talk to the right people, they'll match Jabba's price. Maybe beat it."

Simm looked to Baasen, and the expression on the tough's face told Han it wasn't the first time that idea had been brought up. Baasen shook his head. Another engine roared and faded.

"Pretty thought, but it can't happen."

"Why not? You were never one to leave money on the table."

"Well, you see, I've already taken payment from Jabba. Not the full amount. A third, say. And most of that's spent, so even if I wanted to—"

"Wait," Han said, and for a moment, the blasters and

ship and Empire faded to the back of his mind. "You spent Jabba's money while we've been sitting in here? How does that work?"

"Not while we were here, no. Before. Getting ready."

"Jabba paid in *advance*?"

"Well," Baasen said, "I might have given the impression that you were a bird in hand. There was some overhead needed paying for. Anyway, no harm's done. Present company excepted."

Han's jaw opened a centimeter in real shock. Everything else was forgotten for the moment. He looked at Baasen again, and it was like seeing him for the first time. The redness in his eyes, the angry set of his softening jowls under his facial tattoos. The Baasen Ray he'd known before wouldn't have lied to the Hutt about having merchandise. And he would *never* have taken money for it.

Han laughed. "You're an idiot. Didn't you see what happened to me? I dropped cargo because we were about to get caught, and my life's been three kinds of hell for it. And you thought you'd *scam* a Hutt?"

"It was a risk," Baasen said. "Calculated, but it paid off. And, all respect, but you're going to be five nights of unpleasant floor show at Jabba's place before you're food for a sarlacc. So I think the time for Captain Han Solo to be lecturing me's pretty near its end."

"Simm," Han said. "Did you know he was crossing Jabba?"

"Doesn't matter," Simm said.

"Then you are as stupid as he is. Maybe worse, because you let him call the shots. Oh, I know, he plays the friendly, world-weary part pretty well. But he's tying you to a cherfer and lighting its tail on fire."

"Not your business how I run my crew," Baasen said. "Not anymore."

"Simm," Han said, "if you get me to a communications

array that can reach the Rim, I will see that you get enough money to retire for the rest of your life."

"Don't talk to him," Baasen snapped. Dark blooms appeared on his yellow-green cheeks. "If you talk to anyone, you talk to me, and you *don't* talk to me. You just march yourself to the ship. I've been kind not to break you. Jabba don't care if you still got knees when you reach him. So don't—"

"Really, Simm? Are you listening to this? Is this the kind of brilliant business acumen that says *long-term career* to—"

Baasen's blaster muzzle poked Han's throat. The Mirialan's face was a deep and unhealthy green. The avuncular mask was gone, and all that was left was an angry smuggler, past his prime, over his head, stinking of desperation. And dangerous beyond words. Han swallowed and hoped Baasen remembered what they'd said earlier about blasterfire bringing down the stormtroopers.

"My crew is my crew," Baasen said. "You say aught against me to them . . . well, that's being insulting. You didn't want to insult me, did you now?"

"I didn't," Han said.

Baasen smiled cruelly, stepped back, and lowered his blaster.

"What I *really* wanted was for both of you to keep looking at me," Han said as Chewbacca rose up behind Simm like a mountain made of long brown fur and rage.

CHAPTER FIVE

"OH" WAS ALL Simm had time to say before Chewbacca threw him across the room. The thug went headlong through a pile of crates and disappeared in the collapse. His blaster spun across the floor, stopping a few strides from Han and Baasen.

They looked down at it, then back up at each other at the same moment. Han knew Baasen was reading his face as he calculated his odds of reaching it before the Mirialan shot him. Baasen's hard half grin dared him to try. Neither of them moved until Chewbacca grabbed Garet and lifted him off the ground by the forearms.

Chewbacca's growls were almost drowned out by Garet's panicked shrieks. Baasen kept his blaster aimed at Han's face. "I'll shoot him, Chewbacca. Don't test me."

"Chewie is saying he'll tear your friend's arms off if you do, and he'd love for you to test him," Han replied. They stared at each other for another long, tense moment.

The door to the bay snapped open, and an Imperial officer walked in holding a datapad. "I just need to check one—" He stopped when he looked up and saw the scene. His face went white. Han could see the realization that none of them was walking away from this play across Baasen's face.

"Well, blast," the older smuggler said, and his shoulders dropped. Chewbacca roared and threw Garet at the officer. The mercenary flew across the room like a rag doll and slammed into the Imperial with a meaty thud. Both men went down in a heap. Baasen turned toward the Wookiee, raising his blaster, but Han launched himself in a full-body tackle that took them both to the ground and sent Baasen's blaster sliding across the floor. Baasen slammed a knee into Han's stomach, knocking the air out of him, and pushed him away. The old smuggler started crawling across the floor to the blaster he'd dropped, and Han rolled toward Simm's weapon as fast as he could.

Chewbacca was striding toward Baasen, fury in his eyes, spitting threats of grievous bodily harm at the old smuggler. Baasen reached his weapon first and sprang up to his knees, pointing the blaster at Chewbacca's head. "Sorry about this," he said as he pulled the trigger.

His weapon hand disappeared from the wrist down, his sleeve catching fire from the heat of the blast. Han didn't remember picking Simm's blaster up, but it was in his hand, the barrel smoking with the discharge. He climbed to his feet, keeping the weapon aimed at Baasen.

Chewbacca growled out his thanks and crossed the room to remove Han's cuffs.

"Anytime, pal," Han said, lifting his hands to let the Wookiee work on them, but keeping the blaster pointed at Baasen. The Mirialan's eyes were wide. "You just sit still, old friend, and maybe I'll forget how angry I am right now."

"You shot my hand off," Baasen said. He sounded more surprised than hurt.

"I was aiming at your head. It was kind of a rushed shot."

The cuffs hissed and popped when Chewbacca shorted them out, and a few seconds later they fell to Han's feet with a clank.

"Time to go," Han said to Chewbacca. Every Imperial alert system in the city would be blaring alarms at the unauthorized blasterfire.

The weapons Baasen had taken from them were laid out on a nearby crate, and Chewbacca stopped long enough to grab his bowcaster and Han's blaster. Han pushed Baasen over onto his back with one foot. "You don't want to try and follow us," he said. "The Imperials will throw you in prison, but if I see you again, I'll let Chewie pull you apart."

Baasen stared up at him with amusement and open hatred. "Oh, we'll meet again, boyo."

"You'd better hope not."

"WHERE DO THEY get all those guys?" Han muttered. Chewie huffed a sarcastic reply.

They were hiding in the shadow of a loading crane, about twenty meters off the ground. What looked like a thousand stormtroopers milled around the warehouses and docking bays below. Garet and Simm were both cuffed and kneeling on the ground outside their docking bay while a black-clad Imperial officer questioned them. Han couldn't hear what they were saying, but he could read the sullen expressions on their faces.

So far Baasen hadn't made an appearance. Han kept waiting for the old Mirialan to show up, led out in cuffs by Imperial troops, but it kept not happening. And the more time that passed without Baasen in custody, the more worried Han got. Maybe they were trying to modify the cuffs for a missing hand. That was probably too much to hope for.

"Think he slipped out before the troops arrived?" he asked Chewbacca.

The Wookiee growled.

"He always was a slippery old ghodstag," Han said. "You don't think he'd come after us, do you?"

Chewbacca looked at him out of the side of his eye and grunted.

"Well, looks like the boys in white aren't going to be leaving anytime soon, so we need to slip quietly away now."

Chewbacca chuffed a question.

"No, not the *Falcon.* Not yet. We still need to find our rebel spy, or this was all just a waste of time."

The Wookiee growled out a long response, and Han raised his hands in mock surrender. "Okay, okay, ease down, pal. Yes, I fired the blaster, and so it might seem like our current predicament is my fault. But Baasen was about to shoot you. Should I have let him do that? So, in a way, this is *your* fault."

Chewbacca's low howl was brief and philosophical.

"I mean, you could argue that."

Before Chewbacca could warm up to his rebuttal, Han slid down the crane's ladder to the ground and slipped into the alley between two warehouses. Old, worn-out packing crates littered the space, but there was no sign of any other garbage. For some reason, the utter lack of loose trash in the city was as chilling a sign of Imperial dominance as anything else. Han wondered what happened to people who littered. Whatever it was, clearly it was bad enough that no one did.

At the end of the alley, they hid behind an empty crate while a squad of four stormtroopers walked by on patrol. Chewbacca fingered his bowcaster and looked a question at Han.

"No," Han whispered. "No more shooting."

Chewbacca quietly huffed back at him.

"No, I did not 'start it.'"

The troopers went around a corner, and Han headed off

down the street in the opposite direction. They needed a place to hole up for a while, wait for the manhunt to die down before they picked up their search for Scarlet Hark. Holing up and hiding from the law were two of Han's specialties, but that was out on the Rim, where the Imperial presence was light and the populace cooperative. Cioran was the kind of place where hundreds of stormtroopers responded to a single blaster shot, and Han was willing to bet a lot of credits that there were hundreds more in reserve just waiting for the go signal. And the locals were used to being ground under the Imperial boot heel. They wouldn't dare risk their own safety by hiding fugitives from the law. There wouldn't be seedy bars where a man could slip into the shadows and a few credits in the right hands would keep anyone from asking questions.

Overhead, the traffic of speeders and personal fliers cast fast-moving shadows across gray and glass buildings that reached up so high, they appeared to lean in over the walkways below. Massive structures in a flat institutional style designed to be both functional and oppressive. And everywhere, at every intersection and building corner, the omnipresent eyes of the Empire. Sensor arrays and guard posts dotted the walls of every building. Sleek Imperial speeders cruised overhead, while squads of stormtroopers in urban pacification armor roamed the walkways.

"We may be in a lot of trouble here, Chewie," Han said. He took off his weapons belt and put it and his blaster into Chewbacca's satchel. He pointed at the Wookiee's bowcaster. "Might have to leave that behind, pal."

The Wookiee growled menacingly and clutched the weapon tighter.

"All right, here." Han took off his long coat and handed it to him. Chewbacca wrapped the bowcaster in it until it was just a long cloth parcel that only looked a little bit like a hidden weapon. "Guess that'll have to do."

Chewbacca hefted the wrapped weapon over one shoulder and growled out a question.

"Japet. We'll start with him," Han replied. "He's the one who rolled on her, so maybe he knows where she's hiding. Besides which, we haven't got anything else to go on."

Chewbacca howled and waved his arms around, pointing out the scale of the city and the size of the Imperial presence.

"Well, we'll just be careful, won't we?" Han said, annoyed. "We'll hit the port bars first."

Growling to himself, Chewbacca shrugged and started walking alongside Han.

"And if we keep a bright smile and a jaunty step, we're just two more loyal and happy subjects of the Empire, right? No reason for anyone to stop us."

If Chewbacca was unconvinced, he kept it to himself.

Han walked back toward the dock district where they'd left the *Falcon,* using as a landmark a particularly tall building with a copper-colored top that angled up like a spear point. He hoped there weren't two of them. He kept an eye out for a map or an information kiosk, but this area of the city seemed to be primarily warehouse space; there were far more droids than people, and almost nothing in the way of services for humans. Heavy lifting droids moved massive crates from building to building, and smaller tech droids—R2 and R3 units, for the most part—zipped about on obscure tasks. Occasionally, a squad of stormtroopers moved past in the distance, making Han change course to avoid crossing paths.

A street-sweeping droid rolled by, beeping quietly to itself as it scrubbed a stretch of walkway covered by an oil spill from a malfunctioning lifter. An eye on a long stalk tracked Han and Chewbacca as they walked by it. Han nodded to it as they passed.

"See?" Han began. "You just have to look like you belong—"

"Halt," the cleaning droid said in a deep mechanical voice. "Present valid identification for foot traffic in warehouse sector eleven-B, or wait for Imperial officers to detain you."

"Sorry, but we're pretty busy," Han said, giving the droid his best smile. "So we'll just—"

"Halt," the droid said again. Pieces of its silver shell slid apart, and half a dozen weapons appeared. "Present valid identification for foot traffic in warehouse sector eleven-B, or wait for Imperial officers to detain you."

A port irised open, and a smaller sensor device protruded from it. It waved at them for a moment, then the droid said, "Weapon detected. Drop all weapons and place your hands or manipulating appendages in the air."

Chewbacca dropped the coat-wrapped bowcaster and put his arms in the air. One long, multi-jointed arm darted out from the droid and picked up the package. The stalk-mounted eye stayed locked on Han. "Place your hands or manipulating appendages in the air."

"Yeah," Han said with sigh. "Already been taken captive once today, so pretty much at my limit."

"Raise your hands," the droid insisted stubbornly.

Han took a step toward the droid, and it rolled back an equal distance, its eye never moving.

"I bet you street-sweeping droids aren't really allowed to kill the citizens for something like not having the right identification."

"You'd be correct," a voice said from behind. "But I am."

Chewbacca growled out an angry rebuke.

"I only have eyes on the front," Han said, raising his hands and turning around slowly. "*You're* supposed to be watching behind."

Chewbacca shrugged.

A smiling Imperial soldier held a blaster pointed casually at Han. He wore the black uniform of a junior officer, and carried himself with the smug certainty common to his rank.

"You may carry on with your duties," the officer said, and for a moment Han thought he was being let go. Then he heard the whine of the retreating droid.

"Officer, we're—"

"Involved in that disturbance at the docks, like as not," the officer finished for him.

Han took a step back and to the side, trying to get Chewbacca into the trooper's blind spot. The officer shook his head and stepped back to keep them both in view.

"Please stop," the trooper said. "I have men on their way, and it really does look better on the reports if I take you alive."

Chewbacca roared and the officer spun toward him. He was just starting to turn back when Han hit him with a hard, straight kick in the midsection. The officer stumbled back, but he grabbed Han's boot on the way down, pulling Han with him. The struggle was brief, and afterward Chewbacca helped him drag the dazed trooper into an alley. A few minutes later, Han emerged wearing an Imperial uniform.

Chewbacca eyed him critically and growled.

"Yeah, laugh it up," Han said, straightening his sleeves and pulling on the officer's black cap. "At least this way I can wear a blaster. You're heading back to the ship."

Chewbacca growled.

"Yeah, but we're not going to find one of these Imperial outfits in your size, and they're on the lookout for *us* right now. Not *me*. So head back to the ship and get it warmed up. I'll find Hark and we'll get the hell out of here."

Chewbacca gave a questioning whine.

"I got a better idea," Han said, holding up the officer's

datapad. "I'd be willing to bet our boy Japet is on the Imperial watch lists. Known associates and hangouts. I'm an Imperial now. So I'll just look him up."

Chewbacca barked out another long laugh.

"Come on," Han said. "I can't *always* be wrong."

CHAPTER SIX

KINNEL PERSI, data technician fourth class, sighed, pulled up another entry on his monitor, and shook his head. Around him, the data-control center was busy as a hive. At the next desk, Miki shook her head in sympathy and tried not to grin. Secretly, Kinnel was enjoying her attention.

"How about Japet *Saun,* sir?" he said.

"Maybe," Lieutenant Hannu Sololo said, in the earpiece. "What's his background?"

"His NS-profile, sir?"

"Sure. That."

Kinnel tapped through the screens. "Larceny. Served two years in the work camp on Mangan Three. No present known address."

"Any known . . . um . . . *rebel* associations?"

Kinnel closed his eyes. "Would you like me to check the PF-profile, too, sir?" Miki giggled, pressing the back of her hand to her lips.

"Yes. Do that," Sololo said.

Kinnel clicked through. "You know, you have access to all these files on your datapad, sir."

"Mine's malfunctioning. The encryption protocol, um, needs upgrading."

"Maybe I can help you with that?"

"Just read me his PF-profile."

"*Read* it to you, yes, sir," he said for Miki's benefit. "Just a moment. Here we are. Yes, sir. He was associated peripherally with the resistance cell they caught last year in Port Chait. Questioned but not prosecuted. No records since then."

"Close enough," Sololo said. "Do we have any known associates that we do have addresses for?"

Kinnel hunched forward, his palms over his eyes. He kept his voice bright and pleasant. "Let me check his RQ history for you, sir." Miki was slapping her thigh now, her face dark with repressed hilarity. Kinnel hummed to himself as he worked. "His closest known associate is a Trandoshan dockworker named Cyr Hassk with a berth address of 113-624-e45."

"Hold on. Hold on. Six . . . two . . . four . . . What was the rest?"

"E four five, sir."

"Got it. Thank you. Good work."

The connection dropped. Kinnel pulled off his earpiece and looked over at Miki. She was still shaking with laughter. Tears streamed down her cheeks.

"Where do they *get* these people?" Kinnel asked before the next connection request came through.

Cyr Hassk considered himself in the mirror. The cut on his right head ridge had almost healed, but the scales there were the bright green of an adolescent. He rubbed at the spot with his thumb pad, hoping to scuff the scales to something a little nearer a mature man's gray. He didn't want to get cosmetic abrasives, but maybe if no one saw him—

A knock came at the door of his berth, three strong blows. Cyr lurched back from the mirror, falling into his warning hiss automatically. The berth was tiny. It wasn't more than four steps from his privacy corner to the door.

The human man in the doorway had the uniform of an Imperial officer and the demeanor of a salesperson. Hassk disliked him immediately.

"You're Cyr Hassk?" the man asked.

"Maybe."

"Japet said I'd find you here. That you could maybe help me out."

"He was wrong," Cyr hissed. He tried to close the door, but the officer had already stepped into the berth.

"He seemed pretty certain," the Imperial said, sweeping off his hat. His hair was a shaggy mop of brown, unlike the razor-cut Imperial style. Cyr's pupils narrowed and he flexed his hands. "Maybe we should go talk to him."

"Maybe you should step back out of here," Cyr snarled. "This is my berth."

The man gestured at his uniform. "Do you think I care about whether this is your berth or not?"

Cyr flexed his pectoral muscles and bared his teeth. The man's uniform didn't fit right, either. Too tight at the shoulders and loose at the gut. The lopsided smile was rich with threat, but it was the kind of threat that got settled in the street outside a bar, not in an interrogation chamber.

"Cut the crap," Cyr said. "Who are you, what do you want, and what makes you think I can or will give it to you?"

"I need to find Japet," the man said, dropping the ruse without a hint of chagrin. "You're his friend; you can tell me where to find him."

"If I'm his friend, I'm sure as hell not telling you where to find him. Get out."

"Under other circumstances, I would," the man said. "But he made a decision, and that decision affected me and my job, and now I'm going to need him to make it right."

Cyr weighed a few possible responses. *Japet's a small-time creep who will never make anything right in his whole blasted life*, or *I don't care about you and your problems, so get out*, or *How about we call security and see if they can help you*. In the end, he opted for punching the man in the gut. The fake officer's breath whooshed out, and he doubled over as Cyr brought a knee up to break his descending nose. Only the blow didn't connect. The man wrapped an arm around Cyr's leg and lifted. Cyr windmilled his arms, trying to keep his balance. His claws raked the walls, throwing sparks from the metal, but he went down with a clang. The world went a little quieter for a few seconds, and the universe contracted to the interior of Cyr's body and maybe a few inches past it. The man rolled onto him, putting a forearm lock across Cyr's throat.

"Okay," the man said. "I tried being nice and asking."

"Didn't," Cyr croaked past the choking arm.

"What?"

"Didn't ask. Weren't being nice."

"Oh. Okay. Will you please tell me where I can find Japet?"

"No."

"All right then," the man said, and punched him in the face. The blow was surprisingly strong. Cyr tasted the metallic flavor of his own blood. "Please?"

Cyr twisted, bringing his claws up toward the man's sides. A few more inches and he'd peel back the fake Imperial's skin until the ribs all showed. The man broke off the hold, pushing back just far enough to drop an elbow across Cyr's neck.

"*Pretty* please?"

The lights seemed dimmer than they'd been, and Cyr's breath sounded close and wet in his own ears. He rolled onto his belly, got to his hands and knees. The man kicked again, trying to shove him off balance, but Cyr pushed up. His punch went wide, skinning by the other's head and leaving a dent in the metal of the berth's wall. He pulled his arm back for an open-handed rake that would spill the man's guts on the floor.

The muzzle of a blaster dug into Cyr's neck.

"Sugar on top?"

"You pull that trigger," Cyr said, "and the real security force will be—"

"Yeah, I know. But we could avoid the whole thing if you'd just tell me where to find Japet."

Cyr licked his bloody lips. He could feel the swelling under his scales. When he went to the docks, the one thing no one would be paying attention to was the bright scales on his right head ridge. Cyr grinned.

Japet was an idiot, anyway.

"He's staying with Aminni. That's his girlfriend."

"Great," the man said. "And how do I find *her*?"

WHEN HE'D FIRST come in, Aminni had thought the Imperial officer looked like trouble. Two drinks after that, he was actually starting to seem a little cute. Another drink, and she was wondering if maybe it was going to be an interesting night, after all.

"I don't believe you," he said. His smile was sly and warm, and it made her feel like he was laughing at a joke that she was in on, even though he wasn't. "*You* don't have a boyfriend?"

Aminni drew her fingertip around the lip of her glass.

"We-ell," she said and stuck her tongue out at him a little. Across the bar, her roommate, Khyys, made a mildly obscene gesture of encouragement. Aminni ignored her. "I used to. But he was a jerk. I broke up with him awhile ago."

"Does he know that?" the officer asked, putting his hand on her knee.

"You bet he does. I put him and all his crap in the hall outside my berth."

"Of course you did," he said as if he was talking to himself.

"He'd been stealing my stuff. I told him one more time, and he was out. And then it was one more time. And then he was out. I kind of miss him, though. Not *him* him. I just kind of . . . y'know." She locked her gaze on his. *"Miss."*

The smile came again, long, and slow, and Aminni felt herself blush a little. She tried to count back how many drinks she'd had. It might have been more than three. Well, what the hell. Only live once. She moved forward in the seat, lost her balance a little, caught herself, and kissed his cheek. His arm curled around her, his hand against her waist as if it belonged there. She bit her lips a little and lifted an eyebrow.

"Probably I shouldn't have kicked him out," she said, her voice a little lower than usual. "Probably I should have called you. You deal with things like that, don't you?"

"Missing, you mean?"

"Thieves."

"That, too," he agreed.

"How long have you been in security?" she asked.

He chuckled. "Depends on how you count it."

She excused herself to the women's room to check her makeup, and when she came back out he was gone. She spent the rest of the night sitting with Khyys and her friends from resource management, feeling cranky and let down. Her night didn't hit bottom until it was almost time to go home.

"What's the matter?" Khyys asked.

"My datapad," Aminni said, pressing a hand to her belt. "I thought I brought it, but it must be back at . . ."

Even drunk, she had the physical memory of a man's hand around her waist, his fingers against her body.

"Son of a *bantha,*" she said.

"BABY?" JAPET SAID, stepping into the corridor. He was wearing a splash of cologne and held a fistful of flowers he'd bought for half a credit from a vending machine on the fourth level. "Minni-baby? I got your message. You here?"

In the shadows, something moved, and Japet smiled a little.

"I see you back there," he said. "I knew you were gonna call me. I told you, you remember? I told you you'd call me. You can't go without your big Japet man, can you? No, you can't."

"You might be surprised," a man's voice said behind him.

Japet whirled. The man in the shadows wore an Imperial officer's uniform, but the face was wrong. Not deformed or anything; it just belonged someplace else.

"Who are you?" Japet demanded. "Where's Aminni?"

The man smiled. "Wait for it. It'll come."

Japet narrowed his eyes. He knew the guy. He'd seen him before, and recently. And then with a rush of ice in his veins, he knew. He spun around, half expecting the Wookiee to be standing behind him. Fear lit his nerves and he stumbled back.

"Please, Captain Solo, don't kill me," Japet said. "I'm sorry. It was Baasen. He made me."

Solo spread his hands, smiling without the expression ever reaching his eyes. "You know *nobody* ever believes that line, right? No offense taken. I've used it a couple of times myself. I'm just telling you it never works."

"I'm sorry. Please don't shoot me," Japet said. He tripped over his own feet, falling backward. The flowers scattered on the pristine corridor floor. The rebel pilot knelt beside him, blaster in hand.

"So here's the thing. I know why you did it. Baasen promised to pay you. I'm a businessman. I understand that math. But because of you, I missed my cargo. And I have to find it now. You're going to help me."

"I can't," Japet said, tears welling in his eyes. Baasen had sworn that Solo would be offplanet almost as soon as they nabbed him. He didn't want to guess what had happened to the others.

"You should reconsider that," Solo said, his voice getting rough.

"I want to! It's not that I don't want to! I *can't*. I don't know where she is. It's not like she told me anything."

"She told you enough to set a trap for me."

"She didn't tell *me* anything," Japet said. "I found out about the drop because two of the guys from the rebels were talking about it. I did some work for her a few times because the pay was good. Little stuff. Working lookout when the guys were carrying a couple of data disks one place to another. Getting some dirt on some Imperial somebody."

"Enough she started thinking you were on her side," Solo said.

"I've only ever seen Hark a few times. But there's this place down on level eight where these guys hang out sometimes, and I was there and everyone was a little drunk, and someone was talking about how they weren't going to have to deal with any more of Hark's errands because she was pulling out."

"That's the kind of talent she's got to work with?" Solo said, shaking his head. "No wonder it went south."

"I guess. Yeah. They said she was using the fountain drop. I took it to Baasen because he can use things like that sometimes."

"So you didn't mean anything against me, you were just trying to get Hark's operation blown."

"Baasen pays really well," Japet said sorrowfully.

"Don't ask where that money came from. All right. How do I find Hark now?"

"I don't know," Japet said.

"There has to be some way to signal her," Solo said,

looking down the corridor as if he were a hunter on a trail. "Does she know you on sight?"

"Don't know. Like I said, I only met her a few times. But she's got a reputation for remembering stuff you wouldn't think. So maybe. I don't know."

"If I shot you, would it make the local news?"

"You know what you could do?" Japet said, snapping his fingers. "You could talk to the guy who said she was setting up the fountain drop. His name's Wirrit, and his place isn't far from here."

"Maybe," Solo said. "Doesn't have the advantage of shooting you. I'd *really* like to shoot you."

WIRRIT OPENED THE DOOR a fraction of an inch. He was in his underwear, his hair still wild from the pillow and all thought of sleep gone. The Imperial guard had a black jersey, a black-and-gray cap, and an annoyed expression. Wirrit's hand shook as he very carefully, quietly, pressed his blaster against the door. He'd only have one shot. He had to kill the Imperial on the first try.

"I'm with the Rebel Alliance," the Imperial said. "Hark's drop was compromised, and I need to know where she's staying."

Wirrit narrowed his eyes. His finger didn't leave the trigger.

"How do I know you're telling the truth?"

The Imperial shrugged. "One, I didn't come in with fifty stormtroopers behind me. Two, we're talking here instead of a holding cell. Three, an interrogator droid didn't take off half your fingernails before I asked."

Wirrit frowned.

"Oh," he said. "Right."

THE AIR SHAFT went down below Han for what looked like half a kilometer. He hung in the window frame, his fingers aching until they felt as if they were on fire. If he had pulled the window open another few centimeters, the grenade would have triggered.

Windows from the other berths and apartments lined the walls, looking out into one another or else at the bare drop. Five levels up, a catwalk stretched across the void. Han's grapnel line was like a thread of spiderweb between Hark's window and the high, empty walkway above.

He'd tried the door for almost an hour, plagued by visions of Hark inside either dead or held in silence by stormtroopers or Baasen. Or just sleeping deep enough that she didn't hear him. Going around to the back had seemed like a good idea at the time . . .

He shifted his grip on the window. He couldn't hold on much longer. Just inside, the black monofilament thread had pulled at the proton grenade's switch, tugging the little kettle-shaped device to the edge of the cheap breakfast table. He couldn't tell if it was armed, but if so, the drop to the floor would set off an explosion strong enough to breach a ship's hull. Unless it was on a timer, in which case he'd probably have been dead by now.

He pulled himself as close to the window as he could, pressing his mouth to the opening. The air inside smelled like roasted peppers.

"Hello?" he whispered urgently into the apartment. "Could use a little hand here. Hello?"

There was no reply. His knuckles hurt.

Hark was gone, then. She'd left her old place and trapped it against intrusion from the Imperials. The safe play was to go back up the line to the catwalk, but if there were any clues to where Hark had gone, they were going to be on the other side of the window. And he didn't have any other leads to follow.

"All right," Han said to himself. "It's not that hard. I can do this."

He couldn't keep his grip and also work, so he held on with his right hand and stretched his left through the thin gap in the window until it was all the way into the apartment. He made a fist and let his right hand go. His balled left hand was too big to fit back through the space, and the grapnel line was strong enough to support him. It still hurt like blazes, but it freed his right hand. He pulled his blaster and ejected the power cell, catching it between his little finger and the heel of his palm before it dropped into the abyss below him. Shorting out the contacts would have been a lot easier with two hands, but a few seconds later he had the case cracked and the power leads were starting to heat up past the point of comfort.

Pulling from the shoulder, he hauled himself closer to the window. The proton grenade teetered on the edge of the table as he slipped his fingers in through the open window, holding the shorting power cell against the frame just where the monofilament attached. A trickle of blood ran down his left wrist. Voices echoed above him. Someone was approaching the catwalk. He tried to push the power cell a little closer to the line. The hot smell of melting filament began to overpower the scent of peppers.

The voices came closer and clearer. The tinny voices of stormtroopers.

"Come on," Han said. "Come *on* . . ."

Inside the apartment, the monofilament broke, floating down like a wisp of smoke. Han shoved the window open enough to slide through, cut the grapnel line, and haul himself over the sill. He lay on the apartment floor, curled around his protesting hand. The troopers' voices didn't rise in alarm. He sat up, trembling. The proton grenade showed ARMED. Gently, he pushed the switch back, and a second later the readout shifted to INACTIVE.

Across the air shaft, a small figure looked out the opposite window, long dark hair silhouetted against the light. Han waved and gestured. The child went to open her window, paused, and then followed through. Her eyes were wide.

"Lost my keycard," he shouted across the shaft.

"Oh," she said.

He grinned, nodded, and closed the blinds.

All the rooms were trapped in the same way. Simple, fast, efficient. Not foolproof by any means, but effective enough. There were still clothes in the bedroom. The food in the storage unit hadn't gone bad. Scarlet Hark had been there, but she was gone, and there was no note saying where she'd gone.

He examined the bedroom, the bath, the dining area. All the small signs of occupancy, but nothing that helped. Scarlet Hark drank Surian tea. She solved math puzzles before she went to sleep. She ordered breakfast meals of eggs and roasted peppers from a nearby restaurant. Apart from the death traps on the windows and doors, she could have been anyone.

He'd been working all night. Somewhere high above where the city reached the sky, the sun would be coming up soon. Chewbacca was probably pacing the *Falcon* right now, wondering what had happened to him. Han sat at the table. His eyes felt as if someone had rubbed grit into them, and his wrists ached. The Imperial guard's uniform was cheap and uncomfortable. Start to finish, it just hadn't been his best day ever.

When he stretched his neck, the joints cracked. There had to be a way. There had to be something that would point him toward Hark. Or give her a way to find him. He rubbed his eyes with the palms of his hands until blobs of false color danced before him. There had to be a *way*.

His stomach growled. He hadn't eaten since before the

failed drop. The scent of yesterday's roasted peppers started smelling almost good.

He frowned, sat forward. The recycling bin was half full of old tea and the wire remains of a robotic project. Greasy wrapping paper had an order—#29 PEPPERS & EGGS—printed on it with a comm code, the address of Hark's apartment, and the minimalist logo of a Twi'lek female holding a plate of food. KAYI'S GRILL: BEST SANNOS PLATE IN THE EMPIRE! There was another wrapper underneath it from the day before. And another. She had a habit, then. It didn't seem like it could matter, but something tugged at his mind.

He frowned at it for a moment. Why would it have her address on it? Then he knew. She'd had it delivered. And if she'd been getting it delivered here, she *might* be getting it delivered someplace else. Han smiled and tapped his fingertip against the words.

"I ORDERED A number twenty-nine," the scruffy lieutenant said, slapping the back of his hand into his palm. "It was supposed to be *delivered.* And now I have to come all the way down here."

Kayi leaned against the counter. She'd hardly been here two hours, and her feet already hurt. The man scowled at her. His black uniform looked like it had been slept in, and he had a day's worth of stubble on his chin. She comforted herself with the idea that his superior officer would be chewing him out before lunchtime.

The breakfast rush was in full swing, aliens of half a dozen different species pushing and jockeying for a place to stand. None of the sharp-lined, high-official types were here. All of them had the tired expressions of workingbeings facing down another long day. The air was thick with aromatic grease and the voices of the three Twi'lek men, her husband and brothers, shouting obscenities from the kitchen.

"When did you order it?" Kayi asked.

"This morning," the man said, waving his hand vaguely.

"A particular *time* this morning?" she asked, the two lekku that hung from the back of her head twitching in annoyance.

"Long enough," he said. "Plenty long enough."

"Let me check," she said, with the best smile she could manage. She leaned back toward the kitchen and shouted in her own language, *"Tai'mer! This nerf's behind out here says he ordered a twenty-nine sent out."*

"It's almost done," her brother said.

"Why isn't it out yet?"

Her brother leaned out of the kitchen, holding up the wrapping. *"I printed up the order fifteen minutes ago, and we're in the middle of the rush. That's why not."*

A bronze-and-blue delivery droid zoomed past him, two Sannos Plates in its spiderlike silver arms, and flew out over the heads of the crowd. Kayi sighed and turned back to the lieutenant.

"The order must have been delayed, sir," she said in Basic. "It's almost done now. I'm very sorry for the inconvenience."

"It's all right," the man said. His smile was gentler now. He was almost good looking. "Just wrap it up when it's ready, and I'll take it."

"Of course, sir."

"I mean, I don't want to be a nerf's behind about the whole thing."

Kayi blushed, but the man's smile was so warm, his eyes so merry, she found herself smiling, too.

THERE WERE TWO beds in Scarlet Hark's hired rooms. One, she'd slept in. The other had her equipment laid out in neat rows and columns. The magnetic grapnel. Three blasters, each from a different kind of material that could pass Imperial scanners. The false ID array. Her security countermeasure pack, each black-steel tool in place like the legs of a centipede. The data disks with the schedule and internal layout of the intelligence command offices, and the offices above and below them as well. Everything she needed was in place, except for one thing.

The door chimed. When she opened it, a man was standing there, her breakfast in his hand. He looked both exhausted and smug.

"Scarlet Hark," he said, bowing ironically and presenting her meal like he'd done something clever. Her spine went stiff. An Imperial officer . . . only no.

"Aren't you a little old for a delivery boy?"

"Depends what you want delivered," he said. "Leia said you'd called for pickup."

She accepted the wrapped package with a smile. "You're late."

CHAPTER SEVEN

In person, Scarlet Hark looked sharper than the stills in her profile. Sitting cross-legged on the unmade bed, she unwrapped her meal with an economy of motion that gave the slant of her eyebrows and the half smile on her lips a sense of purpose and professionalism. The smell of spiced egg filled the room, reminding Han that he was still hungry. Ignoring the feeling, he stepped over to take another look at the equipment arrayed on the spare bed. Some of the items laid out there he didn't recognize, but he was pretty sure that if a real Imperial security officer had stepped into the room, it would have meant a firing squad for everyone in a half-kilometer radius, just for the sake of completeness.

Scarlet Hark sighed. Her finger was on the take-out wrapper where her address was listed.

"I should have thought of that," she said. "I've been in the field too long. Getting sloppy."

"I wasn't going to say anything," Han said.

A secretary droid with a blue metal casing stepped out of the closet.

"CZ, this is my ride out of here. Ride out of here, this is CZ-Thirty-Three."

"The pleasure is mine," the droid said in a deep, rolling voice.

"Certainly is," Han said, and then turned his attention back to Scarlet. "The name's Solo. Han Solo. Might have heard of me."

"Might have," Scarlet said, the corners of her lips pulling out another millimeter. "In my line of work, that's not necessarily a good thing."

"Well, the sooner we get you out of here, the sooner that stops being a problem. Why don't you pack up your toy box here, and we can get to the dock. Chewie should be ready for us."

Scarlet sighed and leaned back against her pillows. "There's a problem with that. There's something we need to do first."

Han shook his head. "No, there isn't. You called us for a ship out of here. Ship's here. It's time to go."

"True enough," she said around a mouthful of eggs. "But that means it's time to do the work I couldn't do when I didn't have a way out. Do you want some of this? You keep looking at it."

"Since you're offering," Han said.

Scarlet Hark ripped the take-out package in two and put a portion of the meal on one half, talking as she did.

"Have you ever heard of Essio Galassian?"

"No. Why? Is he important?"

Scarlet nodded to the droid. "CZ? Do the honors?"

A holoprojector emerged from the droid's left eye, and tiny figures appeared above the bed. One was a man with an athlete's build and flowing shoulder-length hair. He was screaming at an older man who was cowering before him. As Han watched, two floating droids the size of two balled human fists followed the long-haired man's sweeping gestures, slamming into the older man's ribs and the side of his head. The older man went down, face and knees slack.

"That's him with the sparring floaters," Scarlet said.

"Seems charming," Han said. "I'm guessing not your old boyfriend."

"He's the Emperor's pet astrocartographer. Runs private missions for the highest ranks of the Empire. Answers to no one, but sometimes he shares information with the security services. He's also a megalomaniac, a fanatic, and a murderer."

CZ turned off the hologram and Galassian vanished. Han accepted the rough paper with its load of egg and pepper. It was still warm, and the smell made his stomach feel empty and eager. He scooped up a mouthful with two fingers. It tasted better than he'd expected.

"I've been infiltrating his operations for the last year and a half," Scarlet went on. "He was on an exploratory mission of some sort. Very quiet. And when he showed back up, he was very, very pleased with himself. The rumor was he'd found something interesting. The sort of discovery that the Emperor would give his favorite pet a treat for. Only someone stole the report and all the preliminary data from his private station on Tyybann, and wiped his file system."

"Someone being you," Han said.

"Unfortunately, no," Scarlet Hark said. "An amateur got lucky. No planning ahead of the heist, and no back end once it was over. Galassian figured out he'd been compromised almost at once, and he threw a fit. Had his entire household staff killed or wiped and reprogrammed."

"Harsh," Han said, sitting on the edge of her bed.

"CZ and I were in his household staff at the time," Scarlet Hark said. "So, yes. It was unpleasant. I was three days from getting a covert copy of his whole records system, and he would never have known it happened. Instead, I wound up tracking through an ice jungle for three weeks, breathing stale air out of tubes and drinking recycled water."

"Recycled water doesn't sound good," Han said.

"It was undignified."

"Still very sorry about that, ma'am," the droid said.

"But," Scarlet went on, "it also gave me enough time below Galassian's radar that when I made it back to a civilized port, he'd moved on. Taken his personal Star Destroyer and headed out . . . somewhere. There was a full investigation going, trying to track down what had happened to the data." She finished the last of her eggs and crumpled the paper in her fist. "Security had a task force on it for a month and a half. They must have pulled in a hundred people for interrogation, and probably three-quarters of those came back out in enough pieces that they could get sewn back together." She tossed the wadded paper across the room, and the droid plucked it out of the air.

"Did they find anything?" Han asked despite himself.

"Yes."

"What?"

"Don't know," Scarlet said with a sunny smile. "Whatever it was, it has half the Imperial fleet getting pulled off missions and the security services scrambling like a kikka nest on fire."

"Can I take that for you, sir?" the droid asked, extending its hand. Han put the torn paper with its eggy film into the blue metal palm, still chewing thoughtfully.

"What did this astrocartographer find in the first place?" he asked.

"Good question. That's what I was trying to find out. Only the amateur got it sloppy before I could get it clean."

"Well, did the Imperials get whatever it was back, or did they just find out who stole it?"

Scarlet lifted her hands. "Dunno."

Han scratched the back of his neck. "Well, that's . . ."

"It really is. The good part is that the security forces' complete and final report on the theft is about ten minutes from here by hired flier. Maybe an hour on foot. Losing that data has the security forces throwing a quiet seizure, and everything they know is right there for the taking."

Han smirked. "Unless another bunch of amateurs gets to it before you."

"Not likely. It's on a physically isolated deck in the Imperial Intelligence Service Center. It's encrypted with Galassian's personal cipher. And they have a constant audit routine that sounds the alarm if anyone so much as makes a copy."

"Well, that's too bad then, sister," Han said. "Because I wasn't hired on to have the security service blow my brains out. I was supposed to get in, get you, and get out. And that's what I plan to do."

"Well then, *sister,* you'll have to wait until I'm done. I've spent too long on this to walk away."

"Brother. If I call you sister, you call me brother, see, because—"

"CZ? Let's see the layout."

"Of course, ma'am," the droid said, and five layers of architectural schematics appeared floating above the sheets. The lines glowed in crisp blue. Scarlet reached into the display. "The first problem is getting into the building at all. The intelligence services control the eightieth and eighty-first floors, but there are access ways on seventy and seventy-three. No one gets into the complex without authorization."

"Which you don't have," Han said. Scarlet pulled a card from her pocket and tossed it through the projection to him. Her face looked out from identification for Choya Sebastiao, environmental technician third class. "I was thinking I'd make you my apprentice, but if you're the guard acting as escort, that's probably better. CZ? Can we arrange that?"

"The card is already being programmed, ma'am. I took the liberty of capturing sir's image when he arrived."

"Spiffy."

"Hey!" Han said.

"Once we're in, we make our way here," Scarlet said, tracing her finger through the tiny, glowing corridors. A pathway of soft green followed where she traced. "It's the probe and sensor encoding regulatory council annex. Still part of the intelligence services, but lower security. We'll need to watch for security droids here and here." Two blobs of dull orange appeared in the schematic. "And there are regular patrols that take this path. And this." Two orange pathways appeared, intersecting the green. Tiny orange dots tracked along them, marking the positions of the guards in time.

"This is a terrible plan," Han said.

"There's a cable conduit access here." The green pathway wormed up through the floors. "It carries the main trunk cables from the transmission towers on the roof to the processing levels down in the forties. Bad place to slip and fall, but it'll get us up to the intelligence service center. We'll need to cut our way through."

"Because no one will notice that."

"I have decking tape," she said. "I've got a high-strength grapnel line that will get us up the vertical parts, and that will get us here." A tiny point of brilliant red appeared on the map, very close to the end of the green pathway.

"Where everything will be open and easy, and no one will get hurt," Han said.

"Where I can use the passcodes and identity records I got while I was working with Galassian to get access and drop a copy of the report to a memory chip." Scarlet's mouth twisted into a tiny smile that was as much regret as amusement. Han looked at the little crimson dot, but the glow didn't give him anything that would explain her expression.

"All right," he said. "And then what?"

"And then every alarm on the planet goes off, and we leave very, very quickly."

"Let's go back to *my* last points, which were 'terrible plan' and 'not going to happen.' "

"This is the part where things are a little more problematic," she said. "I haven't been able to get a full breakdown of the intelligence service emergency intrusion protocols. But we'll have the advantage of knowing that it's going to happen. No one will expect that anybody would attempt to breach physical security like this—"

"You know there's a reason they wouldn't expect that, right?"

"—but this is why I needed to wait until I had a way off-planet that could go immediately. There is going to be a gap when people are confused and scrambling. If we're not in hyperspace before they restore order, we're screwed."

Han waved his arms through the hologram, and CZ let the image fade.

"We're in the Galactic Core and we're working for the Rebellion," Han said. "In most contexts, that's screwed enough right there. I can get you out of here right now, but that's because I'm the best pilot there is. If we light up the security arrays before we even get to the ship—"

"You're not *that* good?" Scarlet asked innocently.

"Nobody's that good."

"Not even the man who made the Kessel Run in thirteen parsecs?"

"Twelve," Han said around a grin. "I did it in twelve. So you *have* heard of me."

Scarlet Hark smiled, and then sobered. "I've spent a lot of time trying to find out what Galassian found. And I've watched some good people die because I asked them to. I have to get that before we leave. If you want to wait in the hangar, I won't stop you, but I think my chances would be better if you came with."

"You see now, that's sounding more like you're asking for my help."

"I'm asking for your help."

They were silent for a moment. Han tapped his fingers against the fake leather of the Imperial uniform's boot.

"What do I get out of it?" he asked.

"Bragging rights."

"That's pretty thin."

"Bragging rights and the undying gratitude of the Alliance."

"How about bragging rights, undying gratitude, and three thousand credits as a performance bonus."

"Done," she said.

Han blinked. "Really?"

"I'd have gone to six, if you'd asked."

"I'd take six."

"Three it is," she said, standing up and checking the time. "If we leave here in an hour, that will put us just about where we need to be. What do you need to get the ship ready?"

"The ship's ready," Han said. "What about your pet droid? How does he fit into this?"

"Ma'am?" CZ asked, and the electronic voice seemed to hold some weight of meaning that Han couldn't quite fathom. Scarlet looked at the blue droid, and her face seemed to soften. Han felt a moment of awkwardness and discomfort, as if he was seeing something intimate.

"This is it," she said. "Finish this, and we're square."

"Yes, ma'am," the droid said, and bowed its head. Scarlet put her hand on its shoulder.

"Thank you," she murmured.

Han cleared his throat. "Am I missing something here?"

"Don't worry about it," Scarlet said, her voice crisp and amused again. "Let's go over the plan."

CZ re-formed the schematic hologram, and for half an hour Han and Scarlet Hark went over each detail. Where the entrances to the building were, the schedule of the patrols, the placement of the conduit. CZ interrupted once to deliver a forged identity card with Han's face on it still warm from the fabrication unit. Scarlet packed her equipment from the spare bed with a practiced efficiency. The tools of spycraft folded into the seams of her pants and the sleeves of her jacket.

When they were done, Han called Chewbacca on his comlink. The Wookiee's roar overloaded the tiny speaker, making his words a stuttering crackle.

"Well, I'm checking in now, aren't I?" Han said. "I found her, but there's an errand we need to do before we go."

Chewbacca's growl was a warning.

"I don't like it, either, but I talked her up to a three-thousand-credit bonus if I help her out. You just make sure the engines are warmed up and the clearances are ready. We're probably going out hot."

Chewbacca whined and grunted. Scarlet raised her eyebrows and smiled. Han found himself smiling back.

"Well, we didn't get where we are by playing it safe, did we?" he asked. Chewbacca's shout was louder and more obscene than usual. Han dropped the connection to the soft sound of Scarlet's laughter.

"He knows you pretty well," she said.

"We've shipped together for a long time," Han said. "Are we ready to do this?"

She frowned. "You look like you slept in those clothes," she said. "It'll stand out. CZ? One last favor?"

"Of course, ma'am," the droid said.

"Thank you."

"For what?" Han said. "What are you thanking him for?"

Scarlet tilted her head. "We need to press your uniform. If we had time, we'd get you a haircut, too, but we'll make it work."

"All right, but I'm wearing it," Han said.

"So take it off. We don't have much time."

Han hesitated.

"If it helps, I promise not to look," Scarlet said.

"No," Han said, undoing the belt with a violence born of embarrassment. "Go ahead and look if you want to. Take a great big long stare." Scarlet turned to face the door of the room, her long-fingered hands laced together behind her. Han pulled off the shirt, then the boots, then the pants. He handed them to the droid.

"I'm not looking," Scarlet said in a teasing singsong.

"I'm not embarrassed," Han said to the back of her head. "I am a very good-looking man."

"Indeed you are, sir," the droid replied. "I'll have these for you in a moment."

CHAPTER EIGHT

"YOUR DROID DOES good laundry," Han said as he and Scarlet rode the lift to the roof of her building. Not only was the officer's uniform cleaned and pressed, but it actually seemed to fit better. Han couldn't see any stitches where the droid had made alterations.

"He's not my droid. He's his own," Scarlet said, but didn't elaborate.

The top of the building had a strictly regimented garden space, with planter boxes and fountains. No one was sitting on the benches, which left Han sighing with relief. Someone dressed like an Imperial officer and someone dressed like a maintenance worker climbing into a rental flier together might be odd enough to be remembered, and once Scarlet's plan went off, Imperial security forces would be swarming through the city looking for their trail. Han had left enough of one with the shootout at the docks. No reason to connect the dots from there to Scarlet Hark.

"Over here," Scarlet said, walking to the landing pad on one side of the roof. She hit the key to summon a flier. "You have credits on you?"

"A few," Han replied.

"Give them to me."

"I'm not sure—" he started.

Scarlet stabbed her hand at him impatiently. "Do you think an Imperial officer traveling with someone of a lesser rank ever *pays* for anything?"

Han handed her his few remaining creds. "I've been robbed before, but never without a fight."

"We could fight, if you'd feel better," Scarlet said, raising an eyebrow. Her dark eyes stayed on his as she pulled her long black hair into a practical knot at the back of her neck. She locked it in place by pushing two small sticks through it.

Han crossed his arms and shrugged. "You know, I've never in my life been bossed around as much as I have since I hooked up with you rebels. It makes me wonder if you guys actually know what that word means."

"What word?"

"Rebel."

Scarlet carefully went over her gray maintenance jumpsuit, checking to see if her various tools and patches were all in place. She had a methodical nature Han found grating and familiar at the same time.

"We're not anarchists," she said, tugging at the patch on one sleeve that identified her as a level-three technician. "We have goals. We want to end the Empire."

"And replace it with what?"

"You know what," Scarlet said. Her crossed arms matched his own. "Are you trying to make fun of me?"

"It was rhetorical. I've heard the speech, sweetheart. 'A glorious return to the Republic of old.' To a guy like me, a new boss is still a boss."

"Then why are you helping us?"

"Honestly? Still trying to figure that one out."

If she had a reply, the rumble and air wash of the approaching rental flier drowned it out. She hopped on board and gave the droid driver an address. It waited until Han was seated and Scarlet had dropped a handful of coins into its receptacle, then the flier shot up into the sky, Han's belly sinking.

Scarlet leaned back in her seat not looking at him, so Han assumed the conversation was over. The truth was, it was an argument he'd been having with himself ever since the rebel fleet had left Yavin. The Death Star had been destroyed. He'd been given his reward for the rescue of Leia. Jabba was still out there, putting a price on his head and waiting for either his money or his corpse. But he kept lingering. Running missions for the rebels, spending time with Leia and Luke, taking chances that the old Han Solo would never have taken. Three thousand credits was nice, but it wasn't any more than a good smuggling run someplace besides the Imperial Core might have netted him. He was having a progressively harder time convincing himself that he was still doing it for the money.

Part of it was watching out for Luke. If there was anyone in the galaxy likely to get in over his head, it was the kid. Part of it was the joy of thumbing his nose at the Empire.

But always there was the voice at the back of his head telling him that by joining the Rebellion he'd become less of a rebel than he'd ever been. Flying off to assault yet another impossibly well-defended Imperial stronghold. It was getting to be a bad habit.

"Over there," Scarlet said. She was talking to the droid. The flier dropped between the towering buildings to stop at the pedestrian level below.

They climbed out onto a quiet side street. A walkway wound through carefully cultivated trees and planters set into the narrow strip of sunlight the surrounding buildings allowed in.

"Thank you for choosing—" the droid started, but Han slapped the button to shut the flier's door and cut him off.

"Which way?" he asked.

"Three more intersections that direction," she pointed, her voice cool and professional. "There's an Imperial watch post that we can't avoid at the second intersection. They're going to be looking for traffic offenses and street crime, so I doubt they'll stop an officer and a tech."

"If they do?"

"CZ redid your identification, so it should hold up to casual scrutiny. I've had more time to work on mine, so it's even more solid."

"Great," Han replied, checking how tight the blaster sat in its holster at his side. The Imperial sidearm was a clumsy thing. The weight felt wrong in his hand. He worried that if he had to pull it, it would slow him down and throw off his aim.

"Stop fidgeting with your weapon," Scarlet whispered at him as they walked. Han bit back his retort with a smile. The uniform didn't have pockets, so he hooked his thumbs on the belt and tried to match the stiff swagger of the other Imperials.

The few pedestrians they passed wore business attire and moved quickly. No one looked at them for more than a second. At first Han thought it was his uniform that frightened them, but then he noticed that they didn't look at one another, either. This was the heart of the Empire. People didn't need a reason to be frightened; fear was just part of the lifestyle. So maybe that was why he was working with the rebels. It was as good a reason as any.

Half a dozen stormtroopers and a junior lieutenant manned the observation post. The officer nodded to Han as they walked by, then shot a questioning look at Scarlet. Han shrugged and rolled his eyes in a what-are-you-going-to-do gesture. The officer smiled and shrugged back, a gesture of solidarity. Yeah, just a couple of low-ranking whip crackers, doing their bit for the glory of the Empire. It left Han feeling dirty.

No one stopped them until they reached the entrance to the Imperial Intelligence Service Center. The doors were massive and metallic, and looked as if they could stop a blast from a Star Destroyer–grade turbolaser. And while they were open when Han and Scarlet arrived, they were also guarded by a full score of stormtroopers and two officers, one of whom stood next to a large red button on the wall. Han guessed the button would set off the alarm and slam the blast doors shut fast enough to cut a bantha in half.

"Halt," one of the officers said, holding up an imperious hand. The stormtroopers stood behind him in postures of boredom, though their helmets hid their faces. "Identification."

"Lieutenant Sololo," Han said, handing over his freshly minted identity card and trying to match the boredom of the guards.

"Choya Sebastiao," Scarlet said after the guard looked up from Han's card at her. "Environmental tech, third class."

"Business?"

"Ventilation failure," Scarlet said, tapping one hand on the tools in her belt.

"It's in a secured area," Han added. "So guess who gets to waste his day watching her pull cable and patch ventilation holes?"

"We can have one of our people escort her," the officer said. *Oops,* Han thought, *may have overplayed the annoyed card.*

"No, no, I'm already here. You men keep doing, you know, guarding. That's important work." Han gave the man a smile and a nod.

"They check out," the officer said, and the knot of stormtroopers parted to let them through.

"See?" Scarlet whispered once they were in and walking down a long hallway toward the turbolifts. "No problem."

"Saying 'no problem' is a sure sign that everything is about to go terribly wrong," Han said.

He hit the lift button, and a mechanism on the other side of the doors whirred to life.

"I'm so glad I brought you along to tell me these things," Scarlet replied.

A man in civilian clothes walked down a side hall and came to stand next to them. He was short, thick through the middle, and balding. He smiled at them without ever meeting their eyes and then rocked back and forth on the balls of his feet whistling tunelessly. When the lift arrived, Han let Scarlet enter first, then stepped in after her and put a hand on the man's chest. "Take the next one."

"What? I—" the man started but the doors snapped shut and cut off whatever else he was about to say.

"He might complain to someone," Scarlet said as they rode up.

"Naw, he's a good citizen of the Empire. If he started complaining every time an officer was rude to him, he wouldn't have time for anything else."

"Or they'd shoot him," Scarlet said.

"Or that."

Scarlet began pulling tools off her belt and out of her sleeves for the job to come. Cutters, sensors, the grapnel for climbing the long shaft up to the security level. Each tool exactly the right one for the job, each perfectly maintained and ready for use. Han thought of the random boxes of tools lying around the *Falcon* and made a mental note to have Chewbacca clean up a bit before they boarded.

The lift doors snapped open, revealing a long Imperial-gray corridor with many smaller doors leading off to either side. "Lots of places to get ambushed in here," Han said, dropping his hand to rest on the butt of his blaster.

"It's eleven doors up on the right," Scarlet whispered, and headed off down the corridor at a fast walk. Han followed, looking over his shoulder as he went.

"What are you doing on this level?" a voice demanded, and Han's head whipped around. A high-ranking Imperial officer stood looking at Scarlet with open disdain, his arms crossed behind his back and his chest puffed out with authority. Scarlet lowered her gaze and tried to walk past him. He stepped in front of her, blocking the path with his body. "I said, what are you doing on this level? No non-military personnel above level ten at any time."

"Well, I—" Scarlet said, but the officer turned his attention to Han.

"You! You should know the regulations regarding non-military personnel on secured levels. Who's your commanding officer?"

"Sir," Han replied, trying for a meek and chastened tone of voice. "This is just to fix a ventilation thing—"

"Captain!" the officer bellowed. "I will be addressed as captain, *Lieutenant.*" He managed to squeeze more contempt into the word *lieutenant* than Han would have thought possible.

"Yes, Captain, sir. I was just saying—"

"You," the captain said, spinning on his heel to thrust his chin at Scarlet, "are under arrest. I will have you in a detention cell and talking to an interrogator droid before the hour is out."

"I think that's a mistake," Han said.

"And *you,*" the captain continued, spinning back to Han, "will be lucky not to be shot for dereliction of duty. Give me your commanding officer's name. I plan to have him here immediately to deal with you."

Han gave the captain his most disarming smile and moved to draw his blaster. Time to take care of the loud-mouthed idiot once and for all. The idea felt like coming home.

Before Han's weapon had even cleared his holster, the captain spun sideways and threw his own head against the corridor wall. Scarlet was standing behind him, hands raised and knees bent. It took Han several long heartbeats before he realized she was in a fighting stance.

The captain rebounded from the wall, staggering back toward her, stunned and unsteady on his feet. Scarlet snapped her right foot up into his stomach, dropping him to his knees with a loud *whuff*. She kicked him again, this time between the shoulder blades, and dropped him to the floor. She dived onto his back and locked her arms around his neck. The captain struggled feebly for a few seconds, then went limp.

Scarlet stood up, her cheeks flushed with exertion, but looking none the worse for wear.

"Is he dead?" Han asked.

"Put your blaster away," Scarlet replied. "If you fire it in here, every alarm goes off."

"Right," Han said, and slid it back into his holster. "Is he dead?"

"No. Does your identity card open these doors? We'll need to get him out of the hallway."

Han punched the button next to the nearest door, and it whooshed open. "Yep."

The room turned out to be a meeting space with a small table and six chairs, currently unoccupied. Han dragged the unconscious captain inside and dumped him unceremoniously under the table. Scarlet was already moving down the corridor to their destination.

"Ready?" she asked. Han nodded.

She punched the entry code and the door opened. Inside was a small technical station. The walls were covered with control panels and displays. It looked exactly like the kind of room that would house a cabling junction.

But in the center of the room, where the conduit access should have been, was a large control station with an Imperial officer manning it.

"I told you this was a terrible plan."

"Excuse me?" the officer said.

"Are we in the right room?" Scarlet asked no one in particular.

"Non-military personnel—" the officer started.

"Not allowed on this level," Han finished for him. "We know. Say, there's supposed to be a major trunk line here, with a conduit access point."

The officer nodded. "Yes, but the last security audit noted it as a flaw, so the cable was rerouted. This communications security station was put in to utilize the space. Do you need access to the trunk line?"

"Not as such," Scarlet replied. For the first time since he'd met her, Han thought she looked a little lost.

"So you work on the security detail?" Han asked.

"Yes." The officer nodded again.

"Would your access card get you into the intelligence service center above us?" Han smiled gentle encouragement at the man.

"Sure, but there's no *way* they'd let non-military—" Han drew his blaster and in one smooth motion clubbed the Imperial officer on top of the head. The man slid out of his chair, boneless, and wound up in a heap on the floor.

Scarlet blinked at Han, opened her mouth as if she had something to say, then closed it without speaking.

"We tried your plan," Han said, holding up the access card. "The rest of this, we're doing my way."

CHAPTER NINE

"*THIS* IS YOUR BETTER PLAN?" Scarlet said under her breath.

"It is," Han whispered back.

The intelligence service was the whole planet Cioran—maybe the whole Imperial Core—writ small. There were no colors in the flooring, the walls, the doors. Only shades of gray and black. The air had a sharp, astringent smell that reminded Han of cleaning up blood. The stink of the well-maintained interrogation chamber.

"Steal a keycard and just walk in," Scarlet said. "Why didn't I think of that? You know we're going to die."

"No one'll see us coming," Han said. "And everyone dies sometime."

"Not comforting."

"The alternative is we go spend a bunch of time waiting for you to come up with some other plan that doesn't work. This way, we get all the risk out of the way quickly and get off this sinkhole of a planet."

The guard at the main desk looked up at them, curious but not yet alarmed. "I think you're on the wrong level."

Han grinned and held up the keycard without breaking stride. "Special permission. Someone routed the ventilation power right through the secure facility. We've got to move it back before anyone compromises it."

The guard stood up, frowning. "I wasn't informed about that."

"General Screal doesn't like us announcing security flaws until after they're addressed," Scarlet said.

"*Screal?*" the guard said, his eyebrows reaching for his hairline.

"Just take us a minute," Han said, as they reached a thick steel door. He slid the keycard through the reader, and the display shifted from red to green with a loud beep. The door slid open. "See?"

As they stepped into the data center, Scarlet pulled a storage disk and a diagnostic interface out of her pocket. Around them, a thousand pillars of black ceramic glowed under blue light. The hiss of coolant and the almost inaudible ticking of power relays were the only sounds. She stepped to the nearest pillar, slid her fingers across its surface to open the control panel, and attached the interface. It squealed once, and a bright red warning code blinked on its face.

"Do we have a problem?" Han asked.

"Several," Scarlet said. "But this isn't one of them."

Her fingers moved gracefully over the interface controls. The red gave way to a soft blue. She took a security chit from another pocket, slid it into the interface's spare slot, and fed the disk into the dark pillar.

"Did we get it?"

"Soon," she said. "So how did you wind up joining the Rebellion?"

"What? Why?"

"Just making conversation," she said.

"An old guy and a kid were looking for a ride and I needed the money," Han said. "After that, it was just bad luck."

The pillar chimed and Scarlet took out the disk. The screen of the diagnostic interface flared and started running through a reboot sequence.

"We should get out of the room now," she said.

At the front desk, the guard was scowling and tapping at his console. Han felt a tightness in his gut. His fingertip drifted toward his blaster.

"Right, then," Han said. "We've got the power routing fixed, and—"

The alarm sounded, and the great steel door slammed shut behind them with a deep gonglike clang. The guard rose up, blaster in hand. Han pulled his own and shot him before the Imperial could find his aim. Together he and Scarlet raced for the doors. In the outer corridor, emergency lights flared red, while men and women in Imperial uniforms scuttled in a hundred levels of panic.

"We have to get down to the street level," Scarlet said. "There's a supply conveyor that runs from here to a holding facility close to the docks." She stopped at the lifts. All of them showed the black-and-red symbol of secure lockdown. She took a small crowbar from her belt and popped the access panel free. "We'll be going through the warehouses."

"Actually, I've seen those," Han said.

She deftly stripped three wires, crossed the connections, and reinserted them. When the unit sparked, she ignored it. The indicator on the lift stuttered back to life. The doors slid open. Ten stormtroopers, weapons drawn, looked out at them. For a moment, no one moved.

"Ah," Han said. "Thank goodness we, um, got you guys. Did you know there's been a security breach?"

"Halt in the name of the Empire!" one of the stormtroopers shouted, and Scarlet pulled the wires free. The lift doors closed on a barrage of blasterfire. Scarlet cursed under her breath and popped open a second access panel.

"We don't have time," Han said. "They're going to get those doors open."

"I can do this," Scarlet Hark said between clenched teeth. The lift doors boomed as something struck them from within.

Han shifted his weight from one foot to the other. At the edge of the bank of lifts, a door was marked with the sign for manual access. A stairway. Every muscle in his body was tensed with the need to run. Scarlet spat out an obscenity. The lift doors opened a centimeter, and a blaster barrel stuck out.

"All right. Enough being clever," Han said, taking Scarlet by the shoulder. "Run now."

The stairway dropped down a hundred or more floors below them and rose another twenty above, all lit by the angry red of the security alarms. Han and Scarlet hurried down them three steps at a time. The sound of confused and angry voices echoed behind them. Han's breath was short, his legs burning from effort. The distance beneath them didn't seem to be getting any smaller.

He stopped before he was quite sure why he'd done it. Scarlet went down another half flight, paused, and looked back over her shoulder at him. Her black eyes were confused for a moment, and then she heard it, too: the tramping of booted feet. Han leaned over the railing and looked down. Maybe ten floors below them, the alarm lights threw shadows across the handrails. Soldiers. Coming up.

"Come on," Scarlet said, heading for the closest door, but Han stopped her, his hand on her arm.

"Up," he said. "What about up?"

"Nothing's up there. No flier stations. No walkways. Just transmission towers and air."

The sound of boots grew louder. Han turned and started back up.

"Solo?"

"Come on," he shouted. "I've got an idea."

Running down the stairs had been bad. Running up was a thousand times worse. Every flight felt longer than the one before. They passed the door of the intelligence center, back where they'd come from, and then up past it. Below them, they heard doors being kicked open and the whine of scanning droids. Han forced himself on. His muscles were burning with the effort. Someone below them shouted, and a bright red blaster bolt burned the air in the shaft.

"We should hurry," Scarlet said.

"Am hurrying."

"You should do it faster."

At the foot of the next flight of stairs, she paused, fixing something to the handrail. Han leaned against the wall.

"I didn't get any rest last night," he said.

"All right."

"Just saying, I can usually run better than this."

Scarlet pulled a hair-thin strand of monofilament across the steps, just below waist-high. In the red light, it was practically invisible. The drum of footsteps grew louder.

"What's—" Han said, then swallowed. "What's that?"

"That's a few more seconds," she said. "Let's go."

Han turned back up, pushing himself. They'd made it up another two full flights, both of them running with their shoulders touching the wall, when an electrical discharge crackled through the air. A man's voice rose in panic, and another one shouted it down.

"That was us, right?" Han said. "We did that?"

"Makes them take it a little slower," Scarlet said. "Hope whatever you've got in mind is a really good idea."

"Me, too."

It felt like an hour or a day or a few seconds before they reached the access panel at the top of the stairway. A polished steel grate covered it, but just beyond Han could see the brightness of daylight. Scarlet pulled an electronic lock pick from her belt at the same time Han shot the lock. Smoking and shattered, the grate swung open.

"That works, too," Scarlet said, putting the lock pick back.

The rooftop spread out around them, a landscape of

ducts and conduits, grating walkways and massive transmission towers. The largest tower rose a hundred meters over the rooftop, reaching toward the clouds. Scaffolds and ladders rose up its center. Han pointed to it.

"There," he said. "Go!"

They sprinted over the rough ground, reaching the tower's ladder at the same time the first stormtrooper spilled onto the roof and took aim. Han boosted Scarlet up, then followed her, climbing with one hand and tapping his comlink with the other. Blaster bolts hissed through the air and blackened the steel.

"Was there anything more to this plan?" Scarlet asked as they climbed.

"I'm working on it," he said, and the call went through. "Chewie! It's me. Tell me the *Falcon* is warmed up and ready to go."

The comlink groaned with the Wookiee's voice.

"*Almost* is not a good word," Han said. "I need you up here now. I'm on a transmission tower on top of the Imperial Intelligence Service Center, and there are a lot of people shooting at me."

Chewbacca's howl maxed out the comlink's speaker. Twenty more stormtroopers had come onto the roof. The sharpness of their commander's gestures made him look as if he were very awkwardly waving. Scarlet reached the gantry at the ladder's top and paused, rummaging through her tool belt.

"I've got a better idea," Han said. "Why don't you get in the air and come get me first, and then I'll explain how it happened when no one's shooting at me?"

Scarlet held a black cylinder between her finger and thumb with a pleased smile. Han nodded at it in query, and she shook her head. She mouthed *Keep going* and hunched at the top of the ladder they'd just come up. Chewbacca grumbled. On the rooftop, the stormtroopers were beginning a systematic advance on the tower.

"No, it's all right," Han shouted. "She's here with me. We're both on the tower. But we need you to get us out of here."

He reached the bottom of another ladder and looked back. Scarlet was hunched over and moving toward him quickly. Behind her, a bright orange flare marked the first ladder's top. Chewbacca grumbled again.

"Well, you may have to go *without* clearance. You can take the fine out of my cut."

A volley of blasterfire cut through the gantryway, striking sparks. Han fired half a dozen times, not bothering to aim. Chewbacca howled from the comlink, but Han couldn't hear what he'd said. The connection dropped as Scarlet reached him.

"What did you do?" he asked, nodding back behind her.

"The decking tape I had for getting into the shaft? It's melting down that ladder. We didn't need it, did we?"

"Nope," he said, and they started up again.

Level after level they climbed, the legs of the transmission tower narrowing around them. The stormtroopers surrounded the tower's base, firing up at them, but the steel girders and webwork of ladders and conduits took the damage. Scarlet kept sabotaging the path behind them. The only direction was up, until they reached the tiny platform where all four legs of the tower met. They were seventy meters above the rooftop. The last thirty meters to the top were reachable only by steel handholds welded into the tower's side. That high up, even steel swayed in the wind. Han's legs felt as if they were made of string, and his back ached. Scarlet's hair was plastered to her forehead and neck, and she was shivering. The decking tape had run out, and she had a blaster in either hand. Below them, the stormtroopers looked like white dolls. The tower shifted, the metal groaning.

"Hmm," Scarlet Hark said.

"What?"

"Down there."

Han leaned to the side, peeking down. Four stormtroopers were struggling with a small plasma cannon, their commanding officer screaming at them, his voice made inaudible by distance.

"They can't do that. They'll take down the tower."

Scarlet grinned. For a moment she seemed less like a rational, calculating master of espionage than a force of nature taking joy in the chaos. Not a soldier, but a criminal. "We may have made them feel a little inadequate. I wonder why they aren't bringing in fliers."

"Fliers?"

"That's what I'd do. Get a few two-person fliers. Maybe a combat droid. Shoot us out of this thing without bothering with the ground game."

Han nodded, then rested his head against the metal. Thirty meters was a hell of a long climb, and he wasn't sure his body was up for it. He closed his eyes, listening for the faint but familiar scream of engines. Yes. There it was. "Maybe something's keeping those guys busy."

"Something like?"

"Come on," he said. "We need to hurry."

The city spread out around them in all directions, gray and hazy and bright with the sun. Flocks of birds swirled below them, passing between the massive buildings. The clouds glowed with sunlight. Han felt the first impact of the plasma cannon in his feet and fingers before he heard the explosion. He kept pushing himself up. Scarlet was just below him, grabbing the handholds as he lifted his feet from them. The wind was cold, the air thin. A second explosion made the transmission tower shudder. The glowing yellow navigation light at the tower's top grew brighter with every moment.

"We're almost out of up, Solo," Scarlet Hark said. Her voice was thin and ragged.

"You're never out of up," he said. "Look."

On the horizon, just above the level of the highest buildings, something like an electrical storm was going on. Dark shapes churned and shifted, flashes of brightness too straight to be lightning. And at the front, flying before the storm of fliers and droids, Imperial police and port authority enforcers, the beautiful gray smudge of the *Millennium Falcon.* The tower shuddered again and began to list. Han fired his blaster into the air three times. Four. The *Falcon* shifted, correcting course toward them.

"Get ready," he said. "We don't get to try this twice."

The *Falcon* dipped a fraction when the ramp extended, then corrected. She was coming in fast, but Chewie wouldn't be able to slow down much with half of Cioran getting scorched by his exhaust plume. Han pulled himself up to the top of the tower, ignoring the abyss before him. Scarlet clambered up at his side. Her eyes were bright. She was grinning.

"Not a good plan," she said. "But it's got style."

Bolts of energy rained down from the belly of the *Falcon,* scattering the tiny stormtroopers far below them. The entry ramp was extended, the speed ripping contrails from the moisture in the air. Han breathed deeply, watched his ship grow larger, closer.

"Now!" he shouted, and jumped.

For a terrible moment, he thought his timing was off. A night without sleep. A hundred-meter climb while being shot at the whole way. And the day before hadn't been much better. Being off by a few hundredths of a second could only be expected. He seemed to hang in the void, his death visible between his feet. Scarlet was a blur to his right, her arms thrown high as if in victory.

The ramp hit him in the side, bouncing him up its length. The world went small and quiet for a few seconds, and when he came fully back to consciousness, the only sounds were the shriek of the engines, the hum of the actuators pulling the ramp closed, and Scarlet laughing. He rolled onto his back and looked at her. Her hair was a wild tumble, her mouth a manic grin, and her teeth were bloody where the impact had split her lip. She shook her head as if trying to clear it.

She held out her hand and hauled him up when he took it. Han was uncomfortably aware of her body beside his; that he was a man and she was a woman, and that against all odds, they hadn't just died together.

"Well," she said, wiping the blood from her mouth. "So much for the easy part."

CHAPTER TEN

THE *FALCON* THUMPED with the sounds of blaster fire hitting her shields. The ship rocked as Chewbacca slammed down the throttle to get away from their pursuers. The Wookiee's howl came from the cockpit as if it were a kilometer away. The metal creaked and groaned, the superstructure of the freighter warping under the strain.

"I'm so sorry, honey, I know this has been rough on you," Han said.

"I've had worse," Scarlet said, frowning at him. "And don't call me 'honey.' "

"The ship. I was talking to my ship," Han said as he ran, limping, down the corridor to the cockpit. "This beating she's taking? It's because of you. Be nice to her."

Chewbacca was strapped into the copilot's chair, frantically pulling at the controls as the *Falcon* climbed over the city. Green bolts of plasma and turbolaser fire streaked past as the Imperial fliers gave pursuit. A red light flashed a shield overload warning on the panel behind him.

Han threw himself into the pilot's seat and gestured at the third chair with his head. Scarlet took the hint and buckled in.

"Heya, pal, thanks for the save," Han said.

Chewbacca growled back, waving at all the flashing damage indicators.

"Hey, believe me, Her Royalness will be paying for every scratch when we're done here."

" 'Her Royalness'?" Scarlet said.

"Still not talking about you," Han said, then yanked at a control bar to spin the *Falcon* in a hard bank. A virtual wall of incoming fire flew past them as the ship spun out of its path. When they'd stopped their wild maneuvering, Han looked over his shoulder at Scarlet. "Not everything is about you, you know."

"I *don't* think everything is—" she started.

"Shush," Han said, and she sputtered with indignation. He pointed out ahead of them as the sky went from dark blue to black. "Out of atmosphere now, the fliers can't chase us."

Chewie unbuckled from his seat and headed toward the back of the ship.

"Hey! Where are you going?" Han yelled.

Chewie rumbled back at him and kept walking.

"Ha!" Scarlet said. "I'm not the only one who thinks your plan was terrible."

Han spun his chair to face her. "Hey, I got you off that planet in one piece. *And* got you your precious data from one of the most secure installations in the Empire. Now who's the best?"

She rolled her eyes at him. Something else occurred to him. "Hey, you speak Wookiee?"

"No one speaks Wookiee but Wookiees," she said. "I mean, I can order a drink or find the bathroom okay . . ."

Scarlet trailed off, her eyes wide and her face pale.

"What—" he began.

She shook her head and pointed behind him. He spun his chair around. Four Imperial Star Destroyers were bearing down on them.

"Huh," Han said. "Probably should have seen that coming."

"Hurry," Scarlet said. "Get us out of here."

"I *am* hurrying," Han replied, spinning the ship around and throwing the throttle to full.

"Hurry faster," she said.

"You keep saying that. It's not as helpful as you think." Han opened up the ship's internal comm. "Hey, buddy, gonna need you to get those shields stabilized!"

A loud Wookiee yell reverberated through the ship.

"Well, how do I know you're already working on things when you don't tell me you're already working on things?"

Scarlet unbuckled, moved to the copilot's seat, and strapped in there. "Tell me what you need."

"Keep those rear deflectors angled to bounce the incoming fire," Han said. "We'll need some time to calculate the jump to lightspeed."

"How much time?"

The ship rocked with a lucky long-range shot from one of the Star Destroyers. "More," Han said, and started punching keys on the computer.

"How old *is* this navicomputer? Are you still running the Minashi-Ryu jump protocols?" Scarlet asked, fingers working fast on the deflector controls. She had skills, Han had to admit. He wondered if it would be enough with four big Imperial Destroyers hammering them.

"Not so old," he said defensively. "I've been meaning to upgrade, but I've been busy."

"Busy?"

"Fighting the Empire," Han snapped, keying in the jump data as quickly as the deck would accept it. "You may have heard of it? Stormtroopers, Death Stars, Darth Vader?"

The ship rocked again as the Star Destroyers closed the distance and began landing more hits.

"You're awfully testy," Scarlet said.

"Raise your hand if you've fought all of those things in the last year," Han said, raising his hand.

Scarlet grinned at him. "Maybe you should keep that on the controls." As if to punctuate her point, the ship rocked with a barrage of incoming fire.

"They've got us in their range," Han said. He twisted the controls, sending the *Falcon* spinning off in a hard starboard turn. The Star Destroyers were fast and bristling with firepower, but they turned like drunken banthas. He needed to buy a few more seconds for the navicomputer to do its work.

"Well. That's disappointing," Scarlet said, and the ship shuddered under a new wave of incoming fire.

"What is?"

"Those," she said, as four TIE fighters streaked past in a diamond formation and banked hard to port for a second pass. "Can we out-turn them?"

"We can try."

"Let's do."

The deflector alarm shouted an urgent warning at them as the rear shields started to fail.

"Chewie!" Han yelled into the comm. "We need those shields up!"

A long, loud series of growls echoed through the ship.

"Your friend has a real gift for profanity," Scarlet said. "How's the navicomputer doing?"

"It's fine, almost done," Han yelled. Then he leaned down to whisper, "Come on, baby, be almost done."

The TIE fighters came about and streaked toward the *Falcon*, laser cannons blazing. Han sent the ship into a tight spin, trying to slip the wide but thin hull through the worst of the incoming fire. The view through the window became a series of blinding flashes as the shields took hit after hit. A second alarm started blaring out a warning that the front deflectors were failing, too.

"Chewie!" Han yelled into the comm.

"How about—" Scarlet started, punching something on the computer. She never finished, because the console went dark in a spray of sparks. She patted at her shirt, keeping it from catching on fire.

"What did you do?" Han asked incredulously. "What did you *do*!"

"I didn't do anything," Scarlet yelled back.

Han pounded a fist on the console. "Come on, baby, wake up! We're in the middle of a gunfight here."

The console flickered once, then went dark again. Outside, the TIE fighters rolled through another hard bank and lined up a new strafing run.

Chewbacca howled from the back, and the console lit back up at the same time the shield warnings stopped screeching at them.

"See?" Scarlet said. "I told you it wasn't me!"

"Good job, pal," Han said into the comm. "Now can you convince the navcom to hurry up?"

Chewbacca whined his disappointment at the thin praise.

"Or we could blow up, would that be better?" Han asked.

Chewbacca grumbled.

"He's your only friend, right?" Scarlet asked. "Wonder why."

"Chewie is not my only—" Han started, but he stopped talking to send the *Falcon* into another series of spins to avoid the TIE fighters. A new alarm sounded, warning of the approaching Star Destroyers and their much heavier banks of turbolasers. The *Falcon* could handle the TIE fighters for a while, but the big Imperial ships would chew through her shields in seconds if they got in range.

Han tapped on the navicomputer's console, encouraging it to go faster. "Luke Skywalker, for instance," he said.

"Who?" Scarlet asked as she shifted the deflectors to deal with the new and deadlier threat of the Star Destroyers.

"Another friend of mine," Han said. "Good friend. Hero of the Rebellion, you know. Very close friend. Luke Skywalker."

"I know who he is."

"Then why did you ask who he was?"

"I wasn't actually listening to you," Scarlet said. "Can we jump now?"

The TIE fighters were no longer strafing them. They were maneuvering to force the *Falcon* into a turn. Just like they were supposed to. Drive the ship toward the heavies, and let the big guns of the Star Destroyers take them out. Classic Imperial tactics. Han admired their skill while trying to think of ways to kill them.

"Get into one of the turrets," he said.

Scarlet barked out a laugh. "We're not shooting our way out of this."

"Can it hurt to try?"

"We need a miracle."

As if in answer to her statement, the four TIE fighters peeled off at high speed. The Star Destroyers also began a lumbering turn back toward the planet. One by one, all the various alarms on the *Falcon* stopped squawking.

Han held his breath for a moment, but nothing changed. The Imperial ships kept angling away.

"They're . . . leaving?" Scarlet said in disbelief.

Han leaned back in his chair, hands behind his head. "Did I mention that I'm the best?"

"You're taking credit for this?" she asked.

"I admit," Han continued, unbuckling to stand up and check on the main navigation computer, "it's not my absolute best work. Five is, I think, my personal record."

"Five," Scarlet echoed.

"Star Destroyers. I once evaded five while doing a spice-smuggling run off Tatooine. That was my best, as far I recall. But four is not bad. Four is more than your normal space pilot could possibly hope to deal with."

"You are," Scarlet said, nodding to herself. "You're taking credit for it. You didn't evade them. They *left*. There's clearly something else going on here. Hold on."

She put Chewbacca's headset to her ear, the loop of it reaching almost the full length of her forearm, and tapped through the signal relays. "I don't know. There's a lot of chatter on the military frequencies, but it's all encrypted. Something's got them spooked. Aren't you worried about that?"

"Not even a little," Han said, banging on the navicomputer with the side of one fist, then dropping back into his chair. "Computer had to reset when the power dropped for a second, but she'll be back in a minute, and then we can finish our jump to lightspeed. Have you back with your Rebellion pals in no time."

"You," Scarlet said, "are a crazy person. I'm starting to question how much my 'Rebellion pals' actually like me if they sent you to get me."

Han leaned back, grinning and putting his hands over his heart dramatically. "You wound me. And after I saved you from the vast might of an Evil Empire."

Chewbacca stomped back into the cockpit, growling.

"Yes, that was good work," Han said. "But don't expect any thanks from our friend here. Seems she pays in insults."

Chewbacca growled out a complicated explanation.

"Well," Han said, "then we better fix it fast before our Imperial friends decide to come back."

"What was that?" Scarlet asked as Chewbacca left. "I didn't catch him. I'm behind with technical terms in Wookiee."

"Chewie says the power reboot blew a few circuits in the navicomputer. Not a big deal. He'll have it back up in no time. But we took a beating otherwise. This trip is going to be expensive. I hope whatever you've got is worth it to the rebels."

Scarlet laughed in disbelief. "Please remember that you didn't do anything but get us shot at until the Empire got distracted and left."

"You see, that's an ungenerous view—"

"*And* you're calling into question *my* value after I spent months working on one of the most dangerous worlds in the Empire?"

"Hey, sister, I didn't realize it was so important to you to impress me," Han said with a grin.

Scarlet's lips quirked, but whatever her retort was going to be was lost when the proximity alarm started screeching again.

"Did they come back?" she said.

"No," Han said, looking at the approaching ship. "This is something else."

Scarlet leaned forward, her hands flying over the copilot's console. "It's a Sienar Fleet Systems design," she said. "It's been modified a lot. It looks like an NM-six-hundred series."

"Wait, I know that ship . . ."

The comm crackled and came to life.

"Han Solo, my old friend."

Han shook his head in shock. "Baasen? Didn't I shoot you?"

Baasen Ray laughed. "Surely you did, my boy. I'm trying to take it philosophical. Difficult, though. You said some hurtful things about me back there. Cruel's a terrible thing to be."

Scarlet stared a question at Han. He turned off the comm. "Baasen Ray. Bounty hunter. He's the reason I had a hard time finding you. He screwed up your drop in order to catch me."

"You're being chased by bounty hunters?"

"Hello?" Baasen said. "Tell me we're still on speaking terms, boyo. I'd hate to start shooting you needless."

Han turned the comm back on. "Yeah, uh, hi. So, Baasen, old pal, we're on our way out, but you be sure to let Jabba know when you see him that I'm on my way with the money real soon."

"Boy," Baasen growled at him, all pretense of good humor gone. "I think I explained that. I can't go back without you, or it's my head on Jabba's spike. So be a good lad and prepare to be boarded."

"Yeah," Han said, "I'm going to go with 'no' on that one. What now?"

"I could blow you into vapor and bring you back to Jabba in a bottle," Baasen said, his voice deceptively reasonable.

Han killed the comm again. "Chewie? How's that computer reset going?"

"So just do what I say," Baasen continued, "and maybe I let the Wookiee and the woman go free. That's a deal you won't be offered twice."

"He'd never let you go. He'd sell you to the Empire," Han said to Scarlet.

"I believe you," she replied.

Han turned the comm back on. "So, yeah, Baasen? We're all not very excited about that deal. Here's another scenario. Why don't you go wait for me on Tatooine, and I'll have the money sent directly to you. You can give Jabba his share, explain the misunderstanding, and everyone wins."

Behind him, the navigation computer gave a series of clicks and restarted. Scarlet moved over to it, then whispered to Han, "Where to?"

Anywhere fast, he mouthed back at her.

"Solo, my boy," Baasen said, "it hurts me that you think I'm so dim about the wits. Even the pain of my severed hand is nothing compared with how your contempt makes me feel. If you ever wondered why you're so unpopular, that might be it. You just think you're so much better than everyone else."

"I have lots of friends," Han said.

"No, my dear boy, you don't. What you've got are accomplices."

Scarlet was busily programming the jump computer. Chewbacca seemed to have everything running well. Han leaned back in his chair with a grin Baasen couldn't see and said, "You've got me there. As always, you see right through me."

"I bet you were congratulating yourself on escaping those Star Destroyers, eh?"

Scarlet gave him a narrow I-told-you-so look.

"Well," Han said. "I wouldn't go so far as—"

"That was me, boy. Might have sent a panicky message on the Imperial channel that a rebel fleet was inbound. Bigger threat, needing all the resources available to meet in glorious battle or some such. Bounced it off one of their out-system watch posts. Take them the better part of an hour to be sure you weren't a distraction."

"That worked?" Han asked, wondering why he'd never thought to do it.

"So, are you going to make me kill you, or are you going to shut down your drive and we can handle this in person like gentlemen? You never know, my good word in Jabba's ear might save you a world of pain."

Chewbacca looked into the cockpit and growled out a question. Han pointed up at the top turret. The Wookiee chuffed and shambled off.

"Your concern for my well-being does you credit after I shot your hand off," Han said.

"Are you trying to provoke me?" Baasen asked. "Or are you just stalling for time?"

"No, not at all," Han said. "Just want to make sure I have your attention when I give you my answer."

"Well, you've got it—" Baasen was saying, but Han killed the comm channel to him.

"Let him have it," Han said to Chewbacca on the internal comm.

The upper turret let loose with a barrage of fire that hammered Baasen's ship, and Han threw the throttle to maximum.

"Almost done?" he asked Scarlet.

"Nearly," she said. "I think that guy really hates you."

"I'm not too fond of him. It won't matter in a minute. Chewie! Keep hitting him in the face until we jump!"

The Wookiee growled back, but the fire from the upper turret never let up.

"Okay," Scarlet said. "Just about ready."

"I hope you know what you're doing. Here. We." Han's "Go" was drowned out by the squawking of a proximity alarm. The ship rocked as Baasen unloaded a barrage of laser cannon fire. The blasts struck across the top of the ship, one of them even hitting the cockpit. The shield alarms began blaring again.

"Go go *go!*" Scarlet yelled. She was yelling at the computer, not him. Something physical slammed into the back of the *Falcon* like a hammer blow. Baasen's ship had fired a missile into them, but the damage didn't seem too severe. A dud, but there would be another one in seconds. Chewbacca charged into the cockpit, howling in anger.

"Buckle up," Han told him. "We're leaving right now."

"Wait," Scarlet said. "There's a missile stuck *in* the ship! Won't it blow up if we—"

She never finished. Han pulled back the throttle on the hyperdrive, and the stars disappeared in a swirl of light.

CHAPTER ELEVEN

THE STARS WERE STILL. Half a dozen warning indicators and error codes blinked and whined from the control boards. A jagged crack ran through the screen in front of him, charred where the battle hadn't quite managed to shatter it. Han leaned back in his seat, took a deep breath, and sighed happily. The tension of battle flowed out of his muscles, leaving him relaxed and a little giddy. Beside him, Chewbacca grunted petulantly.

"What?" Han said. "It all worked out."

"It was bracing," Scarlet said. "Are we really all right, or is that missile stuck in your ship going to blow up and kill us all?"

"One or the other," Han said, and pushed himself up. "I'll go find out which. Where are we, Chewie?"

Chewbacca shrugged magnificently.

"Well, see if you can figure it out. We managed one jump. If we can get one more, we'll be fine."

"I need access to your computer," Scarlet said, holding up the stolen data. "I need to get this encryption broken."

"You can have whatever Chewie doesn't need," Han said as he walked out the cabin door. "Calculating the jump gets first priority."

"Yes, Captain," Scarlet said, her tone somewhere between amused and sarcastic.

"Damn right," Han shot back, but nothing could touch his euphoria. Not every fight left him feeling good, but that one had. When the adrenaline had burned its way through his bloodstream and the fatigue kicked in, he'd probably collapse, but until that happened there was plenty of work to do.

He climbed the ladder up to the gunner's turret. If he pressed his cheek almost against the transparisteel, he could just see where Baasen's missile still protruded from the skin of the ship. It was a gray-green oblong. Depending on how much of it had actually penetrated the *Falcon,* it could have been anywhere from a meter and a half to three. Strands of what looked like cable spread around it. He crawled back down and ran a battery of diagnostics and tests. The missile had cut or crushed part of the power grid, and coolant was leaking badly around it, which was probably what made the ropy-looking things around the missile's entry. There were no traces of explosives or invasive proteins. It wasn't injecting tiny droids into the ship to disassemble her or sabotage her in the middle of a jump. If it had a warhead, it wasn't exposed or sparking. Probably a dud, but he'd still feel a lot better once it was off his ship.

Chewbacca shouted out a list of the systems that were complaining. The signal from the passive sensor antenna was cutting in and out. One of the freight barge clamps had come open and jammed. A power fluctuation in the acceleration compensator had the hyperdrive generator in safety shutdown. The port shield generator was overheating, probably because of the coolant leak.

Han cracked his knuckles.

"I've seen her worse," he said.

Chewbacca howled, and from somewhere deep in the

belly of the ship a woman's laughter rose up with the sound of it.

HAN DIDN'T REMEMBER falling asleep. The last thing he could recall clearly was wriggling on his elbows and knees through a crawl space almost too narrow for him, hydro-spanner held in his teeth, to retune a power coupling for the third time. And then he was in his bunk, swimming up from a darkness as deep and black as space. He rolled over, yawned, and sat up slowly. His right side felt like one continuous bruise, and his back was stiff. He was still wearing the rough black of an Imperial officer, the fabric a maze of wrinkles and oil stains. He stripped the uniform off and threw it away. According to the ship's chrono, he'd been asleep for something like fourteen standard hours, and a quick check of the general status board told him Chewie had been hard at work for most of it. Apart from the coolant leak and the occasional hiccup in the passive sensor antenna, the ship was good to go, or as good as could be expected with a missile still stuck in her backside.

Before he pulled his own clothes on, he took stock of his injuries. Black scabs around his wrist from when he'd hung over the shaft outside Scarlet Hark's window. Purple-black bruises on his hip and shoulder where the *Falcon* had scooped him up. A long, angry scratch across his chest whose origin he couldn't remember. He was as beat up as his ship. He put a hand to the decking, felt the gentle vibration of the engines.

"We made it again," he said softly. "Real close that time."

He waited for a long moment as if the ship might answer, and then got dressed.

In the lounge, Scarlet and Chewbacca were sitting together at the single, small table, eating from bone-colored bowls. Scarlet looked up as he stepped down into the space. Her smile was bright and sharp and pleased to see him. She wore dark pants and a pale open-necked shirt that was a little too big for her. He felt as if he'd gone three rounds with a rancor, and she looked like her months of desperation, lies, secrets, and violence had been a long vacation.

"Good morning, Captain Sleepyhead," she said.

"Same to you," Han replied. "Are you wearing my clothes?"

She shrugged. "Not my first choice in sartorial splendor, but I was packing pretty light this trip."

Han turned to Chewbacca. "You gave her my clothes?"

Chewbacca gestured toward his own soft pelt and lifted his massive tawny brows.

"Fair point," Han said.

"If it's a problem—"

"No," Han said. "It's fine. It's a good look for you."

Scarlet pretended to preen for a moment, then went back to her food. The truth was, with her dark hair down and the tension of danger gone, Han found her considerably more attractive than when they'd been on Cioran. Her smile had settled into an expression of mild amusement, and her eyebrows arched high. The quirks and architecture of her face conspired to give her an edge of constant playful challenge. Han felt an answering smile playing at his own lips as he nodded toward the bowls.

"Any of that left?"

"We saved you some," she said, nodding toward the counter behind him. Han reached for the third bowl. A mixture of soft green leaves and dark flecks of meat filled it almost to the halfway point. Scarlet took one of the last bites of hers.

"You made sahbiye?"

Scarlet shook her head and nodded toward Chewbacca.

"I think my friend here has a little crush on you," Han said. "He never makes sahbiye."

Chewbacca grunted and whined.

"I do too appreciate it. Here I am appreciating it right now," Han said around a mouthful. He turned his attention to Scarlet. "So while we still have a missile stuck on our back, it doesn't look like it's about to detonate. Everything else is solid enough that we'll be able to get you to the fleet."

Scarlet nodded, her gaze fixed on the bottom of her bowl. "About that."

"No."

She looked up. Her eyes were bright with feigned innocence. "No?"

"Whatever it is, no. My job was to fly into the heart of the Empire, find you, and get back out. I already added in stealing data from a high-security intelligence installation. I've done plenty of impossible things. Whatever else it is you're about to ask, the answer's no."

"I broke the data encryption. Galassian's codes only got me in partway, but I know some of the security force's habits, and it was enough. The datafile is the full record of the investigation of the data theft, but there are also some hints about what was in the data that got stolen. Galassian's found something big. Maybe useful. Certainly dangerous. He's already gone back out on some kind of follow-up investigation, and the Empire is scared blind that word of it is going to leak out before he's done."

"And I'm sure all the generals in the rebel fleet are looking forward to hearing all about it."

"The important thing is that they found the thief."

Han took another bite of the sahbiye, stopping to pry a bit of the meat from between his teeth with a fingernail. "Answer's still no."

"The man who got it works with the Sendavé Shared Interest Collective. Ever heard of them?"

"Sure. They're small-time gunrunners out of Elkkasinn and Sunin. Mostly K'rrandin, but with some humans thrown into the mix. They amounted to something before the Hutts decided to take their toys away," Han said. "But the information's wrong. Sendavé Collective wouldn't have any use for hot Imperial data, no matter what it was about. They're strictly small fry these days."

"That's not how they see it," Scarlet said. "According to Imperial intelligence, they've got ambitions. The thief is a human named Hunter Maas. And apparently he has plans for taking the collective to the big time. He's trying to parlay the stolen data into a better position for the collective in general or, failing that, himself in particular. And your friends and mine at Imperial Intelligence? They don't like the plan. You want to know what they're going to do about it?"

"I'm guessing something unpleasant," Han said.

"A full strike force. Shock troopers. Five thousand regular stormtroopers. Special permission from the Emperor to clear any space lanes and supersede any standing orders or Imperial protocol."

Han's eyes went wide despite himself, and he covered it by laughing. Chewbacca muttered to himself and started gathering the bowls.

"Sister," Han said, "if this is your idea of talking me *into* getting involved, your technique's a little rusty. Answer was no before, and it's about a hundred times no now."

"This data is critical to the Empire," Scarlet said, sitting forward, her elbows resting on the table. "Whatever Galassian found, they care about it a lot. Enough to bend rules, and they hate bending rules."

Han chewed slowly, a smile tugging at his lips. He didn't

mind the idea of the Empire being the frightened one for once. Chewbacca chuffed, shook his head, and lumbered toward the galley.

"They're willing to kill a lot of people to make sure no one finds out what Galassian's up to," Scarlet said.

"And I won't be one of them. And more to the point, neither will you. Once you get to the fleet—"

"Once I get to the fleet, it will be too late. They staged a dummy strike on the collective's base on Nummunr a week ago. Hunter Maas escaped, but they've mobilized half the long-range scouting ships in the Core. According to the data, their orders are to find him and then call in the full strike force to kill him and anybody he might have shared the data with. They'll slag planets if they have to."

Han shoveled the last of his sahbiye into his mouth, chewed, and swallowed. Scarlet watched him silently. From the pilot's cabin, an alarm squeaked in protest and went silent.

"So," Han said. "You're saying that instead of doing what I agreed to do—and I've already done more than that—you want me to get between a massive Imperial hunting party and the poor jerk they're about to turn into a grease spot. And you want me to do it just because they wouldn't want me to."

"Yes."

"Let me tell you exactly why that's not going to happen. First, because saving every half-wit who thinks he's big enough to take on the Emperor isn't my job. Second, because I've got an unexploded missile stuck in my ship, and I'd like to get to a nice friendly port with some bomb-disposal technicians who can help me pry it out in a reinforced dock. And third, because the answer is—"

"The Empire doesn't know where Maas is going. I do. We can get there before him."

"The answer is *no*," he said. And then, "Hold on. You

know where he's heading and they don't? How did you find out?"

"Chewbacca told me."

"*Chewie?*"

"Well, he brought me up to speed on a lot of things. I'm the one that connected the dots."

"I don't know what dots you're talking about," Han said, and then the next words died in his throat. The coppery taste of fear filled his mouth even before he knew quite why it was there.

A small-time criminal organization looking to parlay stolen Imperial data into a seat at a much larger table. The kind of big table where they decided the future of the galaxy. If he'd been in Hunter Maas's position, there was only one place he'd have gone: the secret conclave of rebels and rogues, criminals and freedom fighters. He'd have gone to Kiamurr and made himself into one of the Rebel Alliance's new allies.

And so when the Imperial hammer came down, it would wipe out not just the remnants of Sendavé Shared Interest Collective, but every prospective ally the rebels could hope for. Even the ones who didn't come would see the corpses of the ones who had.

And more to the point, Leia was there.

"Chewie?" Han said, standing up. "Where are you?"

Han went to the pilot's cabin and started pulling up star charts, figuring the paths that could take them from the depths of nowhere that presently hid them and into Kiamurr. It wasn't the straightest path, but if he could bend a couple degrees off it . . .

Chewbacca appeared in the doorway, wide arms splayed. He groaned and howled, but Han barely heard him. The jump wasn't pretty. It wasn't clean. But it was possible. That would have to be good enough.

"I'm warming her up for jump," he said.

The Wookiee bared his teeth and howled again.

"It didn't blow up last time," Han said. "Maybe it won't blow up this time, either. Baasen always went cheap on ordnance. That's why he's a bottom feeder desperate for a score and we're the heroes of the galaxy."

Chewbacca threw up his hands in exasperation, but Han knew him well enough to see the relief under the theatrics. Scarlet leaned in the doorway, her arms crossed. Her eyes were a little narrowed, her lips a little wide. She looked like a scientist who'd come across some particularly fascinating and amusing new specimen. Han ignored her.

"Where are we jumping to, Captain Solo? The fleet?"

He went down the readouts. The coolant leak was messing with a lot of different systems, but none of them so badly that it would keep them out of hyperspace. He thought. He hoped.

Scarlet dropped into the copilot's seat. She looked tiny in the space that usually held Chewbacca. "Are you going to abandon Kiamurr?"

"You want my answer?"

"I do."

"Here's my answer," Han said, pointing a finger at her and staring from under lowered brows. "Nobody likes a wise guy."

CHAPTER TWELVE

HIGH IN THE ATMOSPHERE of Kiamurr, a thousand species of birds soared on the permanent updrafts of the planet's vast mountain ranges. Long experience had taught the creatures to avoid the ships that sloped down through the planet's thin atmosphere. Flocks of them swirled around the path of the *Millennium Falcon* as it burned through the high air; black dots against white clouds like space in negative. Han leaned in over the controls, certain that the next second would leave a hundred tiny bodies crashing through the cracked screen, into the landing gear and access panels, damaging the already pounded ship a little more and messily. The birds knew better and kept out of his way.

Knifelike mountain ranges of pale stone rose through the cloud cover, veined with green where the local vegetation clung to it like ivy to a wall. The ice caps that topped the mountains were the color of the clouds, and deep valleys between the peaks dropped five, six, even ten kilometers deep. The crosswinds made navigation tricky, and the walls of stone and ice made it dangerous.

"Are you sure we're in the right approach?" Han asked. "Because I'm not seeing anything."

Chewbacca bared his teeth and howled.

"I *know* I'm the pilot," Han said. "But you're the one who—"

"There," Scarlet said, leaning over Han's shoulder to point at an off-colored smear on a cliff face. The gray of metal, with a blocky shape at one side. Laser cannons. The first line of defense of Talastin City, if he didn't count the birds, the wind, or the stone. They sped past it, the fortification swiveling its weapons to track them. The radio squawked to life.

"Hey, unidentified freighter. We expecting you?"

"No," Han said. "We didn't have time to file a flight plan."

"That's gonna be rough, then."

"We're here with the . . . ah . . . Alderaan refugee relief cooperative," Han said. "Part of the delegation."

"Oh, hey. You Rebel Alliance? I can respect that, but it doesn't mean we got anywhere to put you."

Chewbacca whined as the valley narrowed, mountain ranges on either side coming perceptibly closer.

"Think you could check on that for us?" Han asked into the radio. "Because if I need to pull up out of here, I should probably do it soon."

"Sure. Hold on."

Along the cliff face to their left, a massive snakelike creature longer than the *Falcon* clung to the stone, its sides glistening with golden scales. Han tapped the console impatiently. Chewbacca grunted, slowing the airspeed. The snake-thing turned placid black eyes toward them and opened its gigantic mouth.

"How's our fuel?" Han asked.

Chewbacca yowled an answer.

"That's too bad."

"Well," Scarlet said, "you can tell it's not the Empire."

"Yeah," Han agreed. "I'll take inefficiency and corruption over well-regulated malice every time."

A guidance signal clicked on, and the radio squealed back to life. "All right, unidentified freighter. You're in dock four, slip number three. Gonna be a fine for not putting in a flight plan, though."

"A *what*?" Han said.

"I don't make the rules, Papa. You don't like it, you can pull up now."

"How much of a fine?"

"Supposed to be eight hundred credits, but you seem like a nice guy. Four hundred, we'll call it good."

"Inefficiency and corruption *every* time?" Scarlet asked with a sharp smile.

"We're coming in," Han snarled.

"Welcome to Kiamurr," the voice on the radio said. "Enjoy your stay, right?"

Talastin City squatted in the depths of a narrow valley, its buildings pressed close together on the few precious kilometers of nearly flat ground. At the densest part of the city, structures also climbed up the cliff faces to either side. The vast mountains towering above left the streets in near-permanent shadow except for a few hours in the middle of the day when the sun shone straight down into it. It was like a city at the bottom of a well.

Han followed the guide signals into a slip dug into the mountain's side. Across the valley, dozens more like it glowed: arched caves in the pale rock crowded with transports and freighters and low-powered fighters peeking out of them. The air of Kiamurr smelled of moisture and wood, like being in a rain forest. An early-model LOM protocol droid made its way toward them. Its breastplate was mottled by old damage that had been pounded back into shape and covered with a cheap patina. Han let Chewbacca discuss exactly how much they were going to pay in docking fees and taxes while he made his way slowly around the *Falcon*, surveying the damage from the outside. The Imperial fighters and fliers had done a pretty good job. Scorch marks blackened the ship's side, and the smell of burned-out circuit boards and blown actuators was sadly familiar.

The missile—if it really was a missile—was solidly in the skin of the ship. The ropy things around it weren't just frozen coolant. There were visible structures coming from the gray-green oblong and anchoring themselves to the metal hide of the *Falcon.* Scarlet stepped to his side, her arms crossed like a reflection of his own stance.

"Tracking beacon?" she said.

"Yeah."

"So your friend Baasen knows where we are."

"Yeah."

"That's a pity."

"Well," Han said, "maybe we'll get lucky, and he'll jump in during a massive Imperial assault."

They stood together silently for a long moment.

"Seriously, though, I'll get Chewie to pull that out first thing," Han said.

"Good plan," Scarlet said.

Once the accounts were settled and the old droid limped its way back toward the business offices, Chewbacca hauled out the repair kit. Han and Scarlet headed through the carved stone tunnels, down into the city. Thin, awkward rickshaws haunted the streets, hauled by nervous-looking lizards and their handlers. A walrus-faced Aqualish woman paced back and forth along the shadowed pavement, offering ship parts at a discount. The security patrol droids hummed through the air, ignoring everything. High above, the thin strip of actual sky was shifting from the hazy blue of late afternoon toward the gold of evening.

Han had been in a thousand places like it, all across the galaxy. The details were different everywhere, but the sense was the same. Some had been as large as star systems, others as small as a back room in a cantina. They were the niches of the universe where authority meant a little less, where freedom was a little more available and the scope of negotiation might include hiding the bodies of the people who got too aggressive about their pricing. Justice could mean going before some sort of local magistrate, or it could mean doing the obvious thing and tipping the bartender for the trouble of cleaning up the mess. They were violent places, and they were joyful, and they didn't last. The food tended to be worse and the music better. It was the only kind of place where the representatives of a dozen illegal groups and religions and political movements could come to negotiate. Anyplace more controlled—whether the control came from the Empire, or a Hutt, or the Black Sun crime syndicate—would keep away exactly the people who were needed for that conversation. Han breathed deeply and felt a tension he'd barely known was there let go.

"It's good to be home," he said.

"You're from Kiamurr?" Scarlet asked, raising her hand to flag down a lizard rickshaw.

"Never been here before, and I don't aim to stay here long. It's just not the Core."

The rickshaw driver, a Dressellian with a dark green lesion above his left eye, nodded to them and snapped the leather lead of his draft lizard. "Where to?" he asked.

"Same place everyone else has been going," Han said, hauling himself up to the rickshaw's seat. He put his hand down to help Scarlet up, but she was already on the other side, clambering aboard without aid.

"The conclave hive," the driver said. "You with the Arthos House?"

"The who?"

"Arthos House," the driver said, sliding onto the lizard's thin, anxiously shifting back. "Are you missionaries?"

"No," Han said.

"Good," the driver said and spat. "Can't stand the blasted religious."

The lizard started off, going from dead stop to full speed without any transition in between. The streets of the city were narrow, dark, and crowded. Speeders crowded against the lizard rickshaws. Barge droids lumbered through intersections without bothering to check whether traffic on either side looked like it would stop for them. The cushions in the rickshaw were old and stained and sank in at the middle so that Han and Scarlet Hark drifted toward each other, pulled into contact by gravity. Her gaze flickered over the streets, up into the stone-and-ivy terraces they passed, but her attention seemed turned inward. The voices of street vendors called out in a dozen different languages, offering everything from fresh-picked fruit to computer hardware to weapons.

"I have a question," she said. "What you said before about how, if the rebels win, they'll just turn into another thing to rebel against? Did you really mean that, or were you just trying to sound impressive?"

Han smirked. "I can say what I mean and still be impressive." Her eyes weren't hard, but they weren't soft, either. A beggar ran out into the street, and the lizard lurched around her. Han shrugged. "Sure, I meant it."

"So if we win, you'll turn against us?"

"I'm very consistent," he said. "If we wind up on opposite sides of this, it won't be me that changed."

Scarlet thought about that for a moment. "You think all governments are the same."

"I think anyone who's telling me what I can and can't do is the same. I take it you don't."

"I think you can hold water in a cupped hand and you can't in a fist," she said. Then, "That's a metaphor."

"I know it's a metaphor."

"I wasn't sure, because—"

"I know what a metaphor is."

The driver twisted around on the lizard to look back at them. "You two sure you ain't missionaries?" he asked.

"I'm positive," Han said.

The conclave hive was a single, massive dome that stretched from the mountain face at one side of the valley all the way to the other. It was the color of the mountains, with tier after tier of arches rising one above the other until the pale smooth stone of the dome began. At the structure's base, dozens of small fliers and speeders, rickshaws and transports clogged the streets and alleyways. At a glance, Han could see members of a dozen different species, mostly clumped together and eyeing one another warily. Across from the massive worked metal doors, a Gran was focusing all three of its stalked eyes politely on three black-robed Roonans as they gesticulated angrily. Scarlet leaned forward and tapped the driver on the shoulder.

"We'll walk from here," she said.

"Damned right," the old Dressellian said. "Can't park any closer than this anyway."

Han paid the man as Scarlet dropped to the street and made her way toward the Gran. From where he stood, Han could see the interest of the aliens on the street follow her. A new player had arrived, and everyone there was immediately curious about who she was, who she represented, and how she would change the balance of whatever conversations were going on inside the dome.

By the time he reached her, she was thanking the Gran and bowing a formal farewell to the three Roonans. She took Han by the elbow before he could speak and steered him gently but firmly toward the open doors.

"We need to get to the arcade on the third level," Scarlet said. "The Alliance delegation's in the middle of a conference."

"Let's go."

The interior of the conclave hive was as ornate as the outside. Maybe more. Terraced gardens alternated with structures that seemed to grow from the walls. Near the top of the massive dome above them, a circle of twelve brilliant lights glowed and rotated slowly, bathing the interior in a permanent high noon. Everywhere, people were talking or arguing or watching with sullen anger and sly curiosity. Han knew that every extra side that came into a negotiation raised the complexity of the deal exponentially. Just walking across the broad courtyard, he could feel the density of attention like radiant heat. It was the pressure of people trying to play an angle. He was a little surprised that no one had asked him to leave his blaster outside.

Wide, stone stairs led up from the courtyard and around a massive pillar carved with the faces of an alien species Han didn't recognize. Then an open garden where two lines of Gamorreans in different-colored uniforms were squealing and grunting at one another, while a pair of recording droids zipped among them, trying to catch everything that was being said and screamed and muttered. Another set of stairs led to the left, rising to another tier.

"You sure this is the right way?" Han asked as they started up.

"No."

They walked along a wide terrace with a stone railing that looked down over a walled garden. Two men in bright yellow robes with shaved heads and cranial implants stood at the rail, their eyes locked and their implants flickering wildly. Scarlet started to steer Han around them, but he pulled her back.

"Down there," he said, pointing over the rail.

In the walled garden below them, three humans sat across a stone table from a pair of Rodians. The two human men wore the uniforms of Alliance High Command, and between them Leia was in a white gown with a bright blue brooch. Her hair was pulled back, and her face had a pleasant, amused, almost generous expression that he knew at a glance was as fake as a Merian tricorn hoof.

"This way," Scarlet said, ducking into the archway at the terrace's edge. A thinner stairway led down, and they took it three steps at a time. When they reached the alcove at the garden's edge, the Rodians were standing and making small, insincere bows to the humans. Leia's smile gave away nothing. She held herself with the grace and ease of a Twi'lek dancer. Han paused. Another few seconds and they wouldn't be interrupting her meeting.

The bowing finished and the Rodians trooped away, gabbling to each other in their native language. Han stepped out into the garden, Scarlet at his side. One of the commanders glanced his way, eyebrows rising in surprise.

Leia turned. Her face was soft and round, her pale cheeks touched with pink. The fake politeness fell away from her, and a tired, sardonic smile pressed her lips thin. She looked from Han to Scarlet and back again.

"This isn't good news, is it?"

CHAPTER THIRTEEN

"WE HAVE TO LEAVE," Han said. "Right now."

Leia stared at him as if he were gibbering. Her scorn almost had a physical weight to it.

"Fine. You tell her," Han said to Scarlet, trying to get Leia to look at someone other than him. Scarlet took a step forward, nodding respectfully.

"Princess. We're trying to track down a criminal named Hunter Maas. He has information that the Empire badly wants to keep quiet."

"No," Han said, cutting her off. "No, that's not what we're doing at all."

"I don't know the name," Leia said, tapping her chin with one slim finger. "Haven't met him yet. Is he here at the conference?"

"There is an Imperial strike force looking for him, and they might be jumping in system any minute now," Han told her.

"I think he will be," Scarlet said. "Not as an invited delegate, though. He's got something to sell, so he'll probably be setting up private meetings and making the rounds at the bars and parties looking for a buyer."

"Also," Han said. "A bounty hunter put a tracking device on the *Falcon,* so he's probably on his way, too."

"All right," Leia said. "I'll put out inquiries. See if anyone I know has been contacted by him. What information does he have?"

"Or maybe the bounty hunter has sold our location to the Empire for amnesty," Han said. "Or to Jabba. Really, he's in a pretty rough spot, and just about anything's possible, so we should really get our people out of here. Now."

"He has an initial report from an expedition by Essio Galassian," Scarlet said.

"I've heard about him," Leia said. "He's an astrocartographer, isn't he?"

"And a murderous thug who likes beating people to death with his custom droids. I lived at his compound. He impressed me, but not in a good way."

"All right," Leia said. "And I take it we want to buy this stolen report."

"No," Han said. "We want to leave."

"Buy it or steal it," Scarlet said. "The threat of its leaking has mobilized more Imperial resources than anything I've seen."

"Really?" Leia said. "That's interesting."

"I don't know what it says," Scarlet said. "But I know I want it."

Leia nodded to herself, thinking. "Then I want it, too."

"Chewie will have the ship ready to go in a few hours," Han said. "So I think we should all head back to the docks now."

"I've got a meeting I have to take," Leia said. "Once it's done, I'll let you know what I've found."

"No, because—" Han started.

"We'll be here," Scarlet said and walked away, not waiting for Han.

Leia started to leave, but Han caught her arm and pulled her in close. "This is serious," he said in a rough whisper.

"When that Imperial fleet jumps in, they're going to kill this Maas and anyone who's on the same continent with him."

Leia pulled her arm away. "Don't grab me."

"Are you listening to me? Imperial strike force?"

"I heard you," Leia said, crossing her arms. "But Scarlet Hark's reputation as an intelligence agent is beyond reproach. She's spent years on this. If she thinks this Hunter Maas and his information is worth the risk, then it is."

"But once the Imperials jump in—"

"And," Leia went on, cutting him off, "this conference is filled with potential allies of the Rebellion, which means we owe it to them to warn them of the danger. In the right way."

"But—"

"And," Leia said, "I'm not done here. I have a presentation and a number of important meetings."

"Well, don't expect me to come worship at your feet. If giving a speech is more important than—"

"If I leave in the middle of it, I'd have been better off not coming at all. These groups fund the Alliance, Han. Where do you think we get our money? It's from places like this. Groups that want to end the Empire but don't have the will or the weapons or the numbers. They give us money so we can do it for them. If we look scared, that's not going to happen."

"I didn't know that," Han said. The truth was, he'd never much thought about where the rebels got their financing. He'd only ever worried about getting his hands on some of it.

"We'll figure out this Hunter Maas situation, I'll cement a few deals for alliances and financing, and we'll quietly warn the people who need to know about the Empire before their strike force arrives. I can handle this. It's what I do."

He looked down into her eyes. He'd forgotten how dark

they were. *What you do is get in trouble,* he wanted to say, but he could already hear half a dozen of her replies. She lifted her eyebrows.

"Yeah," Han said. "All right, Princess. You talked me into it."

"Oh," Leia said with a sweet smile. "I wasn't asking."

HAN SAT IN a small, parklike courtyard. Large trees deepened the shadows around cool stone benches and fountains. Patches of grass and carefully tended flowers filled the spaces between gently curving walkways. The space was unoccupied, so Han took a seat on a bench, leaned back against a tree, and stretched out. Above, the thin strip of sky was a pale cerulean blue dotted with puffy white clouds. Kiamurr was a beautiful planet. Han pictured Imperial concussion bombs and plasma bolts tearing down through that serene sky like the thunder of an angry god, the carefully tended landscape turned into a nightmare of smoking craters. The Death Star might be gone, the Empire no longer able to destroy an entire world outright, but they could still turn the surface charred and uninhabitable.

Han watched the blue skies, waiting for the ships to appear, the bombardment to begin.

When it didn't, he called Chewbacca.

"Hey, pal, how's it looking?"

The Wookiee growled through a lengthy description of the damaged systems on the *Falcon,* then ended with an angry description of his feelings at being stuck with all the repair work.

"Yeah, sorry about that. We've checked in with Leia, but she doesn't want to leave until she gives another speech, and Scarlet finds this Maas character."

Chewbacca growled and snorted.

"Yes, I did tell her. She apparently doesn't find that as urgent as I do. It's Leia. You can't tell that woman anything."

Chewbacca barked out a Wookiee laugh.

"Speaking of which, you got that torpedo pulled out of the *Falcon*?"

Chewbacca growled at him.

"Yes, I know it would go faster if I was there. I'll be there, but I'm going to poke around here a little bit first. See if I can find out what we're getting ourselves into."

After a final barrage of accusatory barks, Chewbacca closed the connection. Han looked back up at the sky. No Imperial fleet in orbit throwing fire and death. Strolling citizens chatted quietly, not running and screaming. The buildings gleamed in the sun instead of burning. Death had not come to Kiamurr.

Not yet.

The first bar he found was a structure made entirely of blue crystal and soft, velvety moss. He sat with a crew of gray-faced Neimoidians in elaborate hats who were happy to complain about the strictures of Imperial customs officials and how expensive they were to bribe. When Han angled the conversation around to Essio Galassian and Hunter Maas, he got blank stares and shrugs.

The next place was a dive cantina just outside the conclave itself on a narrow side street where the bouncer, a green-scaled reptilian Barabel who looked like he'd have been as happy to start a fight as stop one, let him through with a scowl. Han sat at the bar, with alpif music shrieking out from the stage like a cross between a landslide and the galaxy's longest-running catfight. He struck up conversations with the barkeep and a Sullustan with ornate tattoos on his dewflaps and ears who claimed to have known Essio Galassian personally. It took Han buying three rounds for the diminutive Sullustan to be certain he was a blowhard making up stories to keep the liquor flowing.

The third bar was a temporary structure in a ballroom that was being rearranged. Droids were setting up tables and chairs, enough to seat several hundred. At one end of the room a small stage had been erected with a podium. The room was so large that even with dozens of tables and hundreds of chairs scattered through it, it looked empty. The murals of the jagged mountains surrounding the conference center that adorned the walls struck Han as silly. Why put up a bunch of walls to block the view, and then paint the view on the walls?

At the base of a painted mountain, a droid behind a long bar served drinks to half a dozen people, including two brown-robed delegates. Han ordered a Seikoshan whiskey. The sharp liquor burned his throat going down, but did help clear his head a bit. Knowing he'd have to meet up with Leia again in just a few hours, Han nursed the drink.

"I agree," someone said to his left. A man in plain gray clothes with no badges or sashes designating rank. He was holding up a glass of brandy in salute. When Han nodded to him, the man tipped his glass and tossed off the rest. "The only way to survive these things is with a touch of the liquid excitement."

Han smiled noncommittally and sipped at his drink.

"I'm here with a trade alliance," the man said. "Non-guild."

Smugglers, Han thought. "Me, too."

"I'll drink to that!" the man said.

I'd bet you'd drink to anything. Han smiled and took another tiny sip. "Say, you know a guy named Hunter Maas? Runs with the Sendavé Collective?"

"Weapons," the man replied, showing that he, at least, knew what the collective was. "Don't deal much in weapons."

"I've got some personal business with Maas, so trying to track him down. Heard he'd be here."

"Blood, money, or love?"

"Would you believe none of those?" Han asked.

"No!" The man guffawed at him. "No, I would not. But it's not my business anyway. Only know the collective by reputation, and that's all bad. Sorry I can't help."

"It was a long shot," Han said. "What about Essio Galassian?"

"Name rings a bell. Heard of a human went by something like that. Antiquities dealer. Explorer. But not for his main line. Doing it for love, not money. Hooked up with the Empire somehow."

"That's the one."

"I've heard he's a sadistic animal," the man said with a shrug.

"Well, that'll make him stand out from the Imperial crowd," Han said drily, and his companion laughed. "Let me get you the next one." He waved at the bartender droid and pointed at the smuggler's empty glass.

"Thank you, friend," the man said. "A generous soul is its own reward. You have business with this Galassian, too?"

"Might. It's a little hard to say right now. Sort of depends on how the rest of this conference plays out," Han replied.

The man shrugged, thick shoulders rolling under his loose gray shirt. "It's good for picking up new contracts with like-minded folks. That's why my group comes. But do I think this ends with everyone holding hands and pledging to end the Empire? No. And only a fool thinks otherwise. The Empire isn't going anywhere, no matter how many battle stations the rebels manage to blow up. If that even happened."

"Pretty confident it did."

"That's as it may be, but I haven't seen any rebel fleets winning victories in my stretch of space. We're still sneaking past Star Destroyers to make our runs and dodging Imperial tax collectors at the ports. If the rebels are winning, I can't tell."

It was like talking to an older version of himself. The man sitting next to him was who he would have been in a few years if he'd never dumped that cargo of Jabba's and gotten himself in enough trouble to take Luke and Ben Kenobi on their suicide mission. He'd be sitting in bars, talking about the fact of Imperial rule and the fantasy of a rebellion actually winning. It gave Han a strange sense of disconnection. Like he was watching the conversation from outside.

"That Alderaanian princess, though," the man continued after a few moments. "She's something else, isn't she?"

"Leia Organa?"

"That's the one. Makes me wish I was ten years younger or a billion credits richer."

Han gave the man a false smile through gritted teeth. The server droid offered him another drink, and he waved it off with a quick shake of his head. The two brown-robed delegates he'd noticed in the ballroom had been replaced by a knot of whispering Lannik, who kept their heads together and spoke in urgent tones too low for Han to hear the words. A few people were starting to take places at the tables scattered around the room, and Han suspected the speeches were soon going to begin.

"Everyone loves the Rebellion, though," the smuggler said. "We pine for the glorious freedom of the Republic of old. And she can give a fine speech. I'm sure she's gotten many offers of support and friendship. How many of them are going to hold up in an Imperial interrogation room? Not many. But we got six new contracts, and the Princess was a fine thing to look at while she speechified. And the dinners weren't bad."

"Yeah," Han said. "That's what I would have guessed. The glorious freedom of the Republic: meet the new tax collector, same as the old tax collector."

"Ain't that the truth," the smuggler said and tapped his glass against Han's.

CHAPTER FOURTEEN

THE HALL STRETCHED out as long as a flight hangar. The high, arching ceiling had been shaped from the same pale stone as the mountains and carved by alien hands into complex designs that made Han think of bird bones. A dirty yellow light filtered down through it. Tables of food and liquor for a dozen different species squatted along one side, filling the air with a dizzying rich stink guaranteed to have something to offend any nose. At the other side, a raised stage waited for a speaker. For Leia. All he could think was how little cover there was up there against blasterfire.

He'd expected the seating to be laid out in rows or concentric circles. What was the point in having a speaker if not to watch and listen? But the conclave hall was laid out in small, almost self-contained units. Chairs, tables, squatting couches for the physiognomies that didn't get along well with chairs. Between that and the trio of Bith musicians covering the murmur of conversations with syncopated, reedy music, it felt more like a particularly posh cabaret. An old bronze-colored server droid clacked up beside him with a plate of grain crackers smeared with something green and algal-smelling and half a dozen unlabeled black bottles. Han shook his head. The droid squawked and shifted toward him.

"I said *no,*" Han growled.

The droid made an offended squeak and clanked off. Han plucked at the hem of his vest, straightening it. There were easily a dozen different species present, most in groups of their own kind. They were dressed in silks and formal robes, high-collared and conspicuously free of wrinkles. Han wasn't the only one wearing a sidearm, but the others walking between the tables managed to make their weapons look ceremonial. The Rebel Alliance had a table near the foot of the little stage with half a dozen humans and one Mon Calamari. Scarlet Hark was sitting among them. She'd traded out her borrowed shirt, pants, and vest for a gown of startling red, and her hair was up in a loose, elegant bun held in place by lacquered sticks. She looked perfectly at ease. Han noticed that there wasn't a chair at that table for him. Probably because he'd said he wouldn't come. It seemed a little rude of them to take him at his word.

A Bothan man in pale brown robes that matched his pelt approached Han and wordlessly pressed an empty glass into his hand. The Bothan's deep brown eyes seemed rich with gratitude and a kind of sympathetic sorrow. It wasn't until he'd walked away that Han understood what had just happened.

"I'm not a waiter," he called after the Bothan. "I don't work here."

"Thank you all for coming," Leia said, and Han's gaze shot to the stage. She was standing at the front of the little platform. She'd switched her gown for one with a dark cloak and sash that made her look as though she were in military dress without it actually being a uniform. The unpleasant yellow light that shouldered its way through the bonelike ceiling dimmed to a mellow gold. The musicians didn't stop, but the music softened, fading into the background. Han stepped back, leaning against the wall. After a moment, he put the Bothan's empty glass on the floor at his feet. A small droid no larger than an Erian table-ferret skittered by and scooped it up.

"I hope you're all enjoying the food," Leia said.

"Because a massive Imperial fleet may be descending on us at any second," Han muttered, "and you may all be dead before you can digest it."

"I wanted to take a moment and thank you all for coming to this conclave," Leia continued. "It takes real courage to stand against the Empire, and that is something everyone in this hall shares. Each of us here is dedicated in our own way to fighting Imperial oppression."

"So that you can avoid taxes," Han muttered, "or run your own little religious cult, or just because you're pissed off that you're not the one sitting in Palpatine's chair. And there's an Imperial fleet I'm supposed to warn you about, which I'll get to any minute now."

"We have our differences," Leia went on, smiling at the assembled room. "I'm not saying that we don't. But after Alderaan, I think we can all see that the danger the Empire poses is too great for any of us to ignore. When the Rebel Alliance attacked and destroyed the Death Star, we weren't acting out of vengeance, but to prevent the tyranny and terror that such a base represents. The tyranny and terror that would have been used to control every sentient being in this room."

Leia's smile was gone now, and she lifted her eyebrow.

"We've won our second major battle, but there are many, many more to come before the Empire's power is broken. The truth is, we can't do this alone. Unless we have friends who can support us, the Rebel Alliance will be defeated, and the next tool the Empire creates will go unopposed. And then everyone in this room and outside of it will have reason to mourn."

"And, oh, by the way," Han said under his breath. "Come on, Your Highness. Spit it out. Imperial fleet. Impending attack. You can do it."

"Thank you all again for being here. It's an act of courage, and I appreciate it from each and every one of you. And I look forward to talking about how we can all work together to make the galaxy a safer, freer place for everyone."

There was a round of polite applause, and Leia stepped off the stage toward the Rebel Alliance's group. The light brightened, and the music grew louder. Han ground his teeth and turned to leave. At the Rebel Alliance's table, a Phindian with skin the color of old spinach was shouting at Leia. Han couldn't make out the words of Leia's reply, but the sneering tone carried. The generals and soldiers of the Alliance looked up at the two in various stages of consternation and embarrassment. The Phindian lifted both hands in fists and gabbled out a plume of invective that could have stunned a krayt dragon.

Han pushed off from the wall and started toward the arguing pair, his palm resting on the butt of his blaster. His fingertip tingled and his chest warmed. After all the frustrations Kiamurr had offered him up to now, a little honest violence was sounding pretty good. Dozens of people had turned to watch the argument, some with curiosity, some with apparent glee. Han felt his joints loosening in anticipation.

He didn't see Scarlet approach. She was just suddenly at his right side, her arm around his as if he were escorting her. She smiled up at him, her dark eyes glittering. "Why, Captain Solo. And here I was thinking you weren't going to attend our little shindig."

Leia crossed her arms, her mouth thin and her chin high. She asked something, and a roll of laughter passed through the first rank of spectators. The Phindian's face grew darker.

"Careful, sister," Han said. "That's my gun arm you're on."

"I know, right?" she said, moving half a step in front of him and steering him to their left as if he were a cart animal. "Why don't you come sit with me, and we'll talk about things before you get all dashing and impulsive."

"What are you . . ."

The Phindian pointed a long finger at Leia and muttered something. Leia waved him away and sat down, ignoring him. The Phindian closed his fist. Scarlet reached a small table with a single curved bench on one side and maneuvered Han into it, her hand still on his arm. They looked less like he was politely escorting her now. Other people sitting that close and touching that much would have meant something more intimate by it.

"Do you want to tell me what's going on here?" Han asked.

"I'd love to," Scarlet said. "Thanks for asking. The Phindian is Haverous Mok, and he's the head of an engineering corporation called Sorintechnic. He's a major supplier of ship-grade weapons for the Alliance, but not everyone knows that, because he's tried to keep it off the books. Following that?"

"So why is he yelling at—"

Scarlet nestled in close, looking to anyone walking by as if she were flirting outrageously with him. It let her speak softly and almost directly into his ear.

"Because he thinks she's going to cancel an order that he's almost finished with. He's mistaken, but it took several people a lot of effort to *make* him mistaken, and we're all very glad he is."

"That makes no—"

"If you look about fifteen degrees to port, there's a man in a blue-gray suit with a little mustache that makes him look like a womp rat. You see him?"

The man was sitting in a group of eight others, human and Yaka. The one Scarlet meant was watching Leia and the

Phindian with narrowed, appraising eyes. Han had the feeling that maybe this was the one he should have been looking to shoot all along.

"Syrynys Lamarkin," Scarlet said. "He's been putting pressure on the companies that make bacta to increase their prices when they deal with the Rebellion. Don't scowl at him. He'll see you. He's been telling himself and everyone who'll listen that Leia Organa is so mad with grief over the loss of Alderaan that she's unstable and on the verge of collapse. As good as insane."

The Phindian shouted again, and this time Han could make out the words *faithless* and *promise breaker.* Leia stepped closer and put her hand on the Phindian's arm, her expression polite but implacable. At his table, the rat-faced man turned to one of the cyborg Yakas and said something.

"Right now, a dozen different people are watching Leia deal with an irate partner, and they're seeing that she's keeping her temper, standing her ground, and controlling the situation. And not being the person Lamarkin said she was. Which was what this whole evening has been about."

Unless he had stepped in the middle and screwed things up, Scarlet didn't say. The Phindian gestured accusingly, but there was less force behind the gesture now. Leia nodded and drew him over toward her table, seating him where Scarlet had been. The rat-faced man rose from his seat and walked stiffly toward the side of the room.

"None of this is going to matter when the Imperial fleet comes and shoots all these people," Han said.

Scarlet let out a peal of laughter that could have passed for sincere and shook her head at him as if he'd said something witty and impudent. Leia looked over at them as if seeing them for the first time and nodded. Han was suddenly very aware of being at a small table with a beautiful woman pressed close to him. He smiled at Leia and leaned in toward Scarlet.

"General Chith has worked out an evacuation plan," Scarlet said, ignoring them both. "I'm taking it to everyone who needs to know so that we're ready when they come. And I've found two of the people Hunter Maas is scheduled to meet with. They haven't heard from him, but the first meeting is scheduled for tomorrow night. If you're not going to shoot anybody, I'm going to go back to doing that now."

"I'm . . . You know, someone could have told me about all this."

"If I'd known you'd be here, I would have," she said, and her voice had lost its false flirtatiousness. "There are a dozen things going on here, they're all critical, and they all affect one another. I assumed you'd be in the hangar with Chewbacca."

Han pulled his arm free of hers and leaned forward, his elbows on the table. He felt embarrassed and resentful and embarrassed for feeling resentful, but he wasn't going to let any of it show. Leia said something, and the Phindian laughed ruefully. A server droid trundled up to the table, and Scarlet waved it away.

"I'll get back where I belong, then," Han said.

"I know the danger's real," Scarlet said. "And more than that? *She* knows it is. I respect that you want to protect us both, but you need to trust me. And her. These are risks we have to take."

"You don't need to tell me about taking risks," Han said, standing up. "Taking risks is what I do best."

"I know," Scarlet said. "It's why we need men like you on our side."

"Damn right you do," Han said, the words a little less powerful than he'd meant them to be. He stood for a moment. "Are you teasing me?"

A glimmer came to Scarlet's eyes. "Absolutely not. And I promise as soon as I hear anything important, I'll make sure you know. Peace?"

"Of course, peace," Han said, tugging his vest into trim. "I don't know what you're talking about."

"All right then." Scarlet stood up, too. "I should get back to work."

"I'll be at the ship. For what it's worth, you're really dressed nicely."

"I'm really dressed appropriately," she said.

"Okay, now I *know* you're teasing me."

She laughed and stepped out into the milling crowd. Han hovered for a moment, trying to catch Leia's eye, but she and the Phindian were deep in conversation. Han made his way to the exit, out through the conclave hive, and into the streets. The night air was cool, and the narrow strip of stars above him gave little natural light to the setting. He itched to be out of the city, off Kiamurr, and anywhere that a massive attack force of Imperial fighters wouldn't be anytime soon. An old woman driving an even older cargo droid hailed him. The droid's lift arms had been fitted out with a rough couch. He handed her a few credits and sat on the worn, broken cushions, and in a moment the droid was lumbering through the dim streets. A flock of night birds flew by, their wings rustling in the dark air. Han sighed and opened a connection to the *Millennium Falcon.* Chewbacca answered it with a long, guttural howl of complaint.

"I'm on my way," Han said.

The Wookiee howled.

"Well, do you see a massive clot of ships trying to get out of here? No, she didn't tell them."

Chewbacca wailed.

"Yes, there's a problem. There're always problems. It's nothing we can't handle," Han said, then dropped the connection. "I hope."

CHAPTER FIFTEEN

"WELL," HAN SAID with a sigh, "here's our problem."

The torpedo that had carried the tracking device onto the *Falcon* had cut through the hull and embedded itself in a secondary coolant pump. Thick ropy tangles of congealed cooling fluid stretched across the cramped space around it. Several electrical systems had shorted as the conductive slime grounded them out. A tertiary power cable for the aft shield generator had been cut neatly in two by the head of the torpedo.

Chewbacca growled and waved one hairy paw at the mess.

"Yeah, buddy, I hear you," Han said. He pulled a cutting torch out of his toolbox and crouched next to the missile.

Chewbacca huffed and shook his head.

"Well," Han said, "yeah, if there's also a warhead, it might go off. But I'm sort of betting there isn't. If Baasen wanted us dead, why bother with the tracker? I figure he wants us whole for Jabba."

The torch sparked to life, and Han started cutting off the tip of the torpedo. The edges of the cut glowed white with heat, droplets of liquid metal falling to the decking and cooling to red. When the tip of the missile rolled away without exploding, Han pointed and said, "See? Told you so."

Chewbacca, who had backed out of the small compartment and was peering around the corner of the hatch, chuffed out an agreement and came back in to pick it up.

The work went slowly and systematically for several more hours as they cut the rest of the torpedo out. When Han found the tracking device in its guts—a small unit no larger than his two balled fists together—he smashed it with a hammer. Chewbacca carried the irreparable pieces to the ramp and tossed them outside, where a multi-limbed scrap droid picked them up and trundled off with them.

When that was done, they started patching the hull. Leia's people had scrounged up a few square meters of decent plating, so Chewbacca began cutting the raw metal into the right shapes while Han welded them into place. Smoke and the stink of hot alloy filled the air. Sweat rolled down his back, making his clothes stick to his skin. The compartment was cramped, hot, filled with almost unbreathable air, and after the ballroom, it was where Han Solo finally felt comfortable.

Leia could make her way through both worlds. She could be at home in a soldier's uniform or a formal gown. She could wield a blaster or a diplomatic speech. If the last few weeks had taught Han anything, it was that he didn't belong in the civilized part of her world. His place was in the bowels of the *Falcon,* or the pilot's seat. Of all the smugglers, pirates, and criminals he'd known in his years living outside the law, the ones who survived were the ones who knew their place. The ones who developed pretensions of respectability usually wound up getting eaten alive by a society they didn't ever really fit into.

Han ran a weld down a long plate of hull patch, then inspected his work. Smooth, straight, airtight. It felt good to be in a place where he knew what he was doing.

"Ready for that next piece, Chewie," he said, holding

out his hand. There was no reply. He pulled off his goggles and turned around. Chewbacca was gone.

"Blast it." Han climbed to his feet and stomped off into the corridor. He yelled, "Where'd you go? We're not done here!"

He turned the corner into the lounge and found Chewbacca standing with Scarlet. She'd changed out of her gown and into a pair of snug black pants and a dark gray top. She was wearing the belt covered with the tools of her trade, and she'd added a compact blaster in a quick-draw-style holster. Her hair was still up in a bun with sticks pushed through it, though with the new outfit the style looked functional rather than elegant.

"What's all this?" Han asked.

Chewbacca started to growl out an explanation, but Scarlet cut him off. "You're not done? What's not done? Please tell me the *Falcon* can fly."

Han shrugged. "Got a sliced power cable, but I've capped off the coolant leak until we can replace it. Hull's patched. She can fly. You two finally come to your senses?" Without waiting for an answer, Han handed the torch and goggles to Chewbacca. "See if you can get that cable spliced while we're waiting for Her Worshipfulness to get on board."

Chewbacca took the tools with a growl and headed off. Han began mentally going through the list of rendezvous points for reconnecting with the rebel fleet.

"Hunter Maas has jumped in system," Scarlet said.

"Great. And the Imperial fleet?"

"Not yet." Taking a seat at the dejarik table, Scarlet pulled out a datapad and called up a hologram of a ship. "He's flying in this. We need to go get him and escort him back."

Han sat down with her, swiping his hand through the air to kill the hologram. "Why does he need an escort?"

"Because," she said, "I need to make sure we're the only party he speaks to about selling his data. You fly out, make sure he lands at the dock we want him to, and Leia and I will be waiting for him there. We can't let this turn into a bidding war. And the sooner we get it, the sooner the evacuation can start."

"Well, now you're talking something close to sense. Do we have any reason to think he'll do what I tell him to?"

"Be persuasive," Scarlet said with just a hint of a smile.

Han frowned to keep himself from smiling back. "This is coming from Leia? This is what she wants?"

"It's what needs to happen," Scarlet said, the smile vanishing. "So go do it."

"Hey, I have *one* boss, sweetheart," Han said, tapping his own chest, "and as far as I'm concerned—"

"Call when you're coming back," she said, standing up. "I'll give you a dock assignment then. Don't screw this up, Solo."

"Don't—" he started, but she was already leaving.

Chewbacca wandered back into the room, the smoking welder in one big paw. He cocked his head to one side and howled out a question.

"I am really starting to dislike the level of bossiness hanging with these rebels entails," Han said. "I thought the princess was bad."

THE *FALCON*'S REACTOR wound up with a hum so high-pitched it was almost subliminal, then cycled back down with a sound like grinding gears.

For the third time.

The knowledge that Scarlet was down in the dock's viewing area watching as he vainly tried to get his ship off the ground made each successive failure a little more humiliating.

"It's got to be a short," he said to Chewbacca. For the third time. "It's the only thing that makes sense. Are you sure you scraped all the gunk out of the cabling?"

Chewbacca growled back dangerously.

"Then it's got to be that tertiary power cable splice." Chewbacca rumbled out another terse reply. "Yes, I know *I* was the one who did that. We can sit here all day assigning blame, or we can fix it."

Chewbacca stared at him for several long seconds.

"I have to stay up here! Someone has to be in the pilot's seat to monitor and test."

Chewbacca got up and headed to the back of the ship without a word. The comm came to life with a hiss, and Scarlet said, "Are you pouting? Or does your ship not work?"

"I don't pout," Han said, aware that actually having to say those words out loud automatically made them a lie. "Just need to finalize something and we'll be heading right out." He shut his mouth before *so stop watching* could sneak out.

Chewbacca growled from the back of the ship, and an indicator on Han's panel shifted from yellow to white. The reactor came on with a smoothly rising whine and stayed on. A few moments later the *Falcon* lifted off the dock, not a warning light in sight.

Flying up off the planet was like watching the universe come into being, stars unfolding as the tops of the mountains fell away. The small, ruddy moon hung on the horizon, and then drifted behind them as Han angled the *Falcon* out of the atmosphere to where he could safely bring the throttle up to full.

Han was scanning the space around Kiamurr, looking for Maas's ship, when Chewbacca walked back into the cockpit and plopped into the copilot's chair. The Wookiee growled at him for a minute, waving his big paws around angrily.

"Don't I know it, Chewie," Han said, then shifted the scan to a new vector and started over. "When did we go from having no boss to everyone being our boss? This Hark character isn't even a princess. You can forgive royalty for acting like the universe owes them something, but Scarlet's just a spy. Where does she get off?"

Chewbacca burbled out a reply while he worked on the damage control, double- and triple-checking the various systems they'd just repaired.

"Take my word for it, buddy, there's gonna be trouble there eventually," Han said. "You put two stiff-necked women like that in proximity to a good-looking guy like me? Sooner or later, it comes to blows."

Chewbacca looked at him out of the corner of one eye and barked a laugh.

"Hey, I'm just giving you the heads-up. You don't want to be anywhere nearby when *that* reactor pile goes hot."

Chewbacca turned his chair toward Han and opened his mouth, but whatever he was about to say was lost when a console alert sounded. The *Falcon* had found a fast-moving light freighter headed their direction. Chewbacca swiveled back to his console and started scanning the new contact. He barked out the info as it came up.

"Moving awful fast for a YU-four-ten," Han replied. "Those things usually drive like garbage scows."

A few moments later, the reason became clear. The YU-410 model Corellian freighter was typically slow moving and heavily armed. Someone had stripped off most of the armaments and beefed up the drive. It had a single laser cannon turret instead of the usual four, and the one it had could only fire forward. Fast moving, its armaments pointing forward, it had been refitted from a freighter into a predator. He'd seen a thousand ships like it, and not one of them had been made for respecting the law.

"That's got to be our boy," Han said. "Let's get over alongside him and introduce ourselves."

Chewbacca ramped up power to the drive to close the distance as quickly as possible. Han warmed up the *Falcon*'s concussion missile tubes, just in case. People had a tendency to listen more closely to your arguments when you'd just flattened their ship's shields.

The big YU-410 came straight at them, heading toward Kiamurr at maximum speed. Chewbacca plotted them a looping course that would put the *Falcon* alongside the other freighter as it passed by. Han pulled on his headset and started hailing the other ship. The only reply was static.

"Huh," he said, "it's almost like someone is jamming them—"

A large energy blast hit the stern of the YU-410, lighting up its shields and sending crackling bolts cascading across its hull. When the light show was over, the YU-410 was still flying, though it looked as if the rear hull plating had taken some damage.

"Chewie, get us over there. I'm going to try to cut that jamming. See if you can lock onto whoever's shooting our friend."

Chewbacca growled out a reply and sent the *Falcon* diving at the YU-410 at full speed. Han began cycling the communications controls, dumping more power into his broadcast and trying to force his signal through the jamming field. After a few moments of work, he was rewarded with a tenuous connection. A faint voice said, "Hello? Who is calling Hunter Maas?"

"This is Captain Han Solo, of the *Millennium Falcon.* I've been sent to make sure you get safely to a dock on Kiamurr."

"You," said the voice, "are doing a terrible job."

Han's mouth shut with a click.

"Be there in a second," he said, then shut off the headset microphone. "Chewie, get us over there before this guy makes me want to watch him die."

A new alert began flashing on the console as the *Falcon* found the pursuing ship and locked on. "Great," Han said. "Imperials." He'd hoped against hope that the ship chasing Maas was a jealous rival, or a pirate, or really anything but the first sign that the Imperial fleet was on its way.

The Imperial ship looked like a TIE fighter, which was bad. Han began scanning the sky for the carrier that had brought it. The real threat would be whatever ship the TIE had jumped in on. But after several seconds of scanning, the *Falcon* found nothing.

"Try to put us between that freighter and the TIE," Han said to Chewbacca, and the Wookiee growled out an affirmative. "And angle the rear deflectors. We'll get in there and spoil their shot."

Han went back to the scan of the TIE fighter. It was an unusual design. Bigger than the usual escort ships, and it had a strange bulge as if someone had welded a bus on top of the hull. "I think I know this one, Chewie. I think that's an SR. Experimental TIE with a hyperdrive for long recon. They didn't make very many of them. If so, we're in luck. He could have jumped in on his own, which means we don't have a frigate hiding out here somewhere."

Yet, he didn't say.

Chewbacca growled and yanked hard on the controls. Hunter Maas's freighter loomed in front of them, and the *Falcon* began shaking with incoming fire. The rear deflector alarms started squawking.

"Oh, look," Han said to Chewbacca, and grabbed the controls. "We've just been invited to the dance."

CHAPTER SIXTEEN

HAN THREW THE *FALCON* hard to port, and a stream of laser cannon fire flashed past.

"That almost hit Hunter Maas's ship!" Hunter Maas yelled in Han's headset.

"It almost hit Han Solo's ship," Han muttered to himself, then turned the headset mic back on. "We're handling it; just keep heading to Kiamurr at full speed. We'll get this guy off your tail."

"See that you do!"

Chewbacca growled out a laugh.

"Not a chance, pal," Han said to the Wookiee, and pulled hard at the controls to throw the *Falcon* across the pursuing TIE's field of fire, trying to draw its aim away from the fleeing Maas. "We're not adding a third boss to this trip. Just as soon as we—"

The *Falcon* shuddered as another burst of laser fire hit her rear shields. A warning light started flashing.

"—get rid of *this* guy, we'll make sure Maas knows his place in the pecking order."

The warning light shifted to red, and an alarm shrieked. The rear deflector was collapsing. The recently patched power cabling had burned out, and the energy surge had knocked out the backup generator. As if to highlight this fact, the cockpit of the *Falcon* started to smell like smoke and burning conduit.

"We *just* fixed that," Han said. Chewbacca growled back. Han nodded. "I know it's frustrating."

Another stream of laser fire cut through the space between the ships. Han managed to evade most of it with a hard spiraling dive to starboard, but a few bolts struck the rear of the *Falcon*. The warning indicator shifted to black, and the alarm squealed one last time, then fell into a sullen monotone.

The rear shield was gone.

Han yanked back on the controls, pulling the ship into a tight loop. The moment they were out of the way, the TIE fighter began pouring laser fire into the back of Maas's freighter. The pirate screeched at them.

"Hunter Maas is being fired upon again! You said you came to protect! You are very bad at this job!"

Han continued the loop until the *Falcon* was behind the TIE. "Yeah, but you still have rear shields," he said to Maas, "so you can take it."

Maas wailed his disagreement, but Han killed the headset. "Chewie, start calculating a torpedo shot on that TIE fighter. If, like the rest of them, it doesn't have shields, one concussion blast should be enough to take it out."

Chewbacca worked at the weapons console while Han throttled up to close the distance. The SR-model TIE was fast, and it appeared to have plenty of spare power for the laser cannons. It fired into the fleeing YU-410 without pause.

The Empire's penchant for building fighters without shields had always seemed insane to Han, one of many reasons he didn't fly for that particular corporation, but working for the opposing team, he was grateful for their lack of compassion for their pilots.

Chewbacca yowled in triumph as the *Falcon* buzzed a target lock signal. Han closed the distance to the optimal firing range and let loose two of his eight ST2 concussion missiles. That was fifteen hundred credits on the wing, but he'd make sure to add that to the bill.

The TIE began dodging when the missiles launched. The pilot was good. Han had expected that. The Empire didn't have very many of the SR-class recon fighters, so whoever flew them would be top shelf. Han kept his finger on the trigger, ready to fire two more missiles if he needed to.

He didn't.

The TIE started a hard turn to port, but the YU-410 veered erratically into its path, forcing the pilot to correct in the other direction and into the path of the incoming missiles. Both hit, and the TIE fighter disappeared in a massive concussion blast that blew it into gravel-sized chunks. The forward shields of the *Falcon* flashed as debris sprayed across the ship.

Chewbacca barked a victory laugh at the vanished fighter and climbed out of his seat.

"Yeah," Han said, "check on that generator. See if it can be saved. I don't like the idea of flying without rear shields until we can get back to the fleet."

Chewbacca growled out his assent and vanished into the back of the ship.

"Hunter Maas," Han said, after turning the headset back on. "This is Captain Solo call—"

"You fired torpedoes at Hunter Maas!" the man shouted back. "The *Cosmodium* could have been destroyed!"

"The *Cosmodium*? Is that your ship?"

"Hunter Maas carries precious cargo in fragile data storage devices! The pulse from exploding torpedoes can do irreparable damage to such things!"

"Those were concussion warheads, they don't make a—"

"And pieces of the exploding ship have pierced the *Cosmodium*'s hull! Hunter Maas will require *extensive* repairs to his ship!"

"Hunter Maas," Han said pleasantly.

"Yes?"

"Shut up."

There was a long silence, though it was impossible to tell if this was obedience or shock.

"Thank you," Han said. "Please follow my course to Kiamurr. We'll make sure you get there safely. We have a secure dock picked out for your landing."

"Hunter Maas selects his own dock," the pirate was saying. "Thank you for your offer, but your work is now complete. Take the compliments and salutations of Hunter Maas to whoever your master is. Good-bye."

"Hold on there, pal," Han said. The guy on the other end of the line was finally starting to get on his nerves. "You're going to follow me back to *my* dock, end of story."

"And why would Hunter Maas agree to these terms?"

"Because," Han said, making sure Maas could hear the smile in his voice, "I saved you." When Maas started to interrupt, he talked over him. "*And* I'm sitting behind you right now with six more concussion missiles. So you can fly to Kiamurr, land at my private dock, and meet with my friends. Or I can tow the crippled remains of your ship to that same dock."

The pause was shorter than Han had expected.

"Hunter Maas likes the sound of this private dock! Lead the way, my friend."

Han nodded to himself and stripped off the headset.

"How's that for persuasive?" he said to no one.

TRUE TO HER WORD, Scarlet had a dock assignment waiting for them at a small freight-forwarding warehouse just outside the main city. The warehouse was closed when they arrived, so the dock was empty of ships and employees. She was waiting for them, lounging on a nearby flight of stairs.

Han trotted down the ramp from the *Falcon,* hand on the butt of his blaster. They didn't really have any idea how many people Maas had with him on his ship, or if they'd be angry about Han forcing them to land. If Scarlet was worried, it didn't show. She stretched out on the steps, head cocked to one side so that her black hair fell away from her eyes. She gave Han a grin.

"Good job, Captain."

"He had an Imperial scout ship chasing him," Han said. "The clock's ticking. The invasion has to be on its way."

"We saw," she said, then jumped lightly to her feet and started walking toward Maas's freighter. "Thanks for handling that, Han. But it's possible the scout that was chasing Maas was working on its own. We can't be sure it was an advance ship of an Imperial fleet."

"Are we waiting to find out? Because that seems like a bad hand to bet all our chips on."

"Let's just get this negotiation out of the way," Scarlet said. "That's our priority. Then we'll decide what to do."

"Why do I feel like the 'we' in that statement doesn't include me?"

"Because it doesn't?"

Before Han could formulate a good reply, the ramp to Maas's ship began to open. A thick trickle of smoke and the smell of burned metal drifted out. The *Cosmodium* had taken a beating, no doubt about that.

"Chewie," Han said into his headset, "get your furry backside out here." The Wookiee growled back. "I know I told you to fix it, but get out here anyway. Bring your bowcaster." Chewbacca chuffed in agreement and closed the line.

Hunter Maas appeared at the top of the ramp, bursting

out of the smoky ship's interior like an actor taking the stage. He was a small man, physically speaking, but he managed to take up all the space in the large and mostly empty dock. He didn't walk down the ramp, he swaggered. He didn't smile at them, he grinned a mouthful of sparkling white teeth. He was shirtless, wearing his small middle-aged potbelly with a pride it didn't deserve. His pants were tight black leather. Over his shoulders flowed a floor-length red cape with elaborate gold piping. A meek R3 droid followed after him like a supplicant, and a thin ratlike bird perched on his left shoulder, chittering random words in a dozen different languages.

"Greetings!" Maas boomed at them, throwing his long cape away from his right hip to expose a holstered blaster. Han worked to keep a grin off his face. The blaster was an ancient model so large that he was pretty sure he could draw and fire three shots in the time it would take that aged monstrosity to clear its holster. If the point of all the cape twirling was to be threatening, it wasn't working.

"Hunter Maas," Scarlet said, giving him a hint of a bow. "We're very happy you agreed to join us."

"Agreed?" Maas said, eyebrows crawling up his face. "All of the posturing from this one"—he pointed at Han—"would have been unnecessary had only Hunter Maas been told of your loveliness."

The gunrunner and thief sauntered down the ramp to Scarlet, swept her hand up in a dramatic flourish, and laid a long, wet kiss on it. "Hunter Maas is your servant, my lady. Command him!"

With a smile, Scarlet managed to pull her hand out of his. "I ask only that you join me for a drink and a conversation."

"Ah, my sweetling," Maas replied, grabbing Scarlet's hand again and putting it on his arm, "we are meant to be together. You have read Hunter Maas's innermost thoughts and discerned his own desires. Lead on, lady. Drink and converse we shall."

Scarlet left her hand on his arm and began guiding him out of the dock, the R3 scooting along behind like an attendant at a wedding. Han followed once Chewbacca had caught up to them. The Wookiee carried his bowcaster in both hands and frowned a question. Han nodded toward Maas and shrugged.

As he and Chewbacca followed Scarlet to the meeting place, Maas ignored them completely. He couldn't blame the man. Scarlet definitely had the air of someone in charge. Whenever she was in the room, he and Chewbacca probably looked like hired thugs—the unspoken threat paired to her polite civility. It was a role Han had played before, but it galled him how quickly he fell into it when he was around her.

Scarlet led them to a small cantina at the edge of the docks. The kind of rough place the warehouse workers and ships' crews would go after a shift to spend the day's wages blowing off steam. Chewbacca hung his bowcaster on his back and crossed his arms, over two meters of furry threat to ward off anyone looking for an easy score.

Inside, the place was all black walls and flashing lights. Gaming machines and gambling tables were scattered around the room as if a bored giant had dumped them out of his pockets on the way through. A dozen different species drank and gamed and scuffled in the cramped space.

Hunter Maas looked right at home. Leaving the R3 with them, he sauntered up to the bar and spoke to the bartender for a few moments, though with the deafening rattle of gaming machines and piped-in music, it was impossible to hear what was said. A moment later the bartender handed Maas two glasses, and Maas passed the man a coin. He gave one glass to Scarlet, and drank off the other in one long swallow. He said something Han couldn't make out. Scarlet answered, nodding toward Han and Chewbacca.

Han could feel the approaching Imperial fleet like an itch on top of his scalp. Every second they spent was one they wouldn't have when they needed to run. A pair of three-eyed, goat-faced Gran in orange-and-black flight suits walked toward Scarlet and Maas, but Chewbacca stepped in front of them and growled, and the two Gran beat a hasty retreat.

Han sidled up to Scarlet and whispered in her ear. "Everyone can tell we don't belong in here."

She didn't reply, but a moment later she finished off the last of her drink and said, "Captain Maas. Would you like to join me in our private room in the back?"

The shirtless man smiled and downed his second drink, slamming the glass on the bar. "Hunter Maas would very much like to join you in a private room!"

Scarlet took his arm and led him through the thick knots of bar patrons with practiced ease. She could move people out of her way with just a smile and a polite nod. Han had to use Chewbacca to clear his path to the back of the bar, and still he almost wound up in a fight with a piggish alien of a species he didn't recognize. In the end, Chewbacca picked up the alien by the scruff of the neck and shook it until it calmed down. After that, everyone cleared a path for them. By the time they caught up, Scarlet and Maas were at a small door. Scarlet knocked, and it slid open.

The back room of the cantina was bare stone, with rough-surfaced scratches where the marks of the cutting torch hadn't been smoothed away. A small table with a bottle of liquor and three glasses stood in the middle of the floor under a single hanging light. Boxes of supplies lined the walls—food and drink and other things less familiar.

Leia stood near the middle of the room, wearing a loose

white robe over sand-colored pants. She looked too elegant to be in a port cantina. Han gave her a grin, and one corner of her mouth twitched.

"Thank you for coming, Captain Maas. My name is Leia Organa of Alderaan, and I would like to buy what you're selling."

CHAPTER SEVENTEEN

HUNTER MAAS LOOKED around the room as if he owned it. He bowed to Leia and Scarlet in turn and favored Han and Chewie with a wink before settling into a chair and propping his heels on the table. Now that he was holding still, Han could see that the man's scuffed work boots were decorated with mosaic skulls made of small shards of crystal.

Chewbacca silently turned to Han and lifted a brow. Han looked down and bit his lip to keep from laughing.

"You are the rebel princess then, hey? The lovely miss says you sent these two to help me escape the Imperial ship," Hunter said. "Hunter Maas owes you a debt of honor, and it shall be repaid."

Leia sat across from the man. From her demeanor, she could have been meeting with a president or a king. Scarlet leaned against the back wall, her face blank, her concentration fierce. Han met her gaze and glanced at Hunter Maas. *This guy? Really?* A small line drew itself at the corner of Scarlet's mouth, not a smile but the presentiment of one.

"I'm pleased the Rebellion could be of service," Leia said. "It seems we have a common enemy."

"Hunter Maas has no enemies," Hunter Maas said. "He has only admirers and the jealous."

"And the fighter that was trying to kill you?" Leia asked.

"Jealous. Intimidated by my masculinity."

Han had been around Leia long enough to recognize some of her small, unconscious expressions. The blink that lasted a fraction of a second too long, the smile that began and ended at her eyes because she'd practiced doing that. Hunter Maas didn't see any of it. The rat-bird screeched and hopped from Maas's left shoulder to his right, nipping at his earlobe.

"I understand that you've come to the conference with some information to sell," Leia said.

"Not information. Victory. Hunter Maas holds the key to control over the Empire! Such that even the mad Emperor quakes in his boots like a little girl to contemplate." He swung his boots to the floor with a clunk and lowered his voice to a whisper. "Power such as you have never imagined. Hunter Maas has come not to sell information, no, but to choose his partner in godlike ascendance!"

Han pretended to scratch his nose to hide his smile, but Scarlet's expression had gone serious again. Hunter Maas was a buffoon and a blowhard, but Scarlet, at least, seemed to be taking his bragging very seriously.

"You have Essio Galassian's project notes," the spy said. "The report he was preparing for the Emperor."

Hunter Maas grinned at her and pretended to shoot her with his fingertip. "The beautiful woman is more than she appears. She has heard of Hunter Maas's victory. Yes, yes. The report of the great villain Galassian, despoiler of ancient graves and toady to the mad Emperor. Hunter Maas has the only copy of his greatest work. The master discovery that will remake the galaxy forever. Only Hunter Maas!"

"Galassian's not dead," Scarlet said. "He can write the report again. Whatever you have, the Empire does also."

"All the more reason to act quickly, yes?"

"What is in this report?" Leia asked.

Hunter Maas spread his hands in a wide gesture that took in the room, the city, the world. He leaned forward, his spine straightening. Whatever the man was about to say, Han had the sense he'd rehearsed it a lot.

"The galaxy is filled with thousands of species, royal lady. Thousands of different shapes of minds. Most, they are of a piece, but some? Some are changed. They find those things that no other can see. Most are turned outward, to the stars and the great community of life, but some turn in to block away the stars. To protect themselves from such as you, yes? Or I."

"Silly them," Han said, and Scarlet shot him a sharp look. Hunter Maas, however, wouldn't be derailed.

"Such a species were the K'kybak. Brilliant and fearful. Their race rose, flourished, and passed to the great emptiness of time all within the realm of one small planet. But the mysteries they uncovered there were profound. Deep, yes? Had their temperament been other than it was, we should all still bow down to a K'kybak master. Yes, even Hunter Maas. Such was their power.

"They were a young species when the invaders came. Long before the Empire. Long before the Republic. Their suffering was under stars of a different color, so long ago this happened. With great wars, they cast off oppression's yoke. And once free, the brilliant, twisted minds of the K'kybak bent themselves to protection. They took the oppressor's ships, their weapons, all the technology that had placed the boot upon their necks. And what did they do with it? Did they create a fleet to annihilate? No. They delved deep, deep into the mysteries of physics and built themselves a tool to wrap their star in safety forever. The greatest weapons in the galaxy were as nothing to them then. They lived the span of their people's lives and died undisturbed by even the most vicious conquerors."

Leia nodded. "That's fascinating," she said in a tone that

suggested it might not actually be fascinating. "And I assume you're here to sell whatever defensive technology they discovered?"

"Alas, no. Hunter Maas instead has the map. The secret coordinates that will lead the wise and powerful to the dead world of the K'kybak, there to retrieve the secret that will lay the galaxy at their feet."

"Will this shield protect against something as powerful as the Death Star?" Leia asked.

Hunter Maas sneered. "Death Star? The K'kybak laugh at this Death Star. Ha!"

"It destroyed my home planet," Leia said, and the hardness in her voice caught even Hunter Maas's attention.

"And I grieve with you, but ask yourself this, royal lady. What power would it have if it could not *move*? Could it have destroyed your world from across the galaxy? I think not."

Hunter Maas wagged his eyebrows. Han and Chewie exchanged a puzzled glance. Scarlet's sharp breath cut through the air.

"Why would they be across the . . . Oh. Hyperspace," she said. "They found a way to control passage through hyperspace."

Han felt his gut tighten. Hunter Maas's comic smile suddenly seemed a lot less funny.

"The twiggy little woman is correct," Hunter Maas said. "They had in their hands the key to controlling all of space, yes? Of saying not who is *permitted* to go from there to here, but for whom it is *possible*. Put your Death Star in a system, turn loose its power, and the man who commands it can become the Emperor of gravel. At sub lightspeeds, his grandchildren's grandchildren's grandchildren might perhaps threaten another planet. The Imperial fleet with its host of Destroyers is nothing if it cannot travel. The Emperor himself. If he cannot send his little men where he wishes, what is he? Nothing. Less than nothing. The greatest gun in the galaxy is of no use when you have no one to point it at."

Leia's face was pale, her lips so thin they almost vanished. It was a tribute to her strength that when she spoke, her voice was as calm and friendly as it had been at the meeting's start.

"That could be interesting. What are you asking for that information?"

"Highest bidder," Hunter Maas said. "Who knows how far it could go, yes? Perhaps the Hutts will give Hunter Maas his own planet. Perhaps Black Sun will give him a hundred planets."

"Well, the Empire will give him a blaster shot through his eye," Scarlet said. "And they know where you are. You don't have a great deal of time for this. We've saved you once. If you work with us now, we can guarantee your safety."

"What is safety to a man such as Hunter Maas? He lives through the greatness of his spirit and the nobility of his soul. Plus which, he has meetings scheduled for the next three days. There is no advantage in selling anything to anyone until those conversations are complete."

Leia leaned forward and put her hand on Hunter Maas's wrist. Han could hear the tension in her voice, tight as a tow cable under high load.

"The man you took this from. Galassian. He knows where this thing is. You have to see that the Empire will be moving to secure it."

"They are bureaucrats," Hunter Maas said. "They would take years to clean spilled paint if the forms were not just so."

"They're also a totalitarian dictatorship that will kill people who don't bow to the Emperor's will quickly enough. If they want this thing—and they do—we won't know it until we're all trapped with dead drives in whatever system we happen to be in."

"Then you should all make your offers to Hunter Maas quickly."

"I'll give you fifty million credits for it right now," Leia said. Han felt a moment of dizziness at the idea of such a sum. More than enough to pay off Jabba. More than enough to *buy* Jabba if he felt the need for a pet slug. He'd had no idea the rebels could put their hands on that kind of money.

Hunter Maas's eyes faded into something like pity. "Hunter Maas would like a planet. No less."

Leia's smile twitched. She rubbed her chin like a man checking for stubble.

"A planet?" she said.

"What did you call it? 'Totalitarian dictatorship'? Hunter Maas would like to be emperor of his own little world. Just one. Is it so much? The Emperor holds the power of life and death over half the galaxy. To give Hunter Maas one little world would mean freeing so very many people. Surely that trade would be fair?"

"A hundred million credits and any ship in the Rebel fleet, but you have to take the deal now. Before you leave this room."

"A smallish planet. With many, many beautiful women."

"Fine," Leia said. "You can have it."

"Poor, poor royal miss," Hunter Maas said, patting her hand. The rat-bird hopped down to the table, chirruped, and defecated prodigiously. "You are lying. Hunter Maas understands. Take time to think. Hunter Maas will be making no decision for several days. There will be time for her to make a real offer."

"You can't do this," Leia said.

"Hunter Maas cannot be stopped," he said almost gently.

"Oh, I think he can," Scarlet said. "Captain Solo?"

Han drew his blaster. The R3 droid squeaked in alarm and extruded a small electrical lead that sparked and crackled. Chewbacca bared his teeth and stepped forward. The droid and the rat-bird both moved back, but Hunter Maas curled his lips disdainfully.

"Your Wookiee may kill Hunter Maas," he said, "if you wish to see the Empire win. It will not matter to Hunter Maas. He will be dead! Is that what you want? To see the Empire win?"

"Does it mean pulling your arms off?" Han asked. "Because then maybe."

"Let him go," Leia said.

No one moved except the rat-bird, and it crawled under Hunter Maas's red-and-gold cape and blinked out at them malevolently. Scarlet's eyes were narrow. Chewbacca growled deep in his throat.

"I said let him go," Leia said. "Put your weapons down and let the man go to his meetings."

Han clenched his jaw, but he put the blaster back in its holster. Chewbacca roared and pounded the table with his fist, leaving a dent. The Wookiee paced back to the corner to glower. Hunter Maas rose, stretched, and bowed to Leia.

"You are as gracious to Hunter Maas as you are lovely, royal lady. Do not think I will forget you, oh no. Hunter Maas knows when a debt of honor is due. When I have the bids of the others, I will give you the opportunity to beat them."

"Thank you so much," Leia said. Her sarcasm would have left blisters on a more sensitive man.

"In truth, Hunter Maas would have been disappointed if you had not tried to intimidate him."

The little man blew Scarlet a kiss, flourished his cape, and swaggered from the room, the rat-bird hunched on his shoulder and the R3 rolling at his heels as if it was afraid of being left behind. For a long moment, the only sound was the muted music from the cantina.

Leia leaned back in her seat, laced her hands behind her head, and said something obscene.

"So," Han said, turning to Scarlet. "That was the guy who got the data you were after?"

"He got lucky."

"Oh, hey, no criticism here. There's no shame in being beaten by a smooth operator like that. I mean, did you see his boots? They were shiny. No reason to be embarrassed just because you lost a sensitive operation to a shirtless man with shiny boots."

"You're enjoying this."

"Just the part where *that* guy was better than you," he said. "The rest of it scares the heck out of me."

Leia stood up and cocked an eyebrow. "All right. So. If he takes this to the Hutts or Black Sun, they'll give him whatever he wants. Or the Empire will come rain fire on all our heads. Or they'll get to this device, wherever it is, and none of this will have mattered at all."

"What lovely alternatives," Scarlet said.

"So we steal it from him," Leia said.

"Give me until morning," Scarlet said. "I'll need to find where he's staying. If it's in his ship, that will actually be easier. If he's put himself in the care of the conclave hive . . . trickier, but possible. They've put a lot of thought into keeping people safe and information private."

"All right," Leia said. "I'll be making a series of panicky calls to the Alliance, arguing over how much we can offer him."

"Why?" Han asked.

"So that he thinks we're still at the negotiating table," Leia said. "As long as he believes he's winning, we're on the right track."

"And what do you want us to do?" Han asked, nodding toward Chewbacca.

"Be his bodyguard," Leia said. "Make sure no one kills him before we get this information."

Chewbacca's outraged howl filled the room.

"I don't like it any better than you do," Leia said, her chin tilted all the way up to look the Wookiee full in the face. "But I don't have a choice. Hunter Maas is a terrible, stupid, venal little man who is playing way out of his league. He's probably going to get himself killed, but he's got the upper hand right now. If the Empire gets a power like this—or Black Sun does, or the Hutts—it will mean the end of all freedom in the galaxy *forever.*"

Scarlet nodded, her expression grim.

"So," Han said, "what'll it mean if *we* get it?"

CHAPTER EIGHTEEN

THE CONCLAVE HIVE had four different classes of accommodation. For the attendees of the conference with the greatest number of people and the greatest power, there were seven private buildings where the administrators could simply hand over the passkeys and give people control over—and responsibility for—their own security. Down from that were high-security cells, hardly better than prison, with guards and surveillance and a constant patrol of small, flying droids armed with blasters and strict orders about who could and couldn't walk the hallways. The third were private sleeping rooms available for rent inside the conclave hive itself, convenient to the meeting rooms and bars. And the last were dormitory bunks for groups of soldiers or multi-bodied hive-mind pods that didn't mind being packed into tight spaces with no privacy.

Han wasn't at all surprised to see Hunter Maas sauntering toward the third-class rooms. A man who needed a droid and a rat-bird for his entourage wasn't going to accept the worst rooms, and he couldn't afford the best. Han slumped under a massive, slick-trunked tree across an open courtyard, cleaning his fingernails and watching through a great glass wall as Hunter Maas negotiated with the droid responsible for portioning out the rooms. Scarlet's voice came to him, thin and tinny.

"All right," she said. "I've got him. You can step away."

Han didn't answer directly, but turned his back to the accommodations suite and walked along the pathway through the hive. A crowd of thin-faced, mean-looking humans scowled at him as he passed a little garden. Han touched his forehead in mock salute and didn't break stride.

It was nearing midnight in Talastin City, and the foot traffic in the conclave hive had a furtive feel. People moving between one clandestine rendezvous and another, eyeing one another warily. Everyone trying to see who was nearby without themselves being seen. Right now, everything was for sale on Kiamurr. Weapons and drugs and slaves, loyalty and betrayal. And, thanks to Hunter Maas, the future of the galaxy. The bad thing was that it meant shadowing Hunter Maas had been tricky. The good thing was that it had been possible, and with Han and Scarlet working together to trade off observing and protecting their target, they'd managed without being spotted.

"Hey," a voice whispered. Han glanced over. A rail-thin Noghri with a heavy brow and permanently bared teeth hissed, "I'm looking for transponder IDs. You selling IDs?"

"I'm not selling anything, sister. I'm just a peaceful-minded civilian on a walk," Han said. She smiled and nodded. They were both lying, and they both knew it. At least they could be cheerful about it.

"We're clear," Scarlet said in his ear. "He's paid up and they've assigned him a room. Head back in."

"What about his droid?"

"He took it in with him," Scarlet said. "The common area's clear."

"Not leaving it as a sentry? Wow," Han said. "This guy really is an amateur."

"I think I'd mentioned that."

"It's just that you're such a professional. Still trying to figure how you lost to him."

"Haven't lost yet. Still playing," she said.

Han angled his way back down the path and toward the accommodations suite. Behind him, he heard the Noghri talking to someone else, asking for IDs she almost certainly didn't need. When he got back to his place at the tree, Scarlet was framed by the glass wall. She'd altered her hair and changed her stance in some small, subtle, and extremely effective way. She was wearing the same dark pants, the same gray blouse, but she looked like an entirely different woman. The soldier of fortune was gone, and a friendly tourist had taken her place. He wasn't sure how she did that, but he was getting the feeling that she found it useful to be underestimated. He paused at the tree until she twisted away from the droid, smiled, and waved him over.

He crossed the courtyard with a sense of being vulnerable. There were too many places around here for someone to hide. That he was one of the people looking to sneak through it only made him more aware of the fact.

"This is him," Scarlet told the droid as Han walked up. "He seriously wanted us to spend the whole trip on the same ship we came here in. Can you imagine anything so utterly boring?"

"I'm sure the gentleman had his reasons," the droid said.

"I did," Han said. "They were good reasons, too. Very . . . reasonable."

Scarlet frowned a little, and Han lifted his hands. *What did you want me to say?*

"He was going on about how much safer we'd be onboard ship," Scarlet said.

"Yes," Han said, catching on. "Yes, I was. And I'm still not convinced by the security here. We have sensitive documents. For business. I don't want to see them lost just so we can have a bigger bunk."

"No need for concern," the droid said, shaking its silver-gray head. "The rooms here are securely sealed from the time our guests leave until they return. Not even service droids, if you'd like. Though that does reduce the amenities, of course."

"Not good enough," Han said, starting to get into the role. "I need absolute assurance that my sensitive documents aren't going to be disturbed."

"In addition," the droid went on, "for a very reasonable fee, encryption-locked safes are available in every room. They can even be set for automatic purge in case of an attempted intrusion."

Han scowled and looked at Scarlet. He raised his eyebrows. *I don't know. What else do you want?*

"It's perfect," Scarlet said, handing the droid a credit chit. "We'll take it."

"My gratitude, madam," the droid said. "You will be in 17-C. If you have any concerns, please only ask."

Scarlet put her arm around Han's again as she had in the ballroom, and he pulled it back out, unwilling to be steered. Scarlet's smile was merry. They walked down a short, broad hallway of laser-cut stone. Scarlet tapped her fingertips together, her eyes scanning the other rooms as they passed. Han didn't ask what she was thinking about. Seventeen-C was a wide room with a low ceiling. The bed was larger than the bunks in the *Falcon,* but by less than he'd expected. Scarlet made a quick pass through the place, then opened the closet and accessed the safe. It chirped, accepted her credit chit, and clacked open.

"How's it look?" Han asked.

"Good and bad," she said. "Magnetic locks. It's just a mechanism, not a droid, so none of the programming workarounds apply. I want to see if I can get any information on the encryption unit."

A brilliant white light bloomed around her, sparks like

stars cascading down. Han yelped in surprise and jumped toward her. Scarlet turned to him, concerned.

"Are you all right?" Han asked.

"Sure. I'm just trying to get to the encryption unit," she said, and held up a tiny matte-black tube. "Welding torch."

"Oh," Han said. "Right. Carry on."

The brilliant light came back, and the smell of hot metal. Han lay back on the bed.

"For what it's worth," Scarlet said, "I think she's very lucky."

"Who is?"

"The Princess."

"You do? She just watched her world be destroyed by Darth Vader, and now her begging-for-money mission turned into a get-the-dangerous-information-before-the-Imperial-fleet-slags-the-planet mission. I don't see how you get any less lucky than her without breaking bones."

"Mmm," Scarlet said.

Han twisted on the bed, looking at her over his shoulder. "Why? What were you thinking about?"

"Nothing. Here, hold this," she said, tossing the little welding torch to him. She leaned into the closet. Something groaned and there was a loud ping. She came out with a triumphant expression and a small glowing green square the size of her palm. "Korrison-Mout model eighty."

"Is that good?"

"It's better than good, it's possible. I'm going to need to get the door-seal protocols, too. Hold on."

She sat on the bed beside him and pulled up the computer. The screen displayed a simple login, and she took a small gray chip out of her pocket and slid it into the access port with an audible click. The screen froze, shuddered, and a stream of complex data started scrolling up. Han sat upright, cross-legged. Scarlet tapped the keyboard. A simple prompt appeared. She started typing.

"He got lucky," Scarlet said.

"Who?"

"Hunter Maas. He was working on Galassian's estate as a gardener. He talked one of the security detail into doing something stupid, and then when it went south, he left her to get burned for it."

"Sounds like she made a bad choice in partners."

"She wasn't as narcissistic as Maas, but she was just as overconfident. I don't know what it is about people that they find their own level."

"Well, the smart people try not to work with idiots, and the idiots don't know any better," Han said. "Makes sense to me."

"Do you think they know whether they're the smart kind or the idiots?"

"Nope," Han said. "Hunter Maas is in his room convinced that he's got the galaxy by the hair. The stupidest ones are always sure they're smart."

"So we could both be idiots who just think we're competent?" Scarlet asked, picking up the encryption unit and reading something printed along its side.

"We know the Imperial fleet's lost a ship that was chasing our boy Hunter. And they know what he's selling. We're on the same planetary hemisphere with that moron. I'm pretty sure we're stupid."

Scarlet tapped the keyboard twice. "He's in 24-D. Sole access, keyed to his voice."

Han sighed and sat up. "I'll go make sure no one kills him."

"I'll figure out how to steal his stuff."

"Then can we leave?"

"Oh my, yes," Scarlet said.

"So maybe we're not *that* stupid."

The door hissed open before him and closed again with a

snap. Han rubbed his palms together and sauntered down the hallway, trying to look innocuous. The doors to the other rooms followed only the most general of numbering schemes, so it took Han several minutes to find the hallway with the doors marked 24. It was a little shabbier than the 17s, with worn tiles on the floor and a crack in the pale wall. He had to wonder if the droid that assigned the accommodations had taken a dislike to Hunter Maas.

Where the corridor ended, there was a small atrium with a pair of couches built into the walls. Han sat on one, adjusting his position until he could see the edge of 24-D's doorway, but someone coming out unexpectedly wouldn't be able to see his face. He checked his blaster. It was charged. He sat back and prepared to wait. It was already past midnight. Even if Scarlet found a way in, it would probably mean waiting until Hunter Maas was out at his next meeting. Han wondered where exactly the man had hidden the information when he was meeting with Leia. He hadn't gone back to his ship before coming here, and Han didn't think he was the kind of person who let something important get too far from his hand. Maybe he'd had a datachip sewn into his cape.

A maintenance droid hummed down the corridor, nodded to Han, and continued on its way. Han traced patterns in the grain of the polished stone walls and counted the leaves on the ferns and ivy that struggled to make the waiting area seem natural and welcoming. His leg fell asleep.

The first time the sound came, Han wasn't certain that he'd heard it. A gentle ticking, like a pebble being thrown against a window. The second time, he was listening for it. The third time, he drew his blaster and stood up. It wasn't coming from the same hallway as Hunter Maas's room, but from the next one down. Han peeked around the corner in time to see something at the far intersection. A shape that ducked out of sight before he could tell what he was looking at. Someone else was in the corridors, and they didn't want to be seen any more than he did.

He opened a connection.

"Scarlet?"

"Han?"

"Everything all right with you?"

"What's the matter?" she asked.

"Nothing, maybe. But you're all right?"

"Making progress," she said. "I think I see how to do the thing, but if there's trouble out there—"

"I don't know that yet," Han said. "I'm going to look around a little. If you hear, you know, blasters and screaming . . ."

"I'll keep my ears up."

Han cut the connection. He stepped back to corridor 24. No one. Slowly, rolling his feet heel-to-toe to keep from making any more noise than the minimum, he made his way toward the intersection where the other person had been. His blaster felt light in his hand; his blood sang in his veins. Through one of the doors, he heard deep, chuckling laughter.

At the intersection, he glanced around the corner, pulling his head back quickly in case someone shot at him. Another long corridor, but at its end, a small, huddled shape. Someone—humanoid, maybe even human—hunched down, half hidden by a lush stand of ornamental plants half a meter wide and two meters tall. Han looked again. Whoever it was, they hadn't turned to look at him. The shoulders shifted as if they were doing something.

Han debated for a moment. There were a million things going on in the conclave hive right now that had nothing at all to do with him. Chances were this was one. He could pull back, make his way to his couch, and take up his vigil again. Or he could just make certain that whatever the figure at the end of the hall was building wasn't a bomb. That might be good, too.

He slipped around the corner. The dark, hunched figure didn't react. Han moved forward step by step, his blaster before him. He reached the edge of the stand of plants and leveled his blaster at the hooded figure's head.

"Excuse me, friend," Han said. "Can't help wondering what you are doing there."

The dark-cloaked figure's head came up. It raised its hands and turned around slowly. It was a Bothan. Han frowned. It was a very familiar Bothan. Han's gut went heavy with dread. He turned to look into the ornamental foliage at his side.

A blaster poked out from between the fronds, pointing at his left eye.

"No need to blame poor Sunnim, now," Baasen Ray said. "Lad's just a pilot that fell in with the wrong crowd. You know what that's like. Now, let's try this again."

"You know," Han said, "this is a really bad time."

"Always is, lad, isn't it?"

CHAPTER NINETEEN

HAN WALKED AS slowly as he could, his mind racing. The hallway was quiet and dim. If there were any security droids or monitors, Han couldn't see them, and no alarms sounded. Either his abduction was going unnoticed, or it was beneath the level of violence that caused concern on Kiamurr. Baasen knew better than to actually put the barrel of the blaster against Han's back. Sunnim walked in front, close enough to block him if Han tried to run but not close enough to grab and use as a shield. He considered screaming for Scarlet Hark, but that would spook Hunter Maas.

All in all, it was not turning out to be a good night.

"You'll be needing to call our friend Chewbacca," Baasen said. "Let him know about the change of plan. And he'll be wanting to get the *Falcon* ready to take off. And you can tell him there's no hard feelings about Cioran. I'd have done the same as him."

"Your plan is to take the *Falcon*?" Han said.

"Not my first choice," Baasen said. "But we make do with what the universe gives us, don't we? It's a ship, and we're in need of one."

The hallway reached an intersection, and Sunnim held up a hand for them to stop before he sauntered out into it, looked in all directions, feigning innocence poorly, and then waved them forward.

"You don't have a ship?" Han said. "Did you walk here?"

Baasen's chuckle was low and rueful. "I'm afraid my old boat's seen her last days. Truth is I'm doing you a favor, my boy. Putting you back in the frying pan, it's truth, but I'm hauling you off the fire to do it. I dropped into Kiamurr system hot and came in a borrat's whisker from sliding into the side of an Imperial Destroyer. They've ten of them out there. Well, Sunnim and I put all the power to our shields and lit out for the territories, didn't we? Still sucked down enough plasma to melt our power couplings. Sad end to a good ship. I'd stay and fix the poor dear, but I'm fairly sure this planet and everything on it'll be slag by morning."

Han's throat went tight. The fleet was here, then. They were out of time. He had to warn Leia. And Scarlet. And Chewbacca.

Sunnim opened the service door at the hallway's end and peeked out, his ears shifting forward. A pair of protocol droids were walking together in the distance, their plating made from a clear polymer, and their circuits glowing blue and yellow in the darkness. Sunnim watched them pass, then grunted and waved Han forward.

"Step quick, old friend," Baasen said, his tone less friendly than it had been. "I've got no time or inclination for your cleverness just now."

"Baasen, you're playing this wrong," Han said, not stepping forward. "This thing with Jabba? It's the smallest game on the board."

"For you, p'raps," Baasen said. "Looms rather large for me. Now walk."

Out of the hall, the conclave hive's windows were showing a slightly paler darkness—charcoal instead of black. A tiny bird no larger than Han's thumb darted up into the air of the great dome above them. Sunnim scowled furiously and waved them forward.

"Look, Baasen. I understand where you are. Honestly, I've got no hard feeling about any of it, either. So before we go out there and can't take any of this back, let me tell you what you're walking out on."

"There's not enough honey in the galaxy to sweet-talk your way out of this, old friend," Baasen said. "And don't dream that I'm above shooting you, eh? Now move."

"You're on the losing side of this. I understand being afraid of Jabba. He's made me nervous a couple of times, and I don't scare as easy as you." Baasen laughed. That was a good sign. Han talked faster. "What's going on here is bigger than that. Big enough to shut down all the Hutts. Right now, you and I are maybe a hundred meters from information that will decide who runs the galaxy."

"You're old for fairy tales," Baasen said.

Han lifted his hands to his sides, palms out, and started turning around. His skin tingled where he imagined the blaster bolt would strike.

"Don't you do that, boy, or I'll end your sad life in this hallway!" Baasen hissed, but Han kept turning. Baasen stood in the corridor, blaster leveled at Han's head. His missing hand hadn't been replaced; it was capped with a steel fitting. Baasen's face was dark with anger, and the trembling in the blaster's barrel wasn't fear.

Han gave his best charming smile. "You know this is big," he said. "I'm not asking you to trust me on that. All you have to do is look. Scarlet Hark shut down operations on Cioran. The Imperials sent ten Star Destroyers. And when I got here, Leia Organa didn't just pull up stakes and go. So you know whatever's going on, it's huge. Right?"

"Stop trying to talk your way out of this," Baasen said, but there was less certainty in his voice.

"A tool that can shut down hyperspace jumps. That's

what's at stake here," Han said. "Lets you determine who gets to move from one system to another."

Baasen shrugged, but Han could see the calculations going on behind the man's eyes. Baasen's gaze softened for a moment, turning inward. Part of Han waned to leap forward, grab the blaster. He restrained himself.

"Everyone stuck on whatever system they're in unless you say they can move. Everyone everywhere asking permission to travel. Paying whatever tolls you ask, or just rotting wherever they are if you want."

"You're lying."

"Did I get the Imperial fleet to help me fool you? Because ten Star Destroyers sounds pretty sincere."

Baasen's tongue flicked out, wetting his lips. He lifted the stump of his wrist, scratching at his nose. The Bothan whined, "Boss. We got to go."

"Patience, Sunnim. Cultivate a bit of patience, eh?" Baasen said. And then to Han, "This magic thing. It's here? On Kiamurr?"

"No, but the map to it is. That's what the Imperials are after. They've known where it is for a while now, but they want to make sure no one else does. Man named Hunter Maas has a copy of their surveys. Hark and I are here to steal it from him."

"Pity that's about to fail," Baasen said.

"It's a big pie, Baasen. Biggest one there's ever been. If you want in on it, it'll be worth more than everything Jabba's got."

"Hark's here? On this planet?"

"In a room three corridors from here. I can take you to her right now if you want."

Baasen still wavered. Outside, the windows were half a shade lighter. The Bothan shifted his weight from one foot to the other as if he needed to use the toilet and made a small keening sound under his breath. Han waited.

"Let's go speak with our dear friend Hark," Baasen said. "Maybe there's a bit of room to negotiate."

"You're smarter than you look, old pal," Han said.

Baasen's smile was touched with sadness. "Anything seems even a degree off about this, and I will murder you where you stand, you know."

"Wouldn't expect anything less," Han said.

They walked back to 17-C. Han racked his brain for ways to warn Scarlet what was coming. If he could raise an alarm, she might be able to get the drop on them, but there was no time. He didn't have any tools to work with, and Baasen and the Bothan were watching his every move. All he could do was move forward and hope.

At the door to the room, he paused. Baasen was behind him to the left, Sunnim to the right. If he spun and caught the Bothan's weapon . . .

"Don't," Baasen said. Han sighed and opened the door.

Scarlet sat cross-legged on the bed. Her hair was pulled back, but a stray lock hung down her forehead. Her full attention was on the deck opened before her. The safe gaped on the wall behind her, three layers of black metal and complex circuitry open to the air. The stench of ozone and melted steel stung Han's eyes.

"Han. Good news. I've got a solid workaround on the door seal, and I got far enough into the comm logs to see that Hunter's been trading calls with half a dozen people since he got in. Smart money says he's arranging more meetings. Communications stopped about twenty minutes ago, so either he's even dumber than he looks and he's going to sleep, or he's getting ready to head out to his first sit-down meeting, and we'll be going in as soon as he's gone." She looked up for the first time. "So, who're your friends and why are they holding guns on you? Did you do something bad?"

"Baasen Ray," Han said, walking into the room. "Sunnim. This is Scarlet Hark. Scarlet? You'll remember me talking about Baasen Ray?"

"The one who screwed up the drop back on Cioran," Scarlet said. "Pleasure to meet you."

"We've met once."

"Huh," Scarlet said with a shrug.

"You're hurting my feelings, miss."

"Well, you can put down your weapons and leave quietly," Scarlet said, her welding tools still in her hands, the deck in her lap, "and no one gets anything but their feelings hurt."

"No need for that, no need," Baasen said. "The good Captain Solo's offered me a share in the proceedings here. Come to parley, haven't I?"

The door hissed closed behind them. Sunnim's gaze shifted from it to Baasen to Scarlet and back to the door. Scarlet leaned forward.

"I don't have time to screw around," she said brightly. "So why don't we start with why I shouldn't kill both of you and drop your bodies down the recycler?"

"We've got guns drawn already. Even if you're the fastest draw in the sector, your friend Solo's a dead man."

"We're not actually that close."

"Hey!" Han said.

"Be that as may be," Baasen said, "I'd still guess that this isn't the moment you'd want to start a gunfight? Inconvenient timing, as it were? Besides which, we've come to help. If what this rascal Han's been saying's even half true, I make us for being on the same side of things. For the moment at least."

"Not sure I'm seeing that," Scarlet said, and her deck chirped. A thin, grainy hologram coalesced over the bedspread. In the hallway outside 24-D, Hunter Maas adjusted his cape, shifted a small carrying case from hand to hand, and leaned in, speaking to the doorway. There was no sound with the feed, but from his gestures, Han guessed the shirtless man was practicing his sales pitch. After a moment, the door slid shut.

"You put a monitor on him?" Han asked.

"I went to find you, and you were gone," Scarlet said. "I went to plan B."

"Replaced by a small cam," Baasen said. "It's no universe for you and me anymore, Solo."

"Laugh it up," Han said. "Where's he going?"

"I don't know, and I don't care," Scarlet said. "This is our window. I'm not going to let your baggage screw it up."

"Baggage?" Han said. "I don't have baggage."

"Well, you do a bit," Baasen said. "No offense meant. So we're partners now? Passage off the planet and a share in whatever profit comes from it?"

"Done," Scarlet said, shutting down the deck. "Welcome to the team."

"Pleasure to be here," Baasen said. "Hope you won't mind that I take a bit of precaution. Sunnim, my boy, you go on ahead to the *Falcon*. Make sure everything's shipshape and ready to go, yes? And if our friends here don't show up with me smiling along behind them . . . well, you know what to do."

The Bothan paused. "Kill everyone?"

"See now?" Baasen said. "You *did* know. Good man, and off with you." The Bothan nodded, opened the door, and trotted away. Baasen holstered his blaster and shrugged apologetically. "Hard to find good help in these fallen times."

"That's truth," Scarlet said.

"Once we're done, we'll need to be leaving quickly," Baasen said. "There's a great flock of Imperial trouble winging its way toward us."

"Of course there is," she said. "All right. Let's still give

Hunter Maas a couple minutes to get away from the rooms. I don't want him doubling back and interrupting us."

"Shouldn't we warn Leia about the fleet?" Han said.

"She'll know. Don't worry about that part. Let's just keep focused on getting into that room, getting the data, and getting out again." She looked from Baasen to Han and back again, her eyebrows raised and merriment in her eyes.

This woman is crazy, Han thought.

"Anyone need to use the facilities?" Scarlet asked, "Because I'm not taking time out for pit stops once we start."

Baasen guffawed and clapped Han on the shoulder. "You always do know the most colorful people, don't you, old friend?"

"It's not my fault."

Scarlet stepped off the bed, tugged the wrinkles out of the spread, and began laying out her tools. She hummed to herself, a soft melody just at the edge of hearing. Baasen watched her, and Han watched Baasen. Knowledge of the coming fleet pressed down on the air like a storm. Han told himself that somewhere on the planet, Leia and the leaders of the Rebellion were heading to their ships. Chewbacca was finishing prep of the *Millennium Falcon*. The plans that Scarlet had put in place were unfolding. He didn't know what they were, and he didn't like having faith in them. It was hard not to pace.

Baasen caught his eye. His grin was warm and avuncular and false. "Just like old times, isn't it?"

"Not any times I remember," Han said.

"In spirit, I mean."

"All right. Sure."

"For what it carries, I do hope this works. I wasn't looking ahead to feeding you to the Hutt with any pleasure."

"Enough banter," Scarlet said. "Focus now."

She put her tools into her pockets and onto her belt with

a calm, military efficiency, then gestured to Baasen. "We're going to 24-D. I'll be popping the seal. You and Solo make sure I'm not interrupted."

"Shouldn't be a problem," Baasen said.

"See that it's not."

The Mirialan smiled and pointed at her with his stump. "I like you. Not the type to play safe or overthink. Quick on the uptake. See the value in things, even when they're unexpected."

Scarlet made a small, insincere curtsy. "You know, if it wouldn't have raised an alarm, I would have shot you and your little friend."

Baasen looked at Han. "I don't think she's fond of you, my boy. Your charms are slipping."

Scarlet stepped out to the hallway, her expression quizzical. She closed the room door behind them.

"Oh, he'd have been fine," she said. "I'm a very good shot. Come on, now. Let's get this done."

Scarlet started off at a brisk walk, not running but wasting no time. Han and Baasen had to trot a little to catch up with her. At the corner, Baasen caught Han's gaze and nodded toward the woman's back.

"Was she joking about that?" the Mirialan asked.

"I can never tell," Han said.

CHAPTER TWENTY

THE LONG STONE hallway outside 24-D was empty, for which Han breathed a silent sigh of relief. Baasen had his blaster in his hand, and the bounty hunter wasn't one for subtlety; he wouldn't hesitate to shoot a bystander if he thought it needed doing. Scarlet crouched at the door and started manipulating the locking panel. Baasen rocked on the balls of his feet while she worked.

After a few long seconds, the door to Hunter Maas's room snapped open. "So much for the easy part," Scarlet said and entered, Baasen right on her heels. Han paused a moment in the corridor, looking both directions, making sure they weren't being followed.

"You keep saying that," Han said. "It's not as reassuring as you think it is."

When no one ran into the hall shouting at them or triggering alarms, he followed Scarlet into the room and closed the door. In the very short time he'd had the room, Hunter Maas had managed to trash it. The bed wasn't just unmade, it was dismembered: pillows pounded into unlikely shapes, sheets half pulled off, and blankets in a lumpy pile on the floor. Wet towels lay knotted on the bathroom floor. There were articles of clothing distributed randomly around the room. The R3 that Maas had brought sat in one corner of the room with a wrinkled shirt draped across it and the rat-bird sitting on it. The rat-bird had defecated on the shirt several times, white-green streaks covering the cloth. When it saw them, it shrieked and danced angrily on the little droid's head.

Scarlet was already opening the closet doors and looking for the safe. Baasen poked the pile of blankets with his toe. The rat-bird squawked loudly at him, and he pointed his blaster at it.

"Don't," Han said. "Might set off the hotel's alarms."

"I don't like the ugly thing." Baasen continued to point his blaster at it, but didn't fire.

"If it's scary, you can stand behind me," Han said, smirking at him.

"Keep pushing, boyo," the bounty hunter replied with a smile. "Keep pushing."

The rat-bird screeched and shifted from foot to foot, flapping its wings at them. It noisily relieved itself again.

"I hope Hunter wasn't planning to wear that to the parties tonight," Han said.

"Filthy disgusting creature," Baasen said. "Can you imagine what the inside of this man's ship must look like?"

Han chuckled, remembering a time when he and Baasen hadn't been enemies. When they'd had a few laughs in shady cantinas across the galaxy. Han could imagine himself making the same choices Baasen had made. Reaching a point where there just wasn't enough smuggling work to make ends meet, and the allure of fast cash for bounty hunting became too great. Could he have wound up there? Desperate enough to hold an old friend at blasterpoint for a quick payoff?

If it weren't for running into an old man and a dumb kid in a Tatooine backwater, maybe. Han didn't have much use for mysticism or ancient religions like the Force, but sometimes it did seem as if something was maneuvering events behind the scenes. One chance meeting, and now here he was, working for Leia and the rebels, and not hunting old friends for money.

"Found it," Scarlet said. She rapped on the safe door with her knuckle. It was in the back of the room's largest closet. She dropped to one knee and started pulling tools off her belt. "He probably wasn't stupid enough to leave his keycard lying around, but maybe he was. See if you can find it."

Baasen responded by yanking the sheets off the bed and flipping the mattress over. He holstered his blaster and pulled a large knife, then started cutting the mattress open.

"When," Han said, "would he have had time to sew anything into it?"

Baasen grunted in irritation, but he put the knife away and flipped the bed frame over instead. Han went into the small refresher and opened all the drawers, dumping the contents in the sink. Most were empty, but one had a few personal grooming implements in it. Nothing that looked like a keycard.

Out in the sleeping area, Baasen was banging on the R3 unit and demanding that it speak. It had backed as far into the corner as it could and hunched down, trying to make itself as small as possible. Baasen kicked it, and it beeped forlornly at him. The rat-bird on its head hissed and snapped at Baasen's one good hand.

"Unless you have a protocol droid handy, you won't get much out of that," Han said. "But check the bird."

"You're kidding," Baasen said, squinting back at him. "You trying to cost me the few fingers I've got left?"

Han rolled his eyes and lunged across the room to swat the rat-bird off the droid. It fell on the floor with an undignified squeak and started flapping its leathery wings. Han grabbed it by the back of the neck and picked it up. It hissed and spit and soiled the carpet, but Han didn't let go.

"See anything?" he asked Baasen. The bounty hunter lifted the wings and poked at the wiry body.

"It's got a necklace or something," Baasen said, and yanked it off the bird. Han let the miserable creature go, and it flapped back to its perch on the droid. It gave them an accusatory squawk then fell silent, huddling under its wings and peering out at them with one black eye.

Baasen held the necklace up for Han to look at. A green gemstone in a silver setting spun slowly at the end of a thin silver chain. Han pointed at it and said, "Scarlet. Does this look like anything?"

She looked over her shoulder for a second, then turned back to her work on the safe. "Yeah. It looks like a fake. Cheap glass. He must not love his bird that much."

Baasen examined the green gem closely, holding it up to the light, then tossed it across the room with a snort. "It's a low class of criminal you find these days. No sense of style anymore. No pride."

"Not like us, right?" Han said.

"Joke if you like, Solo, but no matter where we are now, I always respected you. You're like me. You had a code."

"Part of it was not turning on my friends."

"I know it. But I work for the Hutt, so we can't be friends now," Baasen said sadly. "Also, you shot my hand off."

"I do regret that," Han said. Baasen nodded again as if the words were sincere.

"Hey, boys," Scarlet said. "Don't mean to interrupt this romantic moment, but I need some help here. Baasen, I'm betting you've run a magnetic seal bypass once or twice in your time."

Baasen laughed. "Get elbow-deep in that thing so as I can't draw with Solo at my back? Give me some credit, love. I may be stupid, but I'm not dumb."

"I'll do it," Han said and walked over to the closet. Scarlet pointed at a wire dangling from an open panel on the safe with her chin. Her own hands were inside the guts of the device.

"I need you to keep that wire from touching the metal of the safe until I tell you to, and then I need you to do it fast. So stay ready."

"Got it," Han said, grabbing the wire. His finger brushed the exposed end, and he felt a painful tingle shoot up his arm. The panel where Scarlet was working flashed and sparked, and she yelped in surprise.

"Don't touch the exposed end!"

"Yeah," Han said, "sort of figured that out."

Scarlet grunted at him.

"So . . . ," Baasen started, sitting down on the edge of the room's one small table. Whatever he was about to say next stopped when the door to the room snapped open and Hunter Maas rushed in waving a blaster. In his other hand he carried a small plastoid case.

"Thieves!" he screamed, pointing the pistol at Han. "Betrayers! Hunter Maas makes a fair offer and you respond to him by stealing?"

Han raised the hand not holding the wire and smiled. Scarlet, wrists deep in the safe, could only raise her eyebrows.

"Hey, calm down," Han said. "This is all a big misunderstanding."

Maas grunted and fell face-first on the floor. Baasen stood behind him, blaster in hand.

"Please tell me you didn't kill him," Scarlet said.

Baasen knelt by the fallen man and checked his pulse. "No, just gave him a good whack." Maas groaned as if in agreement.

"Up you go, boyo," Baasen said, pulling Maas back to his feet. "Get over there in the corner and stay quiet, and maybe I won't have to hit you again."

"Hunter Maas is *outraged* by this treatment," Maas

started. Baasen cracked him across the forehead with the barrel of his blaster, nearly knocking him to the floor again. "Shush now."

"Almost there," Scarlet said to Han. "Get ready. Now!"

Something popped inside the panel where Scarlet was working, and Han touched the exposed wire to the side of the safe. There was a flash of light and the smell of cooking electronics. An arc of electricity shot off the safe to Han's wrist, and he danced away with a yelp.

"Hey, warn me next time!"

Scarlet smiled and said, "That got the first fail-safe. Two more to go."

"Speaking of which," Baasen said conversationally. "Is there a reason you're still playing with that? This fellow has the key and the passcode, yes?" When no one replied, Baasen gestured at Maas and said, "Give me the key, friend."

"Hunter Maas will not give in to—"

"Or," Baasen continued, his tone light and conversational, "I can shoot you in the leg. Is it in that case there?"

"No," Maas said, and pulled the keycard out of his pocket. He tossed it to Han. "But without the security code, this is useless!"

"Is that true?" Han asked Scarlet, then bent to pick up the key.

She nodded and did something else to the safe that resulted in a shower of sparks and a scorched-metal smell.

"Suppose then you tell us the code," Baasen said.

"Hunter Maas will never tell!" the thief yelled, which earned him a crack across the mouth from Baasen's blaster. Maas's lip split, and a trickle of blood ran down his chin.

"Given time," Baasen said, raising his weapon again, "I really think you will."

"Stop it," Scarlet said, her voice muffled and distorted by the tool she was clenching between her teeth. "These safes have a self-destruct. Punch in the fail-safe code and it destroys the contents."

"You wouldn't give us the wrong one, would you?" Baasen said, voice filled with mock concern. "Not to your pals? Because then I'd have to shoot you, oh, just a lot."

"Maybe he thinks you're going to shoot him anyway," Han said.

"You can be a very rich man," Hunter Maas said through his swollen mouth. "The richest man in the galaxy."

"People keep telling me about these riches," Baasen said.

"Kill them both," Maas said. "Kill them, and Hunter Maas will share this wealth and power with you. All of space will be ours to command."

"Han," Scarlet said, "I need you to keep your eyes on the job here. Pull on this until it resists, then hold it steady."

Han grabbed the wire and did as she asked, though putting his back to Baasen while Maas asked him to switch sides made the spot between his shoulder blades itch.

"I know this play, friend Hunter," Baasen said. "We're bestest pals right up until the next fool comes along and you offer him the universe on a platter to put a plasma bolt through my skull."

"No! Hunter Maas's word is his bond! We will be partners in ruling the galaxy!"

"And if you buy that," Han said, keeping his tone light and mocking, "I've got some fabulous property at the Core I can sell you."

"You got a ship?" Baasen asked Maas.

"We will procure a thousand ships! Armadas to darken the sky!"

"No," Baasen said slowly, as though speaking to a child. "Do you have a ship right now? To leave this planet with?"

"Hunter Maas's ship has taken some damage, but we can find transport if need be . . ."

"Pity that," Baasen said, then laughed. "Maybe you should be quiet now, let the lady work."

"He does wear on a person with all that Hunter Maas this and Hunter Maas that," Han said, forcing a chuckle. He had the uncomfortable feeling a negotiation for his life had just happened behind his back and the fact that the *Falcon* was flight-worthy was the only reason he was still breathing.

"Now," Scarlet said, practically holding her breath while she spoke. "Let go now."

Han released the wire he was holding, and the door to the safe opened with a quiet click.

"Gotcha," Scarlet said in triumph.

"Good work," Han said, slapping her on the shoulder. "I see why Leia likes you."

Baasen drifted in their direction, trying to look past them into the safe. Maas said nothing, huddling miserably in the corner. Scarlet pulled the door of the safe open the rest of the way and looked inside.

"Huh," she said. "It's empty."

Han reached inside, patting the walls of the safe with his hand, looking for a false wall or bottom, or something taped to the sides. Nothing but bare metal. The rat-bird screeched at them with what almost sounded like a laugh.

"Hunter Maas told you," the pirate said. "You will never find the data without him. The price will now be very high, after these many insults and indignities!"

Han frowned a question at Scarlet, and she shook her head. For the first time, she looked lost.

"Okay," Han said, "I guess we—"

From behind came the sound of a blaster shot. Han spun around to face the room, his own blaster already in his hand. Maas was staring down at the smoking hole in his sternum with a look of puzzlement on his face, and then he crumpled gently to the floor.

CHAPTER TWENTY-ONE

"UM," SCARLET SAID. Hunter Maas lay on the floor at Baasen's feet. The thief blinked twice, then fell into the absolute stillness of death. Han realized he was holding his breath and let it go with an effort.

"That shirtless little gentleman was a bit annoying," Baasen said, poking his blaster at the corpse on the floor.

"So you *shot* him?" Han asked. "Now we'll never know where that data is. You've lost your mind, Baasen, and I—"

"We'll know where it is because *I* know where it is," Baasen said, his voice as calm as if he were discussing the weather.

Scarlet nodded at him. "Okay." Her blaster was in her hand and she drifted away from Han, the three of them turning into a triangle where every angle was a weapon.

Baasen smiled and slipped the stump of his shortened arm into the handle of the carrying case. He lifted it until it slid down to his elbow and hung there, swaying. "So, let's go on back to your ship now, eh? We have what we came for."

"Or maybe I leave you here with Maas," Han said. "And we just take what we need."

Scarlet said nothing but kept drifting to Baasen's left. "You'll want to stop there," the Mirialan bounty hunter said to her. "Makes me nervous you trying to get to my blind side. It's a sad world when there's no trust."

"So what now?" Scarlet asked. Han wasn't sure if she was talking to him or to Baasen.

"I think we—" Han started, but his next words were drowned out by a rising high-pitched wail that seemed to come from everywhere at once.

"Out of time, boyo," Baasen yelled at him. "We should have the rest of this conversation elsewhere."

The planetary defense alarms had sounded. The Star Destroyers were in orbit. The Empire didn't need the data Maas had stolen; they just needed to make sure no one else had it. They wouldn't bother landing troops, they'd just bomb the planet to dust and make sure nothing lived to interfere with their plans.

"To the *Falcon,*" Han said to Baasen. The bounty hunter nodded and smiled. Han tapped his comlink, trying to reach Leia, but the connection didn't go through. The relays were already down.

Scarlet darted out the door and waved an impatient hand for them to follow. Baasen started toward her, then stopped and turned to look at the R3 and the rat-bird.

"You two can come along if you like," he said.

The rat-bird hopped down off the droid's head and flapped over to sit next to its dead master. The droid burbled to itself for a second, then lowered its wheels and followed after the bounty hunter. When they left the room, Han looked back and saw that the rat-bird was gnawing on Hunter Maas's leg. No loyalty among thieves.

The defense alert still sounded, nearly deafening, but a new noise was starting to eclipse it. A distant, heavy booming, like thunder.

The orbital bombardment had begun.

People were streaming into the corridor from the occupied rooms, shouting into comlinks and carrying hastily packed luggage. Han saw a diminutive Ugnaught trip over its own bags and fall to the floor, where a passing human stepped on it.

Han gripped Scarlet and Baasen by the backs of their shirts so he didn't lose them in the crush of bodies, and dragged them toward the main assembly hall. He could see that the street outside was quickly becoming packed with ground transport and fleeing people. By cutting through the gardens and then the conference halls, he could get to the spaceport without fighting the traffic.

Scarlet seemed to understand and agree. As soon as she realized where he was leading her, she took point, grabbing his hand in her own and pushing her way through the crowd. Baasen stumbled along behind, content to let them lead.

A burly alien with gray-green skin and tusks the size of daggers ran into them and howled in anger, but before Han could even apologize the air around them compressed in a massive blast wave and knocked down everyone in the corridor. The shock was followed by the loudest noise Han had ever heard. The stone walls all around cracked like overstressed glass, and he felt sure his teeth would vibrate apart in his jaw.

When it was over, he pulled Scarlet and Baasen back to their feet and yelled, "Keep moving!" He could barely hear himself. There was just a high-pitched whine that seemed to be bouncing around inside his skull.

"Keep up or you'll get left behind, Red," Baasen shouted at the little R3. Its stable three-legged design had kept it on its feet during the blast, but it was having difficulty pushing its way through the crowd.

"Forget it," Han yelled.

Baasen followed him, a grin on his face but his skin flushed a deeper green with fear. "That last one was close, eh?" he said, trying to make the words light.

As if in answer, another ripple of blasts echoed through the corridor, though they sounded farther off. Scarlet finally reached the side door to the hotel and burst through into the conference center's garden space.

All three of them looked up. Even something as vast as a Star Destroyer was too small to be seen clearly in orbit, but the ships could be spotted as the origin points of the massive laser and plasma blasts that were streaking out of the sky and pounding the planet. A barrage of fire hit the mountain next to the conference center a dozen times, blowing starship-sized chunks of rock off the mountainside and raining them down on the buildings below.

"They appear to be upset, poor lambs," Baasen said. Even he seemed stunned by the level of violence the Empire was raining down on them. A few mountaintop batteries fired up into the air, golden plasma fire leaving trails of black smoke behind them as they rose.

"Through here," Scarlet said, and tugged Han after her into a side entrance in the conference center. Baasen tagged along, still staring up at the sky with a dazed look.

Han recognized the massive meeting room where Leia had delivered her big speech. It was crowded with fleeing conference members who'd all had the same idea he'd had to stay off the street. He hoped Leia was already off the planet.

As they rushed through the room and down the long corridors that led to the docks, the ground shook, blast after blast falling from the sky. The air in the city stank of smoke and dust. Over the top of the defense alarm and the shriek and rumble of bombardment came new sounds: the throb of starship engines and the scream of supersonic flight.

"Everybody's leaving," Han said.

"Good," Scarlet replied, and pulled him down a side corridor he didn't recognize. "Underground shortcut to the docks."

They'd gone a few hundred meters through the new hallway when they reached a massive metal shield door, closed and locked.

"Good shortcut," Han said, and started looking for another path. "Were you planning for this?"

"Just watch my back," Scarlet replied, and pulled out her compact cutting torch.

Baasen turned to face the corridor behind them and drew his blaster. He held Maas's case close to his chest with the stump of his wrist. "No reason to shoot anyone," Han said, pushing the man's arm down. "Everyone left is just trying to get away like we are. Unless you can shoot down a Star Destroyer with that thing."

"Almost there," Scarlet said over her shoulder, her face framed by the bright blue glow of the torch.

"Might want to—" Han started, and then time seemed to skip. He found himself lying on his back in the corridor, grit and small bits of stone covering him. The hallway was filled with a cloud of dust that stung his eyes when he opened them. He coughed uncontrollably for a few seconds, though he could barely hear himself over the renewed ringing in his ears.

"They're getting closer," Baasen yelled at him, sounding like a very small voice a long way off. The Mirialan was climbing to his feet, brushing off the rubble that covered him. Scarlet was on her knees by the door, patting the floor to find her cutting torch.

"Almost there," she repeated, her voice shaky but loud. She picked up the torch and resumed her work.

Something shadowy moved toward them in the dusty corridor. Han reached for his blaster and came up empty. There was nothing in his holster. He frantically searched the floor for his weapon. By the time he found it, Baasen was saying, "Well, I'll be damned. Red made it."

The little R3 rolled to a stop a few feet away and trilled out a series of notes at them.

"Great," Han said. "Now everything's just fine."

"These things are handy," Baasen said reproachfully. Then to the droid he said, "Help get this door open."

The droid rolled up next to Scarlet, and soon there were two bright blue points of light cutting through the locks.

"See?"

"I stand corrected," Han said.

A few moments later the door pinged with a metallic snapping sound. Han and Baasen grabbed it and pulled it open. On the other side was a long access corridor for the conference center's infrastructure. Conduits of heavy cabling, ducting, environmental systems, and piping covered the walls.

Another barrage shook the hallway, raining down dust from above. A pipe buckled in the corridor ahead, and steam began pouring into the space.

"Time to go," Scarlet said, and trotted off down the hallway.

Han followed, still wondering where Leia was. Surely she'd been in one of the first ships out. They'd given her enough warning. If something had gone wrong, if she was somewhere in the bombardment . . . Han tried to imagine explaining to the Rebel Alliance that he'd left her behind, that she'd died on Kiamurr. Or worse, explaining it to Luke. Or facing himself in the morning, knowing he could have tried but hadn't. He suppressed a shudder and kept running.

"Scarlet!" he shouted. "Leia's already gone, right? She's left the planet."

"I hope not," Scarlet called back over her shoulder.

"What do you mean you hope not? Why do you hope not?"

Scarlet ran and he followed. The service corridor ended at a long flight of steps up, and a door out onto the flight tarmac. Outside they could see the steady stream of ships launching from the docks, desperately trying to get off the doomed planet. As they emerged from the stairwell, a heavy transport lifted slowly off the field, just starting to get some speed. A turbolaser blast nearly cut the ponderous ship in half. It twisted sideways, trailing black smoke from the mortal wound in its side, its engines rising in a dying scream as the ship crashed back down and exploded into a rain of shrapnel.

"Gods be with us," Baasen said, face paling almost to yellow as he watched the ship die.

Han took off at a dead run toward the *Millennium Falcon*'s dock. Scarlet kept close beside him, huffing and puffing. Baasen coughed and lumbered, staring up at the sky, gape-mouthed at the destruction falling from on high, the R3 droid trailing along and burbling to itself in distress.

Han reached the door to the dock and slammed through it. The *Falcon* sat in her berth, untouched by the incoming fire. Han thought again of mystical energy fields and said a quiet thank-you to whoever or whatever might be looking out for them.

At the bottom of the crew ramp, Leia was strapping a belt around her waist, a heavy blaster hanging on her hip. She'd changed out of her diplomatic gown into brown pants and a white shirt.

"Oh, good," she said. "Now I don't have to go looking for you."

"Looking for us?" Han said. "Listen here, Princess. I got the data, escaped the attack, and got Scarlet back to the ship just fine."

"Awww," Scarlet said, "you're my hero. We should leave now."

Another blast rocked the building, and the metal girders of the dock creaked with the shock.

"Yeah," Han said. "That's a really good idea."

Scarlet ran up the ramp, with Baasen and his droid close behind. When they were gone, Leia put her hand on Han's arm and said, "Thank you."

Han looked for the mockery in it, and didn't find any. "You're welcome. Now let's all get off this planet while there still is one."

He ran inside the ship, straight into a Wookiee hug. Chewbacca growled at him reproachfully.

"Missed you, too, buddy. Let's get her off the ground."

Chewbacca had the ship warmed up and ready. It was a matter of seconds before they were strapped in and climbing through the burning air.

"Put all power to the forward deflectors until we get out of the atmosphere," Han said. "Then angle the rear deflectors until we make the jump."

Chewbacca howled at him.

"Why don't we have rear deflectors? I told you to fix that!"

The Wookiee growled back.

"Yes, I know there was time pressure. But you have to—"

Chewbacca barked at him once.

"Okay, okay, buddy. I hear you. Except now we have to fly through an Imperial blockade while somehow not getting shot in the backside."

Leia, sitting in the chair behind him, leaned forward and said, "What? No rear deflectors? You really should have fixed that."

"No time," Han said, not looking at Chewbacca. "He was busy!"

"What can we do to help?" Baasen asked. He and Sunnim were holding on to the hatchway into the cockpit.

"Well," Han said, angling the *Falcon*'s flight path up through a gap in the bombardment, "I can keep us away from the heavies, mostly. They're more interested in blowing Kiamurr into dust. But once we get out of the atmosphere, TIE fighters are going to be swarming all the ships that're leaving."

"Sounds right," Baasen said. "Nice to have lots of company for that. One ship of many, so to speak."

"Right. So I just need you guys to keep the TIEs off us long enough to make the jump. Keep them from getting a clean shot on our hindquarters."

"The *Falcon*'s got those turrets," Baasen said.

"Right again. You boys know how to use them?"

"Believe we can work it out," Baasen said with a grin.

"Great, then get in there. The plan is—"

"Kill everything?" Sunnim said.

"Got it in one."

CHAPTER TWENTY-TWO

ENERGY BOLTS STREAKED across the stars. Han felt the ship resisting under his control, rising and falling as the shields bled energy into thrust. The freighters, fighters, and tugs boiling up from the planetary surface mixed with the Imperial fighters, swirling and dancing like snowflakes in a blizzard. The tactical computer flickered and stuttered, unable to keep track of all the different points of motion.

"We've got a wave at your two," Leia warned.

Han looked over. Four TIE fighters in tight formation spun down from the nearest of the Destroyers, dogging an ancient cruiser as it struggled up from Kiamurr's burning exosphere. Han angled the *Falcon* to keep them in front of him, protecting the unshielded rear of the ship.

"Baasen?"

"Solo!"

"Let's see if we can help that cruiser out."

"How long until we're clear to jump?" Scarlet shouted from the lounge.

"We're not clear to turn around out here," Han shouted back. "We'll try getting to the other side where we can find some space." *Us and everyone else trying to get off that poor rock.*

The *Falcon* screamed and shuddered. Chewbacca howled in protest and rage.

"What did he say?" Baasen called from the turret.

"He said shoot them *before* they shoot us!" Han shouted back.

"Thank him for the pointer."

The Bothan's despairing wail came from the lower turret.

"Could someone see what's wrong with Sunnim?" Han snapped.

"I'm on it," Scarlet said, heading out.

The blasts from the *Falcon* reached the attacking TIE fighters, and two of them peeled off, screaming toward Han like predators falling upon prey. He pulled the ship down, whipping it to spin around them as they passed, keeping his forward shields toward them. A stream of blasterfire poured from the turrets, brushing against one of the TIE's solar arrays and turning the little ship into a ball of ions and fire. Far above, the triangular body of a Star Destroyer loomed. Wide, glowing bolts fell from the Destroyer's belly toward the planet, shearing away mountains and vaporizing seas.

"He's coming around, Han," Leia said. "Han? He's coming around. Han!"

Almost too late, he saw which of the dozens of ships before him she was talking about, and he yanked the controls to compensate. The *Falcon* groaned under the strain. The lower turret spat out fire, and the attacker died.

"All right, everyone hold on," Han called over his shoulder. "I'm getting us out of here."

He took the tactical computer down. It was too swamped to be useful anyway. With the engines at full, he angled the ship up, through the wide swirl of enemies, his sights on the stars beyond them.

"Han, old friend?" Baasen called, his voice tight and nervous. "What is it you're planning here?"

"Just keep shooting," Han said through clenched teeth. The *Falcon* rose through the barrage of energy bolts and debris. The Imperial Destroyer grew larger, swelling until it almost filled the screen. Chewbacca groaned.

"I know," Han said. "But they've got more weapons on the fighters, and they won't shoot at us if missing means damaging their own."

I hope, he didn't add.

The defensive batteries on the Star Destroyer opened up, and Han twirled the ship, dancing between the blasts. It wasn't even thought now. The *Falcon* was an extension of his body, and he moved through space as if he were running through a battlefield. Chewbacca barked once.

"Get ready," Han said.

Another thousand kilometers. At their speeds, it wouldn't take long. A tight grouping of Y-wings shot past him, neither Imperial nor rebel. Just some poor guys who'd been attending the wrong conference. They drew some of the Star Destroyer's fire. He gritted his teeth. And then they were past, the battle behind them, where a stray shot could sail through the missing deflectors and melt the hull to nothing.

He slammed his palm on the control panel, and the stars became streaks. The death throes of Kiamurr vanished behind them, and he sank back in his chair. Scarlet, Baasen, and his Bothan pilot were howling with delight. As if getting away was a victory. As if they'd won something.

And still, they *had* gotten away.

When he looked over his shoulder, Leia was staring out the screen. The light of hyperspace glowed on her skin. The darkness in her eyes was only partly from their color. There was something more in them, too. Something deeper.

"That was why you didn't just tell them all," Han said. "You knew Hunter Maas was coming, and that the Empire would come after him. If you'd warned them all before he showed up, everyone would have left before the battle started."

She turned to look at him directly. He saw that the words had stung her, and that she was trying not to let it show.

"I did what I could. Told who I could. If I'd sounded the general alarm, Hunter Maas would have run, too, and the Empire would have had another chance to catch him. We would have lost everything. No one's responsible for those deaths but the people who pulled the triggers," she said, her voice hard. And then she softened, looked down. "It's a war, Han. And I'm the one trying to end it."

"No, they're trying to end it, too," Han said. "You're just arguing over the terms."

Chewbacca chuffed to himself and moved as unobtrusively out of the cockpit as a mountain of muscle and fur could manage. Leia's gaze didn't leave Han.

"Are you saying I should have cleared the way so that they could have captured Maas and kept the data out of our hands? Because I can't see how that would have ended well."

"I'm not saying that. In the grand scheme of the war, you did what you had to do," Han said.

"But?"

"Grand schemes can excuse a lot of bodies."

"That's not fair—"

"What are you two on about then?" Baasen asked, poking his head in the cockpit. "It's time to celebrate! We've lived to see another day. You can't complain about that."

Han got up, pushing past Baasen. There were too many people on the *Falcon*. Baasen, Scarlet Hark, Sunnim, the R3 droid, Leia, Chewbacca. Him. It made the ship feel close and tight, and he didn't like it. In the lounge, Scarlet was looking at a long gash on Sunnim's right arm. The Bothan blinked as Han brushed past them. He heard Leia and Baasen Ray behind him. He ignored them all.

Leia was right, and he hated it. The Empire had already shown it was willing to destroy planets filled with innocent people in order to prove a point. As he passed through the ship, he found himself going back through every time he'd gotten out of trouble by making the jump to lightspeed. All the fights he'd avoided, all the times he could have died and didn't. If Scarlet's information was correct and the Empire got hold of this artifact, that would stop not just for him, but for everyone. All the ships boiling up off Kiamurr or Haaridin or Tatooine would have no place to go, and the Empire could pour in wave after wave of fighters until whoever the Emperor had decided was his enemy that week was nothing but fused carbon and a few volatile chemicals.

The plastoid case was in Baasen's quarters. Han scooped it up. It wasn't huge. It was hardly a weight in his hand. He carried it back to the lounge and put it down on the dejarik table. The others were all around. Leia and Scarlet stood at the door to the cockpit, Chewbacca in the background between them. Sunnim and Baasen sat on the couches. Baasen's smile could have meant anything.

"We did our part," Han said, thumbing the case's latch. "Let's see if it was worth it."

The case clicked and slid open. The smell of sugar and lemon filled the air. Han leaned close. The cake was a dusting of bright yellow crumbs and gobs of frosting on a small presentation plate of tempered glass.

"Baasen?" Han said carefully. "What is this?"

Leia stepped up beside him, looking down. She made a small sound in the back of her throat. "Maas must have been going to meet with Eanis Malavoy. He's a buyer for Bonadan Heavy Industries."

"And?" Han said.

"And he likes lemon cakes," Leia said.

Han put his fingertips to his eyes. "Baasen, what did you do?"

"Failed to save a lemon cake, apparently," Baasen said lightly.

"This was supposed to be the data," Han said. "You blew the job. You said you knew where the information was. Now what have we got? A world *died* for this."

"Now, not so hot nor so hasty. I never *said* it was in the case, did I? That's a conclusion you drew on your own. Though, in fairness, I did encourage a certain misunderstanding."

Scarlet made a sound between a cough and a laugh. Leia looked over at her. Sunnim looked from one woman to the other, his ears canted forward in confusion.

"It's in the R-3," Leia said.

Baasen clapped his remaining hand against his leg. "Now, that is a smart woman, my friend. Sees right to the heart of things. Most people don't know how easy it is to hide data in an R-3 unit."

"I know," Leia said.

"Well," Baasen continued, "I guessed he—"

"Thanks for that," Han said. "Chewbacca, would you please escort our friend to the air lock. He's walking home."

"Ah!" Baasen said, holding up his palm. "Now, we had an agreement, boyo. And I've kept my part."

Han felt Leia's dark eyes on him. The truth was, he wasn't sure he'd been joking about throwing Baasen out into space. His head felt thick with distress and exhaustion and the aftermath of the battle. He smirked, clapped the Mirialan on the shoulder, and left it at that.

Leia knelt beside the little red droid. The rat-bird droppings still streaked its finish. The R3 squealed and squeaked.

"It's all right," Leia said. "I've done this before. It isn't going to hurt at all."

A cascade of sparks flew from the droid's chest panel, its indicator light dimmed and brightened again. A beam of light shot out, and the rough, jittering hologram of a man appeared standing on the floor in front of the R3. He was younger than Han had expected, with flowing, shoulder-length hair the color of honey and eyes that would have looked at home on a snake. His smile was obsequious and greedy.

Another hissing spark, and Galassian came alive. He pushed his hair back from his face. His grin was broad, and his eyes seemed to flicker in a way that made Han think of fevers. A pair of floating round droids hovered, one over each of the man's shoulders.

"Master," he said. "It is after much hard work and many weeks of effort that I bring this news to you. I was not certain, but now I am pleased to say that our fondest hopes are achieved. With this new toy I've found, your rule will be eternal and utterly, *utterly* absolute."

Leia took in a deep breath. Her chin lifted in defiance. She looked beautiful that way.

HAN REACHED UP into the access panel. The relay under his fingertips was cold, the power light dull and dead.

"Still nothing," he shouted.

Chewbacca's roar rose from the flooring.

"I didn't say it would be," Han said. "But I'm telling you there's no power right now."

The Wookiee's grumbling faded to near inaudibility. Han let himself fall back, massaging his hand. The rear deflector shields were proving harder to repair than he'd hoped, but he and Chewie were making progress. If he'd been able to reroute more of the power from life support, it would have been faster. Which brought him back again to the idea of throwing Baasen out the lock.

It was probably the smart thing. He didn't have any illusions about the bounty hunter's newfound allegiance. As soon as the opportunity arose and it looked like there was even a little bit of profit in it, Baasen would put a hole through Han's chest and be glad that he'd done it. The truth was Han had killed people he liked more for less reason. It was the cold-bloodedness of it that escaped him, or that he told himself escaped him. He wondered whether, if he hadn't snapped at Leia about her tactics on Kiamurr, he'd have had an easier time doing the obvious thing with Baasen. He hoped it would have been just as hard.

"Captain Solo," Scarlet said. "You have a minute?"

"Sure," Han said. "You got the whole thing decrypted, then?"

She nodded. "How are the repairs?"

"We're getting there."

Chewbacca howled and muttered. Scarlet laughed.

"It's not as bad as he says," Han said. "We'll have full power to the deflectors before we jump again."

The meeting was in the cabin Scarlet and Leia were sharing. With him added in, there almost wasn't space, but the door closed and sealed, and Baasen and Sunnim weren't likely to overhear anything they said.

"What've we got?" Leia asked as Han tried to find a comfortable way to squat by the bunks. It was strange being in his private quarters with the two attractive women. In other circumstances, he'd have been turning down the lights and pouring drinks. Now he just felt awkward.

"More than I expected," Scarlet said. "It's coordinates to the system and data from the sensor sweeps, but Galassian also made some exploratory surveys on the planet's surface. Since the K'kybak died out, their planet's pretty much gone to ruin. There are old cities drowned in swamps and fallen into the oceans. It's not a hospitable place, either. Pretty much anything that isn't predatory is poisonous."

"Lovely," Leia said.

"It gets better. The K'kybak left behind an old defense grid. It's been unattended so long it's mostly dead, but every now and then part of it becomes active enough to throw off jumps going out of the system. That's how Galassian found the place and decided it was something more than a swamp planet. The system that the defense grid uses to disable hyperdrives is in a barricaded temple. Galassian has a rough map of the place."

"All right," Leia said.

"He's found the controls for the device, and he's started working out a translation for them."

"He has a *manual* for it already?" Han asked.

"The beginnings of one," Scarlet said. "I'm going through it now. I don't really understand most of it, but I've spent a lot of time studying him. So some of it makes a little sense."

"That's a lot farther along than I'd hoped," Leia said.

"I know. If he's right, the Empire's on the edge of controlling hyperspace jumps for ships, the hyperwave relays for information. Pretty much everything that uses hyperspace."

"That's bad," Han said. "That's really bad."

"The good news is that getting to the device is a royal pain in the butt and viciously dangerous, so Galassian's being very careful. The bad news is it's a pain in the butt. And dangerous."

"And I assume it's in some totally secluded part of the galaxy that's going to be difficult to reach, too," Han said.

"Actually, that part's not so bad," Scarlet said. "It's near some of the major lanes. No one's used it because there's nothing there, and ships kept disappearing when their jumps went wrong."

Han narrowed his eyes. A tingling sensation started crawling up his neck.

"I think it's safe to assume the Empire has exploratory and scientific teams in the system already," Scarlet said. "I assume they have fighter escorts, but I don't know if they'd risk putting in a heavy military presence until they knew the device was secured and inactive."

"Where is it?" Leia asked.

"Fifth planet of the Seymarti system."

Leia frowned.

"I've heard of that system," she said. "Why have I heard of that system?"

"Because," Han said, "you just sent Luke there."

CHAPTER TWENTY-THREE

THEY DRIFTED THROUGH the Trundalki system, an old smugglers' stopover Han had used any number of times. He'd chosen it because it was a relatively short jump from Kiamurr, and because he could be pretty sure no Imperials would be waiting on the other side. The only planet in the system that had any life on it was unimaginatively named Trundalki IV, and was nothing more than a black-market shipyard surrounded by several dozen bars and gambling dens. The Imperials had never bothered with Trundalki because there was nothing there the Imperials wanted. That was how to keep going. Keep your head down, move fast, and when the people looking to shoot you showed up, be somewhere else.

"Red Wave, this is Pointer, come in Red Wave," Leia said for the hundredth time. Han could hear the words echoing down the corridor from her station in the cockpit. *Red Wave* was the call sign for the escort wing Wedge Antilles was commanding, and so far they weren't answering. That could mean a lot of things. Maybe they were out of range of a hyperwave relay, or having comm failures. It might mean they were too close to an Imperial listening post and were maintaining radio silence. It could mean they were dead.

Or it could mean they had jumped into the Seymarti system and been trapped by the Empire's new hyperspace nullifier. Han tried to imagine being trapped in the same star system for his entire life and failed.

He headed to the lounge to get away from Leia's pleading, but her voice followed him like the muttering of a ghost.

Scarlet and Chewbacca sat at the dejarik table with Baasen's dim-witted Bothan thug and pilot. Scarlet was in the process of annihilating Sunnim's side one piece at a time. Chewbacca watched and laughed at each new kill. The Bothan growled and counterattacked ineffectually. Within minutes his last piece was gone, and he stormed away from the table in a huff.

"You can try Chewie," Han said, taking the Bothan's place at the table. "He's not bad."

Scarlet laughed and turned off the board. "I like both my arms right where they are, thanks."

Chewbacca cocked his head to one side and whimpered at her.

"I know you wouldn't hurt me, sweetie," she replied, patting the Wookiee's huge arm. "Han and I are bantering. It's what you do when you can't have a grown-up conversation."

"Hey," Han said. "Are you saying I'm not a grown-up?"

"Is that what I was saying?" Scarlet bounced to her feet, gave Chewbacca one last pat, and wandered off toward the crew quarters, whistling.

Chewbacca growled and narrowed his eyes.

"I did not run her off." Han leaned back in the chair and put his hands behind his head. "I think she's worried Leia will catch the two of us together."

Chewbacca bared his teeth in a Wookiee grin, then broke into a long, honking laugh.

"Laugh it up, but I know women. You didn't see how

Scarlet was at that ballroom back on Kiamurr. This thing will definitely be a problem. And soon. How are you doing on that shield generator?"

Chewbacca gave a massive shrug and howled.

"Yeah, I hear you. Let's hope we don't get shot anytime soon to test that. The *Falcon*'s been taking a beating lately, and at some point she'll be more patch than ship. Probably just in time to really screw us up."

Chewbacca glanced at something behind Han, and he turned in time to see Baasen wander into the lounge carrying a flask and four glasses in a wire mesh box. The Mirialan sat at their table with a friendly nod to Chewbacca and set down his bottle.

"Sunnim gone already, then?"

"Scarlet thumped him at dejarik and he left in a huff," Han said. He picked the flask up and rotated it in his hands, but there was no marking on it. The metal felt cool to the touch, but not cold enough to have been refrigerated. A thin film of condensation had started to form on it.

"That," Baasen said, taking the flask away from him, "is the last of a fantastic brandy I smuggled once. Been carrying it ever since, looking for an excuse. I want you to share it with me, Solo."

"Wait, so while we were running around Kiamurr, you had a bottle secretly stashed down your pants?"

"Well, the universe is an unlikely place filled with unlikely people. Most things, I'm willing to lose, but there's a few I keep near to hand. No pun intended."

He took three of the glasses, set them on the table, then opened the flask with his teeth and poured. The smell of high-grade rocket fuel filled the air. He pushed one across the table with his steel-capped stump, but Han waved it off.

"Don't need a drink."

"Oh, boyo, you surely do," Baasen said, then tossed off his own glass and gave Han a grin. The message was clear:

It's not poison. Chewbacca picked his glass up and sniffed at it, nose crinkling up with disgust.

Han sighed and raised his glass. "To your health."

Baasen refilled his and tapped it against Han's. "And to your own."

They both drank. To Han's surprise, the brandy was mild and vaguely sweet, while still strong enough to drop a charging bantha in its tracks. Chewbacca put his glass down without drinking and pushed his chair back, trying to get away from the smell.

"That's not bad," Han said as Baasen refilled his glass.

"Better than not bad, I'd say." Baasen refilled his own, but didn't drink right away. He just rotated the glass slowly on the tabletop, leaving a small moisture ring on one of the table's black squares. "Solo, we needed to sit down, you and I, as men."

"I'm listening."

"We know this side of the law, and we know how a friend can become an enemy at the wrong word or the right price."

Han nodded but said nothing. Chewbacca narrowed his eyes at Baasen, and his heavy shoulder muscles tensed.

"I won't apologize for trying to take you to the Hutt," Baasen said after a moment. "That was business, and I'd do it again if all things were the same."

"Baasen, you're making me feel all warm and fuzzy inside," Han said. "Why *are* you telling me this?"

"Well," Baasen said, then paused to drain off his glass. "I want you to know where I stand. I've agreed to help find your magic whatsit, and I'll stand by that. We're allies now. But if it turns out to be wishful thinking and broken promises when we get there, I'll have no choice but to fall back on my old intentions and deliver you to Jabba."

"And I'll have no choice but to try and shoot you first," Han replied. Chewbacca was growling so low in his chest it was almost subsonic.

"I'd expect no less," Baasen said. "But that's understood. What I came to say was until that time comes, we're allies, and you can count on my help. And Sunnim's. He's a bit dim, but he follows my lead."

Han drank off his glass, then refilled it. "So we're friends again right up until we find out this thing we're chasing doesn't actually exist, at which point we both immediately try to kill each other."

"Aye."

"Well, that'll be quite the day."

"That it will."

"Han," Leia said from the corridor. He hadn't heard her coming, but the tone of her voice was worrying. Quiet, and just a little frightened.

"What's going on?" he asked, walking over to her. She gave Baasen a look, then gestured toward the cockpit with her head. Han followed her there, his own worry growing.

"No one can find the survey team," she said when they were alone.

"Then they're probably still in the Seymarti system. If it can kill hyperspace travel, could it block the relays, too?"

"Scarlet thinks it could, if Galassian's figured out how to turn it on."

"If he's figured it all out, we wouldn't have gotten here."

Leia waved his reassurance away with an impatient gesture. "We know the Empire has the location. We know Galassian's there. Our ships may have jumped into the middle of anything. It was just supposed to be a survey and scouting mission. The escort wasn't armed for a full-scale conflict."

"Okay," Han said. "What do we do?"

Leia sat down, rubbing the bridge of her nose between her thumb and finger while she thought. Han dropped into the pilot's chair and waited. He knew how much was riding on her decisions right now. If it had been up to him, he'd have taken Scarlet straight back to the rebel fleet, and Leia would have been killed on Kiamurr. It made his head hurt even to think about how close he'd come to a major blunder. And now maybe Luke was in even bigger trouble, and Leia had to weigh that against the needs of the whole Rebellion. Han didn't envy her at all.

"I've contacted the Alliance. They agree that the possibility of this technology falling into the Emperor's hands is too great a threat. A massive strike force is being assembled to assault Seymarti directly and take the relic if we can, destroy it if we can't."

"Sounds like they're taking this seriously," Han said. "If it does turn out to be a wild gundark chase, we're all going to look pretty silly."

"At these stakes, we can lose some dignity."

Han shrugged. "What about Luke?"

"That's the problem. General Rieekan says he can't have the strike force ready for almost a week. And meanwhile Luke and the others may be trapped, or worse."

"Then we're going to get him, right?"

"You'd do that?" Leia asked, frowning. "Risk the *Falcon* to jump into a system we might not be able to jump back out of, filled with an unknown number of Imperial ships? You aren't getting heroic on me, are you?"

Han raised his hands in mock surrender and grinned at her. "I don't believe in heroes. Luke's my friend. I don't like the idea of leaving him there until some general decides the math is right."

Leia stared at him for a moment, searching his face. Then she got up, but stopped at the hatch to say, "I'll go tell the others."

"Besides," Han said, turning back to his console and starting the calculations for a jump to Seymarti, "Luke owes me a couple, and if I let him get killed, how can I collect?"

"There's the Han I know," Leia said to his back, but there was a smile in her voice when she said it.

—

HAN SAT QUIETLY as the navigation computer finished figuring out the jump, watching the occasional smuggling ship bounce out of the system in a hyperjump or arrive suddenly in a spray of light and other energetic particles as they dropped out of hyperspace. Places like Trundalki would die instantly if the Empire could control hyperspace traffic. It was the kind of backwater outpost that survived only because there were people who needed a way station in a quiet corner of the galaxy. People like him. There were a thousand places just like it scattered across populated space. All of them waiting, all unaware, for the death sentence Seymarti might bring.

Voices drifted down the corridor to him. Leia, talking to the rest of the crew in the lounge. The voices laughed, Chewbacca's loud honk mixing with the Bothan's chittering and the various human sounds. Leia being funny, lightening the moment, getting everyone on the same team.

Another ship jumped out of the system. Han wished them a silent good luck, then almost fell out of his seat when he heard the sound of a throat being cleared behind him.

"You all right?" Leia asked. Han realized the laugh he'd heard must have been their meeting breaking up.

"Sure, just stretching a bit while I work," Han said, then tapped on some controls to look like he was busy. He turned the water recycling system off, then on again. "Uh-huh, that's just about done."

"You finished with the calculations?" she asked.

"Yep, pretty much."

She put a hand on his shoulder, leaning close. "Then punch it, flyboy."

CHAPTER TWENTY-FOUR

THE SEYMARTI SYSTEM lay along the space lanes that led from the Core to the Inner Rim. Its sun was a small white star with a tendency to throw off flares massive enough to bathe its three closest planets in nuclear plasma. The fourth and fifth planets orbited beyond that, and then a cluster of four gas giants spun beyond them, each with a constellation of moons surrounding it. Jumping into the system behind the largest of these, Han could see the great smear of the galaxy. Billions of stars so far away that their light melted together into one great, unbroken band. On the display, the tactical computer drew out the planets and their orbits, the moons, the asteroids, the curving masses of high-energy ejecta from the star. Otherwise, the *Falcon* ran dark. Only the bare minimum of life-support and computational resources. If he'd done it right, they wouldn't look like anything more interesting than a rock with a high concentration of metals.

"Nice placement, old friend," Baasen said. "Just here, we're in three different kinds of shadow."

"Complex systems make for lots of cover," Han said. "And more things to run into."

"Trade-offs," Baasen said. "Always trade-offs."

Chewbacca moaned, gesturing toward the glowing planets and moons.

"Yeah, I see 'em," Han said.

Leia ducked in behind them. The light from the display painted her in shades of red and black. "What've we got?" she asked.

"Passive sensors are picking up something in orbit around the fifth planet," Han said. "We don't have great resolution yet, but it's about the right size for a Star Destroyer."

Leia's expression went grim. "Well, we knew there'd be something."

"All respect," Baasen said, "I was hoping for something smaller."

"So was I, but I was expecting we'd see more," Leia said. "What do the active scanners show?"

"They show little dark circles where I haven't turned them on," Han said. "Seems to me that announcing that we're here with an active signal might not be a great plan."

"Could disguise them a bit," Baasen said. "Shift the spectrum, bounce the signal off the atmosphere of that sixth planet for scatter."

Chewbacca snarled and howled, but he also started setting it up. Han sat forward in the pilot's chair, his fingers laced together. The display showed that the gas giant and one of its moons would be blocking them from the Imperial ship's sight for another few minutes at least. He leaned forward and thumbed up the hyperdrive. The whir and hum filled the ship, but even before he looked at the readouts, he knew. It *sounded* wrong.

"What are you doing?" Leia snapped as he shut it back down.

"Seeing what our options are, Your Worship," Han said. "It's not looking like tactical retreat's one of them. Whatever that thing is, it's affecting our hyperdrive."

"That confirms it, then," Leia said. "They've found it. And they've found out how to turn it on."

"And so we're not getting out of this system unless we get down there and turn it off."

"Not unexpected," Baasen said. "But still a bit disappointing. Hey, boyo, at least your magic gizmo exists, eh?"

At least I won't be shooting you in the back today, he meant.

The communications panel flickered to announce an incoming signal. Not from a hyperwave relay, though. Those channels were coming in as unstable and wild as the hyperdrive itself. Instead it was coming in on standard radio, a weak signal, but using a Rebellion encryption code. Han felt the sudden release of tension in his chest that he hadn't even known was there. He scooped up the headset and opened the channel.

"This is the *Millennium Falcon,*" Han said. "Who've we got out there?"

"Han!" Luke said. The relief in the boy's voice was enough to set Han grinning. "What are you doing here?"

Han smiled at Leia and pointed to his earpiece. Leia's eyes were bright, and her relief showed in the way she held herself.

"Looking for you, among other things. What's your status?"

"We're grounded right now. When we got here, we ran into a patrol of Imperial fighters," Luke said, and then paused. "It got a little hot."

"Do the bad guys know where you are?"

"No," Luke said. "We took the fighters that were left and skimmed past one of those solar flares, then killed power. The TIEs looked around for a while after that, but then they stopped. I think they assumed we're all dead."

Leia pointed to the copilot's headset. Chewbacca growled and whined, shaking his head in refusal.

"I'll give it back," Leia said, her hand still out imperiously. Chewbacca coughed and handed it over. Leia put the headset on and adjusted the strap to her much smaller skull. "Luke. It's Leia. How badly is the force hurt? Where's Wedge?"

"We've got seven fighters still ready to go," he said. "We lost Burlis and Chrenn in the first pass. Daawis is still here, but his attitude stabilizer's shot. Wedge is helping him try to get it working right now. I think we could fix it, if we had the parts. But we can't get the hyperdrives to work. None of us."

"We know, kid," Han said. "That's why we're here."

"Is it some kind of new Imperial weapon?" Luke asked.

"No," Han said at the same moment Leia answered, "Not yet."

"Well, whatever it is, we've been trying to transmit a warning and tell everyone to stay away from here."

Scarlet poked her head into the cockpit, and Han held up his palm. The Bothan's bleating voice and the R3's chirrups and whirs came behind her, a chorus of inquiry and concern. The *Falcon* wasn't built to have that many people all wanting to be in the middle of things together.

"Where are you, kid? We'll come have a conversation in person."

"There's an ice cave on the second gas giant's third moon," Luke said. "It's even got a little atmosphere."

"Sounds glorious," Han said. "Hang tight, and we'll be right there."

"I'll tell the guys not to shoot you," Luke said. Han could hear the smile in the boy's voice. *Was I ever that young?* he thought. Han dropped the connection.

"So they've got it already," Scarlet said.

"It can't be that straightforward," Leia replied, handing the headpiece back to Chewbacca. Han noted that she didn't put it back to the Wookiee's size. "If they didn't think it was a risk to be nearby, they'd have more than one Star Destroyer standing guard over it. And if our hyperwave relays are down, it's a safe bet theirs are, too. My guess is they've found it, whatever it is, and they're still trying to figure out how to make it work."

Baasen shifted to give Scarlet enough room in the cockpit. "Interesting day, this'll be."

"Do we think it's still on the planet," Leia asked, "or would they have taken it up to the Destroyer itself?"

"I don't know," Scarlet said. "Galassian doesn't talk about the size of the thing. If it's working—"

Chewbacca howled at Han and nodded toward the tactical display. Han squinted at it as a pale blue arc appeared between the planets.

"—I'd assume it's on the planet, though. Whatever resources it needs to function are down there."

"No," Han said to Chewbacca. "The burn's too long. I want us running as quiet as we can here. Take it up a third of a degree and we can slingshot around that big moon there. Make it to Luke faster, and there's less chance of the Star Destroyer seeing us."

"You think they'll have forces on the ground, then?" Leia asked.

"A science team at least," Scarlet said. "Guard forces, too. Galassian's initial survey showed several different strata of ruins, so I'd expect that it's somewhere under the planetary surface."

"That's not a bad path," Baasen said, leaning past Han to point at the display, "but there's a better one if you aim for this moon here, instead. Longer path, but faster, and you don't spend so much time exposed to the Star Destroyer because of these asteroid fields in the middle."

Chewbacca howled and grunted.

"What did he say?" Baasen asked.

"Stop!" Han shouted. The conversations paused. From the lounge, the R3 whistled. "If you aren't me or Chewie, please get out of the cockpit. Now."

The others scowled or smirked, but they left. When they were gone, Han ran his fingers through his hair.

"We've got too many people on this ship."

Chewbacca shrugged, adjusted his headpiece, tried it on, then adjusted it again. He growled conversationally.

"No," Han said. "There's only one person in charge. Me."

Chewbacca shrugged again. This time his headpiece fit.

THE ICE CAVE was as wide as a hangar deck. Eight X-wings squatted at the back beside a surveying ship with scorch marks down its sides and blistered metal along its landing gear. The emergency lights on the ice beside them threw wide shadows against the pale blue ceiling. None of the fighting ships was unscathed. Long, black char marks streaked their wings and sides, and one of them had a pool of frozen green coolant on the ice under one wing actuator. But the pilots in their dirty orange jumpsuits all waved cheerfully enough as Han brought the *Falcon* gently down beside them.

As Han walked down the cargo ramp, Luke trotted forward to meet them, R2-D2 rolling behind him. The kid was grinning just as if they weren't trapped in a dangerous system, badly outnumbered, with limited food supplies and no way to call for help or know when—or if—support was coming. Chewbacca's roar echoed softly in the thin air as he lifted Luke up off his feet, tossing him lightly in the air. Scarlet, Baasen, Leia, and Sunnim followed behind.

"I'm glad to see you, too," Luke said, patting Chewbacca's arm. "What are you guys doing out here, anyway? I thought you were off in the Core getting a spy back to the fleet."

"We were," Han said. "Scarlet Hark? Luke Skywalker. Luke, this is the spy."

"Nice to meet you," Luke said.

"Likewise," Scarlet said with a smile. R2-D2 squealed, and she nodded to the droid. "And you as well."

"That," Han went on, "is Baasen Ray. He's a bounty hunter who promised Jabba he'd bring me in, and the Bothan is Sunnim, his pilot. I wouldn't trust either too much."

"Oh," Luke said, frowning.

"Any friend of Solo's," Baasen said with a nod, and then didn't finish the sentence.

"Is he on our side?" Luke asked.

"Not really," Han said. "And the R-3 used to belong to a man named Hunter Maas, but Baasen killed him. Now . . . I don't know. Now it's just on my ship."

"I feel like I've missed a lot."

"Luke, I need to speak to Wedge," Leia said, as the pair embraced. Han stepped back, pretending to look at the power leads on the *Falcon*. He caught Scarlet's glance, gauging him, and ignored it.

"Right here, ma'am," Wedge Antilles said, striding up. Han hadn't seen him approach, but the man looked tired. His flight suit was stained by grease and what looked like engine coolant.

"Commander Antilles, we have to get down to the planet," Leia said, stepping back from Luke but keeping one hand on his forearm. "The thing that's broken your hyperdrives and the communication relays is down there."

"Gonna be hard," Han said.

"Won't be *that* hard," Baasen said. "Just need a distraction, as I see it. And here's one now, eh?" He gestured at the fighters.

Leia's expression went perfectly calm. Blank. Han realized she was weighing the options. The chances of safely reaching the surface of Seymarti V against the danger to the fighters. To Luke.

"No problem," Wedge said. "We'll divide into two wings. One can come up from sunward; the other can come in from the gas giants. If we time it right, no one will notice one extra ship dropping in on the far side of the planet."

"And then what?"

"Then we win," Luke said.

Han laughed. "You took out one space station with a lucky shot because I was there running interference for you, kid," he said. "Don't let it go to your head."

"I didn't say it'd be easy." Luke grinned.

That was the thing about Luke. The way he said it, it almost sounded possible.

"All right," Leia said. "We need to move quickly. The ship with the bad attitude stabilizer?"

"That one," Wedge said, pointing. "I've been working at it for hours, but we don't have the parts. I'd take any help I could get putting her back on her feet."

"Han?" Leia said. "Do we have something that will patch that up?"

Han shrugged. "Let me take a look at it. I'll see what I can manage."

"Thank you," she said, and her voice was a little thick. *She knows how dangerous this is,* he thought. *She knows that she's asking the kid to risk death. Or any of the others. Maybe all. Grand causes,* he thought. *All in the name of grand causes.* But he had to give her this much: she was willing to risk the people she cared about just as quickly as the ones in Kiamurr that she barely even knew. Han could admire that, but it didn't make him comfortable.

"Come on then," Baasen said. "I'll give a hand. I've still got the one."

"All right. Thanks," Luke said. And then, to Leia, "Why is he here?"

HAN, BAASEN, AND CHEWBACCA tramped across the thick blue ice of the cave, their shadows shifting around them as they passed the emergency lights. Baasen's expression was unreadable. The fighter, when they reached it, wasn't as bad as Han had feared. The stabilizer was fused, but it was a standard design. Han could pull any of a dozen from one piece of equipment on the *Falcon* or another. The pilot was a young man, even more fresh-faced than Luke. Han hadn't been sure that was possible.

Chewbacca hauled himself up on the fighter's wing while Han and Baasen got a welding torch and soldering alloy. Leia moved among the fighter pilots, talking and asking questions. Seeing her among them reminded him of the halls and gardens of Kiamurr. This was what she did. It was what gave her power. If she wound up running the galaxy, it would be because of moments like this one, asking for the loyalty of people who had no reason to be loyal to her.

People like him.

"Well, old friend, it's a good, good day," Baasen said.

"How do you figure that?" Han asked.

"Scarlet's hyperdrive killer exists, doesn't it? And the chances of you and me gunning each other down have fallen a notch. At least that's how I see it."

"We're about to throw all eight X-wings at a Star Destroyer so that we can sneak down into the ruins of some xenophobic dead species' civilization and try to steal this thing from who knows how many Imperial troops and scientists. And that's a good day?"

Baasen pursed his lips. "Well, put that way, it sounds less so. But better than it could have been for us."

“It’s thinking like that that put you in trouble with Jabba in the first place.”

“Ah, but let this all play out well, and it’ll be him who’s got trouble with us, eh?”

One of the fighter pilots whooped, jumping up to the X-wing’s cockpit and striking a pose while the men around him laughed. Han couldn’t say quite why the sight left a sour taste in his mouth.

“Come on,” he said. “Let’s get this over with.”

CHAPTER TWENTY-FIVE

THE *FALCON* FLEW quietly through the vast emptiness, moving faster than a comet, but small. Han used the maneuvering thrusters lightly, shifting the ship behind whatever debris he could find and pushing to keep the bulk of the planet between him and the Star Destroyer. Long-range fighter patrols might still reach above the planet's curving horizon. He couldn't do anything about that. The best he could manage was to be small and fast and get down to the planet's surface quickly when the time came.

"Galassian's notes put the temple's coordinates just south of the equator," Scarlet said.

"Yeah, that's actually in the middle of an ocean," Han said. "I'm pretty sure he transposed these two readings."

"Why do you think so?" Scarlet asked.

"Because that would put it more or less directly under the Star Destroyer," Han said. "Anything dangerous or inconvenient just seems more likely to be true."

"There's a cynical worldview," Scarlet said.

"Just being realistic."

The small, blue-white sun touched the edge of the planet. Great sheets of light spilled out, caught in billions of motes of dust that surrounded the swamp world. The debris of some shattered moon, the still-uncaptured remnants of the cloud that had spawned the system, or the relic of the inward-facing K'kybak civilization. Han couldn't say, but it was pretty to look at. And then there, in the center of the light, a speck of darkness. The Imperial Star Destroyer hove into view, and Han tensed.

His impulse was to kick the engines into a fast burn, trusting to speed and maneuverability. Restraining himself wasn't easy, but he did it, letting the *Falcon* follow its trajectory like a thrown rock hissing through the darkness. No alarms had sounded yet. There was no sign they'd been noticed.

Chewbacca grunted and moaned.

"I know," Han said. "I see it, too. We'll try to fix it when we get down there."

"Fix what?" Scarlet asked.

"We've still got a coolant leak from where Baasen hit us with the tracking beacon," Han said. "It's not bad. We'll be fine."

Scarlet took in a deep breath, letting it out slowly between her teeth.

"You know," she said, "I love this part."

"This part?" Han said. "Really?"

"Really," she said. "They're right there. Right in front of us, and they don't see the threat. If we do it right, they never will. We'll slide in, do what we came to do, and by the time they understand what's happened, it'll be too late."

"Maybe," Han said. "Or maybe they'll have moved the shaft we expected to find, and we'll wind up climbing a transmission tower while half the stormtroopers in the Core try to shoot us down. It goes that way, too, sometimes."

"And I loved that part, too," Scarlet said ruefully. "This is why I could never be an accountant."

Something glittered off the Star Destroyer's bow. A wing of TIE fighters starting their patrol, or else ending it.

"What about you?" Scarlet asked. "You have to enjoy the fear, too. Just a little?"

"Not the fear," Han said. "I just like being a little smarter than the next guy."

"That's all it is?"

"That, and I really hate paying taxes."

The comm flickered red and came to life. "Red Wave One, this is Red Wave Two," Luke said. "Do you copy?"

"Red Wave Two, this is Red Wave One," Wedge replied. "I've got you loud and clear."

"We're in place and starting our approach, Red Wave One. You should proceed when ready."

"Understood, Red Wave Two. We're going in."

The Star Destroyer, black against the brightness of the sun, began to shift, turning its vast bulk. Glitters of silver and darkness spiraled out around it, and then the tiny red and orange flashes of laserfire. The battle had begun. Han fired up the engines.

"Hold on back there," he shouted. "This could get bumpy."

The R3 whistled and shrieked.

"What's the problem?" Han yelled.

"The droid's not clamped down, boyo," Baasen said, at the same time that Leia shouted, "The restraint's broken."

"Well, someone get it secured," Han said. "I can't do everything here."

"I'll take care of it," Scarlet said, and hurried back toward the lounge. At the Star Destroyer's starboard bow, something flared. A ship dying. Han couldn't tell if it had been one of the enemy's or one of their own. Han tapped his fingertips against the console. Another rapid flurry of bright green fire stuttered against the stars.

"They're shooting at the kid, Chewie."

Chewbacca whined and bared his teeth.

"I know that was what we wanted. It's all going just according to plan, but they're trying to kill the kid up there, and we're down here. You know what I want to do, Chewie? I want to fire up the turrets, get up there, and help out."

The Wookiee's sigh was confirmation enough. The *Falcon*'s sensors lit up, warning them of the approaching atmosphere. Han tested his fingers on the forward deflector shield's controls, waiting until the last second to bring up power. The less time they spent under power, the less likely it was that the fighters would come down. A few more seconds, and they'd be beyond the reach of the TIE fighters and into the thick soup of air where they could find out if the Empire had any anti-aircraft batteries in place.

"Red Wave Two, this is Red Wave Six. I've got one on my tail."

"I see you, Six," Luke shouted. "I'm coming in. I'm coming in—"

The radio cut out as the first of the atmosphere hit the ship. Han clicked on the shields and angled hard down. The *Falcon* bucked and kicked under him, sending his belly into his throat and then his boot and then his throat again. Superheated air streamed off the shields like foam at the crest of a wave.

"What's the problem, boyo?" Baasen called from the lounge.

"No problem," Han shouted back. "It's supposed to be like this."

Slowly, slowly, and then all too fast, the landmasses of Seymarti V rose up toward them. To his right, a vast, mud-colored sea glittered and shone. Red waters hugged the coastlines, fading into the deep brown middle water. On the land, an answering ocean of leaves rippled in the wind. As the *Falcon* drew nearer the ground, huge pillars rose up above the jungle canopy, their dun-colored sides ridged like stone eroded by centuries of rain. As Han passed over one, he saw a black swarm of insects curling out from the tower like living smoke. The waving leaves grew closer, larger. Any one of them would have been wide enough to cover the whole ship, and they rose and fell gently in a breeze he couldn't feel.

Just as they came even with the tops of the trees, a huge green-black shape rose from below. Han had the impression of vast, steely teeth and a dozen bright-red eyes, and then the *Falcon* was past it. The first of the massive leaves smashed into the ship, popping the *Falcon* up on one side almost thirty degrees. The Bothan screamed.

"Is it still supposed to be like this?" Baasen shouted.

"Not quite," Han replied, and pulled back hard on the controls. The ship shuddered, slowed, and dipped down again. The leaves beat against the screen until Han was sure he heard it crack. He went down deeper, dropping beneath the canopy to where massive tree trunks rose like buildings from the floor below. His eyes fixed on the proximity sensor array, his hands moved fast, and the ship ducked among the huge, black trunks. Something popped, sparks flying out from the console above him.

"Chewie! Was that something important?"

Chewbacca howled in complaint.

"Well, could you find out? I'm kind of busy here."

He pulled up the map overlay and fed it through the sensors. Galassian's coordinates glowed green twelve kilometers ahead. Four klicks before that, there was a rough clearing big enough to put the *Falcon* down.

"I can do this," Han said to himself. "Not. A. Problem."

The proximity alarm blared, and he threw the ship hard to the right, a massive trunk skinning by the *Falcon* close enough to touch. Chewbacca howled.

"Thank you for your input," Han said. "Just . . . hold on."

The canopy didn't open, but it thinned. The ground below was a mass of roots like thousands of gigantic, gnarled fingers twined around one another. The jungle with a permanent death grip on itself. Han lowered the ship slowly, watching the altitude readings with skepticism until the actual size of the root cluster became clear.

"Everyone all right back there?"

"Where did you learn how to fly a ship?" Leia shouted.

"What are you talking about?" Han said with a grin. "I'm brilliant."

The ship touched down, shifted, canted at fifteen degrees, and came to rest. Han shut down the engines with a flip of his wrists and unstrapped himself. Chewbacca rose and tugged at the still-smoking panel of the overhead console. Han scowled up at the relay. A small, blue flame danced around the blackened metal.

"We're going to want another one of those," he said.

Chewbacca's growl was short and percussive.

In the lounge area, the passengers were in different stages of recovering themselves. Baasen and Leia were both finding their feet on the *Falcon*'s canted deck. Sunnim was still sitting, his fists wrapped around the straps and his eyes wide. Han thought the Bothan was trembling. Only Scarlet was moving confidently, stepping across the lounge to the storage blocks, her cheeks warm and her eyes bright with pleasure.

"Bad news is it's going to be a little walk," Han said. "Good news is no one shot at us on the way down."

"That's how you fly when you're not under fire, then?" Baasen said.

"It's harder to see us if we're under the canopy," Han replied.

"You know that's where the trees are, though, right?" Leia asked.

The Bothan gave a small whimper.

"It worked out," Han said. "A simple thank-you will be fine."

Scarlet pulled a small black medpac from storage and hung it on her belt. The light from the upper turret slanted through past her as she looked over at Han.

"Who's coming?" she said.

"I'll not be staying behind now," Baasen said. "And where I go, Sunnim comes with. Watch my back."

"And here I thought we were friends," Han said.

"We are," Baasen said, grinning. He still looked a little greener than usual.

Chewbacca grunted and howled from the cockpit.

"No," Han said. "You're staying here."

An instant later a wall of angry Wookiee boiled up from the front of the ship, waving a welding torch and baring his fangs. Han set his feet on the tilted deck and looked up at Chewbacca's outraged eyes.

"It's not going to do any of us any good to go get this whatever-it-is if there's no ship when we get back. I don't want to come up and find there's a company of stormtroopers or corrosive ants or something infesting the place."

Chewbacca crossed his arms, his eyes narrowing stubbornly.

"It's a swamp out there," Han said. "You know how your fur gets when there's mud."

Chewbacca's scowl softened a bit.

"There'll be snakes," Han said, his voice almost gentle. Chewbacca was silent for a long moment, then turned and stalked back to the cockpit. The flare of the welding torch resumed.

"All right, then," Han said. "Chewie'll be here to keep you company, Your Worshipfulness. Scarlet and Baasen and Sunnim and I will—"

Scarlet and Leia chuckled at the same moment. Han's brow furrowed and he held out his hands in a gesture of confusion.

"I believe Princess Leia had her heart a bit set on coming with," Baasen said as he checked his blaster. Sunnim sighed and began unbuckling himself. Han turned toward Leia, ready to fight. Her dark eyes were on him, cold and implacable.

"Fine," he said. "Fine, if you really want to go out into the middle of enemy territory and get killed, who am I to stop you?"

"Why, Captain," Leia said, her voice sweet and unassuming and utterly false, "did you think I only risked *other* people's lives?"

Right, Han thought, feeling slightly chagrined.

A sudden flare of light filled the air. For a moment, he thought Chewbacca's welding torch had malfunctioned, but the brightness came from the turret. From the sky. Han scrambled into the cockpit, crawling over the console to look up. Through the break in the canopy, a swath of bright blue sky was scarred by black smoke and flaring green energy blasts. As he watched, the sky sparkled again, and another handful of bright flares streaked across the blue.

The radio squawked. "This is Red Wave One. This is Red Wave One. Everyone all right?"

Han picked up the headset. "What's going on up there?"

"Mission successful," Wedge replied.

"We got it," Luke added.

"Got it?"

"The Star Destroyer. We got it."

A deep rumbling shook the air, louder than thunder. All around, the jungle canopy shuddered and trembled. A massive, brightly plumed beast rose up from among the gigantic roots and fled into the twilight of the jungle, shrieking.

"Um," Han said. "Good job."

"It's not over. There's still a lot of fighters up here. We're going to have to pull back," Luke told him.

"I don't think anyone can fault you, kid. We'll let you know what we find."

"All right, Han. Good hunting."

He put down the headset. Chewbacca chuffed. "He got it," Han said. The Wookiee stood still for a moment, then went back to welding. Really, what else was there to say?

The others were gathered by the crew ramp. Baasen and Sunnim had their blasters in their hands. Scarlet had a handheld mapping device and a long black-composite blade. Leia was adjusting the seal on thigh-high black boots scavenged from a repair suit. From its clamps, the R3 whirred and whistled. Han nodded to it like he had any idea what it was saying.

"All right," he said, lowering the ramp. "Let's go."

CHAPTER TWENTY-SIX

THE BOTHAN STUMBLED over a thick root and crashed into the trunk of a massive tree. He pushed away from it, shouting curses in three languages. A long, slimy vine came away with him, wrapped around his face and neck. He continued to curse and claw at it for several seconds before Scarlet pulled the knife from her belt and cut the creeper away in two small strokes.

"Lovely planet," Baasen said, waving his hand in front of his face to keep the clouds of tiny biting insects from flying into his mouth when he spoke.

"You could have stayed on the ship," Han said.

"You'd have trusted me on your precious *Falcon*?"

"I'd have trusted Chewie."

Leia had wrapped her face in a gauzy white scarf to keep the bugs away, but she was fighting to keep her tall black boots from sticking in the thick, muddy jungle floor. Han walked at the rear of the group, one hand on his blaster, waiting for something larger and hungrier than the blood-sucking insects to make an appearance. All around them, the air was full of the whine of tiny wings and the calls of unseen animals. Everything stank of rot.

Once the Bothan was freed, Scarlet shifted back to the front of the group and took point again. She moved through the thick undergrowth, finding the most solid footing available and avoiding the tangles of vine and moss that hung from the branches above. Occasionally, she opened up a hologram of the terrain on her datapad and checked their location. She looked like she knew what she was doing, so Han trusted that they were heading on the right path to find the temple. If not, he'd never know. The jungle looked exactly the same in every direction. And the heavy canopy completely blocked off the sky, making his usual tools for orienting useless.

"Watch out," Scarlet said, pointing off to her left and moving right. "Deep mud here."

Leia pulled her boot out of another mud hole with a wet sucking noise. "And that makes it different how?"

Instead of answering, Scarlet shouted in alarm and danced away from the large puddle, yanking out her blaster as she moved. Behind her, the Bothan yelled and backpedaled into Baasen, nearly knocking him down. By the time Han reached the front, Scarlet was pointing her weapon at a large creature in the middle of the puddle. Its wide mouth was large enough to swallow a Wookiee whole, and a cluster of eyes the size of Han's fist sat on top of its broad head. Its brownish gray skin was almost exactly the same color as the mud around it, and when it croaked at them, its mouth was filled with big flat teeth.

"Don't shoot it!" Han yelled as he ran up to it.

Scarlet frowned and cocked her head. "It almost ate me."

"It wasn't going to eat you. Look at it. All the eyes on top of its head and camouflaged skin—it spends most of its time hiding under the mud. And those teeth are for grinding plants, not animals. Don't shoot it for being ugly."

"Sure," Scarlet said, holstering her blaster. "Didn't realize you guys were friends."

Han leaned over and patted the monster's snout. "It's just curious. Never seen a human before, I bet."

"What about Bothans?" Sunnim said, clearly not entirely convinced by Han's explanation.

Han ignored him. "Watch out for us," he told the monster. "We're not very nice."

As if in response, the creature slid back under the mud almost without a sound. Scarlet rolled her eyes at Han and started off again, Sunnim close behind.

"Didn't know you were such an animal lover," Leia said when she caught up to him.

"If everyone got to kill anything that looked big and scary, Chewie would never be able to leave the ship."

Leia laughed and hooked her arm through his, using his support to keep her feet out of the worst of the mud. "Funny, I always took you as a shoot-first sort of fellow."

"Oh," Han said, "trust me. I am if you're waving a blaster in my face. Not for the crime of being slimy and having too many eyes."

"See?" she said. "There, you keep doing that. Surprising me."

"I'm a complicated man. Many layers to me."

Leia jumped over a large tangle of roots, using Han's arm to keep from sliding when she landed on the muddy jungle floor on the other side. A cloud of the little biting insects burst out of tiny holes in the ground when her foot hit, and for a few moments neither of them spoke. Leia clutched her scarf around her head, and Han waved his hand to drive off the insects. After a while, the bugs seemed to get tired of annoying them and left.

"You know what I find?" Leia asked.

"About?" Han responded.

"Things with layers. When you peel off a layer, you usually find another, smaller layer of the same stuff underneath."

Han laughed despite himself. "You asking to look?"

She swatted him, but he could see her smiling under the

veil. If it weren't for the mud, creepers, stinging bugs, and nearby presence of a hyperspace-disrupting alien technology already at least half under the control of the Empire, it might have been a very pleasant walk.

Something the size of Han's hands flapped out of the jungle canopy and landed on the Bothan's shoulder. It had large, diaphanous wings in dozens of bright colors. They seemed to sparkle and radiate even with only the faint light the jungle let in. The body was thin and multi-legged and graceful, with a small, wedge-shaped head and large, black eyes. A long tail curled behind it, quivering gently.

Han froze. "Sunnim," he said loudly, though trying to keep his tone conversational so no one panicked. "Do not move."

Scarlet stopped and turned around, her face lighting up when she saw the fragile-looking creature. "Oh, would you look at that!"

"Kill it, kill it now," Han repeated, still keeping his voice level and light.

Scarlet frowned at him, but to her credit she started to slowly pull the knife off her belt. "Are you sure? It doesn't seem—"

While she was speaking, Sunnim reached up and touched one of the delicate wings. "Pretty" was all he had time to say before the long, curling tail snapped out and struck him in the throat. Scarlet yanked out her knife, but Han already had his blaster in his hand and in one shot blew the creature off the Bothan's shoulder in a shower of flaming bug parts.

Sunnim stood rigid, the color of his skin darkening all around the angry, red wound the stinger had left. He opened his mouth as if to speak, but only a stuttering gasp came out, followed by a spray of foamy saliva. Scarlet and Baasen rushed to him, helping to lay him gently to the ground. The Bothan continued to choke out an increasing spray of white foam, his body stiff and trembling.

Scarlet pulled the medpac off her waist, but by the time she'd opened it, the Bothan's struggle was over. Sunnim lay stiff, staring up at the sky through sightless eyes.

"Sorry, my boy," Baasen said, his hand under Sunnim's head, the stump of his other arm on the dead man's chest.

Scarlet slowly put her medical supplies away, shaking her head. "Great. The things that look like monsters aren't, but one of the most beautiful creatures I've ever seen can kill in seconds with one sting? What kind of world is this?"

"When something hangs out in an environment as dangerous as this in bright, eye-catching colors, it's because it's the meanest thing in the jungle. The brightness is a warning, not an invitation," Han told her.

Leia put a hand on Baasen's shoulder. "I'm sorry about your friend."

"My thanks to you," Baasen said, standing up and brushing the mud from the knees of his pants. "Not that the cheap little bastard was a friend, but I appreciate the courtesy."

"Maybe I should walk up front," Han said. He took the lead with Scarlet when they started moving again. The poor Bothan's rotten cabbage smell didn't seem offensive anymore, only sort of sad. The last of the scent quickly faded behind them, replaced by the jungle's sour dirt stink.

"What makes you such an expert on alien life?" Scarlet asked after a few minutes.

"I've been all over the galaxy. Seen a lot of stuff," Han said, panting with exertion. "Plus, I have common sense." The ground level had started to angle up, and the steep climb only made walking in the mud that much harder.

"Lot of deadly butterflies?" Scarlet asked, half teasing. Han was gratified to hear she was puffing, too.

"There's a million variations of the same things, but they're the things you see over and over," Han said. "The eyes go near the mouth. Dangerous things get warning colors. We've all got eyes and legs, because eyes and legs are useful things to have no matter where you come from."

"Fascinating."

"You asked, sweetheart."

After a few more minutes of climbing they reached the top of a rocky hill. The trees thinned out, and they could see sky again. There were still brightly colored streamers of energy spreading across the blue, and columns of smoke showed where pieces of the Star Destroyer had fallen through the atmosphere.

Off in the distance, in the direction they'd been traveling, a massive construction of cut stone poked up through the jungle canopy.

"Looks like you've got us heading the right way," Han said, pointing out the massive temple to Scarlet.

"Good work," Leia said, coming up to stand beside them. "I'd hate to get lost in this."

"You and me both," Han replied.

"'Bout an hour, you think?" Baasen asked, pulling out his datapad and trying to bounce a rangefinder off the top of the temple.

"Sure," Scarlet said with a shrug. "If we don't fall in a sinkhole, or get eaten by bog monsters, or stung to death by bugs, or run into some new horror we haven't seen yet. I believe someone mentioned snakes earlier."

Baasen laughed and put a companionable arm around Scarlet's shoulder. "I like you, girl. You've got spunk."

Scarlet laughed back. "I don't like you. You're about to lose another hand."

Baasen kept his smile, but he removed his arm from her shoulder.

Half an hour later, they finally found a snake. A massive creature, twice as big around as Han's waist, with bright scales like burnished copper and brass. It lay motionless across their path like a fallen log, the head and tail so far away they weren't visible in the dim light and underbrush.

"Do we shoot it?" Baasen wondered aloud.

"It's not moving," Han said. "It seems perfectly happy. Look." He jumped over the thick body of the snake. "Just leave it alone."

Scarlet hopped over the thick, scaly body, then held out her hand to Leia. The princess was shorter than the rest of them, and leaping over the snake wasn't as easy for her, but with Scarlet's help she made it. Baasen backed up, gave Han a skeptical look, and then ran at the snake. When he pushed off to leap, his leg shot out from under him in the wet mud and he slammed into the snake's side at full speed, bouncing across its back and into the mud on the other side.

While Baasen was sputtering and cursing and trying to get the mud off his face and clothes, Han held his breath, waiting for the giant snake to react.

The reaction, when it came, was just a ripple of muscle under the scales, and then the snake shot away into the underbrush with surprising speed.

"I think you scared it," Han said.

Baasen was still brushing mud out of his hair. "If I'd known that was all it took, I'd have kicked the blasted thing in the ribs and saved myself some embarrassment."

"Maybe we should leave before it realizes its mistake," Scarlet said, already moving off down the path at a jog.

Finally, they reached the edge of a clearing and, peering past the thick, fernlike undergrowth, spotted the massive stone slabs of the temple just a few hundred meters away. A large opening yawned in the side of the structure, twice the height of a human man and four times as wide. It looked big enough to drive a pair of landspeeders into side by side. Not even a door blocked the entrance.

But between them and that opening, Han counted at least a hundred stormtroopers, several vehicle-mounted rapid-fire anti-aircraft cannons, and five AT-ST scout transport walkers.

"Huh," Scarlet said.

"Yeah. I really didn't have a plan for this," Han replied. "We should have had a plan for this."

"When did we start planning?" Leia asked. "Haven't we been making this up as we go?"

"Think they're afraid of snakes?" Baasen said. "Maybe we could send that big fellow into the camp, create a disturbance."

"Well," Han said with a sigh, "we've gone from no-plan to stupid-plan. That's progress of a sort."

"Red Wave," Leia said. She was talking into her comlink. "Red Wave, are you out there? This is Pointer."

"Red Wave Two, here," Luke said. "Everything okay?"

"No, Red Wave, we're going to need a favor."

"Tell me what we can do to help."

CHAPTER TWENTY-SEVEN

HALF A DOZEN X-wing fighters screamed out of the sky, laser cannons blazing.

Han and Leia crouched behind the largest rock they could find, watching the carnage unfold. Baasen and Scarlet were several meters away, taking cover behind a rotted log as big around as Chewbacca was tall.

"First the Star Destroyer, now this. Farmboy went and got himself useful," Han said. "When did that happen?"

"There's more to him than you give him credit for," Leia replied, but most of her words were drowned out by a series of explosions.

The X-wings cut across the stormtrooper encampment at high speed. The strafing run's goal was maximum confusion, not accuracy. Even so, when the X-wings peeled off and streaked back up into the sky, one AT-ST and two of the anti-aircraft cannons were flaming ruins. The haze of smoke mixed with the mist from the swamp.

The stormtroopers had scattered, some running into the temple, more running into the jungle. A few brave souls held their ground, firing their blaster rifles into the sky. It made a pretty light show, but there was little chance the handheld weapons could pierce a T-65's robust shields.

"Give it another pass," Han whispered in Leia's ear.

"Then we go." He waved at Scarlet to get her attention, and when she nodded back, he mimed running with his fingers and pointed at himself. She nodded again and got into a crouch, ready to go, braced like a sprinter waiting for the starting gun.

The high, throaty roar of X-wing engines returned, followed by another barrage of fire. This time the X-wings had split up, each strafing one of the high-value targets. All of the remaining walkers and vehicle-mounted weapons exploded as the X-wings rocketed past, the ground around them detonating with high-energy laser shots that hurled mud and steam into the air. The remaining stormtroopers dived for cover as the ground heaved under the onslaught. Black smoke poured out of the destroyed equipment, clouding the field.

"Now!" Han shouted, and broke from cover at a dead run. Leia ran beside him, head down, legs pumping, blaster in hand. Han risked a glance behind and saw Scarlet and Baasen a few steps back. If anyone noticed them in the confusion and carnage the X-wing attack had brought, they kept it to themselves. No new shouts or alarms rang out, and in seconds all four of them had reached the dark opening into the temple.

Four stormtroopers were huddled just inside the entrance, looking up at the sky, waiting for the deadly X-wings to return. One of them glanced at Han, cocking his helmeted head to the side in confusion.

"Hey, you can't—"

Baasen shot him, then shot two more while they fumbled with their weapons. The fourth got his blaster out and pointed it at Baasen's face, but Scarlet dropped low to the ground and kicked out, sweeping the trooper's legs out from under him. He fell on the stone floor with a loud crack and went still.

Han poked Baasen in the chest. "Avoid shooting if you can. There could be a lot more of them in here."

"In *where,* boyo?" Baasen asked.

It was a good question. The antechamber they'd entered was a square space about the same size as the entrance. The walls were of the same cut stone as the exterior, though in the cool dark of the interior, a profusion of slimy molds and mushrooms grew from the rock. Some of it glowed with its own luminescence. A confusion of tunnels branched off from the entryway, heading in every direction. Except for the four cowering inside the doorway, there were no more troopers in sight.

"You have a map of this?" Han asked.

"Not yet." While the rest of the group moved into a dark corner to hide, Scarlet reached into one of the many pouches on her belt and pulled out half a dozen metal balls the size of human eyeballs. She held them in the palm of her hand, and they uncurled into metallic insect shapes, with translucent wings and glowing red eyes. She tossed them into the air, and they raced off down the various passages.

"The rebels pay for all those nifty toys, do they?" Baasen asked.

Scarlet grunted noncommittally. Han was pretty sure Scarlet's tools had been paid for by the people she'd stolen them from, but he kept the opinion to himself. She pulled out her datapad and fidgeted with the controls, and soon a glowing holographic map of the interior of the temple began to fill in. The corridors appeared as yellow tubes of light, with larger rooms shifting to orange, and occasional red dots scattered through them. Outside, the scream of X-wing engines started to ramp up again.

To Han's eye it was an impossible maze, but with deft gestures Scarlet rotated the map this way and that, nodding and talking to herself under her breath. She rushed into one of the smaller passages, gesturing impatiently for everyone to follow. They did, and moments later a squad of stormtroopers stepped into the antechamber.

Scarlet backed away down the hallway, watching them, then moved everyone into another branching passage, this one quite dark, so that the only light came from the glowing map. She fiddled with the controls, and the image dimmed until it was barely visible and cast no light on the walls.

"Looks like the alarm went out," Scarlet whispered. "There will be a lot of troopers in the central corridor." She pointed at a thick, yellow line on her map, filled with red dots. The dots were moving, and Han realized they must be marking the location of people that Scarlet's bugs had spotted.

"Do you know where we're going?" he asked.

She pointed at a large, glowing orange central room with a very small corridor coming off it and dead-ending. "This, at a guess. Lots of bodies in here, the most in the structure. And that's the only dead end on the map. A door, I'm guessing. And this temple doesn't seem to have any other ways out."

Leia made a quiet noise of agreement, then whispered, "But that's off the central corridor. Stormtroopers everywhere."

"All respect, miss, I see at least two other ways to get there, including this here corridor we're in," Baasen said, pointing at the map. As soon as he did, it was obvious. Han saw the path leading from where they were through a variety of twists and turns and ending up right next to the short dead-end corridor at the center of the temple.

"No troopers in this corridor at all," he pointed out.

"That worries me," Scarlet said.

Han's eyes had begun to adapt to the dark, and the faint glow of the mushrooms on the walls gave him a dim grayscale view of the hallway around him.

"Any reason we should be waiting here?" Baasen asked. He was rocking on the balls of his feet, his grin so faint it might just have been Han's imagination.

"Stay behind me," Scarlet said, poking Baasen hard in the biceps.

"Aye, love."

Scarlet turned off her map and headed down the corridor. The stone beneath their feet felt wet and slimy, though at the creeping pace Scarlet set it was easy to keep their footing. The air smelled of rot and decay, and a faint hint of something hot and metallic. After she'd gone a few dozen meters, Scarlet pulled a small light off her belt and turned it on, twisting the control until it gave off only the dimmest illumination.

A few meters later, they reached a partial blockage of the corridor. A stone cube a meter and a half on a side blocked the hallway from wall to wall, leaving only a one-meter gap above it.

"We can climb over," Scarlet started, but Han touched her arm and pointed at the ceiling above. "Oh." The block looked to have fallen out of a hole exactly its size.

"Temple falling apart, is it?" Baasen asked.

"No," Leia said, pointing at the ground next to the block. A single foot poked out from under the stone, wearing a white stormtrooper's boot. "It was a trap."

Scarlet turned up her light. The hall brightened. The hole above the stone had a complex mechanism for releasing the block onto the corridor below. A printed foil notice had been pasted to the wall: WARNING: DO NOT USE THIS CORRIDOR, IT HAS NOT BEEN CLEARED.

"I'd say," Baasen said, poking the doomed stormtrooper's foot with his toe. "Though this fellow cleared the first trap for us, eh?"

Han put a hand on the stone block. It didn't budge. It must have weighed thousands of kilograms. At least it would have been quick. But something itched at the back of his brain.

"Can we go?" Scarlet asked, trying to get around him to climb on top of the stone cube.

"This doesn't make any sense to me," Han said, thinking through the puzzle as he spoke. "We came here to find this super-high-tech thing that kills hyperspace, and it's in a temple made out of rock? The traps are deadfalls? Unless this hyperspace blocker is made of granite and powered by a waterwheel, I don't think these people built it."

"Ever seen a Ternin tree sling?" Baasen asked. "Don't look down on the damage a low-tech solution can achieve."

"But hyperspace blocking?"

"The K'kybak died out millennia ago," Scarlet said. "Another more primitive species may have followed them."

"And built all of this," Leia added, "to honor the gods that vanished from their world. It's not uncommon to find this sort of layering of civilizations on older worlds."

"I am not going to like it," Han said, then paused to boost Scarlet up onto the stone block, "if I get killed by a bunch of primitives."

Scarlet lay flat on the block and reached down to help pull Leia up. When Baasen moved forward, reaching for Leia's hindquarters, Han thumped him in the chest. "Hands off."

Baasen had the gall to look wounded. "Was just trying to give the lady a boost."

Leia clambered up the stone with ease. "The lady is fine, thanks. Let's move."

Having now seen the first of the ancient builder's deadly traps, Scarlet slowed her pace through the temple, keeping her light turned up. At several points, she had them avoid specific stones set into the floor.

"Pressure plates?" Han had asked at the first.

"Weird looking, and do we want to test?" she'd replied.

Han didn't argue the point, just avoided anything Scarlet

told him to avoid and tried not to touch the slime and mushrooms on the walls.

They reached a junction with two other corridors and Scarlet signaled for them to stop, then pulled out her map. "Almost there," she said, pointing at the room nearby. It was still filled with red dots. "We'll need a plan to get past those guards."

"What've you got in mind?" Han asked.

"My first thought was to send you and Baasen into the room, guns blazing, and then have Leia and me sneak past while the troopers loot your corpses."

"You see?" Han said. "That's a terrible plan. This is why we don't use plans. We're really bad at them."

"Well," Scarlet said, putting her map away, "let's keep moving, we can figure it out wh—"

Her foot came down on the large stone at the corridor's junction point, and it fell away as if it had never been there. A yawning pit gaped below it, opening into darkness. Scarlet paused for one eternal heartbeat, arms pinwheeling as she tried to keep her balance, one leg still on the ledge while the other hung out over nothing, then she fell forward.

Han's arm snapped out with a gunfighter's speed, the tips of two fingers just barely managing to catch a loose fold of her shirt. But it stopped her fall long enough that Baasen and Leia could dart forward and catch her arms. They pulled her back, hard, and she fell on her rump with a grunt.

"Thank you," she gasped as she fought to catch her breath.

"You'll want to watch your step in here, miss," Baasen said. "Traps and whatnot."

Leia crouched by the spy's side. "Are you all right?" She pulled the canteen off her belt and handed it to Scarlet, who nodded and took a sip.

When her breathing had slowed, the spy stood up and

ran a hand through her dark hair. "So, let's not do that again," she said.

A few twists and turns later, they crouched in the darkness of the side passage looking out into the large room beyond. At the far side of the room, what had appeared to be a short corridor on Scarlet's map actually turned out to be a steep ramp down. From their position, they couldn't see what lay at the bottom. A dozen or more Imperial troops were stationed in the room. About half wore the armor of stormtroopers; the rest were in technician's uniforms. They were looking at the main corridor as though expecting an attack from that direction. They were all armed.

"Only about four each," Baasen whispered. "I've faced worse."

Before Han could object, Scarlet said, "Let me give us some help."

Han pulled his blaster and noted that Leia had done the same. She smiled at him, though it was a sad smile. Han tried out a carefree grin and a wink. It felt false and ridiculous, but he tried not to let it show.

Scarlet was doing something with her map. Han heard a faint buzzing, and one of her six bugs flew past his ear into the room. It joined with the other five already there, and each one landed on a different stormtrooper. A second later, they detonated, knocking the six troopers to the ground. The other six spun around, looking for the attackers, but with Han, Baasen, and Leia firing from cover, all six were down before they could fire a shot.

"That was loud," Han said. "So we should go fast now."

He jumped up and ran across the room, hoping the other three were following but not slowing to check. He ran down the ramp, nearly slipping on the slimy wet stone, and flew face-first into a massive metal door.

"Don't touch it," Leia snapped at him.

"Too late," Han replied, probing his nose gingerly with one finger. It didn't seem to be broken.

The hatch was made of a gleaming alloy, almost seeming to glow with its own internal light. A complex-looking locking device was mounted in the center of the door, though it had been disassembled by the Imperial technicians. They'd hung a simple red button from it.

"Wait," Leia said, but Baasen was already reaching out. He pressed the button and the shiny metal hatch slid open, revealing a corridor below, sinking down into the crust of the planet. Baasen bounced on his toes and looked back to Leia.

"Sorry, miss. You said something?"

CHAPTER TWENTY-EIGHT

PAST THE GLOWING HATCH, the corridors changed completely. It was like stepping from one world into another without traveling the space between them. After a steeply descending ramp covered with thin, toothlike silver projections that snagged their toes and seemed to shift as they moved, the passage opened to a tall but almost impossibly thin network of corridors. Han thought the walls seemed to shift whenever he wasn't looking directly at them. The geometry of the corridors was wrong in a way he couldn't quite understand, the floors seeming to tilt in opposite directions at once. He had the eerie and inexplicable sense that the air was tasting him.

Han had seen the products of hundreds, maybe thousands, of alien species. He understood that each one had quirks of body and mind that made their artifacts and architecture unique. Whatever the K'kybak had been physically, their minds were unlike anything Han had ever encountered. The walls were built in curves of shining steel and deep-blue alloy that seemed to shift as they passed. Sometimes strange, flickering lights and sounds came, and Han couldn't say if they were the warnings of some ancient computer system, or art, or an accident of stress and pressure. Everywhere, the angles of the architecture seemed subtly off, the textures of the surfaces unpleasant, intimate, and threatening.

Every few hundred meters the Imperial survey team had left pale marks on the walls, and they crept along, following the path their enemy had established. Everything about the buried K'kybak civilization was beautiful and disturbing and left Han wanting to wash his hands. And apparently, the others were all thinking something very much the same.

"Creepy," Scarlet said as they entered a great, round room, perhaps half a kilometer wide, with long strands of chainlike metallic growths hanging from its ceiling. A clear, watery liquid dripped down the strands, leaving the wide floor slick and shining.

A drop landed on Baasen's shoulder with a splat. He wiped it off with mild, companionable disgust. "I can't say my sorrow these K'kybak aren't still among us runs all that deep."

"Speaking of which," Leia said, "do we have any idea of how far down this is supposed to go? It feels like we've been heading down forever."

"This way," Han said, gesturing with his blaster. At the far end of the dripping chamber, the path was marked by a backpack-sized box with a small red light at the top. Seeing something of recognizably human design in the unsettling place was a comfort, even if the make was Imperial. Tinny, compressed voices echoed down the chamber beyond. Stormtroopers. And they sounded frightened. At a bend in the hallway, Han held up an arm, stopping the others. He ducked his head around the corner, and pulled back. A solid sheet of blasterfire passed close enough that his cheek tingled with it.

"How many?" Scarlet shouted over the sound of the blasts.

"A dozen, maybe? Something like that," Han answered. "They're in front of some kind of machine. I think they're guarding it."

"The device?"

"How would I know? There were a bunch of stormtroopers shooting at me."

Scarlet's attention was already shifting to the walls and passages around them. Her narrowed eyes glittered with excitement and pleasure. Leia's gaze was fixed on the corner, ready to return fire if the enemy appeared. The barrage of energy bolts began to slow. A smoke haze filled the corridor with the smell of battle. Scarlet pulled out her datapad, but the holographic image on it was fuzzy and indistinct. She closed it again.

"I think there's a way to get around their side," she called.

"Good. You two, keep them occupied," Leia said. "Scarlet! With me. Let's find that flank."

Han and Baasen lifted their blasters as the women headed back toward the dripping chamber. Baasen fired casually toward the bend in the corridor and the barrage came again, louder than a landslide.

"Those boys seem a mite anxious," Baasen said.

"Wouldn't you be?"

"Oh, I am, old friend," Baasen said, firing his blaster again. "I very much am."

The minutes stretched as Han and Baasen baited the Imperial forces. Han kept expecting them to charge, but the assault didn't come. Whatever they were guarding, they weren't being drawn away from it.

Something loud happened around the corner, and a chorus of shouts and screams echoed down the chamber. Han and Baasen exchanged a glance, and then Han poked his head around the corner. Ten white-armored bodies lay on a wide grating in front of a vast, black archway. Scarlet and Leia stood over them, blasters in their hands.

"Good to see you ladies again," Baasen said. "We were just about to go looking for you."

"This isn't it," Scarlet said. On the far side of the archway stood a wide chamber. Its side was open like a window, and a massive shaft, wide as the whole room and the archway besides, slanted down into the darkness. A stormtrooper lay beside a complicated panel in the wall where a series of glowing switches showed patterns of red, green, yellow, and blue. Someone had taken a sheet of foil and etched the words GREEN GREEN BLUE RED—DOWN. RED BLUE GREEN YELLOW—UP. DON'T TOUCH ANYTHING ELSE.

"I take it we're at 'up'?" Leia said.

"One way to find out," Scarlet answered.

"Should we perhaps talk about this a bit first? Come to a meeting of the minds?" Baasen asked, but Scarlet was already flipping the top row of switches, the indicator lights shifting under her fingertips. A deep boom came, like the shooting of a vast metal bolt, and the chamber lurched, sliding down into the slanted shaft. The black archway fell away quickly, leaving behind the bodies of the stormtroopers. They descended deep into the darkness. The chamber picked up speed as it went, the breeze growing stronger. A new smell came to the dark air: something hot and sharp that reminded Han of a ship he'd been on as a boy when its engines failed and melted down. It wasn't comforting.

"How long do you think this has all been here?" Leia asked, and Han was ready to make a guess when Scarlet answered.

"Galassian's best guess was a few million years."

"Still works pretty well, all things considered," Leia said.

Five times they passed huge, arching chambers, flying by so quickly that Han got nothing more than a fleeting impression of vast metal lattices filled with shadows and flashes of light, and then the shaft swallowed them again, sloping even farther down into the darkness. The air grew warmer and thick without being heavy. Baasen stood at the leading edge of the chamber, arms folded, looking into the depths. Han stepped up beside him. It was easy to imagine that they were standing still, the passage flowing past them.

"A lot like being swallowed, ain't it?" Baasen commented.

"Now that you say it," Han said. "How deep do you think we've gone?"

"Fifteen, twenty kilometers," Baasen said. "Not much if you're flying a ship."

"A lot if you're climbing stairs."

"There's a truth."

The floor beneath them shifted. Han grunted.

"What is it?" Leia asked.

"We've started braking," Han said. "Wherever we're going, we're almost there."

Far down the slanting shaft, a glimmer of light appeared, fainter than a star. It grew slowly brighter, stronger. The chamber slowed as it came nearer. Han crouched down, wishing there were more cover. If there were another dozen stormtroopers at the bottom of the shaft, the arrival could be uncomfortable. The others all had the same thought, and as the room slid slowly to a halt they'd all taken what little cover there was.

The chamber butted gently up to a black archway the twin of the one at the top. The deep metallic booming came again as they stopped. Han stepped into the corridor beyond. The sound of tapping footsteps came down the hall. He readied his blaster. Baasen, Scarlet, and Leia all took positions along the wall. The echoes made it hard to tell who was coming or how many, but the sound was sharp and percussive. Not the tramping of combat boots. Han hoped it wasn't combat boots.

The protocol droid that came around the corner had a deep blue patina on his plating and a permanently surprised expression in his photoreceptors that seemed to suit the occasion. As soon as he saw the four of them, he paused. For a moment, no one spoke.

"Oh!" the droid said, then turned and started to totter off. Han and Baasen were after him in a flash, Scarlet and Leia guarding the rear. At the end of a corridor, a bank of three-meter-wide circles showed where doors would iris open. The droid was hurrying toward the one farthest on the left. Han skidded in front of him, hands up, palms out, the gesture of goodwill spoiled only by the blaster still hanging from his index finger.

"It's all right," Han said. "We're not going to hurt you."

"*You're* not," Baasen said.

"Master Essio will not have this! You must not disturb him! I will fight you to the death rather than let you through!"

"All respect," Baasen growled, stepping forward, "you're a *protocol* droid."

The droid squeaked in alarm, and a thin, sparking wire shot from his chest and struck Baasen's arm. The bounty hunter convulsed once, staggering, then pulled the tiny dart out, a little knot of blood and skin still on it.

"You see now," Baasen said, all hint of gentleness gone from him, "you just made my point for me."

"No! Don't hurt me!" shouted the droid. "Master Essio! Help! Help! The intruders have—"

"Ell-Three?"

The droid spun, his head clicking side-to-side, searching for the source of the voice. Scarlet and Leia stepped forward, silhouetted by the light from beyond the dark arch.

"Who's there?" the droid cried. "Who is it?"

"Forgot me already?" Scarlet said.

"The . . . the artistic tutor? But you're dead!"

"Not dead," Scarlet said. "And not an artistic tutor. Ladies and gentlemen, may I introduce Ell-Threepio, protocol droid and research assistant to Essio Galassian."

"You!" the droid squeaked. "It was you all along!"

"Actually, it was the gardener," Scarlet said. "Long story. Why don't you tell us what we want to know before my friend here reduces you to a thin, uniform layer of foil?"

"I will not betray the master!"

"Sure you will," Baasen said, and took a step forward.

The droid danced awkwardly back.

"No! Stop! Harming me will gain you nothing! The device has been activated. Master Essio is in the process of decoding its control schema, but the calculating controller is very odd. He . . . hasn't made a great deal of progress as yet. And the device hasn't been used in eons. It is not perfectly stable. I will not allow you to interrupt him. His work is too delicate and important."

"Where is he, Ell-Three?"

The droid looked back over his shoulder at the array of doors, his servomotors whining. His hand fluttered and clanked. Scarlet nodded.

"Ell-Three?" she said. "Do you remember what I said at the garden party?" The droid turned to her again, his eyes glowing suddenly brighter in surprise or alarm. "This is that day."

Scarlet's blaster bolt took the droid in the neck, neatly cleaving the headpiece from the blued shoulders. The droid's body froze and tipped backward, clanking against the floor. The head dropped to the decking, the eyes dimming, but not yet dark.

"You were a *terrible* artist," L-3PO said, and then turned off.

"Garden party?" Han said.

"Long story," Scarlet replied. "Let's go."

Han and Leia took position on one side of the leftmost

door, while Baasen pressed himself against the other. It took Scarlet a moment to find the controls, but a second later the door shuddered and the dozen blades slid apart.

Beyond it, a grate of steel mesh stood out over a cavern too vast to comprehend. A hot wind swirled and pressed, stinking of overheated iron. A dark-cloaked man stood at what looked like a long, glass table, his fingers shifting across its surface. Two spherical droids floated, one over each shoulder, dull red lights tracking slowly along their smooth surfaces. Han stepped out. The grating below his feet seemed too fragile to support his weight, yet it didn't flex at all when he stood on it. Far below, a massive sphere glowed a dull and sullen red. Han's mind struggled to make sense of the scale he was looking at. The wind moving past him murmured like something enormous and old, talking very softly. They were a hundred meters over the glowing orb. They were a thousand meters over it. Something in his mind struggled, and his sense of scale reset. He saw the room as if he were flying the *Falcon,* and then it made sense.

Still, it took his breath away.

"The planet. It's hollow. That down there," he said, pointing with his blaster, "I think that's the *core.*"

"I thought I gave orders to be left alone!" the man at the desk shouted. "Do you have any idea of the energies involved in this? How *delicate* this work is? Your constant interruptions could destroy us all."

"I know," Scarlet said. "But that's not going to happen."

The man straightened and turned. Essio Galassian was even younger than Han had expected, his face rugged and almost handsome. The shoulder-length hair that shifted in the wind was the same honey-blond that it had been in the R3's hologram, and his smile was bright and sharp as a blade's edge. His gaze flickered over them, spending the greatest time on Leia and Scarlet.

"Princess Leia, I presume," Galassian said. "And my former artistic tutor. I have to assume she was working for you."

"Essio Galassian," Leia said. "Toady to the Emperor and professional grave robber."

"Your service," Galassian said sourly.

"We've come for the hyperspace nullifier," Scarlet said. "Hand it over, and we might take you into custody."

"Rather than kill me?"

"Rather than leave you to your disappointed patron," Scarlet said, and Han saw the man flinch. The door irised closed behind them, and Baasen spun, blaster at the ready. The grate they stood on was one of a network that clung to the inner surface of the hollow world. Now that Han understood the scale, he could see platforms hanging from the stone roof that stretched all along the globe. Galassian leaned against the glass table and crossed his arms. The molten core of the planet spun below them like a sun, radiating heat and light, casting shadows up along the man's face.

Galassian looked at Leia for a long time. The two droids shifted, rising and falling, curving up through the air above him and swooping down behind his back in a sideways figure eight. His shoulders began to shake, and a stream of rich laughter poured out. He spread his arms.

"You want it? Fine. Here it is." His gesture encompassed the table, the platforms, the core spinning below. Everything. The humor left his eyes, and he looked like a corpse. "What do you plan to do with it?"

Leia and Scarlet looked at each other, the hot wind tugging at their hair. Baasen coughed and spat down through the grating and into the more-than-oceanic void beneath them.

"I've got to say," Han said, "I'd been picturing something a little smaller."

CHAPTER TWENTY-NINE

SCARLET STEPPED TOWARD Galassian, her blaster pointed at his heart. Han moved forward, too. The man ignored the threat and turned back to the glass table. The light from its display danced across his face.

"Back away from the table. Do it now," Leia said.

"Or else what exactly?" Galassian said.

"At a guess, we kill you," Baasen said from his place beside the door. "That's how these things tend to play out."

He might as well not have been there for all the attention Galassian paid.

"You have interrupted me. Threatened me. I imagine you must have killed some number of my escort? That was rude, Princess. I don't think I care to speak with you further." The spinning droids were going too fast for the eye to follow now, the curving paths seeming like streaks of silver air behind him.

"All right," Han said. "What's the plan?"

"Plan was we get in here," Scarlet said, "kill him, take the hyperspace-blocking device, and head back for the surface. Turns out there's a problem with the middle part."

"Maybe we should make a new one."

"Working on that."

"Once again," Han said. "Planning. Not our strong suit."

"We can hold him as hostage," Baasen said.

"What will happen," Galassian said, his voice calm, almost amused, "is that you will put down your arms, surrender yourselves to me, and hope that I'm feeling merciful. You have blasters? I am wielding the greatest weapon the galaxy has ever seen."

Baasen held up his blaster. "Our matched fours beats your high single, seems to me."

Scarlet shushed him.

"Bigger guns," Galassian went on, returning his gaze to the glass table. "Stronger blasters. Blowing up planets. It's all well and good. Controlling who can speak, now? Who can travel? That's power. The only use of violence is to convince people to do what you demand. If you have the power to simply enforce your will, why bother with wars? Rebellions? The Emperor will disband the fleet. There will be no need for it. Your kind is dead, and I'm at the trigger."

Han shifted to the right. The grating under his feet rang a little with each footstep. Galassian glanced up at him, sneered, and looked away. The wind tugged at his robes.

"You know what the Emperor will do with this," Leia said. "It won't be your power. It'll be his."

"My ambitions are small. Go wherever I wish. Do whatever I wish. Have worlds bow down before me," Galassian said. "I'll do quite well on his table scraps. But thank you for thinking of me."

"Enough of this," Baasen said, raising his blaster, and for once Han agreed. His finger twitched, but as the shot went off, Galassian gestured at him. One of the floating droids whipped out like an extension of his hand and knocked Han back. The bolt from his blaster passed over Galassian's shoulder, and Han struggled to keep his feet. Baasen, struck by the second droid, fell against the steel grating with a crash and a rush of breathless swearing. The droid swung down again, catching him hard in the ribs. Baasen rose to his knees, grabbed his side, and sank back to the floor. His face was flushed with pain and anger.

"Surrender now," Leia said, "and I'll see to it you aren't abused."

"Princess, take your servants, lay down your weapons, and stop wasting my time. I have many, many things to do that are all more interesting than you."

Leia shifted to the left, spreading out the group. It would be harder for Galassian's droids to block them all if they weren't so close together. Han followed her lead, moving a little more to the right.

"Don't flatter yourself," Leia said. "The Star Destroyer that brought you here is already vapor and meteors. A rebel attack group is preparing to jump into the system. And you're outnumbered four to one."

"Three to one," Galassian said, and before any of them could respond, he lifted both hands toward her, shouting. Leia shrieked as the paired droids swooped down, struck her in the belly and chest, lifted her from her feet, and threw her to the edge of the grate. And over it. Han's chest went hollow, and he rushed toward Galassian, blaster firing as Scarlet lunged for Leia.

Galassian turned on Han. The man's face twisted in a mask of inhuman rage. Han shot him.

Galassian stepped back as the bolt struck his chest. The surprise in his expression spoke of affront: *You presume to hurt* me?

"He's wearing armor!" Han shouted.

"So shoot his head, boyo!" Baasen shouted. Leia was screaming. Han glanced past Galassian to the edge of the platform. Scarlet lay flat, her chest and arms out over the void, her legs just beginning to tip up and over. From where Han stood, Leia was a flutter of motion and a sense of determined struggle.

A streak of silver went past him, and Han shot. Years of

practice and reflex paid off, and one of the droids fell out of the air, clanging on the decking and rolling toward the edge of the platform. Han dodged the second one. It seemed to have sprouted knives. Behind him, Baasen yelped.

Galassian's hand closed over Han's like a vise. The bones in Han's wrist popped, and a bright pain shot through his fingers as Galassian twisted the blaster away, holding it loosely in his left hand. The universe seemed to narrow to just the two of them as Han wondered what it would be like to be killed with his own weapon. He swung his other fist, and Galassian blocked it. Hitting the man's arm was like punching concrete, but Han did it again. Galassian struck back, hitting Han's face. His nose stung, and the taste of blood filled his mouth. The world seemed to ring like a gong.

Scarlet shifted. Only one hand was down to Leia. The other scrabbled desperately at her belt, looking for some tool. Galassian followed Han's glance, smiled, and shot Scarlet in the leg with Han's blaster. The spy yelped in pain, but she didn't drop the Princess or stop what she was doing. Han swung his elbow against Galassian's ear, and this time the strike had some effect. Galassian took two steps back and turned the blaster toward Han.

A bright bolt from Baasen burned the air. The old Mirialan was on his knees now, resting his firing hand on his stump. Galassian gestured toward him, and the remaining droid swept in toward Baasen's face, driving him against the wall and then looping around for another attack. The distraction was enough. Han grabbed his blaster, still in Galassian's grip, and twisted. Galassian bent his knees and turned.

The enemy was solid, strong, and implacable. Centimeter by centimeter, the blaster's barrel moved toward Han. Galassian pulled the trigger, and the blast singed Han's ear and filled the air with the stink of burning hair. Behind them something popped, and a thin line of cord, bright as a spiderweb in the gloom, shot up from where Scarlet and Leia struggled. Scarlet's grapnel line. Leia cried out.

Han put all his strength into moving the blaster away, but it continued to turn toward him. Galassian's grin was bloody, his teeth turned crimson. His eyes widened with the prospect of Han's death.

Baasen plowed into them both, slamming his full weight against them. Han sprawled out on the grate, disoriented and half convinced he'd been shot. Galassian kept his feet, but Baasen was before him, hammering at his throat with his one good fist. Behind them, Leia had her hands back on the decking and was pulling up her knee. The thin cord of Scarlet's grapnel was wrapped around her. Scarlet rolled to her side, blaster up, waiting for a chance to end Galassian, but Baasen was blocking her shot.

Galassian fell back a step under the rage and violence of Baasen's attack. There was blood pouring from half a dozen cuts on the man's face and from Baasen's knuckles. When the blaster shots went off—three in close succession—Han thought at first it was Scarlet. Then Baasen slipped down, smoke rising from his chest and a surprised expression on his face. He grabbed at the edge of Galassian's robes with his one hand, the stump of the other brushing against it as the missing fingers tried to find some purchase.

"Han!" Leia cried.

He looked at her as Scarlet fired. Galassian waved his hand, and the women scattered as the remaining droid dove in for them. Han put his head down and ran, charging Galassian with a roar. The impact felt like tackling a wall, but Baasen had hold of Galassian's ankle and, when the man staggered, kept his grip. Like a tree cut at the base, Galassian tipped back. Han saw annoyance turn to surprise, and then disbelief. A volley of blasterfire and a metallic shriek marked the death of the second droid, but Han didn't turn to look.

Baasen let go of Galassian's ankle as the madman disappeared over the edge of the platform with a scream. And then another one. And then another, each growing more distant as Galassian began the long fall to the planet's glowing core thousands of kilometers below them.

Han knelt at Baasen's side. The wounds in the old bounty hunter's chest were deep. The stink of cauterized flesh was bright and greasy. Baasen's yellow-green face was pale and his breathing shallow. He blinked up at Han, and Han was surprised by the thickness in his own throat.

"Hold on, old man," he said. "We're going to have to get you patched up."

"Han, old friend," Baasen said. "You always were a third-rate liar."

"What are you talking about? I lie with the best of them."

"Not that time."

Scarlet came forward, limping. The medpac in her hand looked profoundly insufficient. Han could see from her eyes that she was thinking the same thing.

"We got him, though," he said. "Just like old times."

Baasen bared his teeth in a kind of smile, turning to look through the grate over his shoulder. "I suspect he'll outlive me, for all of it. That is a powerfully long fall," he said, then gasped. "Truth is, if I'd thought for part of a second, I wouldn't have done that."

"The man you used to be is still down in there somewhere."

Scarlet pulled back the ruins of Baasen's shirt and doused the wounds with numbing spray. Baasen sighed and swallowed.

"If that's right and there's a world past this one, me and that man I was are going to have words in it. *Powerful* stupid, he was."

Leia came to stand by them. The glow of the planetary core streamed up past Baasen, casting him in shadows and brightening her face as she looked down. Her expression was calm, gentle, and strong. Baasen coughed again, and it was a deep, wrong sound.

"Y'know, Han, old friend. If I'd had both my hands, I think I'd have taken him," he said with a grin. "So there's a way this is all your fault."

"Same to you," Han said, but he said it to a corpse. He plucked Baasen's blaster up from the steel grating and put it in his own holster. The three of them stood over the Mirialan, silent for a long moment. Memories flooded Han of the times he'd known Baasen before.

"Turned out he was a good man," Scarlet said.

"No, he wasn't," Han said.

"A friend, then," Leia said.

"Not for a long time."

At last, they turned away, walking back to the lighted table that Galassian had been standing over. The bright surface was alive with strange letters and shifting designs. The script was like nothing Han had ever seen, and while some of the images—a circle more than halfway colored in red, a series of bars with triangles at different points along them—had the vaguely familiar, functional look of technical readouts, what they meant was opaque.

"Does any of this make sense to you?" Leia asked, scowling at the readouts as if simple force of will could make them make sense. Han was still shaking a little from the fight, and he tried not to show it.

"Maybe a little?" Scarlet said. "Let me . . . let me look at it."

"I was afraid you were in trouble for a second, Your Highnessness," Han said, but the barb sounded hollow and unconvincing. Leia looked up at him, and the softness in her face told him that she'd heard the relief in his voice. He might just as well have said *I thought I'd lost you.*

"No such luck," she said softly. He was surprised by the

power of his urge to sweep her into his arms and kiss her. For a moment, there was something else in her expression—apprehension or hope or something of both. She blinked and looked away. "Do you think he's still falling?"

"If they excavated the mantle down to the actual planetary core, he'll be falling for about the next five hours," Scarlet said, not looking up from the table. "The heat will probably sear his lungs and light him on fire before he makes impact, though."

"Couldn't happen to a nicer guy," Han said. "So can you work this thing?"

"No," Scarlet said.

"I thought you had the instructions."

"Galassian wrote the instructions, and he couldn't work it all, either. Not completely, anyway. Let me see what I can manage."

Han nodded, stepped away from the table, and tried to comm Chewbacca and the *Falcon,* to get some better idea of what was happening on the other side of the planet's crust. He had the irrational certainty that the full Imperial fleet had jumped into the system just after they'd gotten down to the bottom of the K'kybak ruins, and they'd be going up to a massive, ongoing firefight. There was no signal. He hadn't really expected one.

Baasen Ray's body lay still and silent, his eyes closed and his face the calm that seemed to come over all people in death. At peace. He'd been a good smuggler once, with all the bravado and addiction to excitement that they'd all suffered from to one degree or another. And then the universe had worn him down. Beaten him until he was a third-class bounty hunter carrying bad debts and desperation. Han could have gone down the same path, become another Baasen Ray. That he hadn't was equal parts luck and perversity of character. He didn't really see how he could take credit for either one.

Leia walked to him. Her blaster was still in her hand.

"Thinking about him?" she asked.

"Thinking he's the only man I've ever known who stole from Jabba the Hutt and died of something else," Han said. "And that he saved us."

"Complicated."

"The universe is a complicated place," Han said. "Unless you're Luke."

"You don't think he's complicated?"

"No. He's a farmboy who loves flying his fast ship. You don't get much simpler than that."

"He won't stay that way," she said, and there was regret in her voice.

"No one does."

CHAPTER THIRTY

"LOOKS COMPLICATED," Han said in what he was pretty confident was the universe's greatest understatement.

"It's a planet-scaled mechanism using technology we don't understand in a language that's not only alien, but dead. So a little bit, yeah," Scarlet said, pointing at the blinking device. "He did make some progress, though. If I can figure out which one of these was affecting the relays, I think we can— *Don't touch that one!*"

Han yanked back his finger. "That one? Is it dangerous?"

"I think so," Scarlet said. "This baby's channeling an impressive amount of energy. Galassian has a lot of notes about small imbalances getting big quickly. And, you know, a giant force field keeping the planetary crust from collapsing into the exposed core. Don't want to turn that off."

She tapped something and the screen lit up. She moved through several pages of translations of the control panel's runes and diagrams without slowing to read them.

"Can you tell what he was doing?" Leia asked, trying to read the information flashing across the table.

"Not really, no."

"All right," Leia said, grabbing Scarlet's hands to stop her from touching the panel. "General Rieekan is going to jump in with the strike force. Once he's here we can figure out how to keep any Imperial ships from jumping into the system. Then we'll have time to—"

The first blaster shot passed so close to Leia's face, Han saw the flash reflected in her eyes. A volley of shots followed it, but Han had already grabbed Leia and Scarlet and pulled them to the ground. He tried to cover Leia's body with his own, knowing it would only buy her a few seconds but doing it anyway. The first blaster shots that hit the fragile control board would blow it apart, and then there would be nothing between him and death.

Han turned to find whoever was shooting. The round door had irised open silently behind them, and a mass of stormtroopers had taken position just outside the platform. Several lowered their weapons to aim at him on the ground. *This is it,* he had time to think, and then they opened fire.

After several seconds of continuous fire from half a dozen troopers, they stopped. The thin sheet of what looked like glass that held up the control panel didn't even have a scorch mark on it.

"Huh," Scarlet said.

"I guess they built their stuff to last," Han said, then rolled off Leia and to his knees. He pulled Baasen's blaster and took several shots around the side of the control board. It was actually sort of nice to have cover he could see through. He could place his shots without having to risk sticking his head out. A second later, two troopers were down and the rest had ducked back out of the doorway. They reached their weapons around the edge to take a few indirect shots, but only one of them even hit the panel, and it did no damage.

"Still going to be hard to hold this position," Scarlet said.

"We have to reopen the hyperwave relays," Leia shouted. "If we can signal General Rieekan to start the attack—"

"Little busy right now," Scarlet said.

"We can't let them take control of it," Leia said. She

moved in a crouch to the other side of the panel and began firing at the doorway, forcing the stormtroopers to pull back.

As Han and Leia traded ineffective shots with the stormtroopers, Scarlet studied the control panel. "I think . . . I think I found the thing that's blocking the hyperwave relays from sending messages out. Maybe."

"Do it!" Leia shouted over the top of a fusillade of blasts from the stormtroopers. Han managed to drop one with a shot to the thigh, and the trooper dragged himself away from the doorway and out of sight. Han could see where his shots were landing, but he'd be much more accurate if he actually stood up and sighted down the blaster. Another wave of incoming fire splashing against the control panel convinced him it wasn't worth the risk. He didn't need to win this fight, really. He just needed to survive it.

Han pulled his hand back to avoid the next barrage of shots, but Leia leaned out and fired off a few blasts that downed another stormtrooper.

"How many do you think are left out there?" Han asked.

"Pretty soon it will be all of them on this planet," she replied. Scarlet grunted out a laugh but didn't look up from her work.

"At least Wedge and Luke guaranteed we won't have that Star Destroyer dropping reinforcements," Han said, firing off a couple more shots as punctuation. His blaster started flashing at him, so he pulled a charge pack from his belt and reloaded.

"Luke! We'll call Luke!" Leia shouted, scrabbling at her comlink. "Red Wave, this is Pointer, are you there?"

"Uh-oh," Han said to no one in particular. The stormtroopers were doing something just outside the door. He could only see the edge of their activity, but it looked as if they were setting up some sort of tripod-mounted heavy weapon.

"Red Wave, this is Pointer, come in!"

"Probably getting some interference from being so far underground," Scarlet said.

"One of us has to make a break for it," Leia said. "Get far enough up that we can ask Luke to tell General Rieekan to start the attack. And then get back down here so that we know when he's through."

"Another really bad plan," Han muttered.

Leia said something else, but it was drowned out by the massive concussion of the stormtroopers' heavy weapon. They'd wheeled it around the doorway and fired it. They hadn't taken time to aim, so the blast hit a meter and a half in front of the control panel. The thin grating of the floor instantly turned white with heat.

"I hope our cover can survive a hit from that," Han said.

"I hope the *floor* can," Leia replied.

The big cannon fired again, this time hitting the control panel's single fragile-looking support. The concussion of the blast knocked Han onto his back and sucked the wind out of his lungs. Both Leia and Scarlet were tossed across the floor, rolling to a stop several meters away.

The blast had left a discoloration on the support glass. A vaguely yellowish spot, with tiny hairline cracks running through it. They couldn't afford to let the troopers hit them again with the big gun. Not if it could actually damage the only thing they could hide behind.

Scarlet and Leia began crawling across the floor back to the control table. The stormtrooper crew manning the cannon were lining up a second shot. They seemed to have noticed the damage the first shot had done and were trying to hit the same spot again.

"Hey!" Han shouted. "You know that thing you're shooting at controls the planet, right? What happens if you blow it up? *You* don't know."

The stormtroopers ignored him. Han popped up, his

arms braced on the top of the table to get one clean, accurate shot. The trooper at the back of the cannon was just about to fire when Han's blaster bolt hit one of the supporting legs and blew it apart. The big cannon canted forward, pulling the gunner along with it. Halfway to the floor the weapon fired, hitting the grating just a little over a meter from the crew with a sound like thunder. The blast hurled the entire crew away. Two of them lay motionless and smoking. The third unlucky man went over the edge of the grating and pinwheeled down and out of sight toward the molten core. Han hoped for the stormtrooper's sake that the blast had killed him before he went over. A few other stormtroopers peeked around the corner of the doorway at the carnage. Han drove them back. The K'kybak control panel glowed under his arms.

He hesitated, then tapped at it and ducked back down.

"How are we doing?" he asked.

"I'm okay," Leia said, crawling back over to her side of the control board and taking cover, blaster in hand. She didn't look okay. There was a trickle of blood running from her hairline and down her cheek, and her forehead was bruised. She'd get upset if he pressed the issue, so he let it drop. Scarlet groaned.

"Are you all right?" Han asked the spy. The wound in her leg looked bad.

"I'm fine," she said, but she seemed a little unsteady. "I just need to . . ."

She wobbled up to her feet to look at the control board, which took her out of cover. The stormtroopers crowded the doorway to fire at her, too many for Han and Leia to drive back all at once. Scarlet yelped and dropped to her knee, clutching her elbow. The troopers paid for it, with two more dead before they could withdraw.

"This is getting old," Scarlet said. She was examining her upper arm, where a blaster bolt had burned through the flesh just above her elbow. It was another ugly wound, but it wasn't bleeding. "Can you believe today's the first time I've ever been shot? Years in the field, nothing. Today, shot twice."

"No!" Han said. "Anyone as reckless as you should be getting shot all the time!"

"Sort of thought it would never happen to me," Scarlet continued. Han hoped she wasn't going into shock.

One of the stormtroopers leaned out and tossed an explosive device. It rolled across the floor at them. Han shot it, sending it rolling in the opposite direction. The stormtroopers peeking out ducked back just before it blew up right outside their doorway.

"There might be a pattern, though," Scarlet said. Her eyelids were drooping and she started to sag onto her back. "We should ask him . . ."

"Sure, sweetheart, I'll give him a call. Whoever 'he' is," Han said. "Leia, grab her medpac and give her something to keep her on her feet."

Leia pulled the pack off Scarlet's belt and started rummaging through it.

"Did you hear what she said earlier? Force fields and tricky-to-balance energies?" Han asked. "That means we can blow this place."

"Are you insane?" Leia asked. "If we figure this device out, it ends the war."

"If—"

"It *ends* the war," she repeated, looking up from her work to stare him in the eye. Han didn't know how her eyes could be that soft and that hard at the same time. "No more Alderaans. No more Kiamurrs. Never again, Han. What is that worth? We stay here. We hold *this* position until General Rieekan comes."

A stormtrooper risked a quick look into the room, but

Han put a blaster bolt into the door frame right next to his face and he pulled back.

"We can't do it," he said, keeping his pistol trained on the same spot, waiting to see if the trooper would peek out again. "And even if we could, you're talking about making a government with absolute power to control travel. The first government that can enforce its laws without anybody slipping through the cracks."

Leia pressed an injection ampoule to Scarlet's neck, then began winding a bandage around her arm. The spy mumbled something unintelligible.

"This isn't the time for that conversation," Leia shouted. But a few seconds later she went on, "You say that like it's a *bad* thing. Only criminals would have anything to worry about."

Han laughed and fired a few shots at a trooper who'd looked around the corner to take a few desultory blasts at him.

"Leia, hate to break it to you. *We're criminals*. I'm shooting at the government *right now.* That's why they call it a rebellion!"

"We're fighting to restore—"

"Yeah, yeah, the glorious Republic of old," Han snorted. "I've heard the sales pitch, sister. But tell me this: if that glorious Republic had had this technology, would it have stopped Palpatine from taking control?"

Leia opened her mouth to answer, then closed it and frowned. Han stood up and fired off a few more shots at the doorway. No one was visible, but he wanted it to stay that way. Scarlet blinked and sat forward, rubbing her eyes.

"Probably not," Leia finally admitted. "By the time anyone realized what he was up to, he controlled the bureaucracy."

"And would there now be a Rebel Alliance?" Han asked

gently. He trusted her to see what he saw. He didn't need to browbeat her into it.

"No," she said. Her expression was almost hurt. "I'd never misuse this, you know. I'd never let anyone else, either."

Scarlet coughed and struggled to focus on them. "What are we talking about?" she asked, but they both ignored her.

"I know you wouldn't," Han said. "I trust you, Princess. But the guy who's elected after you? I don't know him."

Leia frowned and looked away. Something moved in the shadows on the other side of the doorway, and Leia took a quick shot at it. Whatever it was stopped moving.

"If we take this," Han said, using his blaster to wave at the massive machine all around them, "the next evil galactic empire that rises never ends. Does the fact that we probably won't be there to see it make you feel better?"

"No," Leia said. "No. You're right. Let's blow it."

Han let out a long breath. "I've got to admit, it's a huge relief to hear you say that," he said with a grin. Leia frowned at him, confused. Her eyes went wide.

"You already set it to collapse?"

"Yeah, that one thing Scarlet told me not to touch? I touched it about a minute ago. But I was having trouble figuring out how to break the news."

CHAPTER THIRTY-ONE

"WHAT DID YOU DO?" Scarlet asked, staring down at the planet's core as it shifted from dull red to a brighter orange. "*What did you do?*"

The platform trembled, and a hot wind blew up from below through the grating—a gentle presentiment of worse things to come. Han stood up, but a barrage of fire from the stormtroopers drove him back into cover.

"We can't get out the way we came in," he said. "Think I could explain to those guys that we should all be leaving?"

Leia didn't answer. "There." She pointed at a nearby platform where there was a set of irising doorways the twins of the ones on their platform. "We need to get to that one."

"Long jump, sweetheart," Han said. It was at least fifteen meters from the edge of their platform to the one she was pointing at.

"Your grapnel," Leia said to Scarlet. "Would it reach that far?"

Scarlet shifted her gaze between them, struggling to put Leia's question together with the one she'd asked.

"Yes," Scarlet said, nodding. She was moving her head too fast. The drugs Leia had pumped into her to keep her from going into shock were making her jittery. "But nothing to secure it to on this side. The magnet's only on the grapple end."

An electronic voice came from the doorway yelling, "Go go go!" and seven stormtroopers rushed into the room, shooting wildly. Han and Leia returned fire from cover, but Scarlet stood up and fired over the top of the control panel. When the troopers were finally driven back to the doorway, they left three of their number behind on the grating. Several blaster bolts had passed close enough to Scarlet to singe her hair and shirt.

"Please stop doing that," Leia said. "Getting shot three times in one day won't be better."

The core below shifted from orange to yellow, and the platform shook more vigorously. A gentle rain of dust and pebbles fell toward the core from the rocks above.

"We should leave now," Han said.

"There!" Leia shouted, pointing up at a bright metal support arm for the platform above them. "Attach it there. We should be able to swing across."

"Swing across," Scarlet repeated. "That's crazy."

"It'll work," Leia insisted. "Trust me."

Scarlet shrugged and handed her blaster to Han. She pulled the grapnel rig off her belt and programmed in the length of line she wanted.

"I'll be exposed while I'm doing this," she said. "And while we're . . . swinging across."

"I've got you covered. Get it set up," Han said. When Scarlet moved off to the edge of the ramp to line up her grapnel shot, Han went with her, keeping his back to her and firing into the open doorway with both blasters as fast as he could pull the triggers. When one started to flash a warning at him, he yelled, "Reloading!" and Leia stood up to take over covering fire while he slapped in a new charge.

The grapnel line flew off with a smooth hiss, the magnetic head striking the support beam with a thud. Whatever the beam was made of, magnets stuck to it. Scarlet leaned all her weight back on the line, and it held.

A few brave stormtroopers poked their heads around the corner to take shots, but the blistering return fire from Han and Leia drove them back. One of them caught a blaster shot in the eye of his helmet and dropped, half in and half out of the round doorway.

"Do we go one at a time, or all at once?" Scarlet asked.

"Oh, we're all leaving right now," Han assured her. "Leia, go, I'm right behind you."

Leia ran past him, but he was too busy firing at the doorway to watch her attach herself to the line. "Han, go!" she shouted, and a wave of blaster fire flew past him as she opened up on the doorway.

Han turned and ran to the edge of the platform, firing back over his shoulder as he went. Scarlet and Leia had both attached the end of the line to their utility belts, so Han just ran at them at full speed, dove into a bear hug around them, and launched all three of them off the edge of the grating.

Scarlet yelped when Han's arm gripped her injured elbow, and Leia gasped as he squeezed all the air out of her. Han looked down, nothing between him and the almost white-hot planetary core but a few thousand kilometers of empty space. Galassian's tumbling body was too far away to see. A second later they were above the next platform and Scarlet released the line. They crashed to the metal grating in a knot. Han wound up on the bottom, with Leia's elbow in his eye and Scarlet's knee in his stomach.

"Ouch," he said as they climbed off him. He didn't have time for more complaining, as a few blaster shots hit the grating and nearby wall.

Scarlet raced to open the platform's door, and Leia dived through, chased by incoming fire. Han stood and fired a few shots back at the stormtroopers, but at that range, any hits on either side would be completely up to luck. One of the remaining troopers wasn't firing, just looking across the gap at them, head cocked to the side in an obvious you've-got-to-be-kidding-me pose.

Han fired off a few more shots to keep them off balance, then followed Scarlet and Leia through the door. Scarlet shut it immediately behind him, and the sound of blaster shots hitting it echoed through the wall.

They were in a small chamber with one long, sloping shaft leading up at the end. A platform like the one they'd ridden down sat at the bottom.

"I hope that thing has power," Han said.

Scarlet limped toward it. "It seems like everything down here is still powered up."

"I hope you're right," Han said. "Because there's no other way out of this room, and going back out onto the platform right now seems like a terrible idea. Also, the planet is imploding."

Scarlet began flipping switches on the control panel, whispering to herself while she worked. Han heard the word "blue" and realized she was repeating the code from their last ride. His first thought was *I hope the same code means up;* his second was *How does she remember it at all?*

When the massive metallic clang came and the elevator started to climb, Han said a silent thank-you to whatever force of the universe protected heroes and fools. A new round of tremors hit, shaking the floor hard enough to knock him to his knees. Scarlet held on to the control panel to stay upright, but Leia was knocked onto her backside with a thump. Hot wind rushed past them, blowing Scarlet's dark hair into wings on the sides of her head. Han smelled hot metal and lubricant. He hoped the K'kybak had built their transport as well as they had their control panels.

When the shaking stopped, Leia climbed to her feet with a grunt and a wince. "I'm going to need a very long soak in a very hot bath after this trip."

"You know," Scarlet said to Han, eyes narrowing, "I spent two years of my life tracking down the leads that eventually led to this place. Two years of dangerous undercover work. And when we found it, you blew it up on a whim."

"Wasn't a whim," he replied. "It was intentional and well thought out."

"Don't blame yourself," Leia said to Scarlet. "With Han, it's easy to mistake well thought out for spur of the moment. They look exactly the same."

"As much as I'd like to argue the point, we don't have time," Han said, then pulled out his comlink. "Chewie, buddy, you there?"

The only answer was static.

"Chewie, I hope you're not sleeping, because we're all going to die."

That got a yowling response.

"We seem to be high enough to get through, if you want to call Luke with an update," Han said to Leia. As she nodded and turned her attention to her comlink, Han went back to Chewbacca. "We need the *Falcon* up right now. Get it over to the temple. Jungle's too thick there to land, so we'll climb up to the top for pickup."

Chewie rumbled out a reply and closed the connection.

"Again with the climbing to get picked up," Scarlet said with a sigh.

"No stormtroopers shooting at us this time," Han replied.

"No, you're right. Instead we get a planet blowing up below us."

"Just saying it's not *exactly* the same."

"You done?" Leia said to them. "We're almost at the top."

The room they found themselves in had a doorway leading out to the narrow, disturbing hallways they'd come in through. The glittering in the strange alloy walls seemed more frenetic now, as if the architecture itself knew it was in danger. Scarlet pulled up her datapad, but the holographic map was as fuzzy and imprecise as a dream. Scarlet closed it out, shut her eyes in concentration, and then a moment later opened them.

"Follow me," she said, and took off at a fast limp. Han shrugged and followed, Leia right behind.

Scarlet did seem to know where she was going. She took several turns that Han didn't remember from the first time, but at the end they wound up at the glowing metal hatch. The planet cooperated by keeping the shaking to a minimum while they made their way to the upper temple. But the minute they stepped foot on the stone floor, all restraint was lost. The planet shuddered like a bantha with spurs in its flanks, bucking and shaking as if it were trying to throw them off. After several seconds of tossing them from one side of the corridor to the other, the quaking settled into a sullen but constant low rumble.

"Run," Scarlet said. Han was already running, Leia's hand in his. He grabbed Scarlet's as he went by. If he lost either of them in the dark of the temple, he'd never have time to track them down.

If there were stormtroopers left at the site, they were hiding or had run off into the jungle. Imperial-issue equipment lay scattered on the ground, much of it knocked over by the quakes, some of it crushed flat by stones falling from the ceiling. As they sprinted, a massive block of stone the size of a landspeeder dropped from above and cut their passage in half.

Scarlet didn't hesitate, turning at the next junction and leading them through a side passage to get around it. Dust was filtering down from the ceiling, thickening the air. A pit in the floor opened a few feet ahead as they ran, and Scarlet yelled, "Jump!"

They didn't break stride as all three leapt across the abyss, then two turns and a long sprint later they were out in the free air of the dying planet.

All around them, the jungle was bucking and rolling like the surface of a stormy ocean. The massive trees cracked and split with the motion. Leaves the size of starships fell out of the sky, crushing anything beneath. Energy fields filled the skies with rainbows where the shear forces were enough to refract the light. The vast planetary mechanism was fighting to regain its equilibrium and failing.

Han jumped up, grabbed the edge of the first level of the pyramid-shaped temple, and pulled himself onto it. He reached down to help Scarlet up, then ran to climb the next level while she hauled Leia up. Far to the east, a cloud of dust rose toward the sky. When they'd gone up a dozen levels or so, the layers got shorter, allowing them to run individually and make much better time.

As he jumped from step to step a hundred meters above the rolling jungle floor, Han pulled out his comlink and yelled to Chewbacca, "Where are you?"

The Wookiee roared back.

"What do you mean the start-up cycle keeps shorting out? You better make this work, pal, or we're all gonna die."

Passing him, Leia pulled herself up onto a square stone block and stopped. They were at the top. Scarlet joined her and bent over at the waist, panting. Han looked around and saw nothing but the pyramid of stone below them and the quivering jungle all around. No ship in sight.

Scarlet gasped. Han followed her gaze. To the east, where the great plume of dust had risen, the ground was crumbling away. Island-sized swaths of jungle fell away, and the white-gold light of the unstable core blazed out. Whatever forces had kept the planet steady until now were failing, and Seymarti V was eating itself.

"Is he going to make it?" Scarlet asked. Han thought she meant Chewbacca, so he started to answer, but Leia cut him off.

"He should be here any second."

As if summoned by her words, an X-wing screeched out of the sky toward them. It came to a hovering stop a few feet from the top of the temple. Out of Leia's comlink Luke's boyish voice yelled, "Get on!"

Leia climbed onto a wing, and Scarlet followed.

"This is not a permanent solution," Han said. They couldn't exactly ride off the planet on the wing of a starfighter. But he followed. Buying himself a few extra seconds was what he did when it was all he could do.

"Hold on," Luke said, and the X-wing pulled up away from the temple.

The planet gave a massive shudder that blew trees the size of office towers into the sky, and the entire temple beneath them fell into the planet in a cloud of dust and stone and scorching hot air.

A black dot on the rapidly eroding horizon turned into a disk and then into the *Falcon,* flying at them at high speed. A cloud of pale yellow dust bloomed up around them, obscuring the ship for a moment. A hot wind stinking of sulfur whipped them, pressing grit into Han's eyes.

"I'm not going to be able to hold on for much longer," Scarlet said, her voice as calm as if she were talking about getting lunch rather than plunging to her death as the planet below her tore itself apart.

"You won't need to," Han said, and a dark shadow rose through the dust below them. The *Falcon* edged up a centimeter at a time until all three could drop onto it and scramble through the hatch.

"Punch it, Chewie," Han yelled as he ran to the cockpit. Chewbacca already had the *Falcon* flying straight up at its fastest atmospheric speed.

"Get belted in!" Han yelled to Scarlet and Leia.

"Hyperdrive working?" he asked as he settled into his seat. The Wookiee growled out an affirmative. "Get us a calculation for the current fleet position. We're going there in a hurry."

While Chewbacca worked, Han scanned the space around them. Eight X-wings flew in honor guard formation behind them. There were no Imperial ships in sight. The blue sky was streaked with clouds as jagged as claw marks. As he watched, the blue deepened to indigo, and the first scattering of stars showed through.

"Looks like we're all good for jump," Luke said, his voice compressed and flattened by the headset.

"That planet is looking unstable," Wedge's voice said.

"Noticed that," Han replied, throwing the throttle to maximum to put as much space as possible between the *Falcon* and the planet while Chewbacca finished prepping the jump.

"Be nice," Luke said. The sky was almost black now, the stars bright and wide and scattered.

"Be ready to jump," Han said to all the following ships, "in five . . . four . . . three . . . two . . ."

The planet detonated behind them, hurling a massive shock wave of energy and vaporized matter after them.

"One."

The stars disappeared in a swirl of light.

CHAPTER THIRTY-TWO

THE VAST, DARK OCEAN of space glittered with light. Each star was the chance of a habitable planet or moon, an independent station or asteroid base. The brightness beckoned and consoled, promising that there was life and energy and civilization all around. That the void could be overcome. And when the violence that life and stars carried with them was too much, the emptiness also offered safety.

The *Falcon* had jumped into the middle of General Rieekan's battle preparations. The young fighter pilots had been disappointed that a pitched battle around Seymarti had been avoided. The admirals had been relieved. The sting at losing the great new weapon was pulled by knowing that the Emperor didn't have it. If there were people who were relieved that the Rebellion hadn't captured the prize, either, they were quiet about it.

That didn't mean there was no joy to be taken.

"I've read the reports, Captain Solo," Colonel Harcen said, tapping uncomfortably on his desk. "You certainly went above and beyond any of our expectations of you."

"Thanks," Han said, ignoring the implied criticism. "So you're ready to pay me?"

Harcen's jaw stiffened and he looked at the decking. "I wanted to discuss that with you. I notice that your requested payment was somewhat larger than—"

"I signed on for a jump to Cioran," Han said. "We went from there to Kiamurr to Seymarti. Scenic route has more overhead."

"But the agreement—"

Chewbacca growled and leaned forward. Harcen flinched and leaned back.

"The option was to let the Empire kill everyone on Kiamurr, break the Rebellion, and get control of the K'kybak weapon," Han said. "If next time you want me to stop and renegotiate, we can do that, too."

"Of course not," Harcen said. "It may simply take a few days to arrange the transfer of the balance. I'll need to get approval."

"You do that," Han said.

Chewbacca howled and waved a massive fist. Han thought he was overplaying it a little, but he didn't complain. It was the simple pleasures, after all, that made life worth living. Han stood up, touched two fingers to his temple in mock salute, and headed out to the corridor.

The comfort he felt getting back to the rebel fleet with its cobbled-together ships and thirdhand air recyclers made Han a little nervous. He didn't like to think he was getting too attached, but so far he'd dealt with that by not thinking about it, and the strategy seemed to be working. Together, he and Chewbacca headed down the narrow metal stairway, then turned to port and headed for the fighter hangar and the *Millennium Falcon*. Neither spoke, but Chewbacca huffed quietly under his breath. It was something he did when he was feeling particularly self-satisfied. There was even a little spring in the Wookiee's step. As they stepped out into the chaos of ships, tool kits, coolant-delivery tubes, service droids, and orange-jumpsuited pilots, Han leaned in toward him.

"And what's got you in such a good mood?"

Chewbacca yelped twice, lifting his chin to indicate the hangar and everyone in it.

"Of course we didn't die," Han said. "We were safe the whole time."

Chewbacca let out a chuffing whine.

"Because *I* was there," Han said. "That's why."

"Han!"

He turned. Luke waved from the side of the hangar, and beside him, C-3PO echoed the gesture. Half a dozen other fighter pilots were gathered around them. Han thought he saw the glimmer of hero worship in some of their eyes. Han waved back, then looked toward the *Millennium Falcon.* The scar where Baasen's homing beacon had struck home was still bright, and the panels above the rear deflector shield were off, exposing the wires and energy couplings beneath. The thought of the hours of work ahead made Han's shoulders ache. It could wait a little bit longer.

"Hold on a minute, Chewie," he said. He sauntered over to the group. "Hey, kid. What's going on?"

"I was just telling Gram and Ardana about what happened at Seymarti," Luke said.

Han nodded, a knowing half smile on his face. He turned to the other pilots. "He tell you how he took down an Imperial Star Destroyer by himself?"

"I didn't do it by myself," Luke said. "There were eight of us, and Wedge led the attack. And no, I was telling them about how you and Leia blew up the planet in order to stop the Empire."

"Yeah. Well, all right. That's a good story."

"Did you really ride up out of the atmosphere on the outside of an X-wing?" one of the pilots asked. She looked even younger than Luke. Pretty soon the Rebellion was going to be taking them out of diapers and putting them straight into pilot's seats, Han thought. He shrugged.

"It wasn't as impressive as it sounds," he said. "Chewie was right there to catch us."

The pilots' gazes all turned to Chewbacca, who stood a little taller and preened.

"What are you guys doing next?" Luke asked.

"If there's not another emergency, we're fixing the ship," Han said.

"What about after?" the younger pilot asked.

"I'm pretty sure there'll be another emergency by then," Han said. They all laughed like it had been a joke. And it had been, mostly.

"I was just going to go see Leia," Luke said, stowing his helmet. "You want to come?"

"You want me to?" Han said, and then when he saw Luke thinking about the question, quickly added, "Sure, why not? Her Worshipfulness might be able to get them to shake my credits loose a little faster."

As they passed through the ship, Han listened to the chatter around them. Most of it was about Kiamurr and Seymarti, but there was other news and gossip. A fleet of unidentified black ships had been sighted near Thedavio VII, and no one knew if they were some kind of new Imperial design or something different. The uncle of a friend on Dantooine had been in a cantina when a bunch of Imperial troops had swooped in and carried off the barkeep. The survey mission to Cerroban had run into Imperial probes, taking it off the list of possible locations for the new base.

The Rebel Alliance was built on stories as much as it was steel or hyperspace engines. What had happened on Kiamurr and Seymarti was thick in the air right now, but new events would come and wash it away. It wouldn't be long before the fact that Han could have ended the war and didn't, or that the Empire could have had its foot on the neck of the galaxy forever and he'd stopped it, were just bits of trivia, easy to forget in the press of stories that the Rebellion told about itself.

They found Leia in a meeting room off the command center. The screens around the walls were bright with schematics of the ships in the fleet, a map of the galaxy with half a dozen tiny sectors marked off in blue, and a constant feed from the sensor logs. The little red R3 unit that Hunter Maas had owned was in a corner with R2-D2, the pair of them whistling and chirping away to each other while C-3PO shifted his head back and forth between them, trying to keep track of the machine-language conversation.

Leia was wearing a simple gray jumpsuit, and her hair was pulled back. Scarlet Hark, sitting across from her, was a thousand times gaudier in a flowing gown of emerald and crimson, with her hair braided in an elaborate curve that made her seem like a human flower that had just bloomed.

"Solo!" the spy said. "I was hoping I'd see you before I left."

"Sure," Han said. "You're looking . . . ah . . ."

"Ridiculous, isn't it?" Scarlet said, a mad gleam in her eyes. "I'm Feyyata Baskalada, queen of the Emurrian opera, on tour with the company. We're going to Surdapan Station."

"A very dangerous place," C-3PO said, waving a golden arm. "I have tried to warn them, but no one ever seems to listen to me."

"Uh-huh. What's happening there?" Luke asked, visibly trying not to stare at her.

"Rumor has it that an engineer out there built a blaster that ignores deflector shields," Scarlet said. "It's probably bantha fodder, but if it's not, I want to make sure we have it and no one else does."

Leia frowned. "Can you sing opera?"

"No," Scarlet said. "Not even a little bit. This should be *hilarious*."

From the corner, Hunter Maas's R3 squealed. Scarlet stood up, her dress clinking like a crystal chandelier in a breeze.

"Thank you, R-Three," she said. "I know we're short on time."

"Wait," Han said. "You understand what it's saying?"

"No, but I guess well," she said, putting out her hand. "Thanks for the ride, Captain. I hope we can work together again sometime."

"It'll cost double," he said, shaking her hand. "You're a pain in the behind."

"Likewise."

Chewbacca grunted and muttered, folding his arms across his chest. Scarlet paused in front of him, her palm on his hand.

"Me, too, sweetheart," she said. "But I'll be in touch. When I can."

Chewbacca swept Scarlet up in a massive hug. She wrapped her arms around his neck, and they stayed that way for long enough that Han started feeling a little uncomfortable. When the Wookiee put her down, Scarlet gestured to the R3 unit, and the two of them left together.

"Are you tearing up?" Han asked.

Chewbacca barked a sharp reply.

"All right," Han said. "Just asking. No need to get hot about it."

"We just wanted to come make sure you were doing okay," Luke said, touching Leia's arm. "After you got back, you seemed a little . . . upset."

Han looked up at Chewbacca and mouthed *She did?* Chewbacca rolled his eyes and nodded. Leia patted Luke's hand and sat down.

"I'll be fine. There's been a lot of fallout after Kiamurr. We lost a lot of people," she said, and her voice had a cold tone that Han thought he might understand. "But the ones who did survive have renewed their hatred of the Empire. I've had contacts from several people and groups that I hadn't expected to hear from. We'll come out of this stronger than we went in."

"That can only be a good thing," C-3PO said.

"It will be if we win, Threepio," Leia said. *And if we lose, it's just more bodies in the graveyard.* She didn't say the words, but Han understood her humorless smile. He thought of Baasen again. The least likely martyr of the Rebellion. The universe was a big place, and strange things happened there.

From the command center, Commander Ackbar's voice grated and snapped. Han didn't recognize the voices that responded.

"Any regrets?" Luke asked. From anyone else, the question would have seemed like prying. From the kid, it was too openhearted and sincere to take offense at. Leia shrugged. "Some," she said. "But I don't know what I'd have done differently. Regret that I couldn't find a better way through than the one I found. Does that count?"

"What about you?" Luke asked, and it took Han a few seconds to realize Luke was talking to him. He opened his mouth to say no, then paused, shrugged.

"You know," he said. "There were a bunch of critters on Seymarti who were just trying to make it through another day in their crappy little swamp. They didn't deserve what happened to them."

Leia raised an eyebrow.

"That's your regret?" she said.

"Why not? It's a good one."

"What about having the key to end the war in your hand and choosing to throw it away?" Leia said, her voice a little hard with sorrow. Just for a moment, he saw behind her façade. From this moment on, she would be carrying a little more of every death in the war. Every adolescent fighter pilot who got shot down by a TIE fighter, every spy who got exposed and executed in an Imperial prison, every foot soldier who fell under a stormtrooper's blaster rifle would be in part because she'd had the chance to take the power of the K'kybak and Seymarti V, and she hadn't.

It was easy to forget that she'd seen Alderaan die. She hid the guilt of surviving so well that it could blend right in with the normal pressures of commanding an army. Or leading a rebellion.

He thought back to all the things he'd said about Kiamurr. He wanted to say something comforting, but he wasn't sure what that would be. Han made do with answering the question.

"It wasn't the key to stopping the war," he said. "It was the key to stopping anyone ever from doing something I didn't like. Stopping the war would just have been the start. And who wouldn't have done that? Who wouldn't have used it to keep some innocent people alive and stop the thugs from getting more power? Something like that, though, you can't stop once you've started."

"Too much responsibility?" Leia asked. The barb felt almost like he'd offered her an apology. Almost like she'd accepted it.

"The responsibility's not the problem," he said. "A galaxy without smugglers and thieves? How's that a better place? No, Your Worship, you've got to leave some room for people like me."

"Do I really?" she said.

"You really do," Han said. "Sometimes you *are* people like me."

Leia's gaze softened a degree. Luke looked from one to the other of them, a hint of confusion in his bright blue eyes. For a trembling moment, something dangerous seemed about to happen, but then Leia pulled back. Her smile turned sardonic and the façade fell back in place.

"Sometimes I am," she agreed. "But then I bathe."

Chewbacca snorted and Luke chuckled, looking relieved. Han held up his hands. "Fine, sweetheart. You can say anything you want. We both know how you really feel."

"You aren't still pretending I was jealous of Scarlet Hark, are you?"

"It's nothing to be ashamed of," Han said. "I'm a good-looking guy. And back on Cioran, I really didn't have a choice. I had to take my clothes off."

"Why did you have to take your clothes off?" Luke asked.

Han shrugged. "They were wrinkled. That's not the point. The point is it's perfectly normal for a woman—or in this case two women—like her to be attracted to a man like me."

Chewbacca howled.

"She did turn away, yeah," Han said. "But, you know. She probably peeked."

"She did," Leia said.

For a moment, the room went silent. Han felt a blush rising up his neck and fought it back.

"See?" he said, poking Chewbacca's knee with a finger. "She peeked."

The Wookiee didn't answer. Around them, the business of the war went on, as it would for the months or years until one side or the other won. Han wondered, when that time came, if he'd still be a rebel, and whom he'd be rebelling against.

"You know," Luke said after a while, "with Seymarti and Cerroban out of the running, there aren't a lot of places left we can build the new base."

"As long as it's not Hoth," Han said. "That's a miserable planet."

"We'll find something," Leia said. "It won't be easy, and it won't come without a cost, but we'll find it. We always do."

STAR WARS™

SILVER AND SCARLET

JAMES S. A. COREY

"SEDDIA CHAAN," the guard said, repeating the name on my identification papers.

"Yes," I lied.

He handed the papers back, nodded his massive green-gray head, and stepped aside. I tried for the cool, polite smile I imagined a high-level arms manufacturer would spare to a doorman and walked into the club. After the heat and humidity, stepping into the cool, dry air was like arriving on another world. Oolan was a barge city on an open sea, its buildings linked by bridges and separated by canals in a constantly shifting architecture. This month, the currents had taken it north, almost to the planetary equator. Next, it might drift south until blue-green ice pounded against the buildings' foundations and frost covered the bridges' handrails. By then I planned to be back with the rebel fleet, deliveries made and my latest false-self a fading memory. If I was still in Oolan tomorrow, it would mean something unexpected had happened.

Given my track record, it could go either way.

The private club was built as a single wide circular room with windows three meters high at the outer edge. At the center, a hub of black made up the private meeting rooms and lifts to the upper levels. A recording of Bith harp music filled the air, the reproduction so clean the notes felt like they had edges. Outside the great windows, the city curved up, shifted, fell away, then curved up again, carried by the ocean swell. A dozen brightly colored skimmers buzzed along the canal, the human and Quarren drivers seemingly in competition to see who could be the most reckless. I tugged down on the hem of my jacket and looked around casually at the dozen or so club members lounging at tables and couches. The man I was looking for was human, older, and I'd seen only pictures and holograms of him. Trying to seem nonchalant, I touched my comlink.

"Elfour?"

"Ma'am," the droid's deep, gravelly voice came.

"How sure are we that he's here?"

"Ninety-six percent certainty."

"Okay, so run down that last four percent for me."

"The general might have been discovered, and the individual who rode his flyer down from the orbital base might have been an impostor," my lookout droid said. "Trouble inside, ma'am?"

"Just trying to find him. Let me take another pass," I said, and dropped the connection. Seddia Chaan, security engineer for the Salantech Cooperative, would have marched around the room with the crisp, studied movement and impassive expression of the ex–military operative that she was. Since I was playing her, I faked it. A serving droid floated to me and asked in a carefully designed voice whether it could bring me anything to drink. Seddia Chaan didn't use intoxicants, so I asked for tea. The men and women at the tables and couches glanced at me and then away, polite and distant in a way that would have told me I was at the heart of the Empire even if I'd woken up there with my mind blanked.

I'd started the operation months before, following a rumor that the warden of an Imperial political prison might have been growing sympathetic to some of his prisoners. It had taken weeks to run down, since it wasn't an Imperial warden, there wasn't a prison involved, and General Cascaan didn't actually have much sympathy for the Rebellion. But apart from every single bit of information being wrong, things had gone pretty well. I'd tracked Cascaan to the Entiia system, found his clandestine lover in Oolan, and opened negotiations. The whole process had been about as safe and certain as balancing a Verdorian fire rat on my nose, but I'd managed it, all except the last part. The actual meeting and exchange.

I was on my third time around the room and almost done with my cup of tea when I recognized him. He was sitting alone at a small, high table almost against the window. His hand was pressed to his mouth, his gaze fixed on the glittering crystal and silver of the complex across the canal from us. Once I spotted him, I could forgive myself for not recognizing him at once. All the pictures I'd seen had been of a straight-backed, high-chinned man with bright black eyes and a challenging glare. The man at the table was slumped over. His dark skin had an ashen tone, and his eyes were wet and rheumy. When he shifted in his seat, I could see the physical power in his body, but when he was still, he looked like someone's grandpa.

In my work I'd seen the whole spectrum of betrayers, from the ones who were afraid of getting caught to those who were excited by being naughty to others for whom it was just business. The man at the table wasn't any of those. He looked sickened by it. That was bad. I put on Seddia Chaan's cool smile and started over.

"Ma'am?" L4-3PO said.

"It's all right. I found him."

"We have another problem. A flyer has landed on the tower's upper pad. Registration identifies it as the private craft of Nuuian Sulannis."

"Maybe he's a club member," I said, not breaking stride.

"The chances of the Imperial interrogator who has been

investigating the general arriving at the meeting by coincidence are—"

"I was joking, sweetie. Thank you for the warning. Talk to the club's computer system if you can, and try to slow him down. I'll be quick."

"Yes, ma'am."

I slid into the chair across from Cascaan. He looked up, and for a moment surprise registered in his eyes. Then a slow, rueful smile. "You're Hark, then?"

"Yes, sir," I said.

"I was expecting a man."

"That's a common prejudice," I said. "I won't take it personally."

I plucked the credit chit out of my jacket pocket and placed it on the table. The black tabletop made the silver chit seem brighter than it was. The general scowled at it and took a red-enameled memory crystal from his pocket. I waited, forcing my body to stay relaxed and calm while the sense of the chief interrogator landing his ship five levels above me crawled up my spine.

"I take it those are the plans we discussed?" I said, trying to make it sound casual and still keep the ball rolling.

The general scowled and nodded at the same time. The grip of his finger and thumb on the memory crystal didn't relax. I had the sense that if I reached out for it, he'd pluck it away from me. When he spoke, his voice was low and precise.

"Have you ever betrayed something?"

I felt my heart drop into my belly. Last-minute changes of heart were always a hazard in this kind of operation. Usually, I could budget a few hours to get the target drunk and maudlin, sing a few songs about glory and lost love, and pretty much provide whatever hand-holding and consolation they needed to make the exchange. This was not one of those times. If he decided to turn me down, the plans for the next-generation Star Destroyers would fade away from me like smoke in a fist. Also, I'd probably get killed. Not the outcomes I was aiming for.

"I have, but not lightly," I said. "I always had my reasons."

"Do you regret them? Your betrayals?"

"No."

He dropped the memory crystal into his palm and closed his fist around it. There were tears in his eyes. In other circumstances I would have found the gesture less frustrating. "I have been a loyal subject of the Emperor. I have followed the orders of my commanders. I told myself we were bringing order to the galaxy because that was what they told us. Who was I to disagree?"

I leaned forward and put my hand gently on his wrist. "I understand," I said.

"If we do this thing," Cascaan said, "I will be responsible for the deaths of thousands of soldiers."

"And if we don't? How many people will die if we call the whole thing off? And will they be soldiers or innocent people who happen to live on worlds the Emperor has decided don't pay him enough respect?"

"No one else has access to these. When they get out, it will be known that I have turned against them. They will slaughter me for this."

His fingers didn't loosen their grip. I switched tack, taking my hand off his and tapping the silver chit. "There is enough money on this to make you safe. You'll be able to fade into the Rim, find a quiet spot, a new name. A new face. You'll be all right."

"Will I, Hark? Does my conscience count for nothing?"

Don't rush him, I told myself. *He's already halfway to spooked, and if you hurry him, he's just going to freeze up.* I took a deep breath, let it out slowly, made my shoulders relax and my expression soften. The serving droid hissed up to my left with a fresh cup of tea. The city outside the windows rose and fell.

I had maybe two minutes.

"Of course it counts," I said. "I'm getting the sense, sir, that there's something you want to tell me."

"You know I commanded the assault on Buruunin."

"I do," I said. "I lost people I cared about in that attack."

"The cities were undefended," he said. "As soon as we received the order for the bombardment, I knew I would have to betray my Emperor. My Empire. Those deaths brought no order. Only fear. They were wrong."

"Didn't call off the attack, though," I said, more sharply than I should have. He didn't flinch or tighten his grip on the plans.

"It would have made no difference. I would have been executed, and my second in command would have given the order. Insubordination is a fool's way to die. I have my honor, but I am not a fool."

I had maybe a minute and a half. This wasn't going well.

"Afterward," General Cascaan said, "there were any number of collaborators. They came to every outpost we made, mewling and crying, telling us that they had information for sale. Where the rebels were hiding, who had aided them, where their caches of weapons were. For a few credits, they would have informed on their mothers."

"They were desperate," I said. "They were afraid."

He turned to look at me straight on. I hadn't realized until now that he'd been avoiding my eyes. There was a pain in his expression that took my breath away. I'd been working underground for a long time, and somewhere along the way, I'd let Cascaan and men like him turn into a kind of faceless enemy to me. Well, here was his face, and the four-square leader of soldiers wasn't in him.

"*I* am desperate," he said softly. "*I* am afraid. Those people I despised—and I *despised* them, Hark—I have now become. I am selling the trust I have been given for money. For safety. For the beautiful lie that I can be a better man by making this devil's bargain."

"They were refugees of a planet-wide military attack. You're one of the most powerful men in the Empire," I said. "Seems to me, you're in a kind of a different position."

"And does that speak better of me? Or worse?"

"Better," I said, mostly because it seemed like the answer most likely to get him to open his fingers. I wondered, if I lunged for him, if I'd be able to get the plans and run out the door before anyone tackled me. It didn't seem likely. And if I told him we were both about to get arrested by the Empire, I didn't like my chances for moving the process forward.

"I disagree," the general said. "This trade is ignoble. It leaves me no better than them. I cannot take your money."

He was backing out. My comlink chimed. Grimacing, I touched it. "Bad time, Elfour. Kind of in the middle of something."

"Ma'am, I have done all that I could. That . . . *situation* will require your attention."

Cascaan had opened his grip. The red enamel caught the light from the window, shining in his palm like he was cupping a handful of blood. I looked over to the dark wall of private rooms and lifts at the club's center.

Time for plan C.

"Can you hold that thought?" I said, holding up a finger. "I'll be right back."

I walked toward the lifts, thinking through all the ways this could go and how I could affect which one actually happened. The serving droid swooped in to see if I wanted something for my tea, and I waved it away. I couldn't tell if my unsteadiness was caused by the adrenaline or if the city had hit some bigger waves than usual.

"Elfour," I said into my comlink. "Do we know where he is?"

"Interrogator Sulannis is in a lift, coming toward the main floor, ma'am."

"Can we shut down the lift?"

"I have already done so once, ma'am. He is using his security override. I am locked out."

A whole host of solutions crumbled and died. On the one hand, less to think about. On the other, they were the ones I liked best. I was over halfway to the center. "Which lift is he in?"

To my right, a lift door slid open and an older Quarren woman stepped out. Not Sulannis.

"Elfour, which lift is he in?"

"Querying, ma'am."

"Sooner's better."

"Six."

I angled off to my left, not running but walking faster. My choices were getting thin quickly. The coppery taste of panic filled my mouth, and I ignored it.

The lift doors were black enamel and smooth as a mirror. I made my reflection look calm, prim, maybe a little bored. The difference between safe and too late was going be seconds. The doors shuddered and slid open. Nuuian Sulannis stood in the lift car, the light seeming to fall into his black uniform as if it was woven out of black holes. He started to step out, and I faked my way in front of him, then corrected when he did, making it into a little dance of awkwardness and social misstep. His scowl could have peeled the shell off a Keeb beetle.

"Sorry," I said. And then, "Aren't you Interrogator Sulannis?"

He had time to register surprise, and I planted a straight kick just above his pelvis. The blow was designed to stagger him back, and it worked. The lift doors slid closed, and I slipped between them as he regained his balance. I pushed the controls for the landing pad.

Close-quarters fighting, especially when the opponent was so much bigger than me, meant grappling techniques. I started with an elbow lock, but he shrugged it off through equal parts luck and brute strength. He hit me twice in the ribs, but the cramped lift car made it hard to get much power behind the blows, giving me the opportunity for a leg sweep that took him down. Once I got my arm around his neck, it was over, but the choke took long, terrible seconds to take effect. When he finally went limp under me, we were already at the landing pad. I hit the controls to take me back down before anyone could see a disheveled weapons engineer straddling the uncoscious body of an Imperial interrogator.

I had one dose of sedative left in my shoe. I used it on him, stopped the car on the third level, dragged Sulannis to the women's room, and propped him in a stall. All in all, it took less than five minutes.

On the way back down, I tugged my costume back into place, smoothing out the wrinkles while I tried to think how to coax the general back into making the trade. As soon as the lift doors opened, I knew it was over. The little table we'd been sitting at was empty. Cascaan was nowhere I could see. Little wisps of steam wafted from my cup of tea as I came close. The sinking in my gut was disappointment and anger and frustration, but there was something else, too. Some part of my mind that told me I was missing something. This wasn't what it looked like.

"Ma'am?" L4-3PO said on my com link. "Is all well?"

On the black table, the silver chit with Cascaan's payment glowed. Beside it, the bright red of the memory crystal. He'd left the plans and the payment, too. He was going to get caught, and he knew it, and there was nothing I could do to stop it. When I looked up, he was there. Outside the window, walking across the canal bridge and away from me. His back was straight and proud, his head high. It was the first time he'd seemed like the man from the holograms. A warrior, ready to fight. Ready to die.

I scooped up silver and red and put them in my pocket before I touched my comlink. "Time to go. Get the skimmer warmed up, and let's get back to the ship. We need to be out of here before Sulannis wakes up."

"Yes, ma'am," the droid said. "May I ask whether you got what you came for?"

"I did," I said.

"And the general?"

Cascaan reached the other side of the bridge, turned right, and stepped out of my line of sight.

"He did, too."

ACKNOWLEDGMENTS

The authors would like to thank Shelly and Jen, and Anne Groell for making the introduction, and all the *Star Wars* fans who still have their seven-year-old selves sitting in a dark theater in wonder and delight. And Danny, because he rocks.

The STAR WARS Legends Novels Timeline

BEFORE THE REPUBLIC
37,000–25,000 YEARS BEFORE *STAR WARS: A NEW HOPE*

c. 25,793 YEARS BEFORE *STAR WARS: A NEW HOPE*

Dawn of the Jedi: Into the Void

OLD REPUBLIC
5,000–67 YEARS BEFORE *STAR WARS: A NEW HOPE*

Lost Tribe of the Sith: The Collected Stories

3,954 YEARS BEFORE *STAR WARS: A NEW HOPE*

The Old Republic: Revan

3,650 YEARS BEFORE *STAR WARS: A NEW HOPE*

The Old Republic: Deceived
Red Harvest
The Old Republic: Fatal Alliance
The Old Republic: Annihilation

1,032 YEARS BEFORE *STAR WARS: A NEW HOPE*

Knight Errant
Darth Bane: Path of Destruction
Darth Bane: Rule of Two
Darth Bane: Dynasty of Evil

RISE OF THE EMPIRE
67–0 YEARS BEFORE *STAR WARS: A NEW HOPE*

67 YEARS BEFORE *STAR WARS: A NEW HOPE*

Darth Plagueis

33 YEARS BEFORE *STAR WARS: A NEW HOPE*

Cloak of Deception
Darth Maul: Shadow Hunter
Maul: Lockdown

32 YEARS BEFORE *STAR WARS: A NEW HOPE*

***STAR WARS:* EPISODE I**
THE PHANTOM MENACE

Rogue Planet
Outbound Flight
The Approaching Storm

22 YEARS BEFORE *STAR WARS: A NEW HOPE*

***STAR WARS:* EPISODE II**
ATTACK OF THE CLONES

22–19 YEARS BEFORE *STAR WARS: A NEW HOPE*

***STAR WARS:* THE CLONE WARS**

The Clone Wars: Wild Space
The Clone Wars: No Prisoners

Clone Wars Gambit
Stealth
Siege

Republic Commando
Hard Contact
Triple Zero
True Colors
Order 66

Shatterpoint
The Cestus Deception
MedStar I: Battle Surgeons
MedStar II: Jedi Healer
Jedi Trial
Yoda: Dark Rendezvous
Labyrinth of Evil

19 YEARS BEFORE *STAR WARS: A NEW HOPE*

***STAR WARS:* EPISODE III**
REVENGE OF THE SITH

Kenobi
Dark Lord: The Rise of Darth Vader
Imperial Commando 501st

Coruscant Nights
Jedi Twilight
Street of Shadows
Patterns of Force

The Last Jedi

10 YEARS BEFORE *STAR WARS: A NEW HOPE*

The Han Solo Trilogy
The Paradise Snare
The Hutt Gambit
Rebel Dawn

The Adventures of Lando Calrissian
The Force Unleashed
The Han Solo Adventures
Death Troopers
The Force Unleashed II

The STAR WARS Legends Novels Timeline

REBELLION
0–5 YEARS AFTER *STAR WARS: A NEW HOPE*

Death Star
Shadow Games

0

***STAR WARS:* EPISODE IV**
A NEW HOPE

Tales from the Mos Eisley Cantina
Tales from the Empire
Tales from the New Republic
Scoundrels
Allegiance
Choices of One
Honor Among Thieves
Galaxies: The Ruins of Dantooine
Splinter of the Mind's Eye
Razor's Edge

3 YEARS AFTER *STAR WARS: A NEW HOPE*

***STAR WARS:* EPISODE V**
THE EMPIRE STRIKES BACK

Tales of the Bounty Hunters
Shadows of the Empire

4 YEARS AFTER *STAR WARS: A NEW HOPE*

***STAR WARS:* EPISODE VI**
THE RETURN OF THE JEDI

Tales from Jabba's Palace

The Bounty Hunter Wars
- The Mandalorian Armor
- Slave Ship
- Hard Merchandise

The Truce at Bakura
Luke Skywalker and the Shadows of Mindor

NEW REPUBLIC
5–25 YEARS AFTER *STAR WARS: A NEW HOPE*

X-Wing
- Rogue Squadron
- Wedge's Gamble
- The Krytos Trap
- The Bacta War
- Wraith Squadron
- Iron Fist
- Solo Command

The Courtship of Princess Leia
Tatooine Ghost

The Thrawn Trilogy
- Heir to the Empire
- Dark Force Rising
- The Last Command

X-Wing: Isard's Revenge

The Jedi Academy Trilogy
- Jedi Search
- Dark Apprentice
- Champions of the Force

I, Jedi
Children of the Jedi
Darksaber
Planet of Twilight
X-Wing: Starfighters of Adumar
The Crystal Star

The Black Fleet Crisis Trilogy
- Before the Storm
- Shield of Lies
- Tyrant's Test

The New Rebellion

The Corellian Trilogy
- Ambush at Corellia
- Assault at Selonia
- Showdown at Centerpoint

The Hand of Thrawn Duology
- Specter of the Past
- Vision of the Future

Scourge
Survivor's Quest

NEW JEDI ORDER
25–40 YEARS AFTER *STAR WARS: A NEW HOPE*

The New Jedi Order

Vector Prime
Dark Tide I: Onslaught
Dark Tide II: Ruin
Agents of Chaos I: Hero's Trial
Agents of Chaos II: Jedi Eclipse
Balance Point
Edge of Victory I: Conquest
Edge of Victory II: Rebirth
Star by Star
Dark Journey
Enemy Lines I: Rebel Dream
Enemy Lines II: Rebel Stand
Traitor
Destiny's Way
Force Heretic I: Remnant
Force Heretic II: Refugee
Force Heretic III: Reunion
The Final Prophecy
The Unifying Force

35 YEARS AFTER *STAR WARS: A NEW HOPE*

The Dark Nest Trilogy

The Joiner King
The Unseen Queen
The Swarm War

LEGACY
40+ YEARS AFTER *STAR WARS: A NEW HOPE*

Legacy of the Force

Betrayal
Bloodlines
Tempest
Exile
Sacrifice
Inferno
Fury
Revelation
Invincible

Crosscurrent
Riptide
Millennium Falcon

43 YEARS AFTER *STAR WARS: A NEW HOPE*

Fate of the Jedi

Outcast
Omen
Abyss
Backlash
Allies
Vortex
Conviction
Ascension
Apocalypse

X-Wing: Mercy Kill

45 YEARS AFTER *STAR WARS: A NEW HOPE*

Crucible

ABOUT THE AUTHOR

JAMES S. A. COREY is the pen name used by collaborators Daniel Abraham and Ty Franck. Under that name, they have written *Leviathan Wakes*, *Caliban's War*, *Abaddon's Gate*, and *Cibola Burn*.

Read on for an excerpt from

STAR WARS™

LAST SHOT

BY DANIEL JOSÉ OLDER

PROLOGUE

BESPIN, NOW

THE DARKENING SKY stretched out forever and ever around Cloud City. Cumulus kingdoms rose and fell in the purple-blue haze below, parting now and then to reveal the twinkling lights of Ugnorgrad.

Protocol droid DRX-7 chortled to himself. It had been a good day. Impresario Calrissian had entertained an entire diplomatic brigade of young Twi'leks, and the little fellows had been enthusiastic and eager to learn—full of questions, in fact. And of course the new head of Calrissian Enterprises, with his trademark charm, had been happy to comply. This meant that plenty of translating had been needed, and with more than four million languages at his disposal, DRX considered translation his favorite part of being a protocol droid.

Why is Cloud City in the clouds? asked one tiny girl with long eyelashes and her two lekku wrapped into a dazzling swirl above her head.

This most basic of questions would normally have elicited an eye roll or sarcastic reply from the impresario. He would deliver it with a winning smile, and the shine of those perfect teeth would somehow counteract whatever slight could've been perceived. In fact, DRX had wondered if that would happen, and if the girl would somehow take offense.

Then he'd have to go into diplomatic overdrive to make sure she felt better, and DRX considered *that* his least favorite part of being a protocol droid.

"Beena," one of the Twi'lek guardians had said, with a touch of menace in her voice, "we covered Cloud City history in class on the flight here; I'm sure Mr. Calrissian has more important matters to attend to."

"Not at all," Calrissian had interrupted with a lively chuckle before DRX could finish translating. "I'm not even the baron administrator anymore, technically. I still get to live in the fancy house, though." With that, his grin had widened amiably. "But anyway, what could be more important than imparting knowledge to the future generations of our friends the Twi'leks?"

And then the guardian, Kaasha Bateen was her name, had shot the impresario a look that DRX was pretty sure indicated extreme skepticism with a hint of possible attraction. But Calrissian hadn't seemed to notice, instead launching into a lengthy and impressively detailed rendering of the travails and adventures of the diminutive Ugnaughts, Cloud City's original architects, and their partnership with Corellian space explorer Ecclessis Figg.

The little Twi'lek eyes had lit up as Calrissian went on to detail his own escapades. Even Kaasha Bateen, who had been standing with her arms crossed over her chest, mouth twisted to one side of her face, seemed to lose herself in the story, and even corrected DRX on a translation matter. (It had been one open to interpretation, like most translation issues, and DRX had opted to concede the point rather than launch into a lengthy discussion of its nuances. Anyway, he loved a good challenge.)

And now the little ones had all been tucked into their sleeping quarters and the Bespin night was sweeping slowly across the sky. DRX was alone, accompanied only by the gentle hum of Cloud City and occasional blips and whirs from the nearby gas mining rigs. At any moment, the Bespin Wing Guard would be zipping past in their bright-orange twin-pod cloud cars, making sure the city was safe and sound.

In fact, now that DRX thought about it, they should've already zipped past. He'd been standing at the rail of his favorite platform for exactly fourteen minutes and twenty-nine seconds. It was nine thirteen.

He gazed out into the gathering night; nothing stirred, no lights blinked.

Odd.

Perhaps, DRX thought, *Master Calrissian knows what's going on.* He raised him on the comm and received a curt and immediate response from Lobot, the city's computer liaison officer: *Calrissian is busy. Relay message through me, Dee-Arrex.*

How rude, DRX thought. *Status check on Bespin Wing Guard,* he messaged back.

And then: nothing. Minute after minute passed with no reply.

Very odd.

He turned back to the night sky, the clouds, the faraway stars, and then took a step backward, arms raised. A tall figure in a dark-green hooded cloak stood at the edge of the platform.

"Greetings," DRX said. "I am protocol droid Dee-Arrex Seven, at your service." He didn't really feel like putting himself at the service of this stranger, who had, after all, appeared without so much as a noise of warning and seemed to care not a whit for the basic mores of decent interaction. But rules were rules.

"Is there anything I can do for you this evening?" DRX asked, when a few moments had gone by without a reply to his initial salutation.

"Oh yes indeed," a gravelly voice said.

The stranger did something with his hands, and DRX felt all his gears, wiring, and synapses tighten at the same time. A hazy shade of red covered the world. And then everything was very simple: He had to kill.

The vast night sky, the teeming galaxy beyond, the billion blips and clacks of Cloud City: All spiraled together and resolved into a single, pulsing need. Somewhere in that complex, Impresario Calrissian dwelled. Probably asleep in his chambers. *Perfect,* DRX thought. A tiny voice cried out from the depths of his programming, a notion, a desperate wail, the single word: *No*. But it was too distant and tiny to bother with, and DRX had a singular mission: *Kill.*

He pushed forward, barely aware of the dark figure slinking along just behind him. He entered the bright hallways of the central throughway, swerved into a side corridor reserved for staff and administrators, and then bustled along past servers, soldiers, and casino droids until he reached the shadowy side entrance to the baron administrator's palace.

"Protocol droid Dee-Arrex Seven for the impresario," DRX said to the two guards. "With one guest."

They saluted and stepped to the side and the wide door slid open. DRX whirred in and navigated quickly through the narrow back hallways, past the kitchen, and up into an elaborate front room where Calrissian received guests.

Kill.

A simple, shrill mandate that pulsed unceasingly through him.

Kill.

And he would, he would. But first he had to get to Calrissian, and that was about to become difficult: Lobot stepped out from a curtain, face creased beneath his bald head, the red light of his cyborg tech headgear blinking in the shadows.

Lobot's expression indicated disappointment and ire, DRX knew, and a memory surfaced from somewhere deep inside:

how crushed DRX would've been to see that face directed at him any other time. The memory was followed by that same distant, urgent cry: *No!* But it was still too tiny to bother with, especially when things were heating up and the resolution to this urge, the only way to feed this hunger, was so close.

Then Lobot caught sight of whoever it was that had been trailing DRX like a shadow, and his expression went from exasperated to shocked, then hardened quickly to enraged. Lobot advanced and DRX swung an arm forward, clobbering the liaison officer across the face, dropping him.

Kill.

But not this one, this was not DRX's target. He surged forward toward the door, toward Calrissian, toward the answer to the thundering demand within him for blood. And then stopped. Lobot had him by the ankle. He wasn't letting go. Pesky cyborg.

DRX was about to clobber him again (*No!* the tiny voice within screamed, *no!*) when a blast sounded and the room lit up as Lobot slumped forward, unconscious. The figure seemed enwrapped in some kind of blur, as if the atmosphere clouded around his dark robes. He lowered an old Imperial blaster and then handed it to DRX.

Kill.

The blaster was set to stun, but that would do. That would be a start. And then the door flew open and the impresario himself came barreling out, wearing only a towel but with a blaster in each hand. DRX didn't wait, firing once, hitting Calrissian in the shoulder, and again, the second shot blasting him backward against the wall. And then the whole world crackled to life as a red shard of light sizzled past, then another.

The Twi'lek: Kaasha Bateen. Also garbed in a towel, also armed, and in fact blasting away, teeth clenched, jaw set. The third shot flung toward DRX and found its mark, and the room spun as he tumbled backward and landed in a heap.

Kill, the voice raged, but it was a little quieter now, and the other voice, the deeper one, had grown, strengthened: *No!*

DRX looked up just in time to see the Twi'lek woman thrown back by a shot from the shadowy stranger, who then strode forward to the two crumpled bodies and let out a raspy, chilling cackle.

The *kill* voice was just a whisper now, and everything else in DRX screamed *No!* as another blaster shot echoed into the night.

PART ONE

CHANDRILA, NOW

". . . FOR PRINCESS LEIA ORGANA. Urgent message. Urgent message for Princess Leia Organa. Please respond. Urgent—"

"Hngh . . ." Han Solo woke with a tiny foot in his face and an irritating droid voice in his ear. "What?" The tiny foot was attached to the tiny body of Ben Solo, mercifully sleeping for what seemed like the first time in days. Han's eyes went wide. Would the boy wake?

"I will transfer the holo from Chancellor Mon Mothma immediately," Leia's protocol droid T-2LC droned.

"What? No!" Han sat up, still trying not to move Ben too much. He was shirtless, and his hair was almost certainly pointing in eight different directions. He probably had crust on his face. He didn't much want to talk to Mon Mothma under regular circumstances, let alone half naked and bedheaded.

"You replied, *What,* Master Solo," T-2LC replied. He was standing way too close. Droids had no sense of boundaries, especially protocol droids. "Therefore I—"

"Leia?" a voice said as the room lit up with the ghostly blue holoprojection.

Ben stirred, kicked Han once in the face.

"Oh," Mon Mothma said, squinting at the projection

that was being transmitted to wherever she was. "Excuse me, General Solo."

"I'm not a general anymore," Han growled, still trying to keep his voice down.

Mon Mothma nodded. "I am aware." She already struck Han as a sort of spectral presence, all those flowy robes and that faraway look of hers. Being a see-through blue holoform only enhanced that. "It is my habit to refer to our veterans by their rank regardless of their status."

"Right," Han said.

"Is Leia around?"

"I could retrieve her for you," T-2LC suggested, turning just enough so the bright hologram Mon Mothma landed on Ben's sleeping face.

"Elsie!" Han snapped.

Ben's eyes sprang open to a shining blue form dancing around him. He burst into tears. Han shook his head; couldn't blame the kid, really—Han probably would've done the same thing if he'd suddenly woken to find himself enveloped in a Mon Mothma glow cloud. Which in a way he almost had, now that he thought about it. "Shh, come here, big guy." He reached his hands under his son's little arms and pulled him up so Ben was sobbing into Han's chest. Han felt that tiny heartbeat pitter-pattering away as Ben snorfled and sniffed.

"Why didn't you just do that in the first place?" Han whisperyelled.

"I am sorry, sir. My programming indicates that when an urgent message is received I am to immediately alert the nearest member of the household, which in this case—"

"All right, can it, Elsie. Go find Leia."

"As you wish, sir."

"Just a moment, Elsie," Mon Mothma said. Han raised an eyebrow at the sternness in her voice. "General Solo, may I offer the admittedly unsolicited advice that you not be so brusque with your droids? They are, after all, committed to the service of all of our safety and comfo—"

"No," Han said.

"Excuse me?"

"You asked if you could offer unsolicited advice and I answered your question."

"I see."

"You're not going to come over to *my* house and tell *me* how to trea—"

"I am certainly not at your house, and I would further—"

"You know what I mean," Han snarled. Ben, whose sobs had begun simmering to a quiet moan, started bawling all over again. "Great! Thanks, Your Mothfulness. You've been a great help this morning."

Mon Mothma narrowed her eyes, exhaled sharply, and then motioned to T-2LC. "I bid you good day," she said, shaking her head as the droid wandered off, splattering the ghostly blue lights across the walls as she went.

"The nerve," Han grumbled, holding the still-crying Ben against his chest as he hoisted himself off the couch. "Ooh." A flash of pain simmered along his lower back. Old battle wounds. Or just oldness. Or both. Fantastic. The holoscreen across the room said it was 0430. He had a pile of boring meetings today, kicking off a week of planning and preparing for the inaugural meeting of the New Republic Pilots Commission, which Han had grudgingly accepted the leadership of—a mistake he was still trying to figure out how he'd been suckered into. Han hated planning. He also hated preparing. But what he really hated above everything else, besides maybe the Empire itself, was meetings. And now the Empire had been gone for more than two years, the remnants of their fleet blasted out of the sky over Jakku just as Ben was being born, in fact, and that cleared the way for meetings to take the number one slot on the Things Han Hates list.

And if there was one thing this fledgling republic loved, it was meetings.

Ben's sobbing had once again settled to a whimper and now became snores. Han laid him ever so gently on the couch and made his way toward the counter at the far end of the room. "Kriff," he whispered as the sharp edges of one of his son's cyrilform cambiblocks, and then another, dug into his socked foot. "Kriff kriff!" He glanced back at the couch, but Ben slept on.

"Caf," Han muttered to BX the kitchen droid, whose photoreceptors lit up in response. Mon Mothma's know-it-all voice rang through his mind: *They are, after all, committed to our safety and comfort.* "Please," he added grudgingly.

"Right away, Master Solo! It is my absolute pleasure to be of service."

BX-778, a brand-new class 3 culinary septoid droid, was supposedly an expert gourmet chef in more than fifteen thousand different styles of cuisine (although that remained to be seen). He was also way too enthusiastic about his job. Unlike the old WED septoid repair droids the Imperials used on their battlements, BX-778 had a rounded head planted among his seven arms. And since he was a household unit, Lando's creepy geniuses at Calrissian Enterprises, or perhaps Lando himself, had imbued BX-778 with a personality. Of sorts.

"Coagulating the finest Endorian caf beans," he chirped jauntily as one of his appendages swung open a floor hatch and another plunged into the crawl space below, appearing moments later with a scoop of the dark-brown beans. "Ah! Picked from the cliffs of the Campalan mountain range on the southeastern peninsula of the forest moon by well-compensated, humanely treated Ewok caf farmers!"

"Okay, okay, keep it down, scrap heap," Han said. "We're trying to keep this kid asleep for a minute."

"Ah!" BX-778 exclaimed.

Han rubbed his eyes and groaned.

"Apologies, Master Solo. Now lowering volume by twelve percent."

"Fantastic."

BX-778 poured the beans into a cylinder at the end of a third appendage. "Caf beans roasted at the gourmet artisanal factories of Hosnian Prime by the finest culinary master droids in the galaxy." He paused, directing those wide, yellow-lit eyes at Han.

"What?"

"Except you, Beex," the droid said, shaking his head. "You're supposed to say, *The finest culinary master droids except you, Beex.*"

"Is there a mute button on you?" Han asked, but his voice was drowned out by the whir of the caf grinder. "Keep it down, I said!"

"In order to make caf, caf beans must be ground." Han was pretty sure he detected a sour note in the droid's voice. He opted to ignore it. "Put another way," the droid continued, "a culinary droid must grind the beans to make the caf, Master Solo."

The first hint of morning crept along the dark-purple sky over the towering spires and domes of Hanna City. From the bedroom, he heard the faint, urgent mutterings of Leia and Mon Mothma as they debated whatever new crisis had rocked the Senate. Han sighed. The endless series of meetings and paperwork of the day ahead jabbered through his mind like an angry ghost. How did Leia do it? His wife seemed to have been born for the tedium and drear of politics. Sure, she griped to Han late into the night about intricate Senate intrigues and intergalactic wrangling, but even when she was frustrated, the thrill of it seemed to somehow light her up—a world she understood completely and was intimately a part of.

Han, on the other hand, could barely make it through a

whole paragraph of that mindless bureaucratic jargon. He tried to keep the thread, especially when it was Leia talking, but his mind inevitably spun toward thoughts of open space, the escalating tremble of a ship about to enter hyperspace, the thrill of flitting carefree from moon to moon. Everything had seemed so simple during those heady, breathless years of rebellion. It wasn't, of course—torture and death awaited any wrong move, and life in the grip of a seemingly unending war had ground them all down over time. But there was a mandate, a clear enemy to evade and destroy, a sense of mission, and with it all the reckless freedom of life in the underground.

Now . . . Han glanced at the small sleeping form of his son on the couch. The boy had seemed to light up the whole world when he'd first arrived: this simple, impossible sliver of hope amid so much death and destruction. But after all those years of war, Han was still braced for battle, and a new, fragile life meant a whole new sense of vulnerability. Leia had proven again and again she could fend for herself, even saving Han's life more than a couple of times, and Han had finally managed to stop worrying so much about her all the time. Now there was a small, squirmy extension of himself out in the world and he honestly had no idea what to do about it.

A burst of steam erupted from the other side of the counter. "One piping-hot and delicious mug of Endorian-harvested, Hosnian-roasted, and Chandrilan-brewed caf, Master Solo," BX-778 announced, now back to normal volume. "Get it? Because I brewed it here!" The droid placed the ceramic cup on the counter and threw all seven of his arms up, releasing a raucous peal of laughter. "On Chandrila!"

Across the room, Ben erupted into tears once again.

"Beex!" Han hollered. "I told you . . ." He sighed, rubbing his face, and headed back to the couch. What was the point? "I'm gonna bring you in for a personality makeover and a memory wipe."

"Oh dear," BX-778 warbled. "You seem testy, Master Solo."

"Han," Leia said, bursting into the room with her hands tangled in her long brown hair.

"Huh?"

"I need the room, love. Gotta use the holomaps, and the bedroom projector isn't big enough."

"Big enough? What are you—"

Leia shot him a look, the one that canceled out whatever he was about to say without a word, and Han held up both hands. "Say no more, Princess."

"Han," Leia warned.

The room glowed with blue light again. "If we triangulate the coordinates, we should be able to . . . oh!" Mon Mothma's flickering image entered a few seconds before T-2LC rolled through the door. "Excuse me once again, General Solo."

"Han," Leia said. "Put a shirt on, would you?"

"Caf for Senator Organa?" BX-778 chimed.

"Sure," Leia said, and then she slipped into a gentle coo, opening her arms to the still-crying toddler on the couch. "And what's wrong with my baby boy, hm?" She swept him up into her arms, groaning a little as she lifted him. "Ooh, he's getting heavy so fast. Come here, little man, hush." She rocked him back and forth, her braids dangling around him like a canopy, then shot a sharp glare at Han. "Did you feed him?"

Han raised his eyebrows. "Feed him? I . . . we were sleeping peacefully until the honorable chancellor here decided to—"

"Coagulating the finest Endoran caf beans," BX-778 announced.

"Oh, here we go," Han groaned.

Leia passed Ben to him as a map of the galaxy spun wild shadows and lights across the walls. "Take him in the bedroom, please? We'll talk about this later. There's something going on that Mon and I have to attend to."

Red and yellow lights flashed urgently at various points on the holomap, and Han recognized the converging blips of the New Republic fleet. "Are you mobilizing?"

"Han," Leia said. "Go."

"All right, all right!" He hoisted Ben onto his shoulder and headed for the bedroom.

"And put a shirt on, please!" Leia called over BX's babble about Ewok caf farmers.

PEACE.

Han took a deep breath. After all that fuss, he'd gone and left his caf in the front room. He sat on the bed, adjusting Ben in his arms. No way was he going back out there. Not even for caf. And anyway, the bed was so comfortable. Leia had been up late the night before going over some boring statistical analysis of crop production on Yavin 4 and Han had volunteered to keep Ben out of her hair, partially just to preempt any kind of, Force forbid, conversation about agriculture. He'd flipped on a holoshow, some cartoon they had now called *Moray and Faz,* and the next thing he knew it was half past four and the flickering chancellor was monmothmaing all over his living room.

He could probably catch a tiny snooze before he had to get ready, he thought, lying back. Little Ben looked up groggily, those dark eyes settling on Han, studying him. Han had no idea how a two-year-old could have such ancient eyes. It was as if Ben had been waiting around for a millennium to show up at just this moment in history.

Slowly, Ben Solo's eyes drifted closed as his chin settled on Han's shoulder.

Han shook his head, smiling. Here he was thinking about fates and destinies. He was starting to sound like Luke.

The thought simultaneously made him smile and unsettled him, and it was that muddle of feelings that drifted along with him as sleep crept up without warning once again, and dissolved the bedroom, the fussing on the other side of the wall, the chirps of morning birds outside, the half-light of a new day, all into a pleasant haze . . .

. . . Right up until a frantic knocking shoved Han rudely back into the world of awake.

"What?" He slid Ben carefully off him and stood, heart pounding.

Bang bang bang!

The balcony. It was coming from the door to the balcony. Keeping out of sight of the tall windows, Han picked up Ben and laid him ever so gently on the carpeted floor, on the far side of the room from the knocking. Then he crept to the bedside table, slid open the drawer, and retrieved his blaster. Disengaged the safety. Made his way to the door.

Bang bang bang!

In the corner now, one hand on the doorknob, the other on the trigger, he glanced at Ben. Still asleep. Everything in Han wanted to just kick through the nearest window and let loose a barrage of blasterfire. But that wasn't the way, and if this was any threat at all, such recklessness would probably get himself and Ben killed.

Slowly, smoothly, he craned his neck to look at the small datascreen showing the balcony security feed.

All the tightened muscles in his body eased at the same time as he threw open the door, a huge smile breaking out across his face. There, in the purple haze of morning, stood Lando Calrissian, decked out as always in an impeccable dress shirt, half cape, shined boots, and a perfectly trimmed goatee.

"If it isn't . . ." Han started, but he let his voice trail off.

One thing that was different about Lando: that wide scoundrel grin was not stretching across his face. In fact, he looked downright pissed.

"What'sa matter, old buddy? And why are you—?"

Han didn't finish because now Lando was reaching back, winding up, fist tight, and then swinging forward with what looked like all his strength. And then, sure enough, fist met face and Han flew backward with a shocked grunt, thinking, as the world flushed to darkness: *I should've probably seen that coming.*

ABOUT THE TYPE

This book was set in Sabon, a typeface designed by the well-known German typographer Jan Tschichold (1902–74). Sabon's design is based upon the original letter forms of sixteenth-century French type designer Claude Garamond and was created specifically to be used for three sources: foundry type for hand composition, Linotype, and Monotype. Tschichold named his typeface for the famous Frankfurt typefounder Jacques Sabon (c. 1520–80).